A ROBERT CURTIS MYSTERY

I0588176

SOLDIERS OF THE KING
THE BRAMSHILL AFFAIR

David Martyn

BLUE FORGE PRESS
Port Orchard, Washington

Blue Forge Press is the print division of the volunteer-run, federal 501(c)3 nonprofit company, Blue Legacy, founded in 1989 and dedicated to bringing light to the shadows and voice to the silence. We strive to empower storytellers across all walks of life with our four divisions: Blue Forge Press, Blue Forge Films, Blue Forge Gaming, and Blue Forge Records. Find out more at www.MyBlueLegacy.com

Blue Forge Press
7419 Ebbert Drive Southeast
Port Orchard, Washington 98367
blueforgepress@gmail.com
360-550-2071 ph.txt

*Dedicated to
Larry Martyn,
man of faith.*

Acknowledgements

I am grateful for the support, help, and suggestions of Doug Knapp and fellow Gig Harbor writers: Pauli Pedersen, Ken Malich, Max and Loren Aikens, Larry Rabideau, Katrinka Mannelly, Patrick Lowinger, and Cassandra Amouack-Hale.

ALSO BY DAVID MARTYN

THE HALL OF FAITH

The Praise Singer:
A Disciple of Melchizedek

The Oak of Weeping:
The Story of Isaac, Rebekah, and Deborah

The Epistle:
A Story of the Early Church

ROBERT CURTIS MYSTERIES

Called Into Service
Soldiers of the King: The Bramshill Affair
Lords and Ladies: The Banqueting House Plot
For God and King: The Deadly Pamphleteer

NOVELLAS & SHORT STORY COLLECTIONS

Huldah and the Last Righteous King
A Light in the Darkest Night

www.BlueForgePress.com

SOLDIERS OF THE KING

OF THE KING

THE BRAMSHILL AFFAIR

CHAPTER 1
THE SENTENCE

London in February 1622 was cold and dreary. The damp gray skies mirrored the darkness of the soul when hope is lost. The warmth of the happiest Christmas both Robert and Barkley had ever known was a distant memory displaced by the events of their first week in London. Both men watched and waited in silence as a detail of guards prepared the site on Tower Hill. A new rope was thrown over the gallows. A fire was lit in a brazier alongside a crude six-foot by three-foot table. Knives, swords, and axes were honed sharp, and their blades reflected the orange and crimson flames. The crowd of bystanders continued to grow.

Captain Robert Curtis and Sergeant Edward Barkley sat erect on horseback, watching the road to the Tower of London—waiting. The guard detail had finished their preparations and stood around the fire, warming faces and hands. The crowd milled about impatiently rubbing their hands against the winter cold. A light breeze carried the sweet smell of wood fire. But a cold draft arose, and

Robert first tasted the foul, acrid, sooty coal smoke which began to burn the back of his throat.

"What is taking them so long?" Robert asked himself softly.

"Hasn't the army taught you how to wait, Robbie?"

Barkley's reply startled Robert. He hadn't intended his comment to be heard. "Just wish they'd get on with it. Let it be over. We have better things to do, better places…"

Robert's words were interrupted by the beat of a drum and the sound of hooves and boots upon the pavement. A procession was making its way slowly up the hill from the Tower. Soon every eye on Tower Hill was following the slow marching detail as the mounted Captain of the Tower Guard came into view. Behind him, two columns of armed guards, four on horseback, and four more on foot walked on either side of a horse, pulling a crude framed stretcher with a man bound across it. The monotone voice of a black-robed priest carried on the wind as he mechanically read from the Book of Common Prayer. The priest's eyes never wandered from his text, ignoring the man strapped to the litter beside him. The condemned had neither coat nor shoes to shield him against the cold. Only a thin woolen tunic covered his frail blue and purple bruised body. When the detail reached the summit of the hill, they halted with military precision. The mounted Captain of the Guard turned his horse around and commanded, "Stand the prisoner!"

The wild-eyed unkempt man was untied from the

litter and dragged to his feet. As he stumbled forward, a guard walked behind him and grasped hold of each of his hands. A sharp knee to the small of prisoner's back, a tug on the man's hands, and soon they were tied tightly behind him.

The Captain of the Guard shouted, "Howard Fitzhugh, you have been found guilty of high treason and by a warrant signed by His Majesty, King James, you are to be publicly executed this day—hanged, drawn and quartered. Speak now if you will.

The prisoner stared blindly at the guard.

"Detail hang the prisoner!"

The Reverend Doctor Howard Fitzhugh, a don of theology at Cambridge University and a confessed Roman Catholic, was dragged to the gallows. A rope with a simple slip knot noose was placed around his neck and pulled by the guard detail until his feet dangled three feet above the ground. Fitzhugh screamed once before his voice was reduced to loud gasps echoing in the darkening smog. He continued to gasp and thrash about in agony, his eyes wide in fear and pain. After a minute or so, his thrashing stopped, and only a vacant stare remained in his eyes.

"Drop him!" the Captain of the Guard commanded, his voice loud over the silent crowd.

Fitzhugh's body fell to the ground in a pile. The detail lifted him and carried him to the table. A bucket of cold water on his face quickened his recovery, and he was bound hand and foot to the table. A guard shoved Fitzhugh's face towards the blazing brazier beside him and tied his head there.

As the battered body was bound, Robert noticed a nobleman riding a prancing white charger, slowly making his way past. The richly attired man in a jewel-studded deep blue robe with white ermine stole was followed by a barefoot, brown-robed monk riding a donkey. The nobleman coldly eyed the half-dead man on the table, but the monk stared intently and then crossed himself as they rode by. Robert said softly to Barkley, "It's them. Diego Sarmiento de Acuna, the Count of Gondomar, ambassador of Spain, and Simon Stock his renegade English priest."

Barkley stared at the two as they rode by. "Aye, the two plotters and they walk free in the face of the man they led to treason."

Robert and Barkley returned their gaze upon Fitzhugh and watched as another guard with mail gloved hands cut open the condemned man's flimsy tunic and with one quick slash of his sword severed his genitals. His other gloved hand retrieved them and tossed them into the fire beside the screaming man's face. His screams had not yet subsided when a knife slashed open his gut, and his intestines were scooped out and thrown into the fire before his very eyes. Robert gasped, and groans arose from those unfortunate enough to witness the brutality. It seemed an eternity before the screams stopped, but mere minutes had passed before Fitzhugh's eyes rolled back into his head, and his mouth gaped open in silence.

No one spoke. The priest finished his prayers. The only sound now was the sizzling of his bowels in the fire. The putrid smell of burning flesh lingered, suspended in the dirty, humid air.

"Off with his head," came the order, and an ax took it in one stroke.

"Send his quarters to the four corners of London. Spike his head at the Tower Gate!"

A guard took the ax and chopped the bloodied body into four quarters. Each was strapped to a horse and ridden off. Fitzhugh's head was picked up by his hair, dropped in a basket, and handed to a guard. The bloodied garment was thrown into the fire while the remaining guards washed the blood off the table with two buckets of water. The drummer resumed his slow cadence, and the detail silently followed the horse-drawn litter back down the road.

The fire in the brazier continued to burn. Its foul smoke spilling over the hill as the priest followed the empty litter and guard detail away from the desecrated site. The crowd made their way back to the inns and pubs of London in small groups, their voices muted as they went their separate ways.

Robert opened his eyes and lifted his lowered head. "Come, Barkley, let us be away from this hellish place."

Barkley nodded and asked as they descended the hill, "The man was traitor and deserving of death, but Robbie...but Robbie, there is no justice in butchering a man alive. Just ain't right."

"No, Barkley, it's not right. And it gives me no pleasure that we found the evidence to convict them— Fitzhugh and the others: one my cousin and one my friend. And soon, we are off to find their collaborators. I can abide by the justice of an eye for an eye, but this— this is beyond vengeance."

Riding down Tower Hill past the Tower of London and over the old bridge, Robert remembered all the disturbing events of the past week. He and Barkley had been summoned after Christmas and left the warmth of his uncle's house in Berwick-upon-Tweed. Oh, how he had rejoiced in the long in coming reconciliation between his father and his uncle the Viscount and the special Christmas day with his close friend Father Wilhelm Hahn and the always warm and gentle-hearted Katharina.

The mood in the city's pubs and inns and the sitting rooms of the courtiers and officials were uniformly as bleak as the weather. Only one man had shown Robert and Barkley that hope was possible. But the events of the last week buried that hope as they marched through his memory to the cadence of the executioner's drums.

Robert and Barkley rode into London a week earlier, laughing with expectation and excitement. But soon, the dank, gritty fog began to collect its toll. The blank faces of Londoners bent over against the chill wind, clutching their cloaks as they navigated the half-frozen mud streets spoke differently. Perhaps it was his religious training or guilt over not finding his calling, but dark images came to mind. A vision of purgatory, a city of lost souls awaiting judgment.

The two went directly to Westminster Palace, where

Robert quickly learned that the King and Parliament were no longer talking. The Parliament James called with so much hope, had fervently rejected his visionary foreign policy. His privy council failed to persuade James to respect the will of his subjects. England was in crisis. A war raged within—not the bloody conflict that raged across the continent, but a widening gulf between King and Parliament and his subjects. A battle of wills, tearing at the heart of the nation.

The gloom that engulfed London penetrated and filled the empty halls of Westminster Palace with a quiet, unseen malaise. Wide corridors, once busy with Lords and members of Parliament, now echoed with the occasional footsteps of a court clerk. The emptiness of the grand palace after King James I dismissed Parliament the previous November told every visitor that King and Parliament had stopped talking. Unwilling to provide James adequate funding for an army to defend his daughter Countess Elizabeth's Palatinate and opposed to an alliance by marriage to Spain, James sent them home.

Although Westminster was still a Royal Palace, James no longer kept rooms in the majestic building along the Thames River. Once the King's chamber, his ornate sitting room and office, was now the meeting room of the House of Commons. The House of Lords met in the Queen's bedroom. The many chambers intended for courtiers now housed officials of the royal court. Lieutenant Robert Curtis and Sergeant Edward Barkley, aware of the emptiness and hearing only the cadence of their boots on the stone floor, silently made their way to the office of Sir John Doddridge, Justice of the King's Bench.

Curtis and Barkley introduced themselves to Sir John, and he silently pointed to the open door of his office. When he closed the door behind them, Sir John said, "Treason is a serious charge. I will need signed statements."

As he made his way towards the seat to which Sir John pointed, Robert answered brusquely, "The Marquess of Buckingham has the letters to the conspirators. He has the cipher key to their code. He has their names and their plan. He has had them since December!"

Sir John nodded as he sat behind his large desk. "Yes, I have seen the letters. Fitzhugh is at the tower being questioned. His inquisitors have improved his memory, but we must be thorough. I want to know how the Reverend Doctor Fitzhugh came under suspicion. Who else did you speak to at Cambridge? And the man you subdued in Fitzhugh's room, who was he?"

Surprised, Robert stared at Barkley. "I—we don't know the man found watching Fitzhugh's room. Was he not arrested with Fitzhugh? Surely, the college could identify him…"

Robert's eyes widened. He blurted, "They know! The conspirators all know. The Spanish Ambassador, Count Gondomar, he could not be arrested—returned to Spain, no doubt. They are all warned."

Sir John brought his hands together, stared, and said, "And this man, Sharpe, carrying the letters, bad luck that he is dead. Write everything you remember about him as well."

Robert nodded. "Yes, of course. Tell me, the co-conspirators Captain Curtis and Captain Richard with Colonel Sir Horace Vere's regiment in Heidelberg and Mannheim, were they arrested?"

Sir John continued, not betraying any emotion. "Word was sent to Sir Horace. Now, where are you staying? I may need to contact you. I want you to return with complete statements—no more than two days. No detail is too small."

Edward followed Robert's lead and stood up. Robert said, "We stay at Lambeth Palace, guests of the Archbishop of Canterbury, His Grace George Abbot."

Sir John sighed. "Yes, His Grace, the Archbishop, is involved."

Doddridge added as he shook his head. "As if he doesn't have enough problems of his own. Go then. Two days!"

Before Robert was out the door, Sir John added, "Count Gondomar and his renegade English priest—what was his name?"

"Simon Stock, a Carmelite priest. He is brother to Captain Donald Stock, adjutant to Colonel Vere—the Marquess Buckingham's man."

"Yes, Stock. He and Gondomar remain in London. King James has merely banned the ambassador from court—for a time. The negotiation of the marriage of Prince Charles to the Infanta Maria Anna of Spain continues."

Once outside of Sir John's office in the empty hall,

Robert turned to Barkley. "You were quiet. I never knew you to hold your tongue."

Barkley laughed. "You're my senior officer, Robbie. Better you take the heat."

After a pause, Barkley continued, "Who was that thug in Fitzhugh's room? If there are other conspirators, he is our key to finding them. We must find him first."

Robert replied, "We can't touch Count Gondomar or Simon Strock. My cousin Sir Geoffrey and Captain Richard are safely behind the walls of Frankenthal and Heidelberg, so…"

Barkley interrupted, "Or so you hope. What if they were warned before Colonel Vere was told?"

Robert snorted. "And no word from the Marquess of Buckingham or Captain Stock. We have to find Fitzhugh's guard."

Lambeth Palace was on the opposite side of the Thames from Westminster Palace. The guard at the door glared at Barkley as they approached.

Edward Barkley smiled at the guard as they stepped up to the door. "Keeping Archbishop Woolsey's figs safe, are we? Pity no fresh ones for me today."

The guard gritted his teeth, opened the door, and announced Lieutenant of Cuirassiers Curtis and Sergeant Barkley.

Once the guard stepped back out and closed the door behind him, Robert turned to Barkley and asked, "Why do you badger that man?"

"Robbie, he and I have an understanding. He thinks himself something, but I remind him he's a horse's ass."

Robert scowled. "Must I remind you that His Grace, the Archbishop, is our host and the one man we can trust? I will abide by no conduct that would cost us his goodwill."

"Aye, Robbie. I hear ye—speak no more of it."

Archbishop George Abbot appeared and greeted both men warmly. "Just arrived, have you? Glad you are here. Did you make it home to Berwick-upon-Tweed in time for Christmas? And the trip back here—miserable time to travel. But come in. Join me in a glass of wine."

Barkley silently followed Robert as they walked to the sitting room. Robert returned the archbishop's smile and said, "Splendid Christmas, thank you. Wouldn't you agree, Barkley?"

Barkley managed a simple, "Aye. Splendid it was."

Robert continued, "Your Grace, we stopped at Westminster and met with Sir John Doddridge as your letter suggested. Other than the Reverend Doctor Fitzhugh, all the conspirators are still at large. They know we are on to them, but I fear the birds have flown the coop."

"Sit down, Robert—and you also Edward. The wine is warmed. It will take the chill from your bones."

Robert and Barkley sat as Archbishop Abbot poured each a cup of wine. Handing the cups to them, he asked, "Tell me. What did you make of Sir John?"

"He was familiar with the facts. He mentioned Fitzhugh is in the tower and has begun to talk. He seemed unmoved by it all—reminded me of the scholars at Cambridge coldly repeating old facts by rote."

Archbishop Abbot smiled. "A good man—thorough. I recommended Marquess Buckingham take the case to him. He has the patience and persistence of a hound fixed on the scent."

Robert looked at the Archbishop, cocked his head quizzically, and said, "He mentioned you. Said you were involved and as aside said you have enough troubles of your own."

"Oh, that. Sir John leads the inquiry into my homicide case—a gamekeeper, poor soul, I killed him with an errant crossbow shaft. I mentioned that to you before. Well, that is why I recommended Sir John. He is both dispassionate and thorough, and—and we have a relationship—a reason to meet."

Edward cleared his throat. "Beggin' your pardon Your Grace, but he reminded us we left behind Fitzhugh's thug, never thinkin' he might know somethin' and we not knowin' who he is."

Robert nodded. "We are to return in two days with our written statements. Then Barkley and I are off to Cambridge to find him. Have you any word from Marquess Buckingham? Have the conspirators in Colonel Vere's regiment been arrested?"

"The Marquess of Buckingham informs me they are secure in Colonel Vere's custody."

Robert smiled. "At last some good news! So, Buckingham has been in contact. What else does he report?"

"More wine, Edward? The Archbishop asked, lifting a ladle from the bowl. Barkley held up his cup as the

Archbishop poured. "You are both to remain here until the Marquess gives you leave. You will find paper and pens in your rooms. Now I have duties I must attend. When you finish your wine, my housekeeper will show you to your rooms. One other word—Edward, my guard, Thomas—as a sergeant in Colonel Vere's regiment in the field with the Prince of Orange—he fought off a dozen Spaniards helping the Colonel escape when he was found surrounded. Sergeant Thomas is a most accomplished, vigilant, and loyal man. He is armed. Not the man to push. Until dinner then. Good day."

After the Archbishop had left the room, Robert shook his head and said with a smile, "It seems another man you have misjudged, Barkley!"

Barkley grunted, "Yes—wait—another? Who else?"

Robert laughed. "Why me, of course!"

"Robbie, a friend wouldn't be remindin' a friend of his mistakes!"

"Finish your wine. We have those statements to write—and I will be reading yours before you sign it."

Three days later, Robert and Barkley were still waiting for word from Buckingham. They spent two full days answering Sir John's questions 'for clarification,' he insisted. Barkley was known to slip away in the evening for an ale with his new friend Sergeant Thomas, who he now reported to be "a regular bloke and fine soldier."

Robert and Barkley, waiting in the Archbishop's receiving room, were surprised to hear Sergeant Thomas bellow, "Your Grace, the Marquess of Buckingham requests an audience." George Villiers, the King's favorite and now Marquess of Buckingham, strode into the receiving room like a peacock showing his feathers. His velvet and satin robe, embroidered in gold and shimmering in jewels, was crowned by his feathered hat of matching burgundy. His eyes were bright and cheerful, his face reddened from the winter wind after a brisk ride. Seeing Robert and Barkley waiting, the Marquess remarked brightly, "Most excellent! Gentlemen—good to see you hale and hearty!"

Barkley followed Robert's lead and bowed to the Marquess. Robert answered, "We are honored, my Lord."

"Well now, as soon as His Grace is here—ah, he comes as we speak. Your Grace, I was about to tell these good fellows the plan for tomorrow. The audience will take place in the Tower. You can tell them how to behave. You should arrive before ten. His Highness will have a few questions and hear each of you before he signs the warrant. Yes. I believe that is the sum of it. I am afraid I must return directly to Whitehall."

Archbishop Abbot nodded. "My Lord, am I to understand the King will receive me as well?"

Buckingham smiled. "An advantage to the audience at the Tower. Yes, this will not be a meeting of the Privy Council."

Robert cautiously asked, "Sign the warrant, my Lord?"

Buckingham seemed surprised. "Why, Fitzhugh's death warrant, of course—a traitor's execution. He is to be hanged, drawn, and quartered. Right. Well, I must be moving along. Tomorrow then."

The Marquess of Buckingham was out the door as

quickly as he entered. Archbishop Abbot stared at Robert, then Barkley. "There it is gentlemen. You have an audience with the King."

The Archbishop rubbed his bearded chin with his left hand. "Are those the best clothes you have? Well, a clean uniform and polished boots are always proper. You are soldiers. Now, this is how you approach him—wait to be summoned. Then kneel and bow until he says you may rise. You will address him as 'Your Majesty.' And never speak unless asked. Follow his lead—he will tell you what he expects. One last thing—when dismissed bow and remain bowed as you back out of the room. Quite simple, really."

Robert and Barkley stared at each other. Finally, Robert said, "Barkley, you have boots to polish!"

The next morning, Robert and Barkley rode with Archbishop Abbot in his most elegant coach to the Tower of London. Sergeant Thomas, dressed in his formal uniform, sat alongside the driver. The fortress gate opened as the carriage approached, and they drove to the front of the White Tower, rising three stories above the earthen ramped entrance to the square keep in the center of the court. Sergeant Thomas stepped down and opened the door. Robert waited for Archbishop Abbot to step out before carefully following him. Barkley took a deep breath and brought up the rear.

The small procession was led up the stairs to the third floor and into a reception room overlooking the grounds. The walls were covered in rich tapestries, and only one chair in the middle of a luxurious wool rug sat not far from the window. Several courtiers were standing along the back wall near the doorway. Archbishop Abbot whispered in Robert's ear, "The King enjoys watching the condemned caged next to the lions' pen directly below the window. If you look you, likely you will see Fitzhugh there now."

After ten minutes, Lord Calvert entered the room and announced, "His Majesty, King James I of England, Scotland, Ireland, and Wales."

Everyone in the room went to one knee and bowed as James walked into the room and sat on the lone chair. "Very good, gentlemen, rise. Calvert, would you fetch the satchel I left downstairs?"

Secretary Geroge Calvert bowed and walked back out the door as James continued, "Now, Lieutenant Curtis and Sergeant Barkley, come forward."

Robert and Barkley approached knelt and bowed. "Please rise. Tell me, Curtis. have you ever seen Secretary Calvert before?"

Robert replied, "Yes, Your Majesty."

"Tell me where."

"Cambridge, Your Majesty."

"Please, enlighten me."

Robert took a deep breath. "I saw him in the room of the Reverend Doctor Fitzhugh the summer before last. Just before graduation."

"Who else was in the room?"

"Your majesty, those I saw included Lord Calvert, the Reverend Doctor Fitzhugh, Count Gondomar, the Spanish ambassador, and a priest, Father Simon Stock.

There may have been others I did not see."

"Thank you, Lieutenant Curtis. Please step to the window. There is a man in the cage below. Do you recognize him? Sergeant Barkley, you look as well."

Robert and Barkley stepped to the window and looked. Fitzhugh was barely recognizable in tattered clothes, unkempt hair, and blank eyes staring at the lions caged nearby. "Yes, Your Majesty. I see the Reverend Doctor Fitzhugh."

King James nodded. "Very well, come back. Lieutenant Curtis, are you any relation to Captain Sir Geoffrey Curtis, Baron of Cawmills?"

"He is my cousin, Your Majesty."

"He is a traitor and an outlaw! His title and lands are forfeit to the crown. Tell me, Lieutenant Curtis, are you familiar with his lands?"

"Your majesty, I have visited but twice."

"Good hunting land, perhaps?"

"Your majesty, it is just as you say."

King James stared at Robert for several seconds and then smiled. "Lieutenant Curtis, I offer you the office, sheriff of Cawmills Forest. Do you accept?"

"It is an honor, Your Majesty."

The King looked to Barkley. "Sergeant Barkley, I am told that in your past you subverted my customs inspectors. You have never poached, I pray?"

Barkley coughed and replied, "Your majesty, I confess to some youthful indiscretions—that was before my service as a volunteer to my King and Colonel Sir Horace Vere. But poaching! No, Majesty, never could such thing be said about a Barkley!"

The King laughed. "Then an honest office would serve you well. Do you accept office as Under-Sheriff of Cawmills Forest?"

"Your Majesty, it is a great honor. I accept."

"The Lord High Treasurer, Baron Cranfield, will instruct you, Curtis, collecting from my new tenants in Cawmills, and your sundry duties and expenses—and the rights of a Royal Forest. Lieutenant, no, I say, Captain— Captain of Royal Cawmills Cuirassiers. Yes, build me a militia company from my new lands in Scotland. Your office comes with an emolument, five hundred pounds a year and say, Three hundred fifty pounds for your under-sheriff. These amounts awarded for life."

Turning to Archbishop Abbot, King James said, "Archbishop, I have missed your wisdom at the Council. I do hope you shall return soon. They tell me Captain Curtis is a priest. Surely, you can find some office within the church as the coffers of state are so sorely stretched."

Archbishop Abbot nodded. "Your Majesty, as soon as the inquiry into the unfortunate accident with the gamekeeper is resolved, and my authority to appoint clergy is fully restored, I shall at once honor your request."

The King smiled and returned his gaze towards Robert and Barkley. "Your commissions have been prepared. Tell me, Sheriff Curtis, do you suspect others in the plot you uncovered."

Robert's eyes widened. "Your Majesty, there must be others. There was a guard in Doctor Fitzhugh's room. He escaped. I truly fear, there are others. We intended to investigate further—that is, Your Majesty, with your permission."

"Of course, proceed. You will keep Marquess Buckingham informed."

The King looked around the room. "That will be all Captain Curtis, your rank is now as a King's man—you too Under-Sheriff Barkley.

James walked over to the window and looked down at Howard Fitzhugh. "Pitiful little man."

Walking back and scanning the courtiers lining the room, he said impatiently, "Now where is Lord Calvert with the warrant. I would sign it and be gone."

CHAPTER 2
BRAMSHILL

During the carriage ride back to Lambeth Palace, Archbishop Abbot congratulated Robert and Barkley. "King James always rewards service to the state and crown. But what he did today was most exceptional. It is no secret that Parliament has not granted nearly enough funding to make a difference in the Palatinate. His Majesty could easily have sold the Barony of Cawmills for a handsome sum and granted you some small office of little cost to him. Yet he chose to retain the estate intact as a Royal Forest and you two as its wardens."

Robert wondered aloud, "Yes, and he inferred a greater reward was due. A reward he passed on to you, Your Grace."

The Archbishop laughed. "That was more to his normal. Though he is right—Robert, I should find you a place in the church before you are lost to me forever."

Edward Barkley cleared his throat.

Archbishop Abbot smiled. "Edward, the best I could do for you is working for my man Thomas. I certainly could not turn my poor boxes over to a smuggler. I will leave your further reward to Captain Curtis."

Robert laughed. "Barkley, I'm sure as my under-sheriff, you can also serve as a paid recruiter and sergeant major of the Royal Cawmills Cuirassiers. I would not want to risk further temptation on your newly found integrity."

Barkly grumbled, "It seems someone questioned my integrity before the King, but he rightly saw past those the ugly comments and has rewarded me with a position of trust. I am an honorable 'King's man!'"

His Grace laughed. "Angels in heaven rejoice over every repentant sinner."

Robert looked out the carriage window and sighed. "Your Grace, can you arrange for me to visit Bramshill House? The actions of that gamekeeper gnaw at me. Who was he? Why was he there? Barkley and I could visit before we travel to Cambridge and Cawmills."

"Bramshill House belongs to Baron Zouche. He had recently finished the new grand house and invited me to consecrate the chapel. The stag hunt invitation was made after the consecration ceremony. I was not aware of it beforehand, but it was included in the invitation to His Majesty, the King. King James did not make the consecration, but a stag hunt is always a favorite of His Majesty. The King came that morning from Windsor some twenty miles away, where he was on a hunting holiday with members of his court. I recall him saying in jest, he was tired of the courtiers arguing over rooms in Windsor and sought new woods to hunt. As for the gamekeeper, his name was Peter Hawkins. A good Christian man, I support his widow and fast one Tuesday every month in his memory."

"Who was the first to his body? Were there any statements as to why he was out of place?"

"A new hired man was first there. Never did catch his name. Kept repeating, 'Hawkins should have known better.' All the man ever said."

Robert nodded. "And a list of the nobles who were there when the homicide occurred. Who would have had a list, or knew who was invited to the hunt? The procedures for a royal visit, who coordinates servants and retainers?"

Archbishop Abbot studied Robert carefully, "I thought you were most concerned with finding the aid to Fitzhugh in Cambridge. Why this sudden desire to investigate the hunting accident?"

Robert was looking through the window as they passed over the Thames. "I overlooked one servant who was more than we believed at the time. This new hired man and the gamekeeper in the wrong place—with access to the King—no, his death only begs the question. Why was Peter Hawkins, an experienced gamekeeper in the wrong place? And a nameless new hired man first to find him?"

Barkley nodded. "And then there is the placement you can bring Robert when the inquiry is over."

Archbishop Abbot ignored Barkley and answered Robert, "Let me put together the list, and I will ask my secretary to document the procedures for a visit.

Bramshill House is five hours at fast trot south of London in Hampshire. You have time to visit there before your duties in Westminster are complete. You must schedule your visit to Baron Cranfield, who will instruct you on your new duties under the Royal Treasurer."

Robert nodded. "What do you remember about the incident? I find writing the details helps me remember. Start with your invitation to Bramshill House. How long in advance was it planned? Who knew of it? Then record everything that occurred there. And the gamekeeper— Peter Hawkins? What do you know of him? And write everything you recall about the hired man. Is the widow Hawkins still at Bramshill? I should like to speak with her if you feel she would be up to it."

Archbishop Abbot looked up, but his eyes were focused inward on memories. "I shall endeavor to do as you say, and write every detail. As for the hired man, I don't recall hearing his name or anything about him. 'New man,' is all they said. Never heard anything more since the day of the accident. It seems strange now that you mention it. I will write to Mrs. Hawkins. I am sure she will be willing to speak with you. She always insisted her husband was a cautious man, aware of the danger of an errant crossbow bolt."

Robert took a breath. "With your permission, Your Grace, I will pay another visit to the Justice of the King's Bench, Sir John Doddridge."

Archbishop Abbot glanced up at Robert. "Yes. Tell him you investigate on my behalf."

The Archbishop's brow curled, his face serious, and his

eyes focused on Robert. He continued, "Remind Sir John of His Majesty's impatience. Last we spoke, his council of ten lawyers and clergy were split on the issue that hunting as blood sport is incompatible with a clerical office. They have long ago determined there was no criminal intent on my part. Advise him his inquiry might be better received by His Majesty if focused on the King's safety."

Robert was surprised. "A divided council?"

The Archbishop turned to Robert. "I have my enemies. It comes with my position. Bishop Laud has sought the See of Canterbury his whole life. He is the most ambitious and ruthless man for a churchman. He curries the favor of the Marquess of Buckingham and is championed by members of Parliament and the church who would move us closer to Rome. But I have the strong support of Bishop Lancelot Andrewes. A man favored by the King for his leadership in the translation of Holy Scripture into English. We have been friends for years."

The coach stopped at the entrance to Lambeth Palace. The Archbishop stepped out first and made his way through the door as his guard Thomas held it open. Robert followed, and Edward was the last to enter. "Good day to ye, Thomas," Barkley said as he stepped inside.

Thomas replied, "Fine day, it is, Sergeant Barkley."

"Aye it is a fine day, Sergeant Thomas, and make that Under-Sheriff of Cawmills Forest and Sergeant Major of the Royal Cawmills Cuirassiers. There is always a place for a good man if you become interested."

Thomas smiled. "Can't be leavin' His Grace the Archbishop unguarded and then there is this notorious poacher of Archbishop Woolsey's precious figs lurkin' about."

"A real scoundrel, that one! You'll be havin' no more trouble from him—hear moved up in the world, he has!" Barkley replied.

Inside the sitting room, the three men stood before the fire warming their hands. His eyes on the crackling fire, Robert asked, "Does the King suspect Lord Calvert. His questions…"

Archbishop Abbot, also drawn to the flame, sighed. "He knows Calvert remains steadfast in his desire for an alliance with Spain and the Emperor. The King also knows Lord Calvert has no support in the privy council or Parliament. Lord Calvert may be a secret Catholic, but even so, his loyalty is beyond question. It is the embarrassment of Gondomar using Lord Calvert that upsets the King. Count Gondomar will not shirk in his determination to force King James into accepting terms to the best benefit of Spain. You can be sure those present today will be counting the days until Lord Secretary Calvert is retired."

"The surrender of the English in the Palatinate would bring great embarrassment upon King James."

"And perhaps force his hand." Archbishop Abbot paused for a deep breath and turned to Robert. "The danger lies with King James himself. He considers himself the wisest and most clever of men. He cannot imagine being outwitted by the Count."

Barkley interrupted, "Seems His Majesty is at loggerheads with his privy council, Parliament, and the very ambassador he needs to prove them wrong."

"Quite. Saving the Palatinate for The Elector Frederick V and the King's daughter Countess Elizabeth while forging the alliance which he believes will save Europe may be beyond the ability of even the wisest of mortal men."

Robert opened his hands to the warming fire again, "Countless motives from countless enemies."

Sir John Doddridge was surprised to see Robert and Barkley waiting for him in his anteroom. "If this is about, Fitzhugh, the death warrant is signed. His execution is imminent, Doddridge said as the two men stood.

Robert replied, "Yes, we were at the Tower when His Majesty signed the warrant. No. We are here concerning His Grace, Archbishop Abbot. His Grace appointed me to investigate and review the death of Peter Hawkins at Bramshill House. I have come to collect your notes and statements to aid in my inquiries."

For the first time, Robert detected confusion in the ordinarily stoic face of Sir John, "Give my notes to you? Investigate the death of Peter Hawkins? I've been appointed to lead the inquiry…"

Robert nodded. "And your inquiry has determined it was an accidental death under common law, and your inquiry now considers if His Grace can resume his holy office and rejoin the privy council. I can assure you, Sir John, the King is anxious for His Grace to be restored to the privy council. I heard His Majesty say just that at the Tower. I have heard your council of inquiry is divided. Now is an auspicious time to give the King the deciding vote and turn your inquiry towards questions more pertinent to the King. Would he not reward you for the return of Archbishop Abbott, the very result he earnestly desires?"

Sir John's mind was racing. "But why are you investigating? Why my notes and statement?"

Robert smiled. "To make a proper inquiry. Your council has investigated the wrong man. It is not Archbishop Abbot who should be investigated but this new hired man who no one knows. A stranger in the field with the gamekeeper—first man to his aid, and no one knows him! A new man from where? And Peter Hawkins, an experienced man, a cautious man—somewhere he should not have been. And most importantly, this stranger, out of place, is within bowshot of the King!"

"You think…"

"Do you have confirmation of his identity? Who engaged his service? Upon whose authority? Sir John, answering these questions will bring more favor from the King than withholding the counsel of a churchman he needs."

Sir John nodded with certainty. "Yes. But we will make this inquiry together. Come, I will show you the notes and interview statements."

Robert said, "We are off to Bramshill House tomorrow. You are welcome if you can still mount a horse."

Sir John's presence assured Robert and Barkley of a courteous reception at Bramshill house. The approach to the house was from the south requiring a long ride around the forested grounds, past a lake with a pleasant island. Upon sighting Bramshill, Robert called to Sir John, "Lord Zouche is either the humblest of men or enjoys understatement. Bramshill is no mere house!"

Doddridge nodded. "Lord Zouche has built perhaps the finest houses of Elizabethan Architecture in England! It is a wonder to behold—and wait until you enter. He has spared no expense inside or out."

"I am no student of architecture. What style would you say he chose?"

"You see before us his architect, John Thorpe's expression of new Italian palaces. Lord Zouche, like his father before him, was a diplomat in service to the King. His house is the talk of the court, perhaps that is why His Majesty chose to join the hunt following the consecration of the chapel. Half the court was here for the event."

They rode up an open plateau to the grand entrance on the south side of the three-story red-brick mansion. The door was set back in the center between flanking wings to the east and west. The center façade was covered from side to side with columns and friezes. A tall, two-story oriel, an ornate window protruding like a carved sculpture from the facade with half-cupolas above and below, gave shelter over the door. Large mullion windows pierced the walls on either side, flooding the hall behind them with light. An intricately carved white marble parapet crowned the entire roof of the majestic manor.

Sir John Doddridge was immediately recognized, and a servant led the three visitors to the library. The oak-paneled room well-lit by mullion windows was home to an extensive library of two hundred fifty leather-bound and gilded books prominently displayed on shelves. Between the shelves of books, tapestries of Greek and Roman themes hung on the wall. As they entered, Robert thought, '*Karl Schroeder would surely make many sales here! I wonder how my friend is doing—Katharina must be worried. Eberbach and the Palatine—Colonel Vere and the regiment. It seems like a dream.*'

Baron Edward La Zouche was resting after a ride through the forest but soon came down to meet his callers. "Sir John! Does the inquiry continue? We have answered all your questions."

"Lord Zouche, the inquiry into the Archbishop's role in the unfortunate accident shall soon be reported to His Majesty. These gentlemen, Captain Curtis, recently made Sheriff of Cawmills by His Majesty, and Sergeant Barkley, Under-Sheriff of Cawmills, have questions about the hired man assisting your gamekeeper, Peter Hawkins."

A voice from behind a reading chair in an alcove spoke up. "Sir Geoffrey? Is that you? When did you return from the Palatine?"

Two women stood up and turned to greet the visitors. Lord Zouche answered, "Lady Eleanor and my daughter Lady Mary. Forgive us. We did not know you were here. Is Captain Curtis an acquaintance, Lady Eleanor?"

Robert cleared his throat lightly. "Perhaps Lady Eleanor has mistaken me for my cousin, Geoffrey Curtis, formerly Baron of Cawmills and Captain with Sir Horace Vere's volunteers, who is indeed in the Palatine. No, my Lady, I am his cousin Captain Robert Curtis, of Berwick-upon-Tweed, now Sheriff of Cawmills Forest, my cousin's former estate."

Lady Eleanor, a tall young woman with auburn hair, coifed high above her head wearing a pearl and intricately embroidered emerald green dress stared at Robert. Her brow curled in confusion, she asked, "Formerly Baron of Cawmills?"

Robert nodded. "It is shocking news to many. My cousin is a traitor. King James has stripped him of his title, and his lands are forfeit to the crown. He is being held in Frankenthal with the regiment under siege at this very time."

Lady Mary, a small woman with brown hair and anxious blue eyes, asked, "Eleanor, your friend, a traitor?"

Lady Eleanor turned to Lady Mary. "He was a suitor. Like so many, most interested in my inheritance. Not a bad looking man, but it was easy to see he loved only himself. No, Mary, I was not about to follow in your mistake. We are fortunate, you and I, we have no brothers or male cousins to inherit the family house. We need no man to secure our future. We are free to remain as we are or marry whomever we will. You settled too easily, my dear."

"Sir Thomas is a good man! Honored by the King. He makes me happy. I will not hear such talk!"

"Mary, such talk is why we are friends! I am free to say what you think but dare not speak. Sir Thomas enjoys his life in London—he makes merry at the balls at court, while he leaves you here, alone."

"Lady Eleanor, that is enough!" Lord Zouche scolded.

"Forgive me, Mary. I came here to console you not to embarrass you. I will only say that I prefer a man anxious for my company."

Mary scowled and said, "Console me? Or has your boorish behavior made your company unwelcome?"

Lady Eleanor ignored Lady Mary's comment, walked over to Robert, and held out her hand. "I am Lady Eleanor Montclair, daughter of the Earl of Montclair."

Robert bowed, kissed her hand, and said, "My Lady."

"You are far more handsome and younger than your cousin, Captain Curtis."

Lady Eleanor turned to Lord Zouche and said, "Lord Edward, please invite your guests to stay for dinner. I would like to hear how Captain Curtis now oversees his cousin's property in the name of the Crown. Come, Lady Mary. We should leave your father to conduct his business."

CHAPTER 3
NEW EVIDENCE

The Bramshill gamekeeper lived in the village west of the grand house and hidden from view by the thick forest. Tenants farmed the Baron's property west of the village. Tom Farrow, the new gamekeeper, received Sir John, Robert, and Barkley politely. "I have told you everything. Peter Hawkins, God rest his soul, was killed by a bolt from His Grace, the Archbishop. It was a terrible accident—I saw the stag. I am certain His Grace let go at the stag—a terrible thing. Peter was down under cover of the brush, and then, I saw him stand and run. Next, I hear the new hire shout, "Hold! A man is down!"

Robert asked, "Where were you when you saw Peter Hawkins stand and run?"

"I was ten yards behind him. I saw him stand and run, but he was out of my sight when he fell."

Robert asked, "Where was the new hire, the man who first found Hawkins?"

"I could not see. He was somewhere on the other side

of the hunting party."

"Tell me about the new hire. What was his name? How long had he been here? When did he leave?"

"Showed his face that morning—never saw him before. Came from Windsor sayin' the King and his courtiers would join the hunt, would be needin' more keepers to drive game. Couldn't disappoint His Majesty—left directly after the accident. Heard his name was Will Smith. Gone he was, soon as the questioning was over."

"Did Peter Hawkins say anything before he stood and ran?"

The gamekeeper nodded. "Thought I heard Peter say, 'No.' Nothing more, just no, and then he ran."

"How long have you worked here? And Peter Hawkins—would you say he was a cautious man?"

"Worked under Hawkins for ten years, I did. Cautious man? Aye, Peter would have no gamekeeper takin' foolish risks. No excuses. He was a cautious man and knew his business. A good man too. Church goin'. Sober. A hard worker. Never asked for anything he would not do himself. Every hunt he reminded us, 'Careful men, I want you all goin' home safe to your wives tonight.'"

Robert asked, "Can you take us to where Peter Hawkins fell."

"Yes. Beyond the lake, a bit of a walk, but I will show you."

A half-hour later, they stopped in thick woods in a small hollow surrounded by dense brush. Tom Farrow pointed down and said, "I was here, in the safety of the hollow. Hawkins was down along the path, just ahead."

Robert nodded. "Barkley, sit here where Mister Farrow waited."

Turning to the gamekeeper, he said, "Now take us to where you found Peter Hawkins."

Beyond the hollow in the thicket, the woods cleared of underbrush. The gamekeeper stopped and pointed at the ground. "Found him here. The new hire was standin' over him, leaning on his crossbow."

"The new hire was armed?" Robert asked.

"Of course. We all were. Often one bolt will not take a stag down. Can't have his lordship chasin' a wounded stag through the woods. Must keep his Lordship's guests safe. Aye, a good gamekeeper, must be armed and a good shot as well."

Robert asked, "Where was the hunting party?"

The gamekeeper pointed towards a rise in the forest, "Atop the rise. Best view in the woods. We drive the game in front."

Robert called out, "Barkley, what do you see?"

"Trees. It's a bloody forest, Robbie. I just see trees."

Turning to Sir John, Robert said, "Sir John, wait here while I walk up the hill." To Tom Farrow, he said, "Take me to where the hunting party was waiting."

"I can show you where they should have been. I could not see who made the shot."

Robert stopped. "Tom, you told me you were certain that His Grace made the shot."

Tom closed his eyes and nodded. "Everyone said he did. Even His Grace claims he made the shot at the stag—but no, I did not see him."

Robert sighed. "And so he did. But please be careful to tell me what you know and saw apart from what you heard from others—let the others speak for themselves."

They trudged up the hill to a patch of ground hardened from many horse hooves. "Likely, the hunting party was here. The King would invite someone from the party to make the first shot. That day it was His Grace the Archbishop of Canterbury."

Robert looked down the hill to Sir John, his presence just visible through the leafless trees. He called out, "Barkley, what can you make out up the hill?"

After a few moments, Barkley answered, "I'm standing—walk around a bit. Aye, I can make you out now."

"Sir John, you can join us up the hill." Looking off to the right, Robert pointed. "So the new man would have been off in that direction." Other than one large bush, the woods to the right were thin and clear of underbrush.

"Barkley, walk ahead to Sir John and then continue around the base of the hill. Let me know what you see."

"Tell me, the stag you saw, where did it come from?"

"Aye, the stag surprised me—ran across between Hawkins and me. It broke when Hawkins ran. Peter Hawkins probably never saw the stag before it broke."

Barkley called out, "What am I looking for, Robbie?"

"Evidence!"

Sir John joined Robert at the top of the hill. "Evidence? The accident was over six months ago."

Robert nodded. "Why did Hawkins run? He shouted

'no' and then ran. He spooked the stag. The stag bolts and Hawkins is shot. The only person ahead of him was the new hire, Will Smith. Was Smith in danger? Was he carelessly moving in front of the party? Or was Smith, who was armed, hunting for King James?"

Robert called out, "Barkley, you are looking for a crossbow bolt. Make your way up the hill. Sir John and I shall work our way down. Do you see the thicket? We will meet there."

The gamekeeper stopped. "Wait! If Will Smith took a shot, the bolt might have gone long. Let me look up here."

Sir John and Robert started to move slowly down the hill. Doddridge glanced up, pointed, and said, "There. In that tree—crossbow bolt!"

Robert looked up and saw a crossbow bolt embedded in the tree about eight feet above the ground. He called out to the gamekeeper, "Crossbow bolt, brown feather fletching."

The gamekeeper ran over and said, "Your every-day bolt has no fletching. His Lordship prefers brown feathers for Bramshill hunts. Same as the one that killed Peter Hawkins."

As he reached the tree, he stopped. "No. This is not from Bramshill—black threading around the nock. At Bramshill, we use brown."

"Are you certain, Tom? Sorry, I am sure you are. Did you see the bolt that killed Hawkins?"

"Yes, I mean, I don't remember the nock threading. It was Peter Hawkins I was lookin' at, and the Archbishop took his shot at the stag."

"Barkley, you see anything behind that thicket?"

"Looks like a regular hole for the gamekeepers. The ground is beaten down."

Sir John spoke. "The shaft in the tree could have been shot from the thicket. The line is true. But two shots, Robbie? The first for the King and another Peter Hawkins?"

Tom Farrow ventured, "We could search for another bolt in line with where Hawkins fell. The Archbishop was not a seasoned hunter. His bolt could be anywhere."

"Or his bolt may have killed Peter Hawkins as he confessed," Sir John added.

The gamekeeper looked up. "We are losing daylight. I can have my men search tomorrow. You best be returnin' to the house."

Robert sighed. "Yes. You're right. Search tomorrow. Tell me, Peter Hawkins' widow—would she see me, answer a few questions?"

"Widow Hawkins would be pleased someone is asking questions. Tells everyone Peter was a cautious man. Not one to take risks."

Lord Zouche was a gracious host. Having served as an ambassador, like his father before him, welcoming government officials was second nature. In truth, he enjoyed the company of men like himself, servants of the Crown. As Sir John was a Justice of the King's Bench, he sat in the place of honor beside Lord Zouche, and the two of them led the conversation. Lord Zouche began,

"Sir John, it pains me to ask, but the view from Westminster—is Parliament's dispute with His Majesty as troubled as one hears? It seems one's duty is honest advice to His Majesty, but he is our sovereign, and we are his servants, and we must follow where he leads."

"Indeed, Sir Edward, it is most disappointing. Parliament has authorized only the most meager funds for soldiers to defend the Elector Frederick V and Countess Elizabeth. They openly reject the King's desire for an alliance with Spain by the marriage of the Prince of Wales to the Infanta Maria—despite all assurances that the heir to the throne would be raised protestant."

Sir Edward nodded. "Diplomacy is a slow business, and Count Gondomar is most skilled. King James is the wisest of men. He will not be bullied or rushed. The negotiation has gone on for years. If the match comes to naught, Parliament's petulance will only bring the King's displeasure to fall heavily upon them."

"As you say, Sir Edward—and the privy council as well. They plead for His Majesty to hear the concerns of his nobles and Parliament. They do their best to embarrass Lord Secretary Calvert, his only defender of the Spanish alliance."

Robert found himself joining the conversation. "Lord Calvert makes the council's case against him by his careless trust of Count Gondomar, proven to have recruited secret English Catholics in a plot to betray Colonel Vere's regiment in the Palatine. That is why it is urgent for His Grace, the Archbishop, to return to the privy council. The King favors the Archbishop, and he is untainted by the Spaniard Gondomar."

Lady Eleanor spoke up. "If this conversation is going to dwell on politics, my dear Lord Z, let us hear more of this plot. Captain Curtis, are we to understand that Sir Geoffrey was among the plotters? I gather you and the silent Sergeant Barkley played some role in uncovering the conspiracy?"

Robert turned to Lady Eleanor and saw behind her intelligent blue eyes a sharp mind and wit. "Indeed, Lady Eleanor, Sir Geoffrey, was among the plotters. Count Gondomar was certainly the master. He recruited the Reverend Doctor Fitzhugh at Cambridge to run his conspiracy. Fitzhugh used a man named Sharpe, a most evil and despicable man, to carry instructions to three officers within the regiment. Captains all, Sir Geoffrey in Frankenthal with Colonel Burroughs, Captain Richard in Heidelberg, and Captain Donald Stock in Mannheim. Captain Stock was recruited by his brother, Simon Stock, Count Gondomar's aide, an English priest who abandoned his King and country for the pope. Captain Donald Stock proved a loyal Englishman and reported his brother's actions to the Marquess of Buckingham but was unable to uncover the other conspirators."

"But you were—able, that is. And the King has rewarded you," Lady Eleanor replied.

Robert nodded. "By the grace of God. Their mistake was sending their man Sharpe to kill me and a dear friend and godly man from Cambridge who passed by an open door when the conspirators were meeting. The better man—a faultless priest in our Church of England, was killed. I was with the regiment in the Palatine. He shot me and left me in the field for dead. But I was saved by... well it is a very long story, but with the help of Sergeant Barkley and a company of good people, I am alive and here tonight."

Lady Eleanor smiled at Barkley and then turned back to Robert. "Captain, someday you must tell me the whole story."

Sir John added, "Fitzhugh was tried and convicted. He awaits execution. The man will hang, then drawn and quartered as a traitor. The others are in the custody of the regiment. However, Colonel Vere's position is not good. His men are besieged behind stone walls but not immune to cannon fire."

Lord Zouche sighed. "So you are here to clear His Grace Archbishop Abbot and allow his return to the privy council."

Sir John nodded. "The inquiry has determined that Peter Hawkins' death was an accident. But some have questioned if His Grace's participation in the hunt, a blood sport, disqualifies him from his clerical office. Sadly, the council of inquiry split. I have decided to take the decision to His Majesty and ask that he make the deciding vote."

Lord Zouche replied, "The Archbishop is certainly no skilled hunter. He joined the hunt on the invitation of His Majesty, the King. It was King James that offered the shot at the stag to the Archbishop, who only then made the shot."

"And so, your gamekeeper has told us." Sir John

paused and glanced down at his plate before continuing.
"I have learned King James desires the return of His
Grace to the privy council. But that is not why we are
here. Perhaps the death of Peter Hawkins was not the
accident we perceived. There are questions…events that
we did not consider. The new hire, who was he? He
certainly left in a hurry. And the actions of Peter
Hawkins—out of character for the cautious and
experienced gamekeeper. And then today…"

Lady Eleanor interrupted, "You found something
today—excuse me, Lord Z. Don't let me interrupt."

Sir Edward cast a cold stare at Lady Eleanor and then
said, "You were about to say something Sir John, some
new evidence?"

"Yes. We found a crossbow arrow in a tree shot from
below where the hunting party gathered—on the other
side of the field from Peter Hawkins' position. The shot
came from where the new hire was waiting. It was not a
Bramshill bolt. The nock threadings were of a different
color."

Lord Zouche could not hide his surprise. "You think
an assassination attempt?"

Edward Barkley spoke. "The gamekeeper insists Peter
Hawkins called out 'No' before springing up and running
across the field. It seems it was Hawkins who surprised
the stag causing the beast to run in the open, leading to
the Archbishop's shot. We think perhaps Peter Hawkins
witnessed the gamekeeper's attempt."

Lady Mary had been sitting quietly, spoke softly but
urgently. "So Peter Hawkins died a hero's death. He gave

his life for the King! Oh, Papa, we must see that he is honored!"

Sir Edward nodded to his daughter. "If that is the case, my dear, we will certainly do as you suggest." Turning to Sir John, he asked, "So where will your inquiry take you next?"

Sir John took a drink of wine and replied, "Captain Curtis and I will follow up on the new hire, called himself 'Will Smith' claimed to be from Windsor. Tom Farrow and his men will search the field for Archbishop Abbot's bolt. Perhaps Will Smith murdered Hawkins as well."

Robert added, "I will call upon the widow Hawkins tomorrow before we depart. I want her to know we seek the truth and justice for her husband."

Mrs. Hawkins was much younger than Robert expected. She kept a clean house for her two adolescent sons and a daughter. His visit interrupted her daily reading and writing lessons for her children. As she excused them, she reminded them that they could have a better life only with schooling. She bobbed her head down to Sir John in a half-hearted attempt to bow as she pointed her arm inside. "Sir John, finally going to hear me out? 'Twas no carelessness by my Mr. Hawkins. Careful man he was— always warnin' the others, remindin' 'em they have wives and families waitin' at home. Well, come in. Took you long enough to get here."

Sir John stepped in and turned to Robert. "This is Captain Curtis and his Sergeant Barkley. They are investigating the death of your husband for His Grace, Archbishop Abbot—seems they found some new evidence and were hoping you would not object to answering their questions."

"I don't mind answering questions so long as they hear me out. Nobody comes to hear what I have to say!"

Robert smiled. "Mrs. Hawkins, please know that Archbishop Abbot is most sorry for your loss. He fasts and prays regularly for you and your children. He assures you he will continue in his support."

Mrs. Hawkins pointed to benches by the table. "Please sit down. I shouldn't leave gentlemen standing. I hold no grudge against His Grace, the Archbishop. I have forgiven the man—I know he meant no harm. But an inexperienced man should never be given a crossbow! He is a godly man, kind and generous. Even so, he can't bring my husband back. But it is the others—those charged to inquire. They don't listen."

Robert nodded. "I will listen. Others have spoken up for you. They say Peter Hawkins was a cautious man who knew his business. But I would hear from you all that you have to say, and well, please, tell me all you have to say."

Mrs. Hawkins sighed. "Peter Hawkins was a good man. As good a husband that any wife could want. Loving, he was, and God-fearing. He loved his work—loved the woods and caring for the game. Made sure the bows were in good order—everything safe. But he loved his children, and here they are with no father to make them strong and good Christians. My Peter was careful, never took chances. Took his time in everything—'worth doin' right,' he always said. Ask his assistant, Tom Farrow—he'll tell ye. Something happened. Something happened that made my Peter run into the shooting lane. Wasn't right! Something wasn't right at all!"

Robert nodded. "That is why we are here. The Archbishop doesn't think it was right, either. Tell me, did your husband say anything about a new man that joined him for the hunt that day?"

"Mrs. Hawkins looked up in concentration, "I remember a man knockin' on the door that morning. Said he come to help out. Peter wanted nothing to do with him. Peter told him he ran stag hunts here for years without needin' any strangers gettin' in the way. Peter went out, and that's the last I saw of him—never came back to kiss me. 'Only time he left without givin' me a kiss and, and I didn't say good-bye, I didn't give him my love."

"Did you hear the name 'Will Smith?'"

"Could be, but not sure."

"What did he look like?"

"He was a small man. Saw him take off his cap and scratch his head—had sandy-colored hair. Very rough, stood on top of his head like a field of oats. Rosy cheeks—seemed strange in the heat of summer. And, well, he talked different. Wasn't from around here."

Robert smiled. "Thank you, Mrs. Hawkins. Your children—I see you want them to read and write. Would you let them go to school, a real school if I could arrange with His Grace?"

"I would be missin' them most terrible. Could I live

near them? Watch them grow up?"

"I believe the Archbishop would honor that. Now we have other inquiries to make, so..."

Edward Barkley spoke up. "Robbie, you're forgettin' to tell Mrs. Hawkins all we saw yesterday, in the forest."

Mrs. Hawkins shouted, "Like him! The stranger talked like him!" And she pointed to Barkley.

Robert stared at Barkley. "He's from the north. Our man is from the north, perhaps Scotland. Thank you, Mrs. Hawkins. And as my sergeant reminded me, yesterday Tom Farrow took us to where it happened. We found new evidence. We found a crossbow bolt in a tree near where the King and the hunting party were stalking. The arrow came from below, across from where your husband was found, meaning..."

"Meaning my Peter saw him and shouted, 'No!' as Tom told me and ran to do something about it."

Sir John spoke. "We think Peter may have died trying to save the King. We will not give up the inquiry until we know the truth. I will do my best as a gentleman and Justice of the King's Bench to secure justice for you and your children."

Mary Hawkins buried her face in her hands and began to cry.

CHAPTER 4
WINDSOR CONNECTION

Riding back to Bramshill House, Sir John, suggested they return to the wooded hill-top and learn if Tom Farrow had found anything. While looking down the open dale, the perceived events played in each man's mind. Edward Barkley broke the silence, "No gamekeeper would venture across that opening without good cause."

Barkley paused and said softly, "It just ain't right. It just ain't right for widows and orphans in this world. Don't He care? Young widow, three children orphaned, and what of them? Tell me, Robbie; you're the priest if He is the good Lord why does He leave widows and orphans to fend for themselves?"

Robert closed his eyes and sighed. "I can't give you an answer that will take away the hurt or explain the injustice. God tells us to remember—to care for the widow and the orphans and the strangers among us. He tells us He cares but, but He gives the responsibility to us. God never promises to stop injustice, sickness, or death. He just tells us He loves us, and He will be there with us as we struggle. Perhaps He wants us to see each other as He sees us—hurting, vulnerable, and in need of compassion. She reminds you of your mother, doesn't she—young Mrs. Hawkins? She is a good woman. I am confident Archbishop Abbot and Lord Zouche will look after her."

Barkley replied, "Doesn't make it right. Still ain't fair."

Robert answered, "No. It doesn't make it right. But seeing the injustice and being determined to do something about it, well, maybe that's doing the Lord's work."

Tom Farrow climbed the hill and addressed the three. "No crossbow shaft yet, but if we find one, what would it prove? Could have been shot anytime."

Sir John nodded. "Yes, that's true, but it would be another piece of the picture and lend support to what we think happened last July."

Tom looked up. "Did you stop by the widow Hawkins? 'Seems she still grieves."

Robert replied, "She is a strong woman. She will have the support of His Grace and Lord Zouche. Tell me, Tom, do many of the people in the village read and write? We interrupted her lessons to her children."

Tom laughed. "Not much need for readin' and writin' in this village. Just tenant farmers, a smith, a brewer, a cooper, and a miller. No, Mary Hawkins is the only one in the village who can read—convinced Peter the young ones should read. Well, Peter never could say no to his Mary. She offered to teach all the children, parents, too, but no one else saw the need."

"Where did Mrs. Hawkins learn to read and write?" Robert asked.

"Don't know. Peter brought her here. Never talked of where she came from or who her people were. Peter and Mary—good folks. Always neighborly—willing to lend a hand or what they had. Glad news, it is—she and the children bein' looked after."

Sir John nodded. "Right. If you find anything or hear any news, you be sure and tell Lord Zouche. He knows where to find me. Carry on then."

Approaching the great house, Bramshill, Robert asked, "Sir John, can you talk our way into Windsor Castle?"

"As soon as we give our regards to Sir Edward, we shall be on our way. It's just the head gamekeeper we need to question."

Turning to Robert, he said, "Was it your idea, or His Grace, Archbishop Abbot, who wanted me to join this inquiry? 'Seems I have been recruited just to get you inside where you want to go."

"The access that your office provides has been most satisfactory indeed. But I assure you, Sir John, His Grace is an admirer of your skill and persistence in inquiries. I am honored to serve alongside you."

Then nodding to Barkley, he continued, "And your presence tames the tongue of my good friend Sergeant Barkley."

Barkley scowled and muttered, "Calls himself a gentleman."

That afternoon they arrived in Windsor, where a simple inquiry at the guardhouse confirmed the King's gamekeeper lived in the village outside the fortress walls. "No, he replied to Sir John's question, "Never heard of a gamekeeper assistant named 'Will Smith.' Don't know the man—would be lunacy to send a gamekeeper to another estate. Man would not know the ground or the habits of the game. Would only get in the way. Wouldn't be havin' any stranger wanderin' about during a hunt here. Get somebody killed, he would. Lunacy!"

Robert smiled. "Your crossbow bolts. What color fletching and thread around the nock do you use here?"

The gamekeeper replied, "Most of the bolts have no fletching, though if requested, I provide short brown feathered ones. As for the threading around the nock, why every Englishman knows to use brown—easy to come by and holds up well."

"Have you ever known anyone to use black thread around the nock?"

"His Highness brought one back once—brought it back from a hunt in Scotland. All fancy, it was, with three brown feathered fletching and black thread around the nock. Scots still have peculiar ways."

Robert turned to Sir John and smiled. Sir John nodded and said, "We won't keep you any longer. Good day."

They rode to an inn, deciding to journey to London in the morning. With the King and his court in London, the Windsor village inn was like any other in England. The regular collection of local merchants, farmers, and travelers on the road sat in conversation with large mugs of ale in front of them. Travelers ate the bread, cheese, and whatever passed for a stew that day.

Seated around a table not far from the warming fire with their foamy ale while they waited for their meal, Robert leaned back with his eyes closed and said, "Sir John, as I recall, the inquiry report states that Peter Hawkins was shot in the chest. He likely saw his attacker."

"It is possible he saw someone and was shot as he ran towards him, but it is also possible he turned and looked up the hill where he knew the hunting party waited."

Robert continued, "The reports, the witness statements, none reported seeing Peter Hawkins before his body was found..."

"Remember, it was July. The leaves, the foliage, and the underbrush were all much thicker. They did not see clearly to the bottom."

"But they all saw the stag."

"That is true. And it agrees with Tom Farrow's account that the stag broke across the hill above where Hawkins was watching."

"Well, we learned one thing. This stranger, the new hire, Will Smith, is a Scott."

Edward Barkley nodded. "And a fair description, she gave us—short with coarse light brown hair, probably a cowlick."

The innkeeper appeared with three bowls of stew, a loaf of bread, and a brick of cheese. Robert moved the mugs out of the way. He turned to the innkeeper and said, "Much busier when the King and his court are at the castle."

The innkeeper nodded. "The villagers know well enough to stay home when the royal party is in residence. A rowdy bunch they are. Bring their women to stay here; not wives mind you. Their gambling—stakes too high for a workin' man. Aye, I have two sets of regulars. The good people here tonight and the scoundrels from the court. I ain't sayin' nothin' against His Majesty, mind you, only the dogs lookin' for scraps from his table."

"The courtiers and their retinue, they are regular as well?"

"As regular as the King's favorites and his council. Don't change too much."

"Someone new would standout then?"

"Aye, if he weren't one 'em, he'd be out of place—not quick to accept outsiders unless it is an attractive wench."

Robert nodded and lifted his mug and said, "Last July, the King was here for a hunt."

"Aye, his last visit."

"He went south a couple of days to Bramshill. Only a few went with him."

"His Majesty is known to hunt other lands of his lords. Windsor is a strong castle and fortress, but the palace is small, not many rooms. Courtiers fight for a place to stay. The King makes a game of leaving them bickering behind. Takes only his favorites."

"Does the court know of his plans to hunt other estates?"

"More sport. They would never speak of it to His Majesty, but His Majesty's plans are never well guarded.

Those not invited by the King seek their invitation from the lord. Never wantin' to be far from His Majesty—pigs at a trough, they are."

"Sound like men not to be trusted in the company of a wife or daughter. Tell me, last July, when His Majesty traveled to Bramshill, did any stranger visit the inn, asking about the King's plans or looking to be hired on?"

The innkeeper sighed. "Let me think. Always someone lookin' for work—but askin' about the King's hunts? Now that you ask, yes, there was a man—a strange little man. Alone he was. Never a smile—dead earnest—sought out work in the castle. Turned down, he was. Asked about where the King might go for a hunt."

Barkley asked, "Sandy hair, standin' straight atop his head? A Scot, perhaps?"

"That's him. A strange one that one. One mug, and he was out the door."

Sir John nodded. "Thank you. Most helpful. Another round of ale before we call it a night."

The next day Sir John parted with Robert and Barkley at the Thames River bridge. Robert rode alongside Sir John and said, "I will come to your chamber before I depart. I await my audience with the Lord Treasurer regarding my duties at Cawmills Forest. Do you have a word for His Grace concerning the inquiry?"

Sir John replied, "Tell His Grace I will seek an immediate appointment with His Majesty in the hope King James puts the matter to an end. Yes, do see me before you leave. We must continue our inquiries. Most rewarding, Captain Curtis. Most rewarding, indeed. We shall not give up the hunt. Give my regards to His Grace."

Turning to Barkley, he said, "Sergeant, if you grow weary of Captain Curtis' cuts, you come and work for me. Good day friends!"

As Sir John rode across the old wooden bridge towards Westminster Palace, Barkley said with a smile, "Ye hear that, Robbie? Better be good to me, or you'll be trudgin' along on your own!"

Robert laughed. "There is the matter of three hundred fifty a year."

Dinner with Archbishop Abbot was Robert's opportunity to share what they had learned. His Grace listened as Robert unfolded the story of the new hire, Will Smith, and the suggestion of an attempt on the King. When Robert shared the account of Peter Hawkins giving up his safe position to confront Smith, the Archbishop closed his eyes and whispered, "A good man, just as his widow always insisted."

But when Robert expounded the theory that perhaps the Archbishop did not kill Hawkins, instead the killer was Smith, His Grace shook his head no. "Robert, you need not shield me from my guilt. I let fly my bolt. I should not have done so. I know nothing of the crossbow. I have no experience in such a hunt and should have declined His Majesty's invitation. My very presence at the hunt was prideful."

Robert replied, "Perhaps. I make no judgment, Your Grace. But the evidence now suggests a plot and the actions of Peter Hawkins appear heroic—befitting remembrance on behalf of his widow and three children. Indeed, Lord Zouche has commented he will share in a reward to her."

"To do otherwise in these circumstances would bring dishonor to his house. But I shall not leave her to his care—he is likely to ship them all to the Virginia colony! As a commissioner of the company, he constantly searches for unfortunate souls to send off die in the wilds of that new land."

Robert sighed. "If you will hear me, my grace, the widow Hawkins, a much younger woman than I imagined, quite handsome as well—she is most remarkable in her zeal to teach her children to read and write. She, herself, is so taught and has offered to teach the children in the village, though no others see the need. Proper schooling—if you could provide proper schooling for her children. For herself, she asks only to live near her children to see them grow into good Christians."

"You find her to be a godly woman?"

"Indeed, Your Grace. I do. I would urge compassion for her needs."

"It is not her youth and beauty that persuades you?"

"No. Even Sergeant Barkley has taken her cause—was raised by a widow himself…"

"I know Edward to have a good heart. Tell me, what do you know of her people?"

Robert replied, "I asked. No one knows her people. She has made no mention of them to anyone. She and her husband were said to be good neighbors, liked by all—

but never spoke of her life before Bramshill."

"Certainly, I shall honor her request. We will find a school."

Smiling at Robert, Archbishop Abbot said, "Now Robert, we must consider your placement. You certainly have the gift of an inquiring mind and a determination to see justice done. What should I do with you? Tell me about Cambridge—you took vows, but you never found a place to serve. How would you serve?"

Robert closed his eyes and lowered his face to his tented fingertips. "When I think of men like my late friend Reverend George Cox or my dear friend who rescued me from death's door, Father Wilhelm Hahn, I find my faith—my service lacking. Perhaps Father Hahn would be more deserving of your preferment. He worked as tirelessly as I. He sacrificed his safe position, perhaps a bishopric, motivated only in seeing justice for a young protestant woman and safety for a fugitive English soldier."

"Father Hahn has impressed you."

"He is the best of men! He loves God. He serves selflessly and bravely. Compassion—he is the most compassionate man I have ever met. Do you know he now serves the widows and orphans in Berwick-upon-Tweed? He is a hunted man by the Roman Church he has never renounced. Yet he serves our people with love. He does not argue with any man who loves God. My happiest days—truly days of joy, were when he shared the Church of Eberbach with our friend, the Calvinist Pastor Johann Schroeder. Your Grace, it was an amazing time! Protestants worshipping in the sanctuary as Catholics worshipped in the transept, Latin chants sounding as German hymns were sung. Scripture read to both congregations, but best of all, two pastors joined to teach the people of Eberbach one sermon—a homily of brotherly love."

"Robert, I see your heart for unity in the Church. Oh, for the faith to see reconciliation within my lifetime!"

Robert stared into Archbishop Abbot's eyes. "This war. This cruel war, now spreading across Europe—armies of the Protestant Union and the Catholic League—armies of the churches! Such atrocities! Tell me, Your Grace, is God judging us?"

George Abbot, the pastor, slumped in his chair. "Perhaps it is so. But if it is His judgment, we can take hope in the truth that His judgment clears the way for redemption."

Robert looked up. "You refer to Israel's captivities, first in Egypt and then Babylon. But that was Old Testament, before the gracious atoning gift of our Lord."

His Grace smiled. "We have not lost our redemption from sin in the saving blood of Jesus, but does not our Heavenly Father judge nations and Kingdoms? Does He not reveal His will and show us the penalty of sin—the sin of ignoring His commandments? You speak of the Old and New Testament, is it not a simple truth that the message of the New Testament is first to believe and then to obey? Obey what? I say obey Jesus' command to first Love God and then love our neighbor."

"Love our neighbor, Roman Catholic, or protestant?"

Robert replied.

"And in the Church of England, it is conformist, Calvinist and Puritan."

Robert sighed. "Surely, this madness will not last much longer."

"Tell me, Robert, this friend, the priest, Father Hahn, that you have taken in—you know the penalty for harboring a priest in England."

"Wilhelm is not hiding. He ministers openly in the hospital, workhouse, and orphanage in Berwick-upon-Tweed. He does not conspire with Catholic dissidents. He does not perform the mass or challenge the authority of the Church of England. He ministers faithfully regardless of creed. His is an open heart—open to God and open to an honest discussion on matters of faith. Like the reformers before him, he is awed by the Grace that God bestows upon us. I believe with gentle persuasion that he would minister just as boldly in the Church of England. There is but one complication…"

Robert's voice trailed off and sat silently, praying for his friend whose company he sorely missed.

The Archbishop saw Robert's reluctance to say more. "I should like to meet your friend someday. Perhaps there is a place for him, a man with a gift of mercy. But you, Robert, I must find a preferment that recognizes your gifts and allows me to call upon your exceptional skills as an envoy of the Archbishop of Canterbury."

The two men stood up from the table. Archbishop Abbot asked as they left the room, "The execution tomorrow, will you go and witness it?"

CHAPTER 5
CAPTAIN, WARDEN, AND SHERIFF

The day following the execution of Howard Fitzhugh, Robert and Barkley both were somber and in no mood for their appointment with Baron Cranfield, the Lord High Treasurer. Neither man could eat breakfast or discuss the disturbing memories of the cruelty they saw. The sounds and smell of sausage sizzling on the fire spurred them out into the dreary London morning. Never interested in the common law of England or canon law of the church, Robert struggled to push the ugly memories aside and give his attention to Baron Cranfield's crash course in forest law. Unlike his days at Cambridge, he found his new duties compelled him to listen. Robert noted that as the senior officer, he was the warden and authorized to empower his under-warden, Barkley, to stand in to perform his duties. He was to hire a Justice in Eyre to hear cases of trespass and poaching. His verderers, or foresters, maintained the forest and enforced the law. Their primary duty was to protect the game and habitat, the property of the Crown.

Local nobles and tenants could buy a bailiwick, or right
to hunt the forest for a specified amount of game. Tenant
farmers within the borders of the forest paid rent to the
King and answered to the warden and justice in Eyre in
protecting the King's forest. All commerce and activity in
the forest operated under this special forest law to the
benefit of the King. The royal forest was a royal dominion
set aside for hunting or resources—trees were not a
prerequisite of a royal forest, the game typically was. In a
wooded forest, trees were protected as game habitat or
as a royal resource for the Navy. Oak for shipbuilding and
straight spruce for masts were particularly valued.

Baron Cranfield was noticeably chagrined that King
James had signed commissions naming Curtis and
Barkley as Sheriff and Under Sheriff respectively, "Your
duties as royal officials of the forest are warden and
deputy warden. A Sheriff's commission grants
enforcement authority under common law. Unnecessary
in Cawmills Forest."

Robert stared back at Cranfield. "Do you question the
King's commissions? Did it not occur to you that perhaps
His Majesty had specific common law authority intended
for us?"

Baron Cranfield paused, surprised by Robert's bold
response. "What crimes could he have imagined?"

Edward answered first. "Treason to begin with."

Robert smiled. "It is true, Cawmills is a den of
traitors. We shall make it both secure and an Eden for His
Majesty."

The Lord High Treasurer stared at Robert for a

moment. "You still pursue plotters against His Majesty? Tell me, Sheriff Curtis, is there more to Cawmills than the forest, the former lands of Baron Geoffrey Curtis?"

"Aye, it is the Coastal lands between the Whiteadder River before it enters the Tweed and the Eye Water which enters the sea at Eyemouth. There are villages and the towns, Lamberton and Eyemouth, and the Cottingham Abbey."

"Then I shall write your duties as Sheriff of Cawmills and Warden of Cawmills Forest. Concerning your commission as Captain of the King's Cawmills militia, you may use profits from the royal forest to fund this militia. Still, you may not incur any debt against His Majesty and must account for its costs to me. In any case, the Cawmills Forest must be profitable to His Majesty, or your duties as Warden shall be given to some other deputy I shall appoint. Is that clear?"

Robert nodded. "The King is to see a profit from his Cawmills Forest and proof that his militia is battle-ready. And we shall root out the traitors from the land."

"I have prepared a letter of introduction to carry to the Lord Treasurer in Edinburgh. He will recommend capable men in the land to choose among as Justice in Eyre, Verderers, and foresters."

As Robert and Barkley walked the ornate and hauntingly lonely halls of Westminster and passed under the gaze of a portrait of King James, Robert quipped, "I shall be glad to be on our way north. I have had enough of London and its lords."

"A true word, Robbie! Though Sergeant Thomas and

His Grace are the most splendid company."

Barkley sighed. "Robbie, I still wonder—ever again, will we visit Bramshill House?"

Robert stopped and turned to his friend. "We have what evidence there is from Bramshill. You think of the widow Hawkins. Yes, I share your concern for her cause. There are schools for her boys, but her daughter? Her future? Surely, she is a most capable woman, and we have the assurances of His Grace—let us entreat His Grace more fully this evening. But we must go north soon. The trail grows colder by the day."

Over supper with Archbishop Abbot, Robert presented his request. "Your Grace, Sergeant Barkley, and I have one matter to resolve before we return north to our new duties."

Robert paused and glanced at Barkley. "Edward and I have come to take a personal interest in the justice and care for the widow Mary Hawkins. Please, hear what I propose, for I know you have the most honorable intentions. Her two boys will attend grammar school and prepare for Oxford or Cambridge as they wish. But what of her daughter? And where shall Mrs. Hawkins live? What of her life? I submit, Your Grace, that the lads by sent to Berwick-upon-Tweed Grammar School and Mary Hawkins paid as tutor to the girls of the city. Berwick-upon-Tweed has a hospital and an orphanage. Is there not justice to teach our orphaned daughters to read—widows to have skills that do not leave them fit only for the workhouse?"

George Abbot stared at Robert, then looked at

Edward Barkley attentively, waiting for a response. "The hospital, orphanage and poor house where your priest friend ministers?"

Edward interrupted, "And the good woman, Katherina Schroeder, sister of the pastor of Eberbach—they are right and good company for Mrs. Hawkins. Aye, she and the young girl will be family—become her people. I will look in on her sons, not havin' a father, it is only proper a man be known to them. A man they can ask fatherly things…"

Barkley stopped, worried he had gone too far.

A smile slowly curled the lips of the Archbishop. "Perhaps two good men to look after them. Tell me, Robert, the hospital, the orphanage—does the church administer them?"

"Your Grace, they get by on the goodwill of my uncle, Viscount Berwick. But there is more that could be done."

"I will make your offer known to Mrs. Hawkins. I will respect her wishes in the matter. And Robert, if you can convince your uncle to grant the hospital, orphanage, and workhouse to the Church of England with his current support, tell him I will see that the church shall match his endowment. Tell him when the King restores me, I will request Lord Zouche to match the endowment for as long as Mrs. Hawkins lives. I make this offer on the condition that the Reverend Robert Curtis accepts the vicarage of Berwick Hospital Orphanage and Poor House. And with this office comes one hundred fifty pounds a year. I grant another two hundred pounds for good Christian helpers, cleric or layman."

Robert bowed his head and nodded. "It is most generous, Your Grace. If you trust me to serve..."

"Robert, your strength is in the Lord. I have more trust in a man who questions his walk than one who forgets his need for God. And Edward, my blessings upon you, my son."

"Sir John has caught the scent of the plotters. He will certainly maintain the pursuit at Bramshill, and we will share what we learn with him. I believe he will be a strong advocate with His Majesty on the restoration of your duties. Barkley and I leave in the morning. We thank you for trusting us and showing us the most gracious brotherly love. I— we—"

His Grace stood and put an arm around each man's shoulder. "Where words fail an embrace speaks most loudly. My prayers go with you both. Robert, I will prepare a letter to the Archbishop of York regarding your appointment. Berwick-upon-Tweed is under the Bishop of Durham, and his see under the authority of His Grace, Tobias Matthew."

Two days later, Robert and Barkley were warming themselves by the fire of an inn near Magdalene College, Cambridge. "We will start in the morning with a visit to my friend Doctor Giddings."

Barkley set down his mug, wiped his chin, and said, "Aye, your don. The one whose rooms face towards Fitzhugh's—remember seein' Count Gondomar from his window. 'Didn't seem a friend to the dead traitor. What do you expect from him?"

Robert eyed the mug in front of him. "No. They were not friends. I want to know who his friends were. Doctor Giddings would know Fitzhugh's friends here. Perhaps, he has heard something. We have two collaborators—Will Smith, could be from Scotland—recruited by Cousin Geoffrey and the man in Fitzhugh's room. Could be they are in this together—could be separate plots. What else do we have?"

Barkley swallowed his ale. "The ale in this inn is still weak—watered for children like the night we took down Mr. Sharpe."

Robert looked up, his eyes focusing inward. "Sharpe! He has left a trail. He recruited you..."

"Aye, on the recommendation of the Viscount."

"Sent by my cousin, Sir Geoffrey."

"The traitor Geoffrey Curtis—a nobleman no more."

Robert turned his head and brought his hand to his chin. "I wonder who claimed his body?"

Now Barkley was looking up. "His death was known—Fitzhugh must have known. Friends? Family? Maybe his death isn't the end of his trail!"

"Barkley, you knew Sharpe, before, in Berwick-upon-Tweed. You met him—spent time with him. Did he ever talk about others?"

"Aye, I knew him, mostly by reputation. Sharpe was the man to hire for any foul deed. He sought me out right after I signed the enlistment..."

"Made your mark, more truly."

"Robbie, there's no rule a man has to be a gentleman to read and write! Mother taught me readin' and writin' as a lad. Read the Good Book every day and prayed for me, she did!"

Robert smiled. "My apologies, please go on."

Barkley shook his head. "You're a hard one for friends, Robbie. Sharpe said there was more than soldierin' pay bein' one of Sir Geoffrey's men. Said I was to do as he said—helpin' out movin' people, letters and goods separate from the regiment's supplies. Smugglin' was my job. Not touchin' anything but tellin' Sharpe who to see and where to go—promised good money in return. Never saw a penny. Not one for idle chatter, Sharpe, all business, he was. Asked the questions and told me what he needed—shuttled between the Colonel's Captains and England. Spoke like a northerner—never spoke of his people. No, once—I remember—tossed out a mug of ale and said, 'not like ma's in Eyemouth.' Yes— Eyemouth! Hard to believe a man that evil could have a mother. But Eyemouth was his home."

Robert smiled and turned his attention to the stew placed before him. Nodding as he ate, he said, "Tomorrow I will visit Doctor Giddings while you, Deputy Sheriff of Cawmills, make an official inquiry to the coroner. Find out who claimed Sharpe's body."

Early the next morning, Edward Barkley strode confidently into the office of the coroner. He walked to a clerk in the anteroom and said, "Deputy Sheriff of Cawmills with urgent business for the coroner."

The clerk looked up. "Do you have an appointment?"

"You will address me as Deputy Sheriff! Scoundrel! I said my business is urgent. Will you tell the coroner I am here, or shall I enter on my own?"

The clerk sprang up and replied, "Yes, Deputy Sheriff—Cawmills? I will announce you to the coroner at once!"

Barkley followed the clerk and walked past him into the office as he was announced. "Deputy Sheriff of Cawmills to see you on urgent business, sir."

A little man in black robes looked up from his desk. "Cawmills? Urgent business? What is this about?"

Barkley walked forward, put his hands on the coroner's desk, and looked him in the eye. "Makin' inquiries on a man said found dead in your streets before Christmas it was. Told his name was Mister Sharpe. Trampled after fallin' from his horse, he was. Need to know who claimed his body."

"Sit down, Deputy Sheriff. I recall the man. No one came for his body. Not unusual for a traveler."

Barkley stood, leaned forward on the desk, looked down on the coroner, and said, "Even travelers have a family. Send after 'em when they don't return. What became of the man?"

"Priest took the body. Papist priest, barefoot in the winter. Had papers sayin' he was with the Spanish Ambassador; said he heard about the man and took pity. Made him wait a fortnight in case any family was looking."

Barkley stood up straight. "And no family came?"

The coroner looked up at Barkley. "No. No one claimed the body."

Barkley sighed and turned around to leave.

The coroner stood up and said, "But his horse—a man came all the way from Scotland. Had papers showing the horse was the property of a Baron—Curtis. Yes, Sir Geoffrey Curtis."

Barkley turned around. "Captain Sir Geoffrey Curtis? Baron of Cawmills? The man is with Colonel Vere's volunteers in Frankenthal!"

"That may be, but the paper described the horse and bore the seal of the Justice in Eyre. The man took the horse and left."

The coroner saw the surprise in Barkley's face. "Your inquiry, deputy sheriff—who was this Mister Sharpe?"

"A traitor. A hired man of Geoffrey Curtis, another traitor, stripped of his title, his lands forfeit to the crown. Good day sir!"

Robert's inquiries at the college into the identity of Fitzhugh's guard uncovered nothing new. It seemed only he and Barkley had seen the man. Doctor Giddings did not recall seeing him or ever seeing anyone besides his assigned students, faculty, or the rare visit by Count Gondomar.

"Did Howard Fitzhugh have a favored student—a close assistant?" Robert asked.

"Not since Donald Stock graduated," Giddings answered from across the room.

Robert sighed as he stared out of Doctor Giddings's window across the grounds to the rooms of the late Reverend Doctor Fitzhugh. "Who were you, Fitzhugh? A Catholic, yes, but why a traitor? How did Count

Gondomar find you? Donald Stock? Or did you recruit him?"

Turning to his former don, Robert asked, "What would drive a man like Fitzhugh to treason? You knew the man, Doctor Giddings, where did he come from? What were his politics?"

Thomas Giddings stood up and walked to the window and joint Robert in his stare. "Never a friend, though a clever mind and solid academic. Did well for a man who came off the land. The family had no money—tenants of the Duke of Suffolk. He often boasted that the Countess Suffolk, Lady Catherine Howard, took an interest in him—saw to his education."

Robert stood straight and looked Giddings in the eye. "Being named Howard himself must have begged the question of his parents' identity."

"Yes, and Fitzhugh did not attempt to quell such rumors. I believe he encouraged them. That is until they Lady Catherine and the Earl were expelled from the court for corruption."

Robert bit his lip. "Must have been a hard blow. Rumors. I recall hearing that Lady Catherine led Queen Anne to convert to Catholicism before her death. Could..."

Giddings cut him off. "Rumors. Just rumors, no proof. But it is widely believed Lady Catherine is at least a secret Catholic if not hiding priests in her house. It is true, she is well acquainted with Count Gondomar and has involved herself in campaigning for the Spanish alliance."

"Perhaps she decided to hurry things along and repay James by placing the Prince of Wales on the throne. Tell me, doctor, who would have Fitzhugh's possessions?"

"Would have been collected and returned to the family by now."

"And his Celtic Bible, rosary and icon box from the pope?"

"Would have been seized by the Crown, I suppose."

Robert nodded. "There was no record of them in the inquiry notes by the Justice of the King's Bench."

Giddings shrugged.

"So now I add his missing Catholic relics and rosary to his missing guard."

Barkley was into his third mug of ale when Robert joined him at the inn. "A most satisfactory day, Robbie. Aye, most satisfactory indeed!"

"You appear pleased with yourself, Barkley. What have you learned?"

"I've learned that a Deputy Sheriff gets answers! Yes sir, walked in and demanded to see the coroner. No appointment? Hah! He saw me, he did. Gave me answers!"

"I am pleased your new authority agrees with you. Now, share the answers with me."

"Sit down, have an ale. Not so bad by the third mug."

Robert shook his head and pulled out the stool. "Deputy Sheriff, you are speaking to your Sheriff and Captain, not a smuggler or an innkeeper. What news?"

Barkley looked across at his friend. "Now Robbie, I was just about to tell ye, no need to pull rank. No family claimed him. The traitor priest, Simon Stock, buried the body. Funny thing, someone came for the horse. Papers said it belonged to your cousin, Sir, no, traitor Geoffrey Curtis of Cawmills."

"They came from Scotland for the horse? Three hundred miles? What have we missed?"

CHAPTER 6
CURTIS CASTLE

There was a coach that went north from Cambridge, though coach was too generous a description. Only the meanest of peasant, yeoman, or student would subject their body to the slow hard ride in little more than a hay wagon drawn by four horses and covered with a tarp. Coach roads crisscrossed England with coach inns built along the lanes with feed and water for horses and meals and overnight lodging for travelers. A coach traveler could cross England at five miles an hour, not counting for the stops along the way. Forty miles was a good day.

Neither Robert or Barkley fancied a long ride to the sea with the miserable prospect of an uncomfortable sail north in the stormy winter channel, nor were they willing to suffer the ordeal of the coach trip. Hence, they set off on horseback along the coach road to the Great North Road, intending to reduce their travel time by at least a third.

1621 had been a cold and rainy year. The harvest was

small, little more than seed for the next spring planting. Hunger put many poor on the road in search of work. The early months of 1622 were little better, and even the great, oiled-wool hooded cloaks that enveloped Robert and Barkley did not keep them warm as they rode. For many miles, they rode in silence, wrapped in their thoughts. On the second afternoon, Barkley looked over to Robert and asked, "The widow Hawkins—a good Christian woman..." Barkley's voice trailed off.

Robert, his head bent down against the wind in their face, replied, "Yes, the widow Hawkins is a good Christian woman, what do you ask?"

Barkley rode a bit closer alongside Robert, his face also lowered against the wind. "Me mom prayed I would be a good Christian man, not like me father, hear ye, a drunken scoundrel."

Robert was silent, waiting for his friend to get to the point.

"Is it too late for me, Robbie? I did some things that would bring shame to her. Never meant to harm nobody but did some things—not proud of."

Robert turned to his sergeant. "I'm proud to be your friend."

Robert could not see the smile on Edward's face. "I'm worried about the Good Lord, Robbie. Will He damn my soul forever?"

"God is not in a hurry. He waits for us. In all the warnings of all of His prophets, God simply tells us 'Come back to me and mean it.'"

Barkley nodded. "Can I ever be a good Christian man,

good enough for…"

Robert sat up straight and reached across to Barkley. "Good enough for Mary Hawkins? Yes, or any good Christian woman,"

Robert stopped and waited for Barkley to face him. "Edward, you were baptized into the Church. The good Christians of Berwick-upon-Tweed made an oath to raise you to maturity in the faith. Your mother taught you what it means to be a God-fearing man. She showed you the love of God. In your heart, you know who God calls you to be. And many are your brothers and sisters who would walk beside you. Salvation has been given to you. The Bible says, 'How shall we escape if we ignore so great a salvation?' Edward, my friend, listen to the Spirit speaking to your heart. Your heart is as true as any man I have known."

Barkley rode on in silence, the sleet hiding the tears in his eyes.

After another silent ride, Robert asked, "The widow Hawkins has three children. Even if she would have you, are you ready to step-father Peter Hawkins' children?"

The sleet began to build on Robert's cloak, the whitening hood now matched the gray-white fringes of his black hair. Barkley looked over to his friend and quipped, "For a young man you look old, but I am older and have had enough of young man's games. Aye, it is a hard thing to step in on another man's children—harder when that man was a good and loving father, a hero. But am I ready? God willing, I would give it my best."

Robert replied, "I believe you would—how far we

have come from that night Karl's boat delivered me to Heidelberg Castle."

Barkley laughed. "I was sorely tempted to let the cannoneer put one shot close by. Just close enough to remind you of your baptism."

"What stopped you?"

"I liked being a sergeant. The Colonel was good to me—trusted me."

"You will be a first-rate sergeant major as you are an excellent deputy sheriff."

Five days after leaving Cambridge, Robert and Barkley were in Berwick-upon-Tweed warming themselves beside the fire in the Manor house of Lord James Curtis, Viscount of Berwick, and Baron of Tweedbridge.

Lord Curtis was smiling as he brought a bottle of scotch whiskey and four glasses to warm his nephew and friend. "This will take the chill from your bones—to the Sheriff and Deputy Sheriff or Cawmills!"

When the men put the glasses on the table, Charles Curtis filled them again. "To the Warden and Deputy Warden of Cawmills Forest!"

Barkley poured himself another glass. "Perhaps another and I will be as warm inside, as me bottom is warmed by the fire!"

Robert smiled and said, "Uncle, there is another matter. The works of mercy in Berwick-upon-Tweed, the hospital, the orphanage, and the workhouse—the Archbishop of Canterbury, His Grace George Abbot, offered to match your endowment if you gift them to the church. He has named me their vicar if you agree with an income and funds for a master—I would ask Wilhelm Hahn to accept. His Grace would have you continue your endowment as there will always be poor among us. Consider the poor harvest, which left many in hunger."

Lord Curtis nodded. "Made a vicar as well! My, you have been rewarded. Yes. I will agree to His Grace the Archbishop's terms, but you will need to convince Wilhelm. His heart longs to return to his homeland."

"We must send for him. I will lay it before him at dinner. Barkley and I must leave for Cawmills in the morning—Katharina, Katie—Katie will convince Wilhelm to stay!"

James Curtis sighed. "Katie, too, misses her father and brother. And, well, Wilhelm fears..."

Robert interrupted, "Does Wilhelm still fears his love for Katie violates his vow—that a priest cannot be a husband and a servant of God? Has there ever been a better match? We must make them see."

Barkley took another whiskey, drank it down, and set the glass on the table. "I will show them. Let me be the one."

Lord Curtis nodded and said, "One more scotch, and I fear Edward will replay his Christmas role as the Lord of Misrule passed out on the floor!"

Barkley sighed. "Not you too, Lord Curtis!—a deep cut! I pray ye need not be remindin' me of a painful memory!"

Robert laughed. "Was the pain remembered from the hangover then? For it seems you did not learn to limit your drink. I won't be having a deputy passed out beside the criminal he pursues."

"Laugh all of you. I am a new man. You shall see. An upstandin' servant of the crown. Aye, a gentleman, and the Good Lord willin' soon be raisin' a family!"

Robert walked over to Barkley and hugged him. "You're better than a gentleman—a good man and dear friend!"

Wilhelm and Katie rushed to the manor house as soon they heard the news Robert and Barkley had returned. An afternoon of hugs and tears of joy was followed by a celebration dinner at Sir James' table. All agreed the feast was as joyous as their Christmas dinner—better even with the sober company of Edward. Toasts were made for each of the new royal appointments.

After a toast to the new Vicar of Berwick-upon-Tweed hospital, orphanage, and poor house, Robert stood and said, "His Grace gave me the authority to appoint a headmaster to oversee the works of mercy in Berwick-upon-Tweed. Tonight, it is my great pleasure to recognize and reward the faithful service of a man whose heart it is to serve—a man of compassion and love for all of God's people. Wilhelm Hahn, you shall be the headmaster. And you shall receive an income of one hundred fifty pounds a year for as long as you live! What say you, my brother?"

Viscount Curtis shouted, "And a house—I shall provide a good house -fitting a gentleman—in the city!"

Katie jumped to her feet, rushed behind Wilhelm, bent over, and hugged him. Kissing his cheek, she looked up and shouted, "Oh, Wilhelm, it is wonderful news!

Your work is rewarded! It is your calling."

Wilhelm looked down and wrapped one arm around Katie and reached for her hand with the other. He squeezed her tight for just a moment and then looked up and kissed her cheek. "Brother Robert, you do me much honor, but..." Wilhelm closed his eyes and wept.

Robert's chest rose as his heart ached for Wilhelm. He looked at his friend and said, "Tell me, Will, what ails you? You are loved by all here. Indeed, Katie, Edward, and I would not be here, but by your bravery and goodness. And your good work among our people..."

Wilhelm wiped a tear from his eye, looked up, and smiled. "And I love all of you and find fulfillment serving God's children here." Wilhelm paused. He sighed and said, "I have had it in my mind to return—there is unfinished work for me."

Katie's eyes widened. "Return? You would leave me? Will, you know I love you!"

"And I love you, Katie! But there is a greater love—can we forget Karl? Or Johann? What must be done for all those suffering in the Palatine—throughout the continent? And then there is the war in the church. Surely, our Father in heaven weeps over the bloody battle within his holy catholic Church! Shall I hide here in safety and the comfort and joy of a loving and beautiful woman while others suffer?"

Robert shook his head. "Will, do not be overcome by guilt. We shall not abandon Karl or Johann—or the work of reconciliation. Look at Katie, beside you. Does she not feel as you feel? Does she not share in your passion for service? Brother, hear me: it is no sin to love. It is a gift from God. God gives us joy and blessings at the same time as trial and duty—and these blessings are in greater measure!"

Wilhelm focused on Robert, his mind considering Robert's words. "Will, marry Katie. The two of you are stronger together. You will forever remain a priest in the sight of God, and for those, you make intercession. A godly marriage is a path he has placed before you. Help me, my friend. You have shown me my calling. We will walk this road together."

Wilhelm closed his eyes and leaned his head back. He took a breath opened his eyes turned to face Katie, "Could it be true? Could you marry a man such as I? Confused and uncertain as I am of God's will? And without your father's consent?"

Katie's eyes teared up. "Oh, Will, you know I love you, and my heart desires to marry you. Do you truly believe my father would deny you, my hand? We owe our lives to you. He has seen your love and approves. But, if it pleases you, we can wait until you ask him. It is a good thing to give him that joy. Now please will you kiss me?"

Wilhelm stood up, turned around, and finally embraced the woman he loved.

Edward was the first to rise and raise a toast, "To Will and Katie!"

Sir James echoed, "And to the headmaster of Berwick-upon-Tweed hospital, orphanage, and poor house!"

Robert smiling, stood up, and said, "To my friend, Will, a man of God and priest of compassion, mercy, and reconciliation!"

As they left the table and walked to the warmth of the fire, Robert made his way to Katie. With a bright smile, he was about to speak when she hugged him tightly. "At last," Robert said, "A hug from Katie Schroeder!"

Katie replied, "Robert, in truth? Then let me hug you again and kiss you as well!"

After Katie's kiss on his cheek, Robert teased, "For sure, Katie, you will make poor Will jealous!"

Katie blushed. "Oh, Robert, you know we love you. And you too, Edward! Come here and let me kiss you as well."

"A pleasure, indeed!" Edward said as Katie hugged him and kissed his cheek.

"Now, dear lady, allow me to congratulate Will," Robert said.

Wilhelm came alongside Robert and, after a warm hug, said softly, "I must prepare letters."

"Do you bother writing to your Jesuit superior in Vienna?"

Will shook his head no, "But I owe an explanation to the Archbishop of Mainz—he trusted me and advised me like no other."

Robert nodded. "Truly, he is a godly man. He heard our cause and treated us justly. What shall you say to him?"

"The truth. I will thank him, of course, but I want His Excellency to know I do not forego my vow to God or the Church universal. It is Rome and its war against brother Christians and its unbridled corruption I can no longer abide. I will tell him I dedicate my life to reconciliation, looking forward to that day when all of Christendom can take joy in all expressions of Christian worship—praising God for the faith of their brothers and sisters."

"Brother, your vision sounds of heaven on earth!"

"Perhaps it is in part, heaven, but there remains much else for the church to attack—lost souls, poverty, hunger, disease, and despair. These are the enemies the Church should fight."

Robert grasped Wilhelm's shoulder. "Write the Archbishop. And then, there is another Archbishop who would listen to you. He shares your vision."

A few miles above Berwick, Curtis Castle stood atop a craggy hill facing the German Ocean several miles to the east. A grand manor house stood before an ancient tower rising from the peak of the mountain. The stately home of the Barons of Cawmills reminded every visitor that the Curtis family was both Scottish and Norman. Like many Scottish Baronial houses, Cawmills Manor was three stories of Scottish Baronial splendor. Tall round towers and turrets framed garret chambers corbelled out over the cylinders of their main body. Large windows brought light inside, a precious commodity along the often-gloomy Scottish coast. While the grand manor interpreted the chateaus of France, the old tower, Curtis Castle, went back to the first Norman conquerors who displaced Anglo-Saxon and Scottish lairds alike.

Robert and Barkley rode to the front of the grand

house, dismounted, climbed the steps to the covered entrance, and pound on the door. They stood under the stone-carved Curtis family coat of arms as they waited. Robert nodded, and Barkley pounded on the door a second time—forcefully with the hilt of his sword. The great oak door creaked open a crack, and a voice called out, "The lord is away and accepts no visitors in his absence. Tradesman having business should call at the rear servant's door."

Robert pushed the door open and stepped in. "Indeed, the lord of Cawmills Manor and Cawmills Forest, King James I, is away in London. I am your Warden Captain Robert Curtis, and Sergeant Major Barkley is my deputy. You will see to our horses and tell the Keeper of the Estate to receive me at once."

The man at the door nodded less than a bow and said, "I am Andrew Douglas, Estate Keeper."

Robert looked at the small, well-dressed man before him and said, "See to our horses, then immediately return here."

Douglas turned and called out, "John, see to these officer's horses."

A face peeked from around the corner and replied, "Aye, Mr. Douglas. Will the gents be stayin' awhile?"

Andrew Douglas looked at the stern faces of Robert and Barkley before replying, "They will be staying, Johnny."

As Douglas closed the door behind Barkley, Robert looked up at the royal blue and gold shield of the Curtis family crest. Unlike the Curtis crest in his uncle's great hall, with its garland of Tudor roses, this crest was overlaid with the Scottish Thistle. Douglas walked back towards the grand staircase and said, "This way, gentlemen."

As they walked, Douglas asked, "Captain Robert Curtis, nephew of Viscount James Curtis?"

Robert nodded. "I will see an accounting of the tenants before I meet with them. You will assemble the household for my instructions. We shall tour the house and assign the rooms for His Majesty's use. Deputy Warden Barkley will inspect the outbuildings, kitchen, and armory. Tomorrow we shall ride the Royal Forest. The tower, is it in use?"

"The tower apartment is maintained. It houses the Curtis family armor."

Robert nodded. "Fetch the books."

As Douglas was leaving, Robert called after him, "Have someone remove the Curtis Crest in the hall and hang the crest of His Majesty, King James, in its place."

When they were alone, Robert asked Barkley, "What do you make of him?"

"Not happy to see you, Robbie. Surely, he has been informed. It seems to me he is hiding something."

"We must dig deep then."

Barkley looked about the room. "Take no offense, Robbie, but this house is far grander than the manor of his Lord the Viscount."

"This is the ancestral home of the Curtis family. My uncle was born a twin to my cousin's father. They did not record who was born first, so grandfather decided to divide the estate between the two. With the border running through the family estate, the Barons were forced to yield allegiance to two Kings. In war, he sent men and food to each side, careful not to send Scots and Scottish resources to England and vice versa. Dividing the estate made political sense. He did not foresee that one day England and Scotland would be ruled by the same King."

"And Lord James was given the English lands."

"The smaller estate, but with the harbor access, well suited to a profitable merchant's trade."

"A decision your cousin Geoffrey loathed to accept."

"Does it pain ye, Robbie, to see your family house taken away?"

"This house? No. I never felt any connection. But the tower—aye the tower. It goes back centuries. I think of the first Curtis. He came as a soldier and fought for William the Conqueror, who was forced to fight to take what he had been promised. Even in victory, the earls would not accept William. Oh, they gave him the crown—but not their support. The fools. All that bloodshed and now not an earl left in England with other than Norman blood. I think of the first Curtis who determined to stay here in a fair but hostile land leaving the wealth and warmth of family in Normandy."

Robert sighed. "And who am I if not a loyal Englishman with nothing in common with any Frenchman, be he Norman or not. Sharing only blood that runs red when spilled."

Douglas returned with a large leather-bound ledger

and handed it to Robert, who gave it to Barkley. "Mister Douglas, what are the current funds on hand?"

Douglas replied, "That would be eleven pounds. Captain Curtis."

Robert eyed him carefully. "Then you have not collected the rent for the year?"

Douglas smirked. "The rent was collected after the harvest as is normal in Scotland."

Robert snapped, "Then explain where the money has gone."

"Any fool knows it was a poor harvest. And knowing Sir Geoffrey as a kind and good lord, I required the tenants but half the agreed rent. No use in letting them starve. Who would tend the land?"

Robert stared into Douglas' eyes. "And the rest?"

"I sent the rest to Sir Geoffrey, thinking he may have a need there fighting for His Majesty. Will there be anything else, Captain? The tenants will be here in the morning."

Robert replied, "I will take the apartment in the tower. See that it is made ready. Lay the table for us at sunset. Tell the cook we prefer hearty fare and good ale. I will call for you once I have gone through the ledger. Have our horses saddled now—and raise the Royal standard from the house and the tower. That will be all, Mr. Douglas."

"Captain, the tower apartment has not been used in sometime, it may...."

"Then, you should waste no more of my time and see to it immediately."

Robert paused. "Give me the key. I shall inspect it now."

Douglas fumbled for the key from a large ring. He took one off and handed it to Robert. Robert said, "My Deputy, Sergeant Barkley, shall have a full set of keys this evening," and he walked out the door.

"Sergeant Major Barkley," Barkley added.

"My apologies. He is, indeed, Sergeant Major of the Royal Cawmills Cuirassiers."

Robert and Barkley walked across the low heather that passed as a garden in the salty scrub of coastal Scotland. The heavy oak door creaked as it swung outward. The arrow slits provided dim light in the dusty guard room. Robert closed the door behind them and waited for his eyes to become accustomed to the darkness. Across from the door was an open stone fireplace to warm the guards. A round table stood in the center. To the right, a narrow wood staircase climbed alongside the wall. But as their eyes acclimated, it was the walls that captured their attention. From floor to ceiling, swords, pikes, spears, mace, and armor covered the walls. Above the fireplace, two dozen tall modern arquebuses were mounted and below them two dozen pistols.

Barkley smiled and said, "A good start for the company of cuirassiers, Robbie!"

"Yes, certainly sufficient for training—where there are weapons, there must be powder, flint, and cord. Find them. Let's go up."

The second level was a kitchen not used for some time. A large fireplace, fitted with spits and kettle swings, dominated the room. The table and cookware coated in heavy dust. All around arrow slits provided a safe view of the estate. The third floor was the banquet hall with its high ceiling and massive stone fireplace with the Curtis family crest above it. Tapestries adorned the walls. Two tables filled the room, a small table set on a platform for the lord and his family, and a long semi-circular table for guests.

Robert and Barkley continued climbing the stairs to the top, a private living chamber for the lord and his family. The roof timbers were open to the slate shingles above, and the tapestry covered walls encircled a large bed and several smaller cots. A writing table and chairs stood on an old tapestry rug. A narrow door opened upon a walkway behind the stones of the turret top, offering protection to the chest height of a man. Stepping outside, they saw below them the Whiteadder river course it's way around the steep mount on its way to the Tweedmouth. To the west was a ridge of peaks rising between the Whiteadder and the Blackadder. To the north, the Eye water flowed through a fielded valley past Cottingham Abbey to Eyemouth, to the south lay green valleys divided into fields and pasture. Both men walked the turret full around and stopped to stare off to the German Ocean. "Good place, Robbie. Top of the tallest mount for miles."

"Easy to spot an invader—seeing a traitor, well, not as easy."

They went back inside, and Robert sat at the small table. "Let me look at that ledger."

Robert began with the last entry and worked his way back. After a few minutes, he closed it and said, "Hold onto it. Don't give it to anyone. Now let's take that ride through the Royal Forest before our presence is well known."

At the bottom, Robert met two servants coming to prepare the apartment. "Nothing is to be removed. You may go about your work."

A servant was waiting in front of the house with their horses. Robert nodded to Barkley and said to the servant. "While I'm here, walk me through the stable."

Robert and Barkley carefully looked at each horse as they walked through. "Any other horses owned by my cousin, not here?" Robert asked.

"No, Captain Curtis. There be other horses on the estate, but they would belong to the tenants."

Riding off towards the fields below, Barkley said, "Sharpe's horse wasn't there. You're looking for traitors here?"

CHAPTER 7
CHANGES AT CAWMILLS

The tenant farmers were waiting for Robert in the house. They stood around the cold stone walls of the banquet hall. Their quiet chatter stopped when he came in.

Robert walked to the center of the room and said, "Good men of Cawsmill, I am your new Warden of Cawmills Royal Forest and Sheriff of Cawmills, Captain Robert Curtis, and this is my Deputy Warden and Sheriff, Sergeant Major Edward Barkley. Curtis Castle and the estate of the traitor, former Baron of Cawmills, Captain Geoffrey Curtis, has been forfeited to His Majesty, King James. You are now tenants of His Majesty, and all the estate is now Royal Cawmills Forest. His Majesty, a gracious landlord, is generous to those who serve him well, but most harsh to those who breach his Forest Law or lose his favor. Sergeant Major Barkley will instruct you regarding your privileges and duties. It is your privilege to tend crops and livestock on your leased lands. It is your duty to protect His Majesty's forest against poachers and thieves. You will pay your rent following the harvest and the price set by me."

Robert paused and looked at the men before him. They stood silently listening. None appeared surprised. Robert continued, "Foresters will be appointed to keep the game, the woods, and bounty of the forest. You will be told where you may gather firewood. You shall take no stag, boar, or gamebird from the forest."

One man spoke up. "It has been a fair practice to take game feeding on our crops."

Robert nodded. "That is past. You shall take no game. Fence your fields. You will be taxed grain for the game. The gamekeeper shall feed the game that they do not stray into your fields. I will look into a fair bailiwick for the tenants."

"Another tax?" a voice asked.

"You will find the King fair, but he offers you pay for service to him. King James has commissioned a company of volunteers, the Royal Cawmills Cuirassiers. Each tenant who volunteers will receive the equivalent of one-fifth of his rent. If he has sons who volunteer, he shall receive added pay of one-twentieth his rent for each son. I am the Captain of the company and Edward Barkley, Sergeant Major. The Sergeant Major will train and drill the company."

The tenants began to talk among them. Robert raised his arms and called out, "Good men of Cawmills, what say you to your King? Shall Cawmills be remembered for the treachery of Geoffrey Curtis, or shall it be known for stout men, loyal to their sovereign?"

The man who complained about the tax spoke out, "Sir Geoffrey took us hard at the harvest. I am willing to muster and drill in the winter when there is no other work. But could His Majesty give pay in advance?"

Robert turned and stared at Douglas, who was surprised one of the tenants strayed from what he was told to say. Douglas sputtered, "Now Tom, I explained how Sir Geoffrey paid what he could for your meager harvest."

Tom spat back, "I remember your words, but it was not meager. Our harvest was better than most! Don't think we do not know the price of wheat in Berwick-upon-Tweed."

"Now, you know, Tom, we sold in Eyemouth..." Douglas stopped talking.

Robert spoke. "I will give advances on what money I can. But His Majesty will demand a profit. You men are neither poor nor homeless in need of his charity. Now the Sergeant Major will take the recruitment roll. We will be stopping by each family, looking in to see your lands and your needs."

Robert began to walk off when he stopped, turned around, and asked, "Tell me, is there a church in the village?"

Tom replied, "Aye a kirk but no minister. From the day Sir Geoffrey became baron, he decided not to pay the minister. Kept his popish priest, he did. We were left to walk to Berwick or Lamberton to baptize our young and bury our dead."

Barkley called out, "All ye men ready to enlist, wait here. I need a word with the Captain."

Outside the room, Barkley asked Robert, "With eleven pounds for the year, how will you maintain the house and pay the volunteers?"

Robert glanced to be sure they were not overheard, "I will go to Edinburgh tomorrow. I will put up my pay if I must. Keep an eye on Mr. Douglas. We shall arrest him this very day and take him to Edinburgh castle. And Edward, keep an eye out for the horse—and see if you can find a priest hole. Perhaps more than the papist priest was hidden there."

Robert turned to Andrew Douglas, walking by, "Hold Mr. Douglas! We shall now address the house servants. I shall go with you as you call them. You can show me around the house."

Douglas nodded and walked to the servant's staircase down. His quick steps confirmed his worry, "Captain Curtis, don't be putting too much in the words of Tom. The man is always passing his accusations. He got a fair price for his crop. Of course, the price for grain was dear, but his produce not near the bounty he would have you believe. Don't you be thinking…"

"Not to worry, Mr. Douglas, I heard many a complainer in the army. Tell me, in addition to the house servants, how many men work outside?"

Douglas quickly recounted, "There are two in the stable, a smith, a cooper, a mason, a carpenter, and two gardeners."

"And a gamekeeper?" Robert asked.

"Was one—new man—up and left. Haven't taken on another seein' as Sir Geoffrey was off with the army."

"And you left the tenants to poach after a hard year. Well, we will need an experienced man, perhaps two of them very soon."

Douglas looked at Robert. "Two game wardens?"

"If we are to prevent poaching and keep faith with the tenant farmers, yes, we need them. Then there is the house for the foresters—are there cottages in the village?"

Douglas replied as an estate keeper, "There is the gamekeeper's cottage and one other to let. Unless you board them in the castle, we shall need to build more."

Robert smiled. "See how I will depend on you, Douglas? Yes, we will need to build—the house must be made a suitable hunting lodge for His Majesty and his guests. And then we must find a vicar—the King will not abide by a godless village."

Douglas slowed his steps and looked at Robert. "Hunting lodge? His Majesty would come here?"

"It is the nearest place in all of Scotland to London. His Majesty inquired after the hunting lands, and I vouched for the game and a good hunt."

"A royal visit. I never imagined."

Robert looked straight into his face with as broad a smile as he could force, "So you see, we shall need every penny we can find. Ah! The servant's hall. Please introduce me."

Robert met the cooks, maid, and house-hold servants. Andrew Douglas led him to the stable and down to the village to see the cooper, smith, and carpenters. Along the path, Douglas mentioned, "Captain Curtis, the ledger I gave you yesterday. There are certain entries—well, I never once considered Sir, that is, Mister Curtis was a traitor—you see about the eleven pounds—there may be more to be recovered for the Crown."

Robert nodded, trying not to smile, "Yes, about the ledger."

Douglas coughed lightly and replied, "I was just following instructions.   Geoffrey Curtis' instructions. How was I to know that…"

Robert stepped in front of Douglas and said firmly, "Yes, so you have said. Out with it, man! The money."

"Sir—Mister Curtis instructed me that the ledger should show just enough to cover household costs, food for the servants and materials for repairs and such until your cousin, he is your cousin, Captain? Until he returned, if we ran short, I was to see a gentleman in Eyemouth."

Robert could not hide his impatience, "Does this gentleman have a name?"

Andrew Douglas looked up and replied, "Mister Sharpe. John Sharpe. 'Seems he's gone missing. Traveled back and forth to meet with the Captain, he did, but hasn't returned in months."

Robert closed his eyes, shook his head, and sighed. "Of course. Tomorrow you will take me to his house in Eyemouth. And it is not Sir, not lord or even Captain. He, and yes, he is my cousin to the disgrace of the Curtis family, he is simply Geoffrey Curtis. Do you understand?"

Douglas nodded, and then his face cast down, continued, "Bank of Amsterdam. Sir, that is where Geoffrey Curtis keeps his money, in the Bank of Amsterdam. I would leave word with Mister Sharpe, and he would return with what was needed."

Robert smiled. "Amsterdam, close if he needs funds in the Palatine and safely out of reach if he is found out."

They approached the smithy; its doors open to let the heat of the forge escape into the cold February air. The blacksmith was busy with new plowshares. Robert asked, "New plowshares, expensive items in hard times."

The blacksmith did not look up from his work, "Aye, hard times means plantin' larger fields. New fields mean more stone and new plowshares. Risky, but that's the farmers' lot. But even a meager crop can pay more when the grain is scarce."

Robert nodded. "Well, you'll now be paying your rent to the Crown and be obeying forest law."

The blacksmith used his tongs to take a red-hot plowshare from the forge and place it on his anvil. He picked up a hammer, looked at Robert, and said, "So I hear. Tell me, Captain Curtis, my rent?"

"The same. A reduction if you volunteer for the militia."

The blacksmith began pounding the hot metal with his heavy maul.

Robert and Douglas left. Outside Douglas said, "Don't talk much but a good smith."

They walked towards the cooper next door. Robert stopped and asked, "Where did the gamekeeper live? His name wasn't Will Smith?"

Douglas looked surprised, "Not Will Smith, Will Hugh. He left last summer. Said Sir Geoffrey wouldn't be needin' him. Seein' as he was off to war."

"Where did he come from?"

"One of the Howard estates—came with a letter to Sir Geoffrey. Your cousin visited Lord Howard often. He spoke fondly of Lady Catherine Howard. A great Lady, she—was a tragedy when she lost her beauty to the pox. Smitten, he was, for Lady Catherine."

Robert shook his head. "Lady Catherine Howard is old enough to be his mother! I suppose power and influence have a beauty of their own. What did my cousin say when Lord and Lady Howard were banned from the court for corruption?"

"Banned, was she?"

"Too many bribes for the King to overlook."

"Mister Curtis said she came on hard times—most unfair he said—most unfair."

The cooper was shaving staves when Robert visited. "I hear there's money for volunteering—the militia, I hear. Is that right, Warden Curtis, or should I call you Captain Curtis? Seems odd, Sir Geoffrey was Captain Curtis too. I have three strong sons—good boys, make fine militiamen. You send your sergeant here, Captain Curtis. Yes sir, and the signin' pay too."

Robert walked on to the next shop, a harness maker. Before they entered, Robert turned to Douglas, "Go back and find Sergeant Major Barkley. Ask him to talk to the cooper and then join me here. I need a saddlebag."

The harness maker was sewing a leather bridle when Robert came in. "I am fortunate to find a harness maker here in Cawmills—saves me a trip to Berwick-upon-Tweed."

The harness maker looked up and eyed Robert carefully but said nothing.

"Custom work. I need a man to do some custom work—special, not your everyday bridle, harness or yoke. You ever do custom work, Mister..."

"Cox. Adam Cox. 'Depends on what you call custom. Everything I make is custom. You tell me what you need it for, and I make it. No sense in making what I ain't been paid for."

"I am the warden, Captain Robert Curtis."

"I know who you are—tell me what you need—custom."

"Two saddles, each with a place to carry things—things I don't want to be seen or found by say, thieves or robbers on the road. And other special things. You ever do that kind of work, Mister Cox."

"Tell me what you don't want found. I can tell you what you need. I always say, 'let them find something, and they stop looking."

"My Sergeant Major Barkley will tell you what is needed. Tell me, Mister Cox, Mister Sharpe's saddle, the one with the sewn blanket. Did you make it?"

"Did Sharpe send you here? The man owes me money."

"You won't be seeing any money from Sharpe; the man is dead. Trampled by his horse—though conspiring against the King may have played a part. Good day, Mister Cox."

"Best you and your sergeant keep an eye over your shoulder—many a man hereabouts not happy you're here. Good day Captain Curtis."

As Robert left, Cox called out, "Captain Curtis, the militia—I hear Cuirassiers. They will be mounted militia then?"

"Aye, mounted, needing saddles, bridles, baggage— the lot. Plenty of work for a good harness maker—if he enlists!"

Eyemouth was a fishing town that also traded in smuggling. Unguarded by the high border castle of Berwick-upon-Tweed, Eyemouth had few government men or "eyes" to watch the local fishermen and the odd small trade merchant. There was not a family in Eyemouth that did not benefit from the occasional undocumented imports so that even the sheriff only looked about when a complaint reached him from Edinburgh and then only after passing the word. Only one smuggler was ever apprehended in Eyemouth, an unfortunate outsider that ventured into the wrong cove one moonless night.

John Sharpe was well known in Eyemouth, and rumors of his death had preceded Robert and Barkley as they presented their warrants and commissions while making inquiries. The accusation that Eyemouth's Mister Sharpe was a traitor to King and country brought a sudden change in the frosty reception Robert had received. There was a limit to town loyalty and turning on your King was beyond the pale. The local sheriff wasted no time assuring his full assistance in searching the loathsome traitor's property, widowed mother, or not.

After an unsuccessful search of the Sharpe property and an evening of many ales with Barkley, the sheriff, and mayor at the local inn, Robert and Barkley left for Edinburgh with the full support of the Eyemouth town elders and many recruits for the Royal Cawmills Cuirassiers. Edinburgh presented a different problem, getting money from a Scotsman—the King's royal treasurer of Scotland, a man with a long list of royal warrants and insufficient funds to meet them.

The Lord Treasurer carefully examined Robert's warrants and commissions and said bluntly, "Perhaps next year we can see some payment of your emoluments. I expect a good profit from Royal Cawmills Forest, and only then will I grant funds."

Robert pulled a chair over to where he stood in from of the Lord Treasurer, sat down, and said, "Geoffrey Curtis was a traitor, but not a fool. He carried away his fortune with him and has left Cawmills with but a month's funding. I am convinced we can bring a good profit to His Majesty, but you must provide capital until the harvest. Cawmills Forest must be managed and protected, or there will be nothing. With no protection, the tenants will leave, and then what? What will you report to His Majesty?"

The Lord Treasurer stared at Robert. "This is not a

bank. His Majesty doesn't make loans…"

"Cawmills seeks no loan. Cawmills is His Majesty's property. Here is what I propose: Provide what is due my sergeant and me this year, and we will use what is due us to see the forest through the year. We will recover from the profits our due and still provide much-needed funds to the Royal Treasury."

The lord Treasure kept silent, drumming his fingers on the table as he thought.

Robert continued, "What shall I tell the King? That his new Cawmills Forest is now a wasteland of poachers? Do you have a better plan?"

The Lord Treasurer picked up his quill, dipped it in the ink jar, and wordlessly wrote. When he set down the quill pen, he said without looking up, "Take this to the purser and draw your money. There better be a good profit, or I will see your warrant is short-lived."

Robert smiled. "Now, about the pistols, swords, armor, and horses for the Royal Cawmills Cuirassiers."

The lord Treasurer scribbled another note, handed it to Robert, and said, "We Scots have no shortage of weapons."

Robert stood up, took the notes, and walked towards the door. The lord Treasurer called out, "I expect a good accounting. Return as soon as the harvest is sold."

As Robert and Barkley returned to Curtis Castle at Cawmills, Robert told his friend, "Two things remain. We must find an honest forester, and I must secure my emolument from the church. Then we can follow up on Fitzhugh and Will Smith, or is he Will Hugh? I am sure

there is a connection with Lady Catherine Howard—
how we will gain an introduction, I have not worked
out."

CHAPTER 8
FINANCIAL FOOTINGS

Cold sleet fell on Berwick-upon-Tweed as Robert pounded on the manor door of his uncle James, the Viscount of Berwick. Robert was happy despite the miserable weather and cold, wet ride, delighted to be among friends and family. The door swung open, the servant recognized Robert and said, "You can join the other guests visiting his lordship. They are in warming by the fire in the sitting room."

Robert, smiling brightly, followed the servant. As he was announced, he overheard, "Don't be rushed—careful consideration is best... Ah, Robert! Good to see you, nephew! Talk some sense into our good friend Will! Being pushed to leave us," Lord Curtis said, watching Robert enter.

The group around the fire turned to see Robert. Wilhelm appeared confused, and then he saw, *Could it be him? Yes!* Karl Schroeder was standing beside Katharina and another woman, a stranger, wet and shabby in drab clothing. *Is she a nun or abbess?*

Karl came over and hugged Robert. "Good to see you, my friend! I have heard of your exploits—your recent good fortune and the honors from your King! News! I have urgent news for you. But first, this is sister Hulda. Hulda Hahn. Will's sister. She has come to fetch her brother and take our friend away from us, back to Vienna."

"Will? Go back to Vienna? It would not be safe! He has a life here. He is loved and, well, Katie is here!"

Hulda stared into Robert's face and began in perfect French, "Safe? A life here? Certainly not! He was safe with a good life and calling of God until you and your heretic friends and this woman—this Katie—beguiled him in league with the devil nearly brought to ruin a godly priest!"

Will spoke softly. "Now Hulda, that is not true. These are godly people. I decided to help them. They have not brought me to ruin. They have opened my eyes and helped me understand. There were things that I saw— that we saw, you saw them too, Hulda, and mother as well. We knew it was wrong but chose to go along with Papa. I still serve God and His people. They showed me I had a choice and I made it. You, too, have a choice. Father sent you, and mother to the convent. Was it your choice?"

"Mother and I serve God!"

"Serve God—by all means, serve Him! But is the convent where God calls you to serve Him? And our mother? Was that her desire? Or convenient to Papa's ambition?"

"There are questions that should never be asked! Brother, the devil is behind this! Listen to me. Father has arranged for your pardon. The emperor himself has signed the papers. Return with me to Vienna—bring your dirty mistress if you must. Other priests fallen to sinful lust keep their women. She can be overlooked, but you must return soon. The emperor will not be patient."

Wilhelm took a deep breath and rose his voice, "Enough, Hulda! Do not insult my friends and your hosts. Did not Herr Schroeder bring you here? And you speak so cruelly of his daughter, a righteous woman! Enough. We will speak later. Viscount Curtis has offered you dry clothes and a room to refresh yourself from your journey. Go. Change your clothes and return for supper after you rested and recovered the good manners you were taught!"

Hulda snorted her disgust and said, "I will go. As you say, brother, we shall talk again. Thank you, Viscount Curtis, for the hospitality of your house."

As Hulda walked out, she confronted Robert and huffed. "So you are what passes as a priest in this land of heretics. A tool of the devil."

Will broke the stunned silence after Hulda left. "Forgive my sister. She doesn't know you; she doesn't know what she says."

Viscount Curtis chuckled. "For certain, she has no fear of any man."

Katie, who stood by silently through Hulda's tirade, asked sheepishly, "Papa, why did you bring her here?"

Karl hugged and kissed his daughter tenderly. "Werner

brought her to me. She was loudly making enemies with her questions in Eberbach. He was afraid she might 'disappear,' despite her claims of the emperor's pardon for her brother. What else could I do? Wilhelm has risked so much for us, how could I not risk helping his sister?"

"Werner? How is he? And Johann? Are they safe? And friends and neighbors in Eberbach?"

Karl squeezed Katie again and said, "Safe and well. Johann and many of our friends are in Amsterdam. Many, many protestants have taken refuge there. And Werner— well, Werner knows how to take care of himself. He moves about, as I do. He sends his love—is he not like a second father?"

"O Papa, I am so happy that you are here, no matter what terrible things Hulda says."

"Hulda worries after Will as you worry after Johann. She is a good woman. We just haven't seen her best yet. Wait, you shall see. Someday we will love her as we love Will and Robert and Edward and all the house of Curtis!"

Karl placed a soft kiss on Katie's forehead and turned to Robert. "Well, perhaps not all the house of Curtis— my news. Your cousin Geoffrey has escaped."

"Escaped?" Robert and Lord Curtis asked in unison.

Karl nodded. "I'm afraid it's true. Your Commander of the English volunteers, Colonel Herbert, informed me. It seems the very day he received the King's letter ordering him to arrest Captain Sir Geoffrey and Captain Richard, your cousin Geoffrey went missing. It seems by the time word sent from Mannheim reached Frankenthal,

Sir Geoffrey was nowhere to be found."

"He was warned," Robert replied. "Only Major Donald Stock sees Colonel Vere's mail before him—you don't think…"

"Donald Stock playing both sides? I never trusted him. He is playing the hero to Colonel Vere, boasting it was his information sent to the Marquess of Buckingham that uncovered the plot. He insists the leak to Geoffrey must have come from the court or perhaps you, his cousin."

Robert took a deep breath, "He only confirms my early belief—the man is a liar and never to be trusted."

Karl nodded. "Colonel Vere is no fool. He will not be easily put off from the obvious. We have established another chain of communication that does not pass through his adjutant's office."

Robert looked up and closed his eyes. "Cousin Geoffrey moved his money to the Bank of Amsterdam. He would immediately go there for funds. What about his servant? Is he missing as well?"

"Yes, his servant is gone as well. Your cousin lived well in Frankenthal. He had money. He may wait before going to the bank, or he may send his servant fearing a trap."

Robert thought for a moment and answered, "With his man dead, he has few friends to help him. The papal envoy, Don Lorenzo, he was in contact with the plotters. Don Lorenzo has the means to hide and protect him."

Karl nodded. "Don Lorenzo is still attached to Count Tilly, who is tightening the blockade of Heidelberg as we speak. General von Mansfeld was driven east and will not move until Duke Christian of Brunswick marches in the spring and only after the roads are firm. It is difficult, but I can still get word to Colonel Herbert in Heidelberg."

"What word of Captain Richard?"

"Captain Richard confessed and is being held until trial. He accepts the King's judgment but swears he would not have followed through on orders to murder Colonel Herbert or surrender Heidelberg. He has asked to be permitted to defend the city alongside his comrades before facing execution."

Robert sighed. "It was a hard thing to learn that my friend was among the plotters. I want to believe his confession and his plea to fight for his King is honest. It is to his credit that he did not flee. Wasn't he warned?"

"Yes, he was warned. He told the Colonel that honor demanded that he confess and do the right."

Robert's eyes widened. "How—who warned him?"

"A coded letter—like all communications. He did know the source."

Karl grasped Robert's shoulder. "We will find your cousin Geoffrey. We have many friends in Amsterdam— I'm known in the bank. And Don Lorenzo can be watched. But I fear most for your comrades in Heidelberg. Count Tilly will want his victory before Duke Christian and General von Mansfeld can relieve them."

Robert bowed his head and stared into the fire. The room was quiet; the only sound was the crackling of the embers. Robert lifted his head, turned, and smiled at Katie, who was standing silently off to the side.

"Forgive me, Katie. It seems a hard day for you. Take

joy in the news your brother is safe, and your papa has come to visit. Do not be disheartened by sister Hulda— her words come from her love for her brother Will, and do you not share in that love? Now, as the mistress in my father's house, I look to you to bring good cheer. A hug and a kiss in friendship would do me well."

Katie smiled. "Robert, you say such things! Must you always look for my embrace?"

Robert smiled. "Will has won your heart. Dear Katie, can I not settle for a hug and a kiss now and then?"

Katharina hugged Robert tight and kissed his cheek, "How can I not hug the man who loves Will like a brother. Tell me, where is Edward? He deserves a kiss as well."

"Sergeant Major Barkley is managing things at Cawmills Forest. There is much to do and even more to learn. Barkley, I mean Edward, will be jealous he missed your kiss. But more pleasant things—tell me about your work in the hospital."

Will escorted his sister Hulda down to dinner. Viscount Berwick rose and welcomed her to his table. Hulda nodded meekly, "I must thank you for your hospitality, Lord Curtis. My brother has told me of the great kindness you have shown him."

Everyone watched Hulda in silence. She turned and smiled meekly. "I beg your forgiveness for my rude behavior this afternoon. My brother Wilhelm has told me of your shared plight."

Hulda slid her chair to sit down; her eyes shifted to

Kate, and the smile drained away from her face.

Robert said, "You are truly a brave woman, Hulda, to search for your brother on your own in a country at war."

"I trusted God."

Karl smiled. "Indeed, God was in it! Surely, only by His will did Werner meet her and bring her to me. I tell you the magistrate holds Wilhelm as an accomplice in the murder of Major Ryskamp, the Eberbach garrison commander. If the magistrate could not be trusted to honor Wilhelm's pass signed by the Emperor, we could not trust him to treat Hulda honorably and not hold her hostage for Wilhelm's arrest."

Hulda looked at her brother. "Murder? Are you an accomplice to murder? We heard you ran off with heretics, besot by a foolish girl, but murder?"

Robert interrupted, "I killed Major Ryskamp. It was wrong, but I was enraged to find him—he tried to—he forced himself on Katharina. In her own house, he tried…"

Karl interrupted, "It is true. Your brother Wilhelm merely posted the confession, which proclaimed the killing of the major in defense of my daughter."

Charles Curtis turned to Hulda and asked, "My child, surely you are precious in the sight of your father, tell me, why did your father permit you to undertake such a perilous journey?"

Hulda looked down. "Our brother Maximilian would not go. He hates Wilhelm, always has. Wilhelm questions their greed—Papa's and Max's. Father cares nothing for Wilhelm either, only the family name, titles, and estates.

He would have ignored this had not mama insisted."

Will looked up. "How is mother? Is she well? Has she found peace?"

Hulda reached out and took Will's hand. "She is well. But no. No, she has not found peace. She refuses to take vows. She lives in the convent as in prison. She claims she made a vow as a wife. And a wife and mother she remains, no matter what our father says."

The young woman paused with a sigh and continued, "And there are the rumors..."

"What rumors," Wilhelm asked.

Hulda looked directly into her brother's eyes. "Father told us that the Archbishop would no longer overlook a bishop living with a family after the scandal of the Prince-Archbishop of Salzberg..."

"Yes, yes, he was ordered to separate from his family—but generously. I know this."

"But, brother, what if—what if that was not why we—mother and I—were sent off to the convent? The rumor—and I have heard from several others—the rumor is he has another mistress, a young woman. He tries to hide her, but it seems some have found him out, though the archbishop has said nothing. There you have it. He has put away mother for a younger woman. He is, he is just—just a beast in holy robes."

Wilhelm leaned over and hugged his sister. "And still mother honors her vow as his wife before God. As the Bible says, 'Who can find a virtuous woman, for her price is far above rubies...'"

Will squeezed Hulda's hand and asked, "And you,

Hulda, did you take vows?"

Hulda smiled meekly. "Not yet. I am a novice, but I am not ready—I can't make the vow. I look at mother— at her sacrifice for us and see another calling. I see mother's calling as holy and unto the Lord. Her service is loving and true, not self-serving like father's and Max's."

Will leaned over and kissed his sister's forehead. Hulda looked up and said, "Wilhelm, mama is worried. She longs to see you again—to know you are safe and faithful in your service."

Will closed his eyes to stop the tear welling up. "I know. I owe her that."

Charles Curtis offered, "It might be wise, Will, that you at once write your mother and inform her that Hulda has arrived safely. Give her comfort in that knowledge."

Katie ventured, "Will, why not bring Hulda to the hospital and the orphanage tomorrow that she might see the work our Lord has called you to. Does she not owe you that as well? There is time to determine what you must do."

Hulda looked at her brother. "Please, brother, I would see what draws you away from your family."

Will smiled. "Yes. Please come. There is so much work! But God is good, and needs are being met."

Katie smiled and said, "Hulda, you must allow me to lend you a dress—and perhaps help with your hair. We do not want you to be confused with a girl from the workhouse—though surely they are no less beautiful to our Lord."

Hulda stared at Katie and then said, "It would be nice to wear a dress again."

The conversation turned to the plight of the German protestants in exile in Amsterdam and throughout the United Netherlands. Johann had escorted two groups and would soon undertake a third mission under the guidance of Karl's network of watchers. Robert listened politely but could not take his eyes away from the resolute young woman in a nun's habit.

Robert saw Will, Katie, and Hulda off the next morning after breakfast. Hulda was smiling brightly, her black hair brushed and held high under a blue hat. She wore a blue gown and white bodice, highlighting her soft blue eyes and fair skin. Hulda blushed as Robert bowed before her as they went out the door. "Captain Curtis," she replied, "I have only seen such manners at the court in Vienna."

Robert smiled brightly and replied, "When a lady, nay two ladies of grace and beauty pass through our door, what else can a gentleman do? Good day, my lady, Hulda, and you, Katharina."

Will turned and stared at Robert, shook his head, and said, "What a difference between this new Captain Curtis and my old friend Lieutenant Curtis."

Katie smiled and said, "Good day Robert!"

Later that day, Robert was writing a letter of introduction to the Bishop of Durham whose diocese included Berwick-upon-Tweed, when he received a letter from Archbishop Abbot. He put down his pen, opened the letter, and began to read. He was relieved to learn his visit to the Bishop of Durham would not be necessary. Archbishop Abbot had come to terms with his friend, Bishop Richard Niele. It confirmed support for Robert's preferment, and the emoluments for the new works in Berwick-upon-Tweed would be funded jointly by the Baron of Tweedbridge and the Archbishop of Canterbury. Robert was to acknowledge the pastoral oversight of the Bishop of Durham and keep him informed of the works of mercy in Berwick-upon-Tweed. His Grace recommended a call upon Lord Bishop Niele at a convenient date. Robert had longed to visit Durham Cathedral and honor the memory of Saint Cuthbert of Lindisfarne.

Robert smiled and thought, *Well, my funding is secure here—even so, I cannot fund the militia company. Perhaps my uncle can be persuaded to provide a small loan for me to carry over until harvest.*

Robert noted a small postscript on a second sheet to Archbishop Abbot's letter. When he finished reading it, he set it down and said to himself, "I will need a place for Mrs. Hawkins here in Berwick-upon-Tweed, and I must notify the headmaster of his new students."

CHAPTER 9
COMPANIES AND CLERGY

Edward Barkley's bellowing carried above the staccato blasts of pistols. He acquired the mark of a sergeant, a loud, angry voice of authority. "Eyes open! Arm straight. Aim at the target! The ball will go where it is pointed, not where you wish or hope!"

Barkley walked down the line of his twenty volunteers, barking commands as he went. "Arm out. Aim. Right arm. Which eye? Which eye? Use your right eye to sight along the gun barrel." Walking further, he said, "Straighten that arm—don't squint." At the end of the line, he then commanded, "Reload and wait for my command."

"Careful with that powder, lad—keep the barrel up! Up! Now the ball and wadding. Careful. Pistols up. Trigger set. Ready. Aim—arms out straight, sight down the barrel. Fire!"

When Barkley ordered the targets retrieved, he was not surprised by the few holes in most targets. He was surprised by the tight pattern of holes—no misses from one quiet young man from off the Royal Forest. "What's your name, son? Barkley asked.

"Lilburn, Aiden Lilburn."

"Where did you learn to shoot, Lilburn?"

"No different than lookin' down the shaft of an arrow or bolt of a crossbow, Just can't be worryin' about the kick after the shot."

"Hear that, men?" Barkley bellowed. "No different than lookin' down the shaft of an arrow or the bolt of a crossbow!"

Barkley turned to Lilburn. "Corporal, take the other end of the line, show the men how to aim to hit the target."

Lilburn answered, "Yes, sergeant, wait—corporal?"

"It's Master Sergeant—and stay after drill. I want to speak more with you."

"Aye, Master Sergeant—remain after the drill," Lilburn replied with a smile.

After the pistol drill—after the guns were cleaned and collected and the men lined up at the door of the tower to return the pistols in good order, as Barkley went to insert the iron key into the lock, he turned to his new corporal Lilburn. He said sternly, "Don't be thinkin' you're a cuirassier yet, Lilburn. There's more to soldierin' than a good aim. Won't be so easy ridin' a skittish horse frightened by artillery and shell. No, won't be easy when they're shootin' back at you or chargin' like wild men with pikes. Then there's the waitin'—the wet and the cold—or so hot your throat is too dry to speak. Weeks of boredom interrupted by hours of terror."

Barkley's voice fell off, and his face drained to a blank stare.

"Then why do you do it, Master Sergeant? Why do you soldier?"

Barkley studied the eager young man. "Why do I soldier? While soldierin', I found who I am."

Aiden Lilburn stared at Barkley but dared not question him further. Before Barkley swung open the heavy iron-studded door, there on the ground before him, he saw the short straw, and he knew.

Barkley turned to the line of volunteers and bellowed in his best Sergeant Major voice, "You will enter one at a time, give your name and pistol number and hand your pistol to Corporal Lilburn. The corporal will confirm the number and its condition to me and return the pistol to the rack. All in good order, men—aye, soldierin' is all in good order!"

Once all the weapons were secured and the volunteers released, Barkley said to Lilburn, "You don't live on the estates, that is, in the Royal Forest—why did you volunteer? Where are you from?"

Young Aiden's face was open, and as unguarded as only the youth can be. "I heard in Eyemouth, lookin' for work. Heard there was an enlistment bonus—maybe somethin' could come of it."

Barkley stared at the boy no more than eighteen and waited for him to continue.

"Born on Lindisfarne, a place only a monk could love. Been workin' my way north stoppin' by great houses and estates, doin' what I could find."

"Where did you learn to shoot?"

"Was no great learnin' just something I could do. 'Helped out a gamekeeper. He learned me the crossbow. 'Relax, breathe easy, be patient—that's the trick,' he used to say."

"Did he teach you to track, herd, and care for the game?"

"Aye—'biggest part of the job."

"Go to the manor house—to the back and ask after Mister Douglas. Tell him you are a gamekeeper, and he is to find you a room and place at the table until Captain Curtis returns."

Lilburn smiled and got up to leave. Barkley called out, "A room and food only until the Captain returns, corporal!"

Once the door closed behind Lilburn, Barkley stood up and slowly walked around the armory level of the tower. *What was he looking for? Is anything missing? Out of place? Who has the key?* Barkley slowly searched the tower, level by level.

"I'm told you have urgent news," Will said, as he entered the drawing-room in the Viscount's townhouse.

"Yes, my friend, everything is in order. Your position secured and funds of your own available. No need for me to visit the Bishop of Durham. I can get on with my inquiries for the Archbishop and His Majesty."

Will walked to the window and looked out into the late winter dusk. "Well, that's very good for you, Robert. Get back to your inquiries. I see that the vicar of

Berwick-upon-Tweed hospital, orphanage, and workhouse can accept his title and his money without guilt, knowing he has left the work to others."

Turning to Robert, he said, "You have not once visited the poor, sick and helpless entrusted to your care. You have not prayed among them or offered them the eucharist. You have not seen them or heard their pleas. Just an office to you, one among the many you seek. You assume that I will do the work and be happy. Tell me why I should not return to Vienna with Hulda and fulfill my duties as a priest without the restriction or danger in this land of exile where I am forbidden to say a mass."

Robert's jaw dropped, and stunned, he turned to face his friend's rebuke. "You pierce me, my friend. I do care, I do. I am sorry, I thought—it's just that you have a gift and I struggle, I don't—I can't be the man that you are."

"How do you know if you haven't tried? Most only want someone to listen—to believe you care. Come with me tomorrow. See what must be done—for surely, they need a priest, a vicar to pastor them. What will you do when I leave?"

Robert walked beside his friend. "You must not leave! I will go with you. Doesn't the parish priest serve communion? They remain in the parish."

"He comes—but then why is there a new vicar? It is because there is more than a parish vicar can do. Have you ever spoken to him?"

"Will, you know you cannot return to Vienna. You cannot be the simple, honest priest where your father is a Bishop, and the court is as corrupt as you say. You would be silenced—compromised. You are not one to compromise…"

Will shot back, "And I have not compromised here?"

"But your feelings for Katie—you have an opportunity to live honestly, loving God and loving a wife."

"Truly, is it my love for her and God, or temptation?—a trial that I must endure?"

Robert sighed. "So it remains—you still do not see. I brought you here to see that God calls us into a community. We are stronger together. A good wife—a godly woman—is a gift—strength from our heavenly Father, not a distraction or a temptation. And Hulda— Hulda understands this, she has said as much. You must allow her to serve as she feels called—not as chattel sent off to save your father embarrassment. No, my friend— tomorrow you will show me how to serve. It is true, I must not allow my new-found bent for inquiries to pull me away from serving God—and you will see too, that you have been called here for a purpose."

The next morning found Robert and Wilhelm walking the narrow streets of Berwick-Upon-Tweed down towards the river, through the narrow gate into the lower city and to the U-shaped stone building on the flat river plain. The hospital occupied one large wing and the orphanage the other wing. The kitchen, laundry, physician's surgery, staff rooms, and a small chapel filled the middle between the two wings.

The hospital was two floors of beds in a row. The upper ward was fitted with beds framed into the wall with privacy curtains. These beds were reserved for the merchant class, men and women with no heirs to care for them. In return for their property, they were afforded the best care. The lower ward, with row after row of cots with straw mattresses, housed the poor whose treatment was supplied free by the parish.

Will instructed, "I like to start my day in the chapel, praying for God's grace, preparing my heart to serve His children. I rotate days where I begin my prayer rounds. Neither rich nor poor is more or less deserving of God's grace. Illness, age, and death do not value one above the other."

Robert nodded. "Let me join you in your prayers of preparation—and a psalm—I find a psalm brings my mind to our Lord."

After Wilhelm and Robert prayed and recited Scripture for half an hour, Will said, "The parish vicar keeps elements of the sacraments here. Surely, he would not object to you, a priest, and now Vicar of the hospital to serve the eucharist feast today. Come. I will assist you. Today we start in the lower ward."

Robert stared at the chalice and loaf before him. Will nodded. "I will introduce you and pray with them. Then you offer the bread and cup. Come, our flock awaits."

Robert blessed the cup and the bread, took them, and followed Will to the hospital ward. Will greeted each patient warmly by name, asking after their condition, and listening to their small talk. He smiled and chuckled or frowned as each one shared the last day's events. He introduced his great friend and new Vicar of the Hospital the Reverend Captain Curtis. "He will hear your confession and after our prayers, share the Lord's Supper with you. Now, what shall I pray for?"

More than one patient whispered, "Brother Will, why don't you bring the Lord's Supper, I know you are a priest—I have watched how you bless us. This fellow is nice enough and so too the parish Vicar, but they will never love us as you do."

Robert was surprised but found himself smiling as the patients appeared unconcerned that he overheard their comments. After the second patient spoke likewise, Robert found himself replying, "Soon. Brother Will soon shall be ordained in the Church of England and will find the joy of Christ in administering the sacraments."

Will took the patient's hands and replied, "Thank you, brother, but you do not know my friend Robert as I do—he too is a man of grace and love. When he has spent more time with you, you will love him as much as I do."

The patient stared at Robert and said, "He has a kind face—more kind than the doctor. A Reverend Captain, you say? Never heard such a thing, but Lord Curtis is a kind gentleman. A relative? Learn from Lord Curtis, Captain, and you will do well. Learn from brother Will, and you will do better!"

Robert smiled. "I will do just as you say. Now receive my blessing—the Lord bless you and keep you this day and forever. Amen."

The orphanage was a busy place, filled with the exuberance of youth. The children were given duties at an early age. The youngest- toddlers—filled with curiosity and the wonder of learning, were treated with favored attention by the women charged with their care. Entering the nursery, Robert and Wilhelm found Katie chasing after a giggling toddler running with her diaper in her hand. In the corner, Hulda was singing a French lullaby to two infants in her arms. Robert laughed and said to Will, "So this is how Katie spends her day!"

Will smiled. "She would spend more of it here if she could, but she also accompanies the nurses and sits with patients. And stories! How she enjoys telling the older children Bible stories after they have finished their chores."

Robert nodded. "Tell me, their chores are not onerous, I pray."

"The girls do laundry, help in the kitchen, help with the younger children, and learn domestic skills. When they are ready, by age ten and some as young as seven or eight, they may be put into service in manor houses or inns. They are prepared to become wives and servants, though some become skilled cooks, bakers, and often brewers."

Robert interrupted, "Reading and writing? The catechism?"

Will shook his head. "No. The grammar school is open only to boys, sons of freedmen. But the girls are capable and chaste. There is no dishonor to growing up an orphan."

"But their opportunities are less…"

Will replied, "Less? No less than any girl growing up in Berwick who is not privileged to be born into a noble or merchant family. If a girl wants to learn to read, there are always religious orders."

Robert sighed. "And the orphan boys?"

Will said, "The boys tend animals, cut wood, tend fires, help carry the invalids and labor as they can. They are loaned out for the salmon run to the fishermen along the river. They work in the ropewalk running back forth as hemp is spun first to yarn and laid into rope. Only the oldest are allowed to work the net and rope tarring. They are all put out of the orphanage by ten as laborers, ropemakers, wool cleaners, or farm laborers. Some are apprenticed to a tradesman. Some with the right skills and personality, go into service into the manor houses."

"But again, no school."

"The grammar school will take them in if their master wants them to learn to read or write."

"Is there no hope of adoption?"

"Very little. Sometimes a merchant or tradesman and his wife will adopt if there is a fervent desire for children. And bastard children of the nobility and wealthy are placed in adoption. But orphans? These children can be had very young as laborers without the risk of an unhappy adoption. Most of these children have parents—they have a family name. They just don't have an opportunity."

Hulda wandered over to Will and Robert. "Brother, it is such good work you do here. And Katie, such a heart—a heart of compassion."

Turning to Robert, she said, "I still don't know about you, Captain Curtis. My brother commends your love of

God, and Katie speaks of your bravery. But I see a man unsure of himself hiding behind his duties."

Robert said nothing.

Hulda looked into Robert's eyes. "Do not hurt them." And she went back to her choir of toddlers.

Will turned to Robert and said, "Come with me to the workhouse. And we must see the parish vicar."

As they walked down the wharf street towards the workhouse for the poor and homeless, Will called out to the parish vicar, also making his way there. "Father Witten, you remember Captain Curtis?"

The vicar turned to Robert and said, "So here you are, Curtis. You've done well for yourself with the commission your uncle bought you. Better than you did at Cambridge. Now I hear you have won the patronage of His Grace, Archbishop Abbot. Set you up nicely. Well, there is enough work for all of us."

"My apologies, Father Witten, I should have called sooner. Will was about to introduce me to the poor house. I would have the great benefit of your opinions on the work of mercy here." Robert replied.

The Reverend Gerald Witten had served the parish of Berwick-Upon-Tweed for twenty years. His father was a ship chandler who wanted better for his son. But Gerald was not an ambitious man, he accepted the patronage of Lord Curtis and served the people of Berwick humbly.

"Politics, Reverend Curtis, politics. It is the bane of the church in general and in here in Berwick particularly."

"They're all Calvinists—Presbyterians—behind my

back and in their hearts—the burghers and the people alike. They follow the Scotsman John Knox. Berwick-upon-Tweed, for all its prominence and prosperity, has no bishop. A bishop brings wealth to the church. He brings influence and privilege—and money. The city elders attend Church of the Holy Trinity only to qualify for the vote—and give sparingly. The city—the corporation it is called—for that is what it is—granted a charter in 1604. The city hall and guildhall are the same. The city pays only for the grammar school, leaving charity and works of mercy to the church. The church tax is paltry, and we could not sustain the work without Lord James Curtis. And he is getting on in years.

"Then, you should be pleased with the new appointments; my uncle is to double his support."

The vicar nodded. "Yes, that is most welcome. But if His Grace genuinely wants to help the people of Berwick-upon-Tweed, Tweedmouth, Spittal, the whole of the northeast—give us a bishop! And you, Robert, will you support the work when your uncle's title comes to you?"

"My father is the heir..."

"But a year younger than his Lordship—no Robert, you are heir, but are you committed?"

Reverend Witten stopped and faced Robert. "Do you know the opposition your uncle faces? The merchants and the burghers call him Lord Curtis to his face, but behind his back, they despise him. He did his job for King and country too well. They have not forgotten his efficient collection of the ship tax. Taxes are paid by the wealthy.

The excise taxes make our port more expensive as it is. He is opposed, and you will be tested by them when the day comes."

Witten sighed. "They resent his charity to the poor. They say he puts smugglers above gentlemen."

Robert looked ahead as they walked. "The poor in the workhouse, do they pay their way?"

The vicar kept walking. "That is the intent. And, when times are good, they do. The workhouse accepts the homeless, and in return for their room and board, they are put to profitable work. It is the intent of the church that man should be encouraged to work and not be a burden upon others. We have done well in moving our tenants back into work of their own. The difficulty lies in providing care and opportunity for the homeless without taking work from those who have it."

Robert nodded. "So work must be found that would go begging."

"Robert, there is no work in Berwick today that goes begging as you would say. But we must find them work that allows us to feed them. We do our best to supplement with seasonal work, harvest labor, and salmon fishing. Thank goodness, the River Tweed is the best Salmon river in all of England! We loan out those proven dependable, and they often stay on with their new masters. But we must have work for them all the time, so we employ them in the most loathsome jobs, combing, cleaning and dying wool and in producing cloth from inferior wool with the lowest margin."

The men entered the great door open against the cold

and staggered when they breathed in the foul odor of the wool baths. Robert coughed as they made their way towards a man raking wool from the lye bath, working it up and down until it dripped dirty white.

Father Witten spoke. "The lye bath removes the dirt and the stained oils from the wool. It will be treated with new oils to recover its natural water repellants. Then it will be combed again before being spun and woven into fabric."

He moved on. "Only able men work the lye baths. I find it too dangerous for women and children."

He turned to Robert. "The guildhall makes no such exceptions."

Continuing, he said, "The women do the combing. They must comb out the strands. It is tiresome work, but safe. They also do spin. I try to teach the young men and women the loom—it offers them a future with a skill. There is still the challenge of dealing with the most inferior wool and crude loom. The cloth is suitable only for sackcloth. After the hemp harvest, I try to find enough hemp to teach weaving sailcloth as well as employing the children in the rope yard. I must be careful there, not to upset the guild—very jealous—the ropemakers and sailcloth guild."

Robert nodded and asked, "Do you find work for servants, in the manse or inns?"

Witten nodded. "Aye, but it is risky for the women. Many an innkeeper seeks serving wenches—but in truth, they recruit prostitutes. I will not abide by such foul behavior. The best we can prepare is milkmaids and scullery maids unless they have experience before they come to us. I will not send someone seeking our mercy into sin or slavery."

"And brother Will, you have taught him this as well?"

Reverend Witten placed his arm on Will's shoulder, smiled, and said, "Father, for I have deduced he is a priest—but we shall call him brother. Brother Hahn teaches me. So, I shall not quarrel with his appointment. Be sure, Robert, that I and Church of the Holy Trinity will work with you—all the more so if the work is increased. My question to you is: are you up to it? Are you prepared for the fights to come?"

Robert turned to Will. "If my brother does not abandon me."

CHAPTER 10
NEW ARRIVALS

When Robert returned to Cawmills Forest, Edward introduced him to his new Justice in Eyre and prospective Forester. Colin Gordon held the appointment as Justice in Eyre. He was educated in the law at Saint Andrew's and spent one year as a clerk in Edinburgh. A nephew of the Earl of Huntly, chief of the Clan Gordon, this was his first step in a career guided by his uncle. The prospective Forester was a middle-aged man named Neil Burns. He carried only a letter of introduction from the Lord Treasurer saying, "Mister Burns is an experienced forester, an honest man who can be trusted in your circumstances at Cawmills Forest."

Shaking the hand of Colin Gordon, Robert said, "Welcome to Cawmills Forest Justice Gordon. Shall we find you a place in the village or..."

Gordon replied, "My quarters in Curtis Castle are comfortable enough and will serve me sufficiently for now." Robert nodded. "Curtis Castle is the King's house and the bedrooms set aside for his party. You may stay here for now but know that you must find other quarters in the event of a royal visit."

Gordon nodded. "Of course, Captain Curtis. A visit by His Highness would be a great honor—as he has yet to return to Scotland since he accepted the English crown."

Robert's eyes bore into Colin Gordon. "I am warden here and Sheriff of Cawmills by the appointment of His Majesty, King James. I require everyone serving in Curtis Castle and Cawmills Forest to remember this is the King's estate, and it will be respected and honored as such. Deputy warden, Sergeant Major Barkley, will decide where you hear your trials—it will not be in Curtis Castle. You will present your requests to him. You will make all requests of the Warden first through the Deputy Warden. Sergeant Major Barkley speaks for me."

Gordon stared at Robert before he nodded and walked off.

Robert turned to Neil Burns and extended a hand and said politely, "Mister Burns, come with us. Barkley, Sergeant Major Barkley, and I will show you the forest. You do ride?"

"Aye, Captain. Ridin' covers the grounds quickly. I must ride with the royal party, though I find my work is done best afoot."

"Go to the stables and have them saddle three horses. Barkley and I will join you in a few minutes."

When Robert and Barkley were alone, Barkley asked, "What do make of the Lord Treasurer's letter—special circumstances?"

Robert replied, "Yes, and a Gordon. Why here? The Gordons are known to be fierce Catholics. My cousin, a Catholic, is stripped of his title, yet a Catholic comes here for a minor appointment?"

"He is a cocky fellow," Barkley replied.

"Yes, I want you to keep him in his place. Charge him for food and lodging. For now, if he brings a case to trial, it shall be held in the village church. It is not being used."

Robert sighed. "The preacher of the Kirk in Coldstream told me no one from Cawmills comes to his church. I believe everyone here is Roman Catholic. A Roman Catholic from a prominent family seeks office here? The Lord Treasurer sent Mister Burns as someone to trust."

Turning to Barkley, he added, "Did you find the priest hole?"

Edward Barkley shook his head. "No. But someone has been in the tower. I don't know who has the key or what they were looking for. I found nothing amiss, but someone has a key."

Robert nodded. "Keep on it. Let's go—see what we can learn from Mr. Burns."

Barkley replied, "One bit of good news, found a lad who will make a good gamekeeper. The young man can shoot a pistol truer than any man in our regiment."

Robert asked, "An outsider?"

"From Lindisfarne, heard we were recruiting. Made him a corporal and asked him to stay on as gamekeeper."

"Yes, very good. If Burns is the man that I expect he is, we should have two men we can trust."

Robert stopped and turned once again to face Barkley. "Look about this place—top of the hill—comings, and goings cannot be hidden. What if—what if there is no priest hole? What if there is no priest hole because the priest is hidden in plain sight? My cousin has established a Catholic order on the estate, and their priest lives among them. But who? Whoever he is, he has his chalice, vestments, crucifix, and rosary. Find them, and we find our priest. Find our priest, and we find my cousin's connections to Count Gondomar, Simon Stock, and Catholic conspirators."

Edward replied, "Perhaps something was or is hidden in the tower. We will certainly get no help from anyone here."

Robert smiled. "We now have fresh eyes. Come, let's find the cut of our mister Burns' sail."

Lord James and Charles Curtis wandered about the great hall of Curtis Castle under the watchful eye of Andrew Douglas as they waited for Robert to walk from the tower. Lord James asked, "Tell me, Douglas, what has become of my brother's arms? I remember they were displayed prominently over the fireplace."

Removed on the orders of Captain Curtis—I believe he retains them in the tower, my Lord, but then no one is permitted in the tower."

"Hard news, my nephew, Sir Geoffrey. A most capable man. Converting to Catholicism, I could accept. A man should be free to serve God as his conscience leads, but a traitor to our King?"

"Perhaps his conscience could not permit his service to a King who denied Catholics access to their church, my Lord."

Charles stared at Andrew Douglas, surprised by the presumption of his remark. Sir James said nothing, his eyes on the King's arms above the mantel, moved down to the religious tile affixed to the keystone of the fireplace.

Lord Curtis continued softly, "And now our ancestral home forfeited to the crown. Very hard news. Yet my nephew keeps you all on. Good of him. Good of him indeed."

Robert and Edward came in, and Mister Douglas said, "Here is Captain Curtis. Is there anything else, Lord Curtis?"

Robert looked at Douglas and said, "That will be all, Mister Douglas."

"Father, Uncle! Good to see you! What brings you to Curtis Castle? I am glad that you are here—so much to get done—but pleased—I would be pleased to show you Cawmills once more!"

Lord Curtis spoke. "I brought you a letter."

Robert looked puzzled. "Delivering letters, uncle?"

Lord Curtis smiled. "I believe it a special letter—carried by Mary Hawkins. She is my guest while her children enter their studies at Berwick Grammar School. Lovely woman. My house has become a place of grace and warmth with your friends Robert. I find it hard to let them leave!"

"I have just made her acquaintance, uncle—I have

hardly earned her friendship."

"Well, you and Edward have made a favorable impression—she sees you as saving knights who freed her from the dragon's lair. She gives you this letter from Lady Eleanor Montclair. I thought it might be urgent."

Sir James handed Robert the letter and said, "She also asks a favor. One of her sons believes he wants to become a gamekeeper like his father—she insists he continues his education. She asks that he is apprenticed while still attending studies at the grammar school."

Robert took the letter, and absent-mindedly began, "We perhaps we could arrange…"

Barkley interrupted, "What Robbie meant to say is, we will apprentice the lad under the forester and gamekeeper. He will learn the forest law as well as gamekeeping and have a future as a gentleman forester. I shall see to it myself!"

Lord Curtis smiled. "Splendid, Edward! Mrs. Hawkins will be pleased with your proposal—a gentleman is what she desires for all her sons."

Robert quickly read the letter then stared off, lost in his thoughts.

"Well, son, what does she say?" Charles Curtis asked.

"Lady Montclair is to host a hunt and a gala ball. She intends to reintroduce her friend, Countess Howard, into society after their scandal—she asks me to attend as her escort. She mentions an interest in my inquiries at Bramshill House."

Charles Curtis laughed. "She asked you? Such a thing is never done! Who is this Lady Montclair?"

Barkley laughed. "Nothing Lady Montclair says or does would surprise me. The woman, and a beauty she is, she knows her mind and will have her say—and Robbie, she will always have her way!"

Lord Curtis remarked, "Brother, Edward is quite correct. Lady Eleanor is the daughter and only heir of the Earl of Montclair. She inherits a fortune though no title. She is refreshingly honest and has never shown herself constrained by convention. When is this event? Perhaps I can help prepare you."

"About time, you learned to be a proper gentleman, Robbie!" Barkley laughed.

"A proper gentleman? Well, deputy warden Barkley. You will learn proper English, read the classics, learn etiquette, and you too will become a gentleman."

Berwick-upon-Tweed was only an hour by horse from Curtis Castle. Riding little more than a mile south of the Royal Forest, Robert, Barkley, Charles, and Sir James crossed the English border into the tenant farms of Berwick Bounds, lands of Sir James. As they passed the estate house of Berwick Bounds, Robert turned around and gazed at the tower of old Curtis Castle. "So close yet so different."

Sir James turned to look as well. After a short gaze, he said, "That is why I make my home in Berwick. The Curtis family has been on this land for centuries. We have watched the border change and been careful in our allegiances. Dividing the land was meant to save it. I could not abide living in a manor in sight of the tower—

watching us grow apart. But with Curtis Castle lost, well..."

Lord Curtis smiled. "Perhaps you will be favored by the King, and he will restore and reunite the baronies."

Robert sighed. "I don't feel like an heir—I never believed it would fall upon me, I..."

Sir James nodded. "You will do us proud, Robert, I know you will."

The men rode on into Berwick, towards the high wall above the River Tweed to the grand stone manse built against the wall of the old fortress. They found Mary Hawkins and her three children sitting in the great hall. Mary motioned for her children to stand, and they all bowed politely. "Lord Curtis, we are most grateful for your generous hospitality. Be assured as soon as I find lodgings for my family; we will no further bother you. I have already spoken to the Reverend Witten and have arranged to teach the girls and any boys not enrolled in the grammar school on Sundays after worship. School will not interfere with workhouse or orphanage duties. But lodging is very scarce in the city. I have asked his assistance in finding..."

"My dear Mrs. Hawkins, please be assured you are my most welcome guests. A busy house, one with children, is a happy house. I will hear no more of it. Now I have fetched my nephew and sergeant Barkley. They were most anxious for your safe arrival. Master Sergeant Barkley has a proposal regarding young Peter. Sergeant."

Mary nodded. "Captain Curtis, Master Sergeant Barkley, I am most grateful for all you have done for us."

Putting a hand on the tallest, she said, "This is Peter. He wishes to honor his father, a man who loved the forest and all of God's good creation."

Edward walked over to Peter and said, "Young man, indeed, you shall honor your father, and I will help you. But you must be schooled—as both your father and mother desired. So, grammar school it is, but also, but five miles away is Cawmills Royal Forest, where you shall be apprenticed to the gamekeeper and the forester. Perhaps someday you shall become a warden of the Kingwoods! An officer of the crown and protector of the forest. How does that suit ye, lad?"

Peter replied, "I will do my best, sir!"

Robert smiled as he watched Peter's face brighten. Mary, dressed much finer than he remembered at Bramshill, beamed as she gazed upon Peter.

Barkley smiled. "I will see that you do, lad. Now, who is this fine fellow?"

Edward extended a hand to Peter's brother.

"I am Paul Hawkins, sir."

"And what is to become of you, Master Paul Hawkins?"

"I should desire an education, sir. Oxford or Cambridge and then a career in law or perhaps the church, like..."

Mary stared at Paul, and he corrected, "Like any scholar-gentleman."

Barkley nodded. "Like the honorable Captain Curtis—a Cambridge man and a man of the church."

Mary, surprised, turned, and looked at Robert. For a

moment, their eyes locked. Robert thought, *Who is this woman? She did not become schooled and poised on the land. A gamekeeper's wife? She is not the village woman I met at Bramshill. There is more to her story—and what a handsome woman she is.*

Mary nodded. "Why Captain Curtis—Reverend Curtis, it was you. You influenced His Grace, the Archbishop, on our behalf."

Robert nodded. "Edward, as much as I—His Grace is most fond of Edward." Now, who is this young lady?"

"My name is Lillian. I am pleased to meet you, Captain Curtis, and you, Sergeant Barkley."

Robert smiled. "Peter Hawkins would be proud of each one of you. A good man—a hero."

Turning to Lord Curtis, Robert said, "Uncle, I do hope your guests will dine with us this evening."

Then turning back to Mary Hawkins, he said, "I am curious about the letter Lady Eleanor Montclair asked you to carry. Did she say anything more?"

Mary shook her head. "She only asked I see that you receive it. She was most gracious. She arranged a coach to bring us here."

"Lady Eleanor? Not His Grace or Lord Zouche?"

Lord James Curtis was beaming with joy as he entered his dining hall filled with new friends. He insisted the children be seated at the long table with all of the houseguests. "What a great lie that has been told in the great houses of England, that children should be seen but not heard! Let them stay at least until they become weary of our company. Only then let them pursue their games and make their sport of the evening! Barkley will keep them in good order -eh, Edward?"

Edward smiled at Mary Hawkins and replied, "Aye, Lord Curtis, only a mother keeps better order than a sergeant major! But Mrs. Hawkins need not fret this evening. I say, let her enjoy your table and your guests in full measure!"

Mary Hawkins bowed and said, "You are most kind, my Lord—with Sergeant Major Barkley's help, I pray they will not be a distraction."

The children meekly took their places at the table as Lord Curtis asked Hulda, in French, "Mademoiselle Hahn, I hope you now see the good works of mercy Wilhelm provides here. He is loved by all he serves. Will is free to act and do as our Lord above leads him. He is unhindered by church politics—you see now, there is no calling in Vienna greater than here? Here where he is safe and loved—where he has an income for life."

The servants began to circle the room serving one by one. Mary Hawkins shook her head as young Paul picked up a fork. He set it down and chose another beside it. Mary smiled and nodded yes.

Hulda replied to Sir James, "You are indeed gracious Lord Curtis, but his family..."

Sir James interrupted, "Surely, you sent a letter to your mother. She will be relieved that he is safe, serving God and loved by all who surround him. You must ask her to visit. She is welcome. Let her come share in his joy."

Hulda turned and looked at her brother. He returned her gaze, his eyes fixed on hers, longing for her approval. She sighed and said, "Truly he does the work of our Lord—he has found a place, he has found peace, and—and he is loved. He has found what our mother and I long for. Perhaps—perhaps I shall write her again and wait, yes, wait to hear what she has to say."

Hulda smiled meekly as Wilhelm lowered his head and wiped his eyes.

Hulda glanced at the silent Katie and then turned to Robert. "Is it true English priests can marry? Is it common?"

"Robert nodded. "It is expected. Even bishops and archbishops marry. Marriage is a gift of God given to all his people. It is given for the good—it makes us stronger. How can it be that we sanctify the marriages of others with no understanding of the estate ourselves?"

Mary Hawkins responded in perfect French, "And you, Captain Curtis, a priest—you have no prospects for marriage?"

Robert just stared, with no words to reply.

Lord Curtis laughed. "Here, here- you do come to point! Robert, you should take your own advice—find a wife—find your strength—and give the Curtis name a future heir. Now let us toast to marriage, a great blessing!"

Robert nodded and smiled as he tasted his wine. "You must tell us, Mrs. Hawkins, where did Peter Hawkins find an educated lady, comfortable at the manor table and fluent in French and English? For I have never seen such grace in the home of a gamekeeper. You made no show of these skills at Bramshill House."

Mary Hawkins sighed. "No. Not at Bramshill. We could not. But even there, I could not withhold an education for my children."

Mrs. Hawkins smiled at her children. She stroked the hair atop Lillian's head. "We came here for the children—for their future."

Mary paused and shook her head softly. "Peter was not always a gamekeeper."

Lord James Curtis broke the silence. "You are among friends. Your children shall indeed have the education you desire—and Berwick-upon-Tweed is blessed that you should teach our girls. We shall not compel you any further regarding your past. But God has drawn each of us here—to this place—to this table, and you are welcome!

CHAPTER 11
RESURRECTIONS

March 27, 1622, began as another dreary, not yet spring, morning. The Curtis family and guests made their way across the green towards Church of the Holy Trinity, which commanded the highest ground in Berwick-Upon-Tweed, it's back against the city wall overlooking the Tweedmouth. As they stepped upon the newly green grass, the sun broke through, and glorious light instantly drove the despair of winter away. Climbing the stairs to the church, the Vicar, Reverend Witten, greeted Lord Curtis with the age-old Easter greeting, "He is risen!"

A smiling Lord Curtis replied, "He is risen, indeed!"

The Curtis booth at the front of the church, just below the high pulpit, was filled beyond capacity, and Karl Schroeder insisted upon finding a seat towards the rear. The joyful Easter music lifted Robert's spirits, and he sang along loudly if not always on key. A smiling Barkley, dressed in his clean and bright uniform and highly polished boots, joined in the singing, an arm on the shoulder of young Peter Hawkins, who stood looking about under the watchful eye of his mother. Will, Hulda, and Kate joined Sir James and Charles Curtis in the back pew of the Curtis family booth. The small warming-pan beneath the pew was an afterthought in the special warmth of family and friends in worship.

Robert listened as the otherwise inarticulate Vicar Witten challenged his congregation with the question: 'He is risen, the victory is won—how then shall we live in His victory?'

When the time came for communion, the Curtis family was the first to be led to the altar rail. Hulda watched as Will kneeled and crossed his arms in front of him, a sign that he would not take the sacrament but accept a blessing. Hulda kneeled beside him and crossed her arms as well. Robert smiled as he saw Will uncross his arms, cup his hands, and accept the bread from Reverend Witten. Will closed his eyes and ate the bread. The cup followed, and he drank. Hulda watched her brother and did as he did, her face unable to mask her uncertainty. Katie also watched Will accept the sacraments. She sobbed tears of joy—she knew Will had made his decision.

After the service, Will walked alongside Robert and said, "Oh, that the Church practiced Peter's call for a royal priesthood of believers—even Saint Paul spoke of the priesthood of all believers. What glory that would be! How did it come about those kings and emperors tell us who our priests must be?"

Robert replied without thinking. "You know that Saint

Paul himself established leaders, priests, and bishops—men like Timothy and Titus—they were men of mature faith so that the flock was not led astray."

Robert paused, His eyes widened, and he asked, "Is it because of the Holy Eucharist you ask this question?"

Will sighed. "I could no longer abstain from communion with our Lord and the nourishment to my soul His body and blood provide. It occurred to me as I knelt before the altar, that if the teaching of the church is true—if the sinfulness of the presiding priest does not tarnish the benefits of the sacraments—then I can find grace in the elements based on my faith! God's works of grace and mercy come to me no matter who the server."

"Did you find grace?"

"Yes. God's grace feeds my faith."

Will stopped and faced his dear friend. "The holy catholic church cannot be divided by princes, Kings or emperor—neither can it be divided by bishops, archbishops, metropolitans or popes. But this is the world in which we must dwell. I recall the words of Saint Paul in his first letter to the Corinthians, 'To those under the law I became like one under the law (though I myself am not under the law), so as to win those under the law…'"

Robert completed the passage. "To those not having the law, I became like one not having the law (though I am not free from God's law) to win those not having the law. To the weak, I became weak to win the weak."

Will nodded. "I have become all things to all people so that by all means possible, I might save some. I do this all for the sake of the Gospel that I might share in its blessings."

Robert smiled and looked into his friend's eyes, waiting.

Will nodded. "God's flock has no saying in their Kings and bishops—Robert, do you think the Church of England would grant this priest its authority to serve communion to the poor and sick of Berwick? Would they accept one willing to become one of them for the sake of the gospel?"

Robert hugged his friend and said, "The right man. A holy man whose heart it is to serve would rejoice to welcome you to minister the sacraments to the faithful and serving God and our people."

Robert paused and looked off as he continued, "I would trust no one but Archbishop Abbot himself. I have told him about you. You must go to him."

Robert and Will walked silently back to Sir James' house. Katie had been walking with Mary and Hulda. She came alongside Will and silently slid her arm under his. Will reached over and patted her arm. Katie smiled and rested her head on his shoulder.

Katie softly whispered in Will's ear, "When I saw you take communion this morning. I remembered the worship in Eberbach—you and Johann—and the dream of unity in the church."

Will smiled as they walked home in silence.

Charles Curtis whispered to Karl Schroeder, walking beside him. "I see a wedding in the future."

Karl nodded. "Yes, it's about time."

The sun above warmed the earth and hearts of the band of strangers drawn together by circumstance and providence as they slowly but happily made their way to the great stone house in the ruins of the old castle. Mary Hawkins exclaimed, "Look over there, a daffodil! How it lifts my spirit!"

Lillian Hawkins squealed, "Mommy, I saw a robin!"

An Easter feast awaited Lord Curtis and his joyous guests. Sir James asked Will to bless the food and their time together. After his "Amen," Will remained standing and said, "I have something to share with all of you, my friend Robert, and you too, Edward, who brought me safely from the Palatine."

He turned to Viscount Curtis and continued, "Sir James and Charles, who have welcomed me so warmly, our new friend and co-worker…"

His eyes moved around the table. He came to Mary. "Mrs. Hawkins and your beautiful children…"

To the others, he said, "My dear sister, Hulda, most capable Karl and my dear, dear, Katie. I have decided to stay, for now, here in Berwick, where the Lord has given me His work to do. But it has always been in my heart to serve God and all those He loves as a priest. I have shared with my bother priest, Robert, that I will seek ordination in the Church of England."

Lord Curtis raised his glass. "Hear, hear! God Bless you, Father Hahn!"

Barkley raised his glass. "To Father Will!"

When he emptied his cup, Barkley shouted, "And will you finally take Katie as your bride?"

Will looked at Katie, who sat blushing, at once smiling and crying, and said, "It is in my heart, but I shall not presume upon Katharina—and there remains the question..."

Barkley interrupted, "Yes, yes—approvals and ordinations—but you know Kate's heart. We all know Kate's heart in the matter. Katie Schroeder, will you have this man, Will Hahn, as your husband? Speak, dear Kate! I see your father, poor Karl, bursting. We all know he dare not return to the Palatine until he knows his daughter's future is happy and secure!"

Katie stood up, wiped her eyes, leaned over, and kissed Will on the cheek. "Will has not sought my hand; he must ask Papa!"

Now Karl sat up straight and said sternly, "Wilhelm Hahn, is there something you wish to ask me?"

The bewilderment on Will's face slowly drained, and a bright smile curved his lips. "Herr Schroeder, I have long..."

"Too long," Robert shouted.

Will tried to continue, "For some time, I have desired to reconcile my..."

Now Karl interrupted, "Will, do you want to marry my daughter, Katharina? She is most precious to me. Will you love her and care for her above all, others?"

Will took a deep breath, turned, and gazed at Katie beside him. His face now deadly serious, he said, "Karl, I love Katie and will care for her above all others—and I promise—if you agree—if we marry, we shall be one and I will treasure her above myself."

Karl walked over to Will and hugged him. "You have my blessing,"

Karl turned to Katie, hugged his only daughter tight, tears flowing from his eyes. "O Katie, I pray you to find the happiness your mother brought me. Today is a joyful day, indeed."

Edward called out, "Well, Kate—we still await your word—don't become shy on us now!"

Katie laughed. "Edward—friends…"

Katie turned to Will and said, "Yes. I will marry you."

Congratulations flowed from the Curtis' and a teary-eyed Edward Barkley. Mary Hawkins, who was sitting beside Hulda quietly, translating the conversation to her in French, looked up and warmly add her congratulations to the smiling couple. Hulda Hahn sat silently, scowling over her plate. She pushed her chair away from the table, stood up, and said, "Lord Curtis, please excuse me…"

Will interrupted her, "No, Hulda. You will not insult my friends and our host. You will not judge them. Not Katharina or me. You will sit, and you will listen."

Hulda froze and stood in silence for a few moments before nodding and sitting down. The room was silent, every eye on Will. Wilhelm took a deep breath and said, "Friends, it is important you hear my reasons as well. As Robert and Edward have said, my decision was a long time in coming. I prayed and prayed. I debated my friend Robert, ministered with Pastor Johann Schroeder, and I listened to the counsel of the Archbishop of Mainz, a godly man. I still honor my vow to God. I do not love Katie any less, but I must honor God first. I do not leave the Roman Catholic Church to marry Katie. I will join the Church of England to intercede for the poor and sick of Berwick—to provide them comfort, yes, but the sacraments as well."

Will paused and moved his eyes across the faces of his friends listening. "The table—the Lord's Supper, it does not belong to the priest, the pope, or the church. It is the Lord's. We come to the table not on the invitation of the priest or bishop but in obedience to the command of our Lord Jesus, who said, 'Do this in remembrance of me.' By your word, sister, you tell me of our father's unfaithfulness, yet you would take communion from him. And that is right—for it is not the priest but God who bestows His Spirit and His Grace on us through the elements. How then can God's grace be withheld through communion given by any other servant of God? Lord Curtis, is it true that many of our neighbors in Berwick follow the Scottish Calvinist reformers who acknowledge no bishop?"

Sir Curtis nodded. "It is as you say."

"And these good Christians still attend Church of the Holy Trinity—and receive communion?"

Sir Curtis nodded. "Yes, some receive communion here—they must if they wish to vote."

Will continued, "I understand it is the law—that the King has affirmed the Church of England. And the people comply. Robert, this is a protestant country. I'm told there are still Catholics Christians in England; do they attend church? Do they receive communion?"

Robert looked up. "Some abstain from the Lord's

table, but many receive communion and keep their Catholic faith secret. I do not believe…"

Will interrupted, "No, neither do I believe that Kings or Princes should determine the faith of their subjects, but it is the case, unfair though it is. Now you be the judge, Hulda, does God condemn people because the King chooses their church? And I will insist that my friends Robert and Pastor Johann Schroeder and Katie also have shown me our three faith traditions agree on the historic truths of the faith as we recite in the ancient creeds—if God does not condemn them why should you or I condemn them?"

Hulda sat silently listening to her brother. Will sighed. "The true sin lies with us. We allow the church to be divided. Surely God weeps to see His children at war with each other over churches who put prince above God."

No one interrupted.

Will continued, "Here I can be honest. I can serve. Papa will not push me to be someone else. I can work with brothers and sisters who sometimes see worship differently, yet faithfully. I can work for unity, and yes, I can marry the woman I love. Consider dear sister, our mother—she believes her marriage and motherhood is a sacred calling. Cannot my becoming a husband and someday a father, be equally honoring to our Father in heaven?"

Will stared at Hulda and waited. Hulda sat quietly, considering her brother's words. Then she said softly, "You have given me much to consider. Truly your friends gathered at this table are godly people—I could not condemn them. Perhaps, I could learn…"

Mary Hawkins took Hulda's hand and said, "Sister, stay with us—I will teach you. I will help you understand how these Christian people of many faiths can strive to live together in peace—yes, peace, and even love. While we live in a world, not of our making, we can build lives and friendships on our common love for God and our fellows. We need not be strangled and stunted by hate, the foul fruit of judging others, something our Lord has commanded us to leave to Him only."

Hulda looked into the warm eyes of Mary and said, "You would build on our common faith—an understanding and acceptance of differences so as not to divide?"

"It is where we begin."

Hulda nodded. "There must be trust. Brother, you trust these people—you…"

Will walked behind his sister and put his hands on her shoulders. "Trust them? Yes. I love them—they are my brothers and sisters—true family, and I strive ever to be trustworthy to them."

Hulda smiled weakly. "You would still be a priest in the eyes of God?"

"Brothers and sisters faithful to God are divided by man's sin, not God's plan. Christians in the east, in Africa, and half of Europe remain separated from the Church in Rome, but I believe they are no less faithful and no less loved by our Father in heaven. If the English will have me, I will be a priest and serve God faithfully as

He grants me His power. I will go with Robert—to London, to the Archbishop of Canterbury, prelate of the Church of England and make my case to him."

Hulda sighed and struggled to laugh. "You must increase your skill in English. I will wait here—I will learn English as well—if Frau Hawkins will instruct me. And I will write mother—I will tell her how you follow your calling."

Katie asked, "You are going to London? So soon? How long will you be gone? When…"

Will turned to Katie. "I shall go as soon as Robert is prepared to depart. Do not despair. I shall return quickly. You have preparations to attend—we can marry upon my return. Robert, you can officiate—yes, with Johann? Could Johann come? I leave you and Karl to prepare."

Robert spoke. "Barkley can attend to our duties in Cawmills—he is more than capable."

Barkley's surprise elicited an excited, "Me? Run things at Royal Cawmills Forest?"

Robert ignored him. "Yes, give me a few days with him at Curtis Castle, and we shall be on our way."

Turning to Mary Hawkins, Robert asked, "Mrs. Hawkins, I would like to discuss the letter you carried."

The western horizon was a deep red when Robert and Barkley rode up the hill to Curtis Castle. Robert said, "We can stable our horses this evening—no need to call out for the stable boy, let him enjoy his dinner uninterrupted."

Both men dismounted and led their horses to their

usual stalls. Robert had just unsaddled his horse and was about to place the saddle on its post when Barkley called, "Robbie, come take a look."

In the end stall stood a dappled gray horse. Barkley lowered his voice and said, "That's his horse—Sharpe's—I am certain."

Robert hung the saddle on its rail and joined Barkley at the stall. Robert ran his hand over the horse's neck and then looked at the second saddle on the railing. "Same saddle. The blanket is sewn on."

Robert stroked the face of the gray and said softly, "Where have you been, my friend? Who brought you here?"

CHAPTER 12
HOLY MEN AND THE HOLY ISLAND

The parlor of Estate Manager, Andrew Douglas, in the Curtis Castle manor house was different. Mr. Douglas occupied a suite of rooms set off from the downstairs servant's hall. While it was typical for butlers and housekeepers to be provided comfortable parlors and a separate dining room from the other servants, estate managers rarely roomed in the manor house, and this apartment was as luxurious as any in the house.

Robert and Barkley had no reason to enter these quarters before, but their return at dinner time found Douglas at his table with the Justice in Eyre, Colin Gordon. Robert knocked on the door and hearing conversation in the room; he did not wait to be welcomed in. Opening the door and stepping inside, Robert said, "I find you at your table, Mister Douglas—I shall not be but a moment."

Seeing the nervous look on Gordon's face, Robert

added, "You will excuse the interruption Mister Gordon, I shall not delay you long. I am off in the morning for some time. My deputy, Barkley, has my full authority—he will give me a full report when I return. You will be most busy—much to do. More volunteers—horses. I have the funds—Barkley will hold the money—for enlistments and horses. Pistols and swords shall be delivered. And a canon. Training for the Royal Cuirassiers."

Douglas gave his best servant's smile and replied, "Very good, Captain Curtis. We shall make it happen as you wish."

"Thank you, Douglas—I know I can expect solid support—stabling will be an issue."

Robert walked to the window, which faced the stable and brushed the drapes open wide. A beaded tieback fell to the floor. Robert looked down. He did not see the alarm in Douglas' eyes as he said, "Don't trouble yourself, Captain, I will tend the drapes—you were speaking of stabling the horses."

Robert looked up and out the window, his smile hidden from the others. "Yes, Barkley and I counted twenty stalls, and besides our two horses, eleven others—my memory was ten—but then, I see Mister Gordon is here. Regardless, we shall soon have one hundred mounts. I thought they could be stabled by the tenants—for a price. They will welcome the income, I should think."

Andrew Douglas nodded. "I should think they would—and the cost of a new stable saved."

Robert continued, "A careful accounting of the horses—give Barkley the records. You shall account for all horses as the property of the volunteer company."

Robert turned to the side, his hand on the fine white, green, and gold drapery. "I go to London, I should like to report that all things are well here at Cawmills Forest—and invite His Highness for a hunt. I have every confidence in our Forester, Mister Burns, and our new gamekeeper. But a review of His Majesty's Royal Cawmills Cuirassiers—now that would be a grand event!"

"Grand indeed! And an honor!"

Robert turned and faced Douglas and Gordon, both now standing at the table. He smiled broadly and said, "There you have it, gentleman. I shall do my best, and I depend on you."

Robert started for the door. "Come, Barkley, let us leave these gentlemen to their dinner."

Robert stopped at the door. "The dappled gray, is that your mount, Mister Gordon?"

Colin Gordon hemmed and hawed, "Yes. No. That is—the gray has been made available to me but is property of the estate—that is the Royal Forest."

Robert smiled and said, "I'm certain Barkley and Douglas will sort it all out."

"Captain Curtis," Douglas called. "Shall I arrange dinner for you and deputy warden Barkley?"

Robert answered, "Most thoughtful, yes. Barkley and I shall eat upstairs in his apartment."

Climbing the stairs, Robert whispered to Barkley, "We

found the priest hole—and the priest!"

Barkley replied, "Douglas?—how?"

Robert said, "I want you in this house while I am gone. Don't let Douglas know your schedule. As you come and go—even from training—use your new corporal to cover, but don't let him know of your comings and goings either."

Barkley nodded. "But how do you know?"

Robert patted Barkley's shoulder. "Providence—the beaded tie backs—they are rosaries! And the drapes, vestments. Hidden in plain sight! I would not have noticed if I had not dislodged the tie back. The crucifix end lay under the bottom of the drape when it fell. It occurred to me if the beads, why not the drapes, the cut—unmistakable."

Robert paused as he looked around the darkening house; only a few candles lit the staircase. "Be careful—if you have the opportunity, see what else you can find in Father Douglas' apartment."

"What would I be lookin' for, Robbie? His eucharist cup and plate?"

"Could be anything—but I would start with a cipher key..."

"A box—a box, like Fitzhugh's..."

"Perhaps—it will be hidden in plain sight."

At the top of the stairs, they stopped at the gallery above the hall. Robert said, "Gordon knew we recognized the horse as Sharpe's, and you would find it in the records. See what you find out—perhaps the stable boy—when was the horse returned and when did it become Gordon's mount."

"Aye, I will be careful with the lad. You still leave in the morning?"

Robert turned and smiled at Barkley. "You are the perfect man for the job! Who better at keeping secrets than a smuggler? One last thing—go into Eyemouth and Coldstream see what you can learn about Mister Douglas—stop by the kirks—talk to the Presbyterians. How do so many Catholics find this place?"

"Aye, I will tread lightly."

"The sheriff of Eyemouth can be trusted—and my uncle is but an hour ride if you need help."

Barkley thought for a moment and said, "The lad, Aiden Lilburn, he can carry messages..."

Robert sighed. "What do we know about him? 'Seems too good to be true—marksman, gamekeeper—shows up just when we need one."

Robert paused. "Keep him close—but watch him. No, dare I say it? Young Peter Hawkins will carry the messages. Say nothing to the lad—provide him a saddle—a saddle made special."

Barkley smiled. "You have the mind of a smuggler, Robbie! Aye, only me and Lord Curtis will know of the messages."

The dim light and silence of the hall were violated first by the clear sound of footsteps and then a moving candle as a housemaid approached the stairway with a large dinner tray.

The muddy road south reminded Robert of the Count of Tilly's impending attack on Heidelberg before Duke Christian of Brunswick would move his outmanned, inexperienced new army south to their defense. His thoughts were with the English Volunteer Regiment. He should be there with them, not safely in England. Will sensed his friend's thoughts and interrupted the early April morning. "You worry about your friends in the regiment."

Robert did not lift his head. His eyes focused down on the muddy track before them. He sighed. "Yes—for all of our efforts, what have we accomplished? Their fate is an afterthought."

Will replied, "Robert, you accomplished so much! Duke Christian is a good man—he will do his best. He will move, thanks to you! And you have stopped the treachery within—the plotters will not kill the colonels and surrender the garrisons. And what a heroic thing you have done to save Katie! No, Robert, a man is only accountable for his actions—sometimes we must leave the results to God."

Robert nodded and then laughed. "Do you not find it strange that I ride with my friend, a Roman Catholic, while all of my efforts at Cawmills Forest are to uncover the purposes of the enemies of my King? All Catholics—in league with my cousin!"

"Robert, I know you well enough to say, it is not their Catholic faith that upsets you. It is their loyalty to your cousin's plotting and betrayal."

After riding in silence a few minutes, Robert said, "We

are nearing Lindisfarne. It is an ancient and holy place to the English. I should like to take you there—to the Holy Island. You should learn of Saint Cuthbert, a holy monk—much loved and venerated by the people. The monks of Lindisfarne brought Christianity back to Northumbria and England after the invading Angles and Saxons brought back their paganism when the Romans abandoned the land."

Will replied, "Yes. I should know of your English saints. I have heard stories of the Irish monks who brought Christ back to Europe in the dark times."

"King Oswald, our first Christian King—raised as a hostage by the monks—raised a Christian—invited them. It was a thousand ago. The Irish monk, and Bishop, Aiden, was his close friend. But Cuthbert was not Irish. He was an Angle—of a noble family- who the Lord gave a vision. God stirred his heart to serve Him. Cuthbert spoke our language. He went to the people where other monks feared to go. A truly humble man—such faith! He put his life in the hands of God, and fearlessly served Him only. Do you know what that kind of faith can do?"

"Robert, our King? Our language? You are Norman— the descendant of invaders. But yes. I know the power of faith you speak of. It is the faith of saints! Study the saints, and you will find they were humble men and women. Humbled by sin and their unworthiness—filled with self-doubt. But God gave them the strength—the faith—when it was needed, not before."

Robert stared ahead. "Why, I am as English as any man in Britain!"

Robert turned to his friend. "And I pray what you say is true. I pray when the time comes, I will receive His strength and will not fail our Lord."

Robert looked ahead and then said, "There—You can see the sea and the Holy Island. We must cross at low tide. We should hurry, I see peasants and pilgrims waiting to cross."

Lindisfarne Castle rose from a rocky point on the otherwise low, green island. Robert pointed and said, "You see the castle? It was there. After the priory was sacked and looted by Vikings, Saint Cuthbert's remains were moved to Durham Cathedral, further south, and inland. King Henry VIII closed the priory when he appropriated all the abbeys. He ordered the castle built from the stones of the ruins. But King Henry could not erase the memory—the holiness of Lindisfarne—from the hearts of his subjects."

Robert and Will joined the small column of men, quietly walking the pilgrim's path to Lindisfarne. Halfway across, Robert pointed to another, smaller island. "There is Innerfarne—there Saint Cuthbert lived his last days alone in a small shelter. The story is told there was no water on Innerfarne, but when Saint Cuthbert built his shelter, a spring well opened in the floor of his humble home."

Will smiled. "You see Robert, God provides when our needs arise!"

Robert and Will made their way to the priory ruins. Robert spoke as he stared where the altar once stood. "They made him bishop. But his heart was to bring the gospel to the people. His trial came when new Christians came from the south—bishops and priests from Rome. They did not learn our language or respect our ways. Worship would be in Latin. The monks were told they must bow before the Italians—they must change their worship. Easter was no longer to be celebrated according to the ancient calendar."

Will nodded. "Yes, the whole church changed calendar…"

"Not the Irish or the Northumbrians. The King married a woman of the south—she followed the Roman calendar—but with separate calendars, how could husband feast on Easter while his wife fasted, still observing Lent? The King called a council at Whidbey, and they decided to adopt the Roman calendar. The King put it to Saint Cuthbert to ensure his Bishops and priests led the people to the Roman ways."

Will sighed. "Such a change can be very hard…"

Robert continued, "Many monks abandoned Lindisfarne. They traveled to Ireland. Cuthbert was opposed to the changes—he saw the church hierarchy and Latin as moving his priests away from the people and their cherished worship traditions, but—but he stayed and did his best to bring his flock to the new ways. It was his humility, his love, and his daily walking with the people that are remembered."

Will nodded. "The good shepherd gives his life for his flock."

As they left the abbey ruins, Robert said, his voice no longer reflective, "I must stop in the village before we leave. I must check on someone—a new man to Cawmills—says he is from here,"

In the village, the mayor answered Robert. "Aiden Lilburn? Yes, there are several Lilburn families. Aiden? 'Seems there was a young man, Aiden. 'Ran off. Yes, 'had sharp words with his father and ran off."

"Where can I find his father?"

"Aiden's father lies in the cemetery—died right after young Aiden left. Only rumors of why he ran off like he did. They say he ran off to become a monk. They say he called the King 'another heretic, like Elizabeth the whore and Henry, the pig, made themselves rich from the abbeys—trampled on the monks, the saints, and the church."

"Dangerous words if truly spoken."

The mayor nodded. "A man sayin' such words could not be stayin' in Lindisfarne."

Robert thanked the mayor and left. As he walked out, he thought, *How do they find their way to Cawmills?*

Once again riding the muddy Great North Road south, Robert sighed and turned to Will with uncertainty in his face.

"Well? Out with it! You have something to say. What can be so dire?" Will asked.

Robert muttered, "Durham. The Bishop—our bishop. We should request an audience. I have not met him, and I am not sure…"

"You are not sure of our—*my* reception. His Grace, the Archbishop, has ordained everything we do in Berwick-upon-Tweed, and you fear the Bishop is jealous of his authority in his diocese."

Robert nodded. "As you say. I have never called on the bishop and formally submitted to his authority. I worry…"

Will smiled. "Bishops and church hierarchy, I understand. Waiting will not make our audience any better. We shall go and show him subservience."

Robert shook his head. "I fear it is more than that— Bishop Neile, a man who has climbed higher and higher in the bishoprics, has given several preferments to Bishop William Laud. Laud has long sought the appointment of Archbishop of Canterbury. Bishop Laud seeks to undermine His Grace at every opportunity. He sought His Grace, George Abbot's removal from office on the homicide charge in the accidental death of the gamekeeper. Bishop Neile agrees with Bishop laud on a theological dispute and is fiercely opposed to Calvinism, but where his scholarship may be weak, he is most skilled in politics—and he enjoys the favor of the King."

Will replied, "Surely Bishop Neile knows that the King restored His Grace to the privy council and his holy office. If he is skilled in politics, he will not pursue a lost battle. At least not openly or until a new opportunity arises. We are small players in their game—not viewed as a threat. No, I expect he will seek only information and our assurance of subservience to his authority, now that we minister in Northumberland."

Robert smiled. "Your years in Vienna have taught you well!"

Robert paused. "The Thirty-nine Articles. You should be familiar with them. All clergy must abide by them. Tonight, I shall give you my Book of Common Prayer. The Bishop will surmise that you—a man from Vienna, are or were Catholic. You must assuage his concerns—there are only a few Roman dogmas found unacceptable to the Church of England. We have debated them in the past and can review them once more."

Will laughed. "Debated is a mild term. As I recall, all protestants find the Mass and doctrine of transubstantiation most offensive."

Robert nodded. "Indeed. But we, you and I have come to see that 'the real presence' of Christ in the elements agrees with Scripture and assures us the bread is real food and the wine his blood."

Will nodded. "Yes, what you call the 'middle way.' Only because of how 'it is real' is not defined."

Robert snorted. "Now Will, is not God's Spirit 'real?' Why insist on a fallible interpretation of a mystery of God?"

"Yes, brother, I agree that God's Spirit is real, and our Lord's presence in the elements is real. And I know how the practice of sealing host bread in a crucifix and using it as cudgel -making swear under the body of Christ—a tool to intimidate peasants or unwanted voices has become repugnant to protestants."

"God cannot be used by man. He will not be mocked."

Robert paused and changed the subject. "Then there is purgatory—rather there is no purgatory, no evidence of one in Scripture nor need for one as our salvation comes by grace from God as a result of our faith, not works. The Roman teaching of purgatory is works based. It surmises an atonement that must be earned. And our Lord, himself, taught that upon death, a righteous man's spirit went to the 'bosom of Abraham' (here I speak of the parable of Lazarus) that is—paradise, as told to the thief on the cross—or hell."

Will was silent. He thought before he answered, "I can avow that the Scriptures teach us heaven awaits the resurrection of our body and hell awaits all who deny our Lord Jesus is the son of the Father. I wonder, but I will not say so unless asked, I wonder if we sleep until the resurrection of the body. Sleep with no awareness of time."

Robert looked at his friend. "To the thief, our Lord said, 'Today you will be with me in paradise.' Paradise— and later—after his coming again—a New Heaven and our resurrection. It is a mystery."

"I will answer carefully, Robert. Are there other Catholic views I must beware of?"

Robert smiled. "Celibacy. Celibacy is not necessary for priests, bishops, all clergy. On the contrary, we view marriage as a gift and a blessing for the clergy as well as the people."

Will laughed. "As you have made so clear to me."

Bishop Neile greeted Robert and Will warmly. "Reverend Captain Curtis. Finally, we meet. His Grace has written to me of your faithful service and of our Majesty's desire to find a suitable preferment for you within the church.

How fortunate I am that you serve in Berwick-upon-Tweed! Your uncle has been most generous and gracious to the church!" And Mister Hahn—I have received the most glowing reports from the Vicar Witten of your work! Indeed, my flock in Berwick-upon-Tweed is blessed."

Bishop Neile pointed to two chairs, and Robert and Will sat. The bishop continued, "You are traveling south—to London. Only rumors, but may it be you go to see His Grace, Archbishop Abbot? Very pleased—pleased the unfortunate incident indeed has been put behind."

Robert nodded. "My Lord Bishop Neile, we do travel to see His Grace. I continue in my inquiries of his behalf and on behalf of His Majesty. I have found Cawmills Forest, my cousin's former estate in Scotland, of course, filled with men, Catholics who conspired with Geoffrey Curtis."

Bishop Neile added, "Catholic intrigue! Glad it is Scotland and not Northumberland!"

The Bishop turned to Will. "And you Mister Hahn, headmaster of the hospital, orphanage, and poor-house, why do you travel? Is it true you seek ordination from His Grace?"

Will froze. The bishop smiled. "Come, come, Mister Hahn, you are from Vienna—you must be Catholic. It is believed by many you are a priest. I can see the delicacy of your position. I can understand your friend, Captain Curtis' relationship with His Grace—the preferment His Grace has provided, as directing your purpose. I shall not stand in your way. Indeed, I say only God-speed! God speed—and—remember, Berwick-upon-Tweed is a parish of Durham, as is all of Northumberland. I expect everyone serving in Northumberland to remember their Bishop."

Will nodded and answered honestly, "Lord Bishop Neale, I seek only to serve, humbly the widows, orphans and poor where God has sent me. I find inspiration in the life of Saint Cuthbert."

Bishop Neile smiled. "Well said! A saint to protestant and Catholic alike."

Neile nodded and added, "I believe you do. You will have no problems with me, Father. It is His Grace, who is the Calvinist."

CHAPTER 13
PETWORTH HOUSE

At Lambeth Palace, Sergeant Thomas announced Captain Curtis and Mister Hahn. While they waited, Thomas glanced to see no one would notice his break in protocol and whispered discreetly, "No Sergeant Barkly, Captain Curtis? Is he well?"

Robert replied, "Quite well, Thomas. Attending to his duties in Cawmills—I will pass on your kind thoughts."

"Thank you, Captain," he replied at resumed his rigid posture.

Archbishop Abbot came to greet his visitors. "Welcome, Robert. And you sir, Mister Hahn. Should I address you as Herr Hahn or Father Hahn?"

Will bowed and said, "Your Grace, we are in England, Mister Hahn is appropriate."

The Archbishop smiled and nodded. "You are most welcome. Please come."

The Archbishop turned and walked to his chambers. As Robert and Will followed, His Grace asked, "Edward could not make the trip? He is well, I pray?"

Robert sighed. "Enjoying his new duties in Cawmills, Your Grace."

"Well, we shall miss his company. Mister Hahn, Robert speaks most highly of you and your work in Berwick-upon-Tyne. I am pleased you have come. I would hear your account of events on the continent. You have spoken with the Emperor's Counselor, Archbishop Elector von Kronberg of Mainz."

"Indeed, His Grace is a humble servant of God and a righteous man, known for tolerance and whose desire is peace. As a pastor, I know of none better. I shall always treasure his counsel."

Archbishop Abbot said, "A strong report, indeed. And yet you are here. Brother Hahn, why do you come to me?"

Will answered directly, "I seek ordination that I may continue to serve the widow and orphan, and the sick, the poor and the strangers of Berwick-upon-Tweed. I seek authority to administer the sacraments. I honor my priestly vow to God and will obey lawfully ordained bishops of the church."

"Sit down, my brother. We have much to discuss."

Robert saw the warmth in the Archbishop's eyes and the open heart of his good friend. Archbishop Abbot shared collegially with Will the challenges he faced to bring unity to the divergent views within the Church of England—allowing the English reformation to settle into an acceptable "middle way." A Calvinist himself, Archbishop Abbot saw strength in a broader church at once firm on the historical foundations of faith and welcoming to some liberty of non-essential doctrines. He accepted that this vision permitted open questions, such as the meaning of Christ's 'real presence' in communion, and other unresolved mysteries of faith. Harder issues involved governance—the support of King and Parliament as well as the diverse clergy and congregants. The hierarchy of Bishops was non-negotiable, the partnership of church and state too long established to grant the total independence some of his Calvinist friends and most of the 'nonconformist' or puritan leaders demanded.

When the conversation moved to Will's understanding and acceptance of the Articles of the Church, Robert excused himself to make the short trip across the river to call on Sir John Doddridge at Westminster Palace. Neither the Archbishop nor Will seemed to notice as he slipped out of the room.

Sir John greeted Robert warmly and asked, "Where's sergeant Barkley? Afraid I might poach him from you?"

Robert huffed, "Why does everyone in London ask after Barkley? Is my company so loathsome otherwise?"

Sir John laughed. "Come now, Captain, the fellow is good company—never know what he might say. And then you treat him abominably!"

"Abominably? You have not heard his cuts at me!"

"A strange pair the two of you—settling into his duties at Cawmills, is he?"

"Taking to it like a duck to water—but I dare say he is happy to stay behind, close to the Mary Hawkins."

Sir John pointed to a chair and uttered, "Barkley and

the Widow Hawkins?"

Robert sat down and laughed. "Truly, the good sergeant is smitten!"

Robert paused and said, "Widow Hawkins turns out to be a mystery woman herself. Not only does she read and write, but she seems to have left her country accent behind—speaks French and who knows what else, fluently."

Sir John sat down. "She would not be the first fallen gentlewoman to be placed safely on an estate. Do you think Peter had any involvement?"

Robert interrupted, "No. And I am sure once she feels secure in Berwick-upon-Tweed, she will be more forthcoming. She has great ambition for her children. But I have determined there is a connection between the attempt on King James at Bramshill and the Fitzhugh plotters. I am certain the gamekeeper, Will Smith, if that is his name, was briefly employed by my cousin at Cawmills, called himself Will Hugh there."

Sir John's eyes widened. "Really? Please go on."

"The interrogation of Fitzhugh, what did you learn?"

Sir John looked up, took a breath, and said, "As I recall, he admitted meeting with Count Gondomar, Simon Stock, Captain Donald Stock, and your cousin Geoffrey. He wrote to, but never met Captain Richard."

"You know, my cousin, Geoffrey, escaped."

"No! Is that true? Bad luck!"

"It is true. He was warned—Richard too. Captain Richard did not run. He confessed and remained in Heidelberg. But no other names—from Fitzhugh?"

"Fitzhugh gave us no more than what we already knew. Admitted he was a papist—again something we already knew."

"Who was Fitzhugh? Where did he come from? His family?"

"Raised by an estate manager. One of the Howard estates. A bastard son. The estate manager was John Hugh, a widower. Would never name young Fitzhugh's mother. Rumors would say Lady Catherine Howard—but few believe John Hugh was his true father."

Robert nodded. "And Lord Howard saw to his education?"

Sir John agreed, "And Lady Howard saw that he was raised Catholic."

"Sounds like Cawmills. My cousin permitted only Catholics in his employ or tenancy. I believe his estate manager to be a priest hidden in plain sight. Tell me, Sir John, how do they know? The Catholics, how do they draw papists in every trade and walk of life?"

"They know. Their priests know. They know the papists who will protect them, and they know the secret-Catholics who fearfully hide their faith."

Sir John turned his gaze toward the window as a shaft of the April sunlight found its way through the cloudy sky. "The war goes on. The papists and there are many among our aristocracy. They know they have not yet lost England. They believe people will follow the King. Change the King, and they can change the church. Of course, this ignores the truth that real change did not come to our church through Henry VIII. It came through the demands for a Bible and worship in our language. Henry opened a box, and the reformation emerged. Now to our benefit, the papists are divided, not in faith but nerve. The most fervent among them would replace His Majesty, King James..."

Robert interjected, "Like the gunpowder plot. But that was years ago."

"The King has not forgotten. Why he has only recently—last July, I believe—released the Earl of Northumberland from the tower. Held him twenty years on the suspicion that he knew of his cousin Thomas Percy's plans and held them to himself."

Sir John paused and continued gazing out the window before continuing, "Still the zealots plot. They would hurry to the throne, Prince Charles, who they believe they can manipulate. The more cautious among them prefer to work with Count Gondomar—diplomatically drawing the King into an alliance with Spain and the Emperor. The price is to include both emancipation for Catholics and a return of church property."

Robert said, "The cautious you speak of can in the heart believe their loyalty to the King is unhindered."

Sir John turned and looked Robert in the eyes. "Which makes them all the more dangerous."

Robert smiled. "I've been invited to Petworth House. Lady Montclair has arranged the visit. I am to be the guest of Lord Henry Percy, Earl of Northumberland."

Sir John's eyes widened. "Now that is something!"

Robert waited nervously in the comfortable sitting room

of a large townhouse, a short walk from Whitehall Palace. The door opened, and a servant announced, "Lady Montclair."

Robert stood up and bowed as Eleanor came in. She was more beautiful than he had remembered, dressed in an emerald green velvet dress spilling yards of fabric around her, down to the ground and rising to a high waist, gold bodice with mutton sleeves. Matching lace collars encircled her sleeves above her wrists and encircled the low, rounded cut of the bodice. The pattern repeated on a ruffled neck collar, which rose behind her head and supported a circular crown of heron feathers atop the back of dark red hair. He bent over and kissed her hand, conscious not to stare at the gently rising and falling beauty before his eyes.

Smiling brightly, she said, "Captain Curtis, it is so good of you to come. You left Bramshill without saying goodbye. I wanted to tell you—please, Robert, may I call you Robert? Please sit down."

When Lady Eleanor was seated, Robert sat in a chair alongside. "You were saying, Lady Eleanor. You wanted to tell me…"

"Let me look at you. Robert, you dressed—you look like—well, I can't tell if you dress like a country vicar or a town clerk. You cannot be seen in good company as you are. You are heir to Baron of Tweedbridge. You must dress like a lord, not a tenant!"

"Lady Eleanor, my father is my uncle's heir…"

"Uncle or father, it doesn't matter, they are both old. You will become Baron. Has it not occurred to you that the King favors you? He has granted you offices. Continue to please him, and he may grant you your cousin's titles as well."

"There is something you were going to tell me."

"I will see to your clothes myself. Stylish doesn't need to be bejeweled and weighed down in gold like Buckingham. I see you in long clean lines, black and white doublet, a red, no, silver girdle to enhance the specs of gray in your black hair, and black breeches. You are a captain, tall boots, not shoes."

"Lady Eleanor, your letter."

Lady Eleanor sighed and looked up. "I mean to help you—with your inquiry. Fitzhugh and the gamekeeper. I will introduce you to people, but you must keep your wits about you. At Petworth, Lord Percy will know."

"What will he know?"

"I have heard rumors about Fitzhugh—who he is..."

"That he was raised on a Howard estate, rumored to be the son of Lady Catherine. I know."

Lady Eleanor smiled. "The Howard's saw to his education. Perhaps Lady Catherine was his mother, but it is more important who his father was. And the Bramshill plot on the King—the gamekeeper you cannot find."

"The Earl of Northumberland knows these things?"

"Let's just say I believe he knows who knows—among the Catholics."

Robert's head cocked, his eyes squinted a moment before he turned to Lady Eleanor and asked, "Why would he tell me? Why trust me?"

"Lord Percy has spent twenty years in the tower. He

needs the goodwill of the King. He trusts very few men at court, but he trusts me. I told him about you, but you must earn his trust. Now I will not be escorted by a country vicar!"

Petworth House in West Sussex was forty miles south of London. The sumptuous estate was the southern home of the wealthy Earls of Northumberland for generations. Close ties to the Catholic Scottish Royals had brought the Percy family into disfavor with Henry VIII, Queen Elizabeth, and King James successively. For a time, their ancestral home, Alnwick Castle, was forfeit to the crown, returned, and again the family banned from the north. The ninth Earl, Henry Percy, made the unfortunate decision to appoint his cousin Thomas Percy constable of the castle while his radical protégé plotted with the Gunpowder conspirators against King James and Parliament. After twenty years, King James allowed Lord Percy's stylish imprisonment to move from the Tower of London to Percy's Petworth House.

Lady Eleanor, an avid rider, was constrained by the baggage of her large wardrobe to her ornate carriage. She insisted Robert ride with her, his horse following behind. The hours on the road passed slowly to Robert as he listened to instructions. Robert had survived his audience with the King, surely an earl, and one in disfavor, should not be difficult.

His thoughts were interrupted when Lady Eleanor said, "Robert, are you listening to me? This is important. Lord Percy will invite the gentlemen to a night of cards.

You must play. He believes he can take the measure of a man in a card game."

Robert turned his eyes from the coach window and said, "I don't play cards. I am not one to gamble away what little I have."

Lady Eleanor said, "You will play. I will give you money. I know the stakes for which these gentlemen play. Now listen to me. The Earl will question you during the game—the higher your stakes—when you most need your wits—he will come at you the hardest. Concentrate on him. I will teach you how to play defensively."

"Defensively?"

"You are to play to stay in the game not to win. You can't win. You are fresh quarry for them. They will lead you on—let you win a few hands before they move to take all you have and promise notes for much more. That is the game."

"I am glad I find no urge to gamble."

"Follow Lord Henry deVere, the Earl of Oxford and Sir Thomas Wentworth, the Earl of Strafford closely. They are Lord Percy's closest friends. They never wager against each other. They may question you as well on Lord Percy's behalf."

Robert nodded. "Who else will be guests this evening?"

"I expect Lord Calvert, Sir Thomas and Lady Catherine Howard, the Earl and Countess of Suffolk, also in disfavor, and Lord George Gordon, Marquess of Huntly and Lady Henrietta. You will know if Lord Percy accepts you by the end of the evening."

"Accepts me?"

"Trusts you with what he knows. Even men in disfavor have powerful friends, and the King's disfavor can change quickly. Sir George Gordon, the first Marquess of Huntly, was twice imprisoned by His Majesty and had been stripped of his title as the Earl before returning to favor."

The carriage stopped in front of the great house. A servant opened the coach door, lowered the step board, and helped Lady Eleanor out. A lady's maid met her to escort her to her room. Her hosts would greet her at dinner. Robert followed her out while servants began removing Lady Eleanor's bags. Robert told the stableman to hold his horse, concerned he may have caught a stone in his shoe.

A quick look at the hooves revealed a small pebble beneath a loose shoe. They were unable to dislodge the pebble with their fingers, so the two slowly walked the near lame horse to the stable where the smith could clear the stone and reattach the shoe. The smith quickly went about his work while Robert stroked and quieted his horse. A quick look about the stable reminded him of the special regard aristocrats had for their horses. The prized animals were far better housed than the tenant farmers who provided income to the estate.

Robert paid little attention to another man in the stable until be noticed him pull a saddle from the railing—a saddle with the blanket sewn on. It was identical to the one taken from Sharpe's horse—the 'special' saddle of Cawmills. Robert stepped out of the stall to take a closer look. The man saddling his horse noticed Robert watching him. He stared for only a moment, quickly cinched the saddle, mounted the horse, and gave his mount the spur and ran him out the barn, nearly hitting Robert and the smith in his rush. The man's face was familiar—he had seen the fear in those eyes before—Fitzhugh's thug!

Robert's instinct was to jump on his horse and chase after him. Instead, he turned to the smith. "Who was that man?"

The smith looked up from the shoe he was nailing and said, "That fool Joseph Wright. Lord Percy will hear of this mind, you!"

"You know him?"

"Aye, he runs the messages back and forth to his Lordship's estates in the north—from Alnwick Castle."

Robert spent the afternoon in his room, thinking. *What do I know about any of these people? All Catholics or secret-Catholics certainly. No, Sir Thomas Wentworth I know to be protestant. The King appointed him to raise support for the volunteer regiments supporting Elector Frederick V. And is he best friend to Lord Percy? I hear I must earn Lord Percy's trust—can I trust him? His man, Wright, was in league with Fitzhugh. Why am I here? Lady Eleanor—why her interest in me? Can she be trusted? What is her connection to these Catholic Earls? And the King's secretary of state, George Calvert—trusted by all? Is he?*

The candles were lit before the guests invited down for dinner. Lords and ladies were gathering in the hall outside the dining hall, waiting to be led to the table. Lady Eleanor had not arrived before Robert descended the grand staircase and was greeted by Lord and Lady Percy. "You must be Captain Curtis," Lord Percy said warmly, "I look forward to hearing of your exploits with the volunteers. Lady Eleanor insists you're the right man for the task. Calvert has told me His Majesty favors you. Even Sir John Doddridge has praised your skill."

Robert bowed. "You are most gracious, Lord Percy. Your hospitality honors me."

Percy smiled, looked to the top of the stairs, and said, "Ah, the beautiful Lady Eleanor—always last it seems— Well, we can move along into the dining hall."

Robert waited for the guests to file in. Lady Eleanor walked beside and took his arm. "Captain Curtis—shall we?"

Robert smiled and whispered, "Lord Percy mentioned a task."

Eleanor replied softly, "Friends of the missing Bramshill gamekeeper."

Robert's uncle, Viscount Berwick's table, was no match for the Earl of Northumberland. A footman attended each guest, serving fine wines, fresh fish, fowl, and venison. It was plain that Robert was the only stranger at the table. The others chatted like old friends. George Calvert discussed the latest news from the privy council with no concern for secrecy. There were no secrets between these nobles. Sir Thomas reported the dire situation of the English Regiment in the Palatine, visibly distraught over Parliament's unwillingness to authorize new taxes. Turning to Robert, Sir Thomas said, "Were it not for loyal men like Viscount Curtis and the collection of the ship tax requiring no Parliament action, there would be no Regiment."

The Marquess of Huntly, Lord Gordon, grumbled in his Scottish brogue, "Better off if they were never sent. King James would have accepted Spanish conditions all the sooner. No good losing men and quite possibly the finest Commanders in England and Scotland."

Lord Percy turned to Robert and asked, "Captain Curtis, this plot you uncovered—this Fitzhugh fellow— the traitor, what put you on to them?"

"Lord Percy, I dare not tell you the long story— suffice it to say, by the grace of God, I survived an attempt on my life—an attempt that made no sense. A Catholic priest rescued me—a most amazing man who has become closer to me than any brother. He, too, was being pursued pursuing justice for the brother of a protestant woman whose brother, a pastor, taken unlawfully. It seems our pursuers were in league. Fitzhugh was the key. A friend and I witnessed a meeting of the plotters in Cambridge though we made no note of it at the time. A thug working for my cousin, Sir Geoffrey Curtis, and the plotters, murdered my friend, a better man than me, but God saved me from his several attempts. We caught the scoundrel, intercepted his messages, and found the cipher key in Fitzhugh's apartment. His Grace, Archbishop Abbot, arranged for us to pass the messages through Marquess Buckingham to the King."

Sir Thomas Howard shook his head. "A hard thing to learn your cousin a traitor, and he determined to kill you. But now you are both Sheriff of Cawmills and Warden of a royal forest. Landed on your feet, young Captain Curtis—indeed, you have done well."

Lord Percy smiled. "Captain Curtis, this priest—you call him closer than a brother—I am informed you have taken holy orders in the Church of England—him a Catholic—this does not disturb your conscience?"

"Would all men serve God as my friend Will! I have met none like him in compassion and mercy! As for my conscience, Lord Percy, it is refreshed. I believe God judges a man's heart, not his dogma. Where in Scripture or the church fathers is it written that God requires a perfect theology? Is not our ancient belief—our creeds and tradition filled with mystery? Will God judge a man by his struggle to understand a mystery? I say no. God seeks our love and our faith, Catholic or protestant. We are called to love and worship Him. It is Kings and princes who divide us—Christ's Church is universal whether we pray in Latin, English, or German."

Lord Percy was surprised. "You see no difference between Catholic and protestant?"

Robert shook his head. "Lord Percy, I see much difference in worship, but no difference in faith. My Catholic friend and I see a difference in but three of the thirty-nine articles of the Church of England—celibacy of priests, the existence of purgatory, and how Christ is present in the elements. Other than these, the difference lies in the self-proclaimed authority of the pope.
Together, we agree that celibacy was instituted by the church, with good intention, but not demanded in

Scripture or historically practiced in the apostolic church. It can be withdrawn at any time. Purgatory is not found in Scripture and infers man's requirement to earn his atonement, contrary to reformation teaching, but as doctrine, it is not fundamental to man's salvation. Last, the Church of England's teaching of the 'real presence' of Christ in the eucharist does not decide how that presence occurs."

Lord Henry de Vere interrupted, "Captain Curtis, would you have Catholics and protestants living together as brothers?"

Robert smiled. "Do they not now live together—as friends, sometimes husband and wife? We do a poor job of hiding it. Let me tell you how the Elector Prince-Archbishop of Mainz appointed my friend Vicar General of Eberbach—how as a priest, he invited our Calvinist friend to share the church of Eberbach. Catholics in the transept, protestants in the sanctuary were worshipping together. Latin and German liturgies, both pastors, joined for the Scriptures and sermon but separated for communion. No longer separated by a false curtain of mistrust, all the Christians of Eberbach worshipped as brothers."

Lady Eleanor spoke up. "Why Captain Curtis, you a hopeless romantic—a dreamer of brotherly love between the church at war!"

"I do not find this dream hopeless, Lady Eleanor. I find it God's will for our time."

CHAPTER 14
THE GAME

Lord Percy rose from the table and said, "Gentlemen, it is time we permitted the ladies their evening. What you say you all to cards?"

Lady Eleanor placed her hand on Robert's arm as he rose. He turned and returned her smile. The soft caress of her touch as his arm slid through her hand coursed through his body. He stood beside her chair, leaned over, and silently kissed her cheek. His nostrils drank of her perfume. The sweetness of her skin against his lips lingered as Eleanor whispered, "This is where you belong, Robert. I am so pleased you came. Now go, you have already won the day."

The adjacent chamber to the grand dining room was furnished with card tables. The dark oak paneling and the windows into the dark night left only the fireplace and few candlestands to provide soft light on the playing tables. "What shall it be?" Lord Percy asked.

George Calvert replied, "Maw! It is all the rage in London—it is the King's favorite!"

Lord Percy shook his head. "No four-man trump game—there are seven of us. I say a real man's game—brag! You must know it, Captain Curtis. Surely as a soldier..."

Robert smiled, surprised to be honored for his opinion. "Brag it is, Lord Percy—three-card, four, seven or nine?"

"We are men, not women or children going through the deck, hoping for salvation. Nor will there fooling with two hands at a time. Three cards, no draw—live with your bet!"

The men settled around the table, and Lord Percy slid the deck to the Earl of Oxford. "Lord Henry, you've been quiet this evening, you deal."

Henry de Vere shuffled the deck and moved it in front of Sir Thomas Wentworth, who cut the cards, slid the deck back to de Vere, and said, "From the top Henry—we have guests tonight!"

Lord Howard called out, "Stakes—our usual?"

Lord Percy replied, "Captain Curtis is still a working man, like you Calvert—let's not discourage his play. I say five pounds a chip. One chip to play, one to bet, two to call. Not too rich for you, Curtis?"

The numbers went through Robert's mind—a minimum of twenty pounds a hand. "I should not want to diminish the sport to you, gentlemen. I will play."

Lord Gordon replied, "Winning is its own reward in this company. Tell me Curtis, were the affairs at Sir Geoffrey's Cawmills so dire that you spent your stipend on recruitment pay for your company of volunteers?

Cavalry, I understand?"

Robert smiled and thought, *he tells me of his advantage—for sure they have inquired after me—do they know all?* He answered, "You are well informed, my lord. What you say is true. My cousin removed his fortune to Amsterdam before implementing his notorious plot. The volunteers train as cuirassiers, cavalry with pistol and saber."

Lord Gordon snorted. "Cavalry with pistols—what has become of honor on the battlefield!"

Robert nodded. "As you say, winning is everything."

Now seated, Robert tossed in his ante, and Sir Thomas dealt the first card. One by one, each man tossed in another chip to see a second card. Robert stared at the two of clubs and three of diamonds and tossed in another chip.

The Marquess of Huntly, Lord Gordon, tossed in two chips and said, "Raise." He continued, "Your cousin, Sir Geoffrey should go to the King and petition him for mercy. He is a lord if only a baron—he still can be of value to the King..."

"As you did—more than once—Lord Gordon," Sir Thomas Wentworth replied.

Robert looked once again at his cards. "My cousin has escaped and now roams Germany. He has abandoned his King and his comrades in harm's way. Certainly, that cannot be to his credit. He fears the same fate as Fitzhugh." Robert tossed in two chips and received his third card.

"Fitzhugh had nothing to offer the King other than an

example. It is never the same for us."

Robert looked at his cards—a pair of threes. Lord Percy took his third card and raised. "Captain Curtis or I ask you, Reverend Curtis, should not a man be forgiven and granted another chance following confession and penance?"

Wentworth and de Vere folded. It came to Robert, who sighed. "cover." The kitty was separated. Robert replied, "Forgiveness must follow true confession and repentance—but accountability remains."

The remaining men bid up a second kitty another two rounds before Lord Howard called. Lord Percy took the hand, and the second kitty with a pair of twos before Robert turned his card. His pair of threes gave him the covered kitty."

George Calvert smiled. "Two threes. Our young friend plays well, bold—but not reckless."

Lord Percy nodded. "Yes. A man who understands risk and reward. Tell me, Robert, can you unite with someone with a shared enemy?"

Robert nodded. "I would look for more than a common enemy—I would look to what lies beyond— common interest -common welfare and lasting trust."

Lord Percy replied softly, "I believe you would."

Percy spoke up. "Your deal Secretary Calvert. Give them a good shuffle!"

As Calvert dealt the card, Henry Percy said, "Now, gentlemen, I believe we can tell Captain Curtis why we invited him here."

The growing company of Royal Cawmills Cuirassiers was practicing loading pistols while mounted, a skill new to all the men. Barkley rode beside Corporal Lilburn and said, "Have the men practice loading once more. Then have them form a line and fire on your command. Be safe about it. Watch both the men and the horses. I am off to the tower; I will return shortly."

Lilburn's face lit up. "Aye sergeant. Let's see what they can do!"

Edward rode up the hill to the stable. He entered from the far side, out of view of Mr. Douglas' window. The stable boy was with the volunteers; even so, Edward walked the length of the stable to be sure he was alone. The horses were all with the volunteers. Edward walked to the rail where Colin Gordon's saddle rested. Looking around once more, he lifted the saddle from the rail. The blanket came with it. He carefully unstrapped the lacing of the blanket and looked at the compartment beneath. He smiled as he lifted a leather pouch from the tight void. Inside the pouch was a letter. Barkley opened the letter.

Barkley breathed a quiet, "Yes!" then reached into his pocket and took out a copy of the cipher found in Fitzhugh's Cambridge apartment. Nervously, he deciphered the short message and quickly returned the pouch to the saddle compartment and laced the blanket back onto the saddle.

As Barkley returned the saddle to the rail where he found it, a pail fell from the loft, and several birds flew out the stable door.

Barkley's hand went to the stock of his pistol. His eyes scanned the stable. Once again, the barn was quiet. The silence mocked him as he called out, "Who's there?"

Barkley's heart raced as he again walked the length of the stable. There! His peripheral vision detected movement in the loft above him. Barkley froze. In the dark shadows, above to his left -

Barkley sighed. "A barn cat. 'Got the best of me! A cat!"

Barkley heard a sloppy volley of pistols and rode down to his drilling volunteers. Several men were clutching the necks of wild-eyed horses. Barkley rode to the front and ordered, "Dismount! Hold your mounts by the bridle, reload—these horses must become accustomed to gunfire!"

Turning to Lilburn, he said, "Good work, Lilburn. Come by the house this evening for dinner. There is news I will share with you."

That evening, Barkley met with the forester, Neil Burns; Justice in Eyre, Colin Gordon; Andrew Douglas; and gamekeeper, Aiden Lilburn. "Men, Captain Curtis has determined a young man, the son of a hero to our King, young Peter Hawkins, will apprentice here as gamekeeper and forester. Sunday morning, I shall worship in Berwick-upon-Tweed and return with the lad. His lordship, Viscount Curtis, will escort the lad's mother to assure the good Mrs. Hawkins that all will be well with the lad here at Cawmills. Mister Douglas, I expect you will make them welcome and see to a fine dinner. You will all share the table that evening. Lilburn, I expect you to learn your manners. Mister burns you shall provide them a ride about the forest, answer any questions. Lilburn, you go along with them. Mister Gordon, you can join the conversation at dinner."

Barkley looked about the great hall. "Viscount Curtis is the twin to Geoffrey Curtis' father. Curtis Castle has been in their family for centuries. You will treat him with the honor he is due. And Mrs. Hawkins is—well, she is a special lady, a gentlewoman of refinement. She will not allow her eldest son to be mistreated or humiliated. Captain Curtis has given his word. I need say no more."

"Under warden Barkley, will Mrs. Hawkins and his lordship spend the night?" Douglas asked.

Barkley nodded. "I will make the invitation. Have all prepared."

Lilburn asked, "Will young Hawkins join the regiment?"

"No. Mrs. Hawkins has lost her husband in service to the King. She will not risk her son."

Douglas cleared his throat loudly. "Ahem, how shall I account for these costs?"

Barkley's eyes cut into Douglas, who stammered, "Well, I only…"

Barkley replied, "Captain Curtis has given his emolument—he has bought the horses and pays the costs until harvest. Make a full accounting. Or perhaps the Captain will determine costs can be found in a cut in the house staff. Or Perhaps an estate manager's stipend is unnecessary. That will be all."

The officers of Cawmills forest stood at attention as Barkley, Viscount Curtis, Mary Hawkins, and young Peter arrived at the front of the manor house. The staff welcomed the entourage as nobility. A footman opened the carriage door and assisted Mary Hawkins as she stepped out. Every house servant and the officers of the Forest bowed to Lord Curtis and Mrs. Hawkins.

As they entered the house, Mary, her eyes bright and smiling demurely, turned to Barkley, and nodded. She whispered, "I'm impressed!"

Douglas led the guests on a short tour of the house. Lord Curtis stopped and stared at the King's coat of arms over the fireplace. His eyes focused on the top of the fireplace before he sighed and turned away.

When Mary Hawkins insisted on joining her son on the tour of the forest, Neil Burns said, "Then it is settled we must ride!"

Mary Hawkins gracefully mounted the horse brought forward, and she demonstrated both comfort and skill on horseback. Barkley smiled as he rode beside her. "I thought we might talk as we ride."

"I would be pleased to have you beside me, Master Sergeant, or shall I call you Under Warden Barkley?"

"I am most happy when you call me Edward."

Mary turned, smiling brightly. "Mister Burns and the others await. Let us not fall behind, Edward."

Lord Henry Percy picked up his card and said, "Captain, we pursue the same man. His name is William Wright, a gamekeeper. As you have correctly surmised, he has already made one attempt on the King's life."

Robert ignored the card laid in front of him. His stare told the others he was listening.

Thomas Howard, Earl of Suffolk, continued, "He was an assistant gamekeeper at Charlton Park, my estate in Wiltshire—ran off last spring. Not sure where he went, but he matches the description of the new gamekeeper at Bramshill..."

Robert interrupted, "My lord Howard, I understand the man to be a Scot or northerner—sandy hair, thick, standing straight on his head."

Lord Howard nodded. "Yes, came to us from the north, just as you describe him."

Robert nodded. "He traveled to Cawmills before stopping at Windsor before Bramshill.

Lord Percy looked at Lord Howard and then added, "There is more. Fitzhugh is the son of my cousin, Thomas Percy, a leader of the gunpowder plot. There may be a connection between them."

Robert replied, "Fitzhugh grew up in the house of Lord Howard's gamekeeper..."

Lord Howard sighed. "I was asked to find him a home—I do not discuss my wife's affairs—but the boy was bright, and as High Steward of Cambridge, I found him a place there. Never thought he would turn traitor."

Robert asked, "Why do you suspect a connection? Is there more to connect them than your estate, Lord Howard?"

Lord Percy spoke. "They are both sons of plotters. Thomas Percy and John Wright, their fathers, were guilty in the gunpowder plot to kill the King and his Parliament."

The game was forgotten. Robert sighed. "Why me? You are powerful men. Why not take your suspicions to the King?"

Lord Percy answered first. "I've spent twenty years in the tower trying to regain His Majesty's trust—if I came forward now, it would only affirm his suspicion that I withheld knowledge of the affair."

George Calvert nodded. "Our members are suspected as Catholic sympathizers. In truth, King James would be more tolerant to the Catholics among us but for past plotting."

Looking over to Gordon, Calvert continued, "Sir George Gordon is a past recusant, only recently readmitted to the church by His Grace George Abbot. His sympathy for Rome has been overlooked by King James, who has elevated him in position and peerage to Marquess of Huntly. Every man here is suspect by Parliament, even my good friend Sir Thomas Wentworth, a solid protestant and in favor of England's intervention in support of Frederick V and Elizabeth of Bohemia. We cannot be the ones to uncover a treasonous Catholic plot."

Robert stared over Calvert's head and thought a moment. "Fitzhugh was working with my cousin Geoffrey and Count Gondomar. Is Gondomar playing two games? An alliance by marriage with Spain would come at a price—tolerance towards English Catholics at minimum. Why would Gondomar risk the alliance?"

Henry deVere answered, "No one here has accused Count Gondomar. Though what you mention is troubling. We know His Majesty seeks unity in the realm. The unrest—an attack on the Church of England would bring further restraints. It would keep His Majesty from indulging Catholics for now—until the church is stable. Trust, Robert. The King must trust his lords. Trust must flow down from the nobles to the people. Only when the seed of trust is planted will tolerance flower."

Lord Percy added, "Captain Curtis, you have earned the King's trust and the trust of those sympathetic to the protestant cause on the continent. You are a priest in the Church of England. We trust you to help us prevent a civil war—stop the plot against our King. We are loyal subjects hoping for a better day."

Robert nodded silently.

Lord Percy shoved all the chips in front of Robert, smiled, and said, "A down payment on your expenses."

Robert looked at the chips, then looked up at Lord Percy and asked, "Your messenger—the rider from Alnwick Castle, tell me about him…"

CHAPTER 15
LOOKING FOR ANSWERS

The late April morning found West Sussex blessed with bright warm sunshine. The sweet smell of honeysuckle and daphne wafted on the soft breeze. Robert and Eleanor slowed their mounts from an invigorating lope to an easy walk. "I do love Petworth, Robert, the sun, the gardens—just breathe it in. When I must leave London, there is no finer place."

Robert smiled. "I find leaving London, the best part of the visit. London is dreadful—dirty, squalid, and ugly. The foul air and the mood of the people are one and the same."

"That is not the London of the court. It is gay, full of music and dance parties and balls."

Robert smiled and shook his head no. "I see intrigue and mistrust."

"Perhaps we only see what our fears permit us to see, or perhaps only what we are looking for."

Robert looked in Eleanor's eyes. "What are you looking for, Lady Eleanor?"

Eleanor smiled and said, "Life."

The two rode slowly through the flower carpeted forest, back to the great house of Petworth breathing deeply of the scented air, gazing into the branches of the tall trees with buds opening into early green foliage, trying to spot the songbirds serenading their ride.

Eleanor broke the silence. "I do not recall a more pleasant ride or a more dashing escort. Again—we must do this again and again! I am so pleased you have come into my life! Tomorrow—we will ride again tomorrow morning."

Robert sighed. "I am off to London tomorrow morning. I must be about my business."

Eleanor could not hide her disappointment. "Tomorrow? Then I shall ride with you. Yes, we shall travel together, and I will convince you that you are mistaken about London."

Robert found Lord Percy in his private chamber. "There you are, Captain Curtis, come in- sit. Here is a letter of introduction to the Constable of Alnwick Castle. You will be shown the highest courtesy and cooperation anytime you visit. I send the constable my highest confidence in you."

Robert accepted the letter and asked, "The lad, the messenger, Joseph Wright, will you retain him?"

"Aye, it is best to keep your enemies in sight. His connection to William Winter and Fitzhugh—it never occurred to me before, all sons of traitors. Joseph, the son of John Wright, William Winter, the son of Thomas Wintour and Fitzhugh the son of my cousin Thomas

Percy. All zealous Catholics like their fathers determined to kill King James and perhaps Parliament—the second generation of gunpowder plotters."

"There may be more. Did Robert Catesby have sons? Or Fawkes, or any of the others? And their priest—they must have a priest in their confidence and ties to Count Gondomar. Hate and revenge are powerful motives."

Lord Percy sighed. "Gondomar is the most clever of men. It pains me to learn that I must no longer trust him. Why must he stray from the path of negotiation?"

"Perhaps he tires of negotiation—how long has it gone on? And King James grows old."

Robert paused and said, "Lord Percy, Sir John Doddridge will expect a report. I must tell him that I am pursuing a treasonous plot. How much..."

Lord Percy nodded. "Sir John is a trustworthy man. You may tell him we have uncovered the connection of the plotters—through their fathers. Ask him for discretion—it is Marquess Buckingham you must beware."

Robert stood up. "I leave in the morning. Lady Montclair is determined to accompany me to London."

Lord Percy stood and replied, "God speed, Curtis. It seems you have caught the fancy of the brightest star in the court. Lady Eleanor is an exceptional woman—and you must think of an heir."

"An heir—I have no..."

"Come, come, Robert, you will become Baron of Tweedbridge—and with success perhaps more."

The carriage ride to London gave Robert time to think—to plan his visit to Alnwick Castle. *Was there a connection to Cawmills, to his cousin Geoffrey? And Geoffrey—has there been any word of his whereabouts? And the regiment—has Duke Christian of Brunswick begun his march south? And Wilhelm, his mind will be elsewhere. He contemplates priestly service and perhaps the joys of marriage. Will I ever be fit company for my friend?*

"Robert! Robert!" Lady Eleanor repeated.

Robert turned away from the window and smiled at Eleanor. "Forgive me, Lady Eleanor. You were saying?"

"Do you find my company so boring? I thought you enjoyed my company. If you prefer, your horse trails behind, you can ride off at once."

Robert smiled and took Eleanor's hand. "You are never boring, my lady. Forgive me. My thoughts were on the counsel of Lord Percy. But truly, I am most comfortable in your presence."

"The one thing I cannot abide by, Robert, is being ignored. Promise me that—promise me you will not abandon me to my own amusement."

Robert sighed. "I have wounded you! You must forgive me for I would never be the one to offend…"

Lady Eleanor patted the seat beside her. "Robert, sit here beside me. Having you across is too far—sit close. I must tell you…"

Robert slid across and sat beside Eleanor. She leaned her head on his shoulder and placed her hand over his. "Tell me?" he asked.

Lady Eleanor whispered, "Never leave me to my own company. The loneliness—my parents—my father—my father ignored me. I barely remember my mother. She died giving birth to my brother. I saw my father once a day, for but a few minutes. I was a daughter, not a son—not an heir. He could not accept that I lived, and his son died. His second wife bore him no children. A servant raised me—and she a mean and wicked woman. No, Robert, I cannot live alone."

Robert caressed her shoulder. "You are a lovely woman, so full of life! Men adore you—and you say you are lonely?"

Eleanor replied, "Men seek a beautiful wife to give them an heir and sit with other ladies while they gamble and chase mistresses. I will not become like Lady Catherine Howard pursuing young lovers."

"Is that what you saw in my cousin Geoffrey?"

"Let's not talk any more of him. I would rather talk about you. You are different, Robert. You are someone to be trusted. You see worth in women—like that poor widow, Mary Hawkins. You speak of widows and orphans—perhaps it is the priest in you that appeals to me. But when I saw you with the lords—accepted and trusted—you can become a great man in England."

"If only I were that man. I see no greatness, nor desire to be a great man—just to walk with a heart for God and neighbor."

Eleanor lifted her head off Robert's shoulder. "I can help you. You are too humble. You can be—you will be a great man in England—Lord Chancellor is what I see in you!"

Robert laughed. "Let's not aim too high, my lady."

"Eleanor, call me Eleanor, and you shall be my Robbie."

Robert chuckled. "Sergeant Barkley calls me 'Robbie.'

"The man adores you, Robbie—and he is such fun! Tonight, in London, we shall go…"

Robert turned. "Lady—Eleanor, in London, I must see Sir John Doddridge. I will stay with His Grace, Archbishop Abbot, and then accompany my friend Wilhelm back to Berwick-upon-Tweed."

"But I want to show you the London I love."

Robert smiled. "A few days, perhaps. I can stay a few days, but I must get about the business I share with Lord Percy. It is of the highest importance to the King."

Eleanor kissed his cheek. "First, we shall find you more clothes and then, well, then we'll see."

Sir John Doddridge intently listened as Robert told him what he had learned. "Sons of the gunpowder plotters? And you believe they hope to succeed where their fathers failed?"

"They have tried once already—they are sure to try again. They appear to coordinate with Count Gondomar and my cousin, Geoffrey. Lord Percy has unknowingly brought them together. With Fitzhugh dead, his guard, who we left behind, young Joseph Wright is at Alnwick castle—I suspect our gamekeeper whose name I now know is William Winter, and the evidence we need is there as well. I am off to Alnwick Castle day after tomorrow. The Earl of Northumberland begs your highest discretion—he does not trust Buckingham."

Sir John nodded. "You trust Lord Percy? He is surely a secret Catholic."

"I trust them all: Lord Percy; Howard; Gordon, de Vere; and Calvert. Sir Thomas Wentworth—he protestant and in favor of the cause of Frederick V—is one of them. Their goal is tolerance, not regicide. They risk trusting you. They permit me to keep you informed."

Sir John laughed. "Well, they are right about Marquess Buckingham. Never give him more than the moment requires."

Robert added, "There is something you can do—the other plotters, Guy Fawkes and Robert Catesby to begin, but all who are known. We must know their sons and sons-in-law. We must inquire after all. Someone has brought them together—a priest, perhaps? Their motivation may be zealous Catholic teaching or simple revenge."

"Yes, I will go through the documents and search for their whereabouts. You mentioned evidence at Alnwick?"

Robert nodded. "Where else could it be? What I should have found and taken from Fitzhugh..."

The lights of Westminster Palace reflected on the Thames in frivolous competition with beams of moonlight as Robert approached Lambeth Palace. The tiny green blossoms on Cardinal Woolsey's fig tree were camouflaged in new green leaves. Sergeant Thomas greeted Robert warmly, like family, and led him to the Archbishop's chamber. His Grace, George Abbot, was seated across from Wilhelm Hahn, two cups of wine sitting on the small table between them.

"Robert! Back already? Sit and join us—if your journey has not been too tiring. Our brother Will and I were discussing Paul's letter to the Galatians, the very book he read and discussed with His Excellency, Archbishop Elector of Mainz, von Kronberg. We were considering Saint Paul's challenge of pleasing God rather than pleasing men—and, how Paul chastised Peter when he was wrong."

Will nodded hello to Robert and replied to Archbishop Abbot, "But Saint Paul submitted to Peter and James at the Council in Jerusalem."

Robert sat down and said, "Your Grace, now you see how my friend Will is never easily dissuaded from his argument. I shall merely listen until the point is resolved."

George Abbot laughed. "Fetch a cup of wine and join us."

Abbot turned to Will and said, "It is true Paul submitted to authority as any righteous priest must. Paul loved and honored Peter. His point in Galatians is that all authority flows from God through Christ. We submit to Christ's authority—his Word and his Spirit. That is what Jesus expressed when he first called Simon, 'Peter.' When he said, 'On this rock, I will build my church.' The rock for which Simon was thereafter called, Peter, was the truth revealed by God that Jesus is the Son of God. Jesus confirmed this when he said, 'Blessed are you, Peter, for flesh and blood did not reveal this to you but my Father in heaven.'"

His Grace took a sip of wine and sighed. "Brother, the best of men are sinners. We are called to become like Christ. It is Christ whom we put first and follow. We follow with others who follow Christ—but we imitate them only when they imitate Christ."

Robert looked at Will, still considering the Archbishop's words, and said, "I return north in two days. Are you with me? Or do you have another thirty-eight articles to debate?"

Will looked up. "No, I debate only to learn. I have uttered the Oath of Supremacy. His Grace has ordained me—he recognizes my vow to our God. I have now sat under two Archbishops who love God and would see the holy catholic church restore fellowship with all who hold to our ancient creeds and apostolic faith. This war within the church surely tears at the very heart of our Lord."

Archbishop Abbot sighed. "Perhaps you can help, brother or I say, Father Wilhelm? I will write Archbishop von Kronberg a letter. Can you see that it is delivered to him?"

Will smiled. "Yes. Please write. He is a good and faithful priest. Perhaps he can persuade the emperor or others. Yes—you must send him a letter."

His Grace looked at the tired but smiling, Robert, and said, "When you have rested, you must tell me about your visit to Petworth. It seems you have had some success. But now, finish your wine and retire."

Robert nodded, drank his wine, and stood to leave.

Archbishop Abbot said, "For a man filled with self-doubt, you have a gift of capturing friends of character and heart. First, you bring me Edward, and now you bring Will. Take strength from them."

Robert smiled. "The gift is from the Lord. For you have not yet met Karl, Johann, Werner, or Katie. Our Heavenly Father does not send us to journey alone."

Robert began to walk out, stopped, and turned. "And I thank God he has brought me alongside you, Your Grace."

CHAPTER 16
CASTLES AND WALLED CITIES

Katie and Hulda stood up and ran to the door when Robert and Will were announced. Will opened his arms and hugged them both first kissing Katie's cheek and then the top of Hulda's head. "Such a welcome! I should go away more often." Will joked.

Katie replied, "No more travel! You shall stay here with me. Tell me, Will, are you a priest? Can we live and serve openly here in Berwick-upon-Tweed?"

Will smiled and nodded his head.

Hulda stepped away from her brother, and grunted. "So you stepped away from the true church after all. You abandon your calling and your vows made before God."

Will tried to take Hulda's hand, but she pulled away. "My vow is to make disciples of Jesus—to serve the poor and the sick. Now I can see them receive the grace of our Lord given in the sacraments…"

Hulda would not allow him to continue. She spat back, "English—not Catholic. Not the true church."

Will remained composed; his smile genuine. "The people have no choice in who blesses the sacraments. Are they any less effective? If they accept the eucharist, who am I to judge them?"

Will paused. Hulda's eyes were on the floor, but Will knew she was listening. "Good men, who love God, debate a mystery—and it remains a mystery whatever they believe. The truth is in Christ—His body and His blood. He calls us to faith, not dogma. And I have not abandoned my vow. I serve God, where I am under the authorities of the land."

Will stopped and waited. Hulda sighed but did not answer.

Katie broke the silence. She smiled at Robert and said, "Robert, you have not asked for a kiss. Where is the Robert I know, the man I am so fond of? Where are you? Are you not happy to see us?"

Robert smiled. "I am always happy to see you, but..."

Katie grabbed Robert's sleeve. "Your clothes. You have changed—you look so dashing. It's a woman! A woman has dressed you!"

Robert kissed Katie's cheek. "I must go soon—today. So much has happened. I cannot stay—even until dinner. Give my apologies to..."

Will spoke out. "Stay. They have much to hear. Karl. Is Karl here? I must travel to Mainz with him."

Katie and Hulda replied together, "Mainz?"

Hulda continued, "You will be arrested!"

Katie interrupted, "Your work is here. Why else have you gone to London and accepted new holy orders?"

Will replied, "I must deliver a letter to the Elector Archbishop Von Kronberg of Mainz, A letter from His Grace, Archbishop Abbot."

Hulda screamed, "No. Let Karl deliver the letter. Come home with me to Vienna."

Katie ignored Hulda. "I'm going with you. We can find Johann, bring him here, and be married."

Will turned to Robert. "Robert, help me convince them."

Hulda screamed, "Him? The man who took you from your calling? I hate him!"

Robert shook his head. "They will not listen to me— Karl. They may listen to him. He knows what lies ahead for you. Perhaps they will listen to him. I must go, my friend."

Will clasped Robert's arm. "Forgive her, don't take her words to heart. She doesn't know what she says. I know you must go. I fear for your life, brother. Tell me you will not pursue them alone. Take Edward—others too—men you can trust."

Robert exhaled deeply, stepped back, and tightened his grip on Will's arm. "Brother, outside of this house, who can I trust?"

And Robert was out the door.

At Curtis Castle, Barkley was waiting alone as Robert arrived. Immediately Barkley said, "They sent for him!"

Robert dismounted his horse and asked, "Who sent for who?"

"Why, your cousin Geoffrey of course. I found a letter

in his saddle. Gordon carries the letters. Hides them in the same place—uses the same code."

Robert nodded. "You have been busy. Very good! What did the letter say exactly?"

Barkley smiled. "Short and sweet: 'Come, we have a place for you.'"

Robert replied, "It is not here. They refer to Alnwick Castle, I am certain. Fitzhugh's thug is there. His name is Joseph Wright. He runs messages from Alnwick Castle to Lord Percy, Earl of Northumberland, living at Petworth in West Sussex. His son, Thomas Percy was the link; he is Fitzhugh's father. The gamekeeper is William Winter. They are comrades—all of them. Come to the tower. I will tell you everything. We must be off to Alnwick."

"Who will we leave here? And there's the lad to consider—young Peter Hawkins. We cannot leave him if there be any danger. Why Mrs. Hawkins would..."

"Slow down, Barkley," Robert said, "Where is the lad now?"

"Out about the forest with the forester, Mister Burns and gamekeeper, Aiden Lilburn."

Robert replied, "Go tell Mister Douglas that I have returned and that we are riding the forest—just for a look about and to check on young Peter Hawkins. Say that I will have dinner with him and the Justice in Eyre, Colin Gordon, at sunset. Then come and meet me at the harness makers shop."

Adam Cox was sewing new reins when Robert entered his shop. "Mister Cox, remember we spoke of custom work?"

The harness maker did not look up. He continued slowing, pulling a steel needle through awl driven pinholes. "I told you all my work is custom—did you decide what you want hidden?"

Robert sat on an old chair by the door. "The young lad—apprentice to the gamekeeper and forester. His mother worries after him—I won't be having a young lad riding back and forth to Berwick-upon-Tweed risking bandits. The boy is too young for a pistol and no man with a blade. He'll be carrying his pay and sometimes letters—mail for the Crown and Viscount of Berwick."

Cox kept at his work. "Custom, you say?"

"A saddle with a pouch under the blanket—a place for his coins. Make it a red blanket with a blue border. I say, why not make his mother proud? A gift. Yes. Something to make the young man welcome. And a saddlebag for whatever he might carry. Will it take long? Do you need his old saddle? It is one of my uncle's to be sure, or will it be new?"

Adam cox pulled out the needle and rethreaded the piping. "Sounds like my regular custom saddle. I have one ready. Just bring the blanket."

"Not so regular in the way of Mister Sharpe's saddle or that highwaymen know its secret," Robert said.

Cox replied, "No. Not one like that. The lad and his coins will be safe so long as he does nothing foolish."

Barkley arrived just as Robert was leaving the harness shop. "Come, Barkley, let's find Burns and the lad."

As they rode away, Adam Cox stepped out the door and watched Robert ride away.

Out of Cawmills village, Barkley asked, "What was your business with Adam Cox?"

"A test to see where his loyalties lie." Then turning to Barkley with a smile, Robert teased, "I suspect you have been calling on the widow Mary Hawkins. I'm afraid you must put your courting on hold. The lad can tell her that you have left. Just do not say Alnwick Castle. That is our secret, for now."

Barkley stood up in his stirrups, pointed and said, "There. In the dale near the creek. They place a salt lick."

As they rode down to meet them, Robert said, "Is there something you can tell Lilburn to do? I want to speak with Burns alone. Tell the lad he is to wash up and join us for dinner. Fetch the red blanket with the blue border from my bed and take it to the harness maker, Cox."

"Corporal Lilburn can prepare a drill schedule for say, a week?—while we are gone."

Robert nodded. "Yes, plan for a week. We can always send word."

Burns, Lilburn, and Peter Hawkins waited for Robert and Barkley to dismount. "Welcome back, Captain Curtis," Burns said cordially.

Robert dismounted and walked over to Peter. "I heard our new apprentice had arrived. How are you, Mister Hawkins? Still think this may be the life for you?"

"Oh, very much so, Captain Curtis. Under Warden Barkley has been most helpful and Mister Burns and Lilburn the best of masters."

Robert patted Peter's shoulder. "And your mother,

what does she say of your choice?"

"Mother says she has never seen me so happy since—since Papa..."

Robert took a knee in front of young Hawkins. "I'm sure your father would be proud—very proud indeed, son. Now you go with Barkley, that is Under Warden Barkley to you. I will see you at dinner."

Barkley spoke. "Lilburn, I will be off. You will drill the volunteers in my absence. I want a schedule—seven days. Have it for me at dinner—in the manor. Well, go! Get about it, corporal."

Lilburn sprung up, a broad smile on his ruddy red face. "Aye, Master Sergeant! A week's drill schedule." And he was off at once.

When they were alone, Robert asked Neil Burns, "What do you make of them, Mister Burns?"

Burns watched the others depart and took a deep breath. "Eager. Eager and full of the spirit of youth. Lilburn is green as the grass, though quick to learn and capable. A reliable man. Young Peter knows his business already. Lad says he spent time in the woods with his father. Worshipped his father if you ask me. He will do fine. A sharp mind, that young one. Schooled, he says."

Burns turned to Robert and said, "Found a good one, Captain. Tell his mother that I'll watch over him."

Burns nodded and repeated softly, "You found a good one."

Robert stood with his hands on his hips, staring at the salt block. "Mister Burns, Barkley and I have urgent business. We will be gone perhaps a week. You will take charge. Take no lip from Mister Douglas or Mister Gordon. Cawmills is a Royal Forest, and you are the forester. If you need us for any reason, send off to my uncle, the Viscount of Berwick. Keep your business to yourself, don't share with Douglas or Gordon."

Burns turned and looked into Robert's eyes. "Goes without saying, Captain Curtis. You can trust the lad and me."

Robert smiled. "There are few here I can trust. But nothing to the lad—he is too precious to his mother."

Robert mounted his horse. "Dinner tonight, Mister Burns." And he rode back towards Curtis Castle.

At dinner, Robert engaged young Peter Hawkins, asking a report on the game of the forest. "Good, hearty stags, Captain, they have at least three harems of does. Tenants have been good—no signs of poachers, even though times have been hard. I've seen evidence of a boar, though I have not spotted him yet."

Robert smiled. "And how are you getting on with the others?"

"Most splendid. Only my mother ever treated me better."

Robert laughed. "Well, gentlemen, we must not spoil the lad."

Hawkins and Barkley blushed, and Burns laughed, the others smiled. Robert looked around the table and said, "Gentlemen, Barkley, and I have business for the Crown. We are off tomorrow for a week. Mister Burns will make the decisions in our absence..."

The Justice in Eyre, Gordon interrupted, "Surely, as an

officer of the crown, I should…"

Robert interrupted, "You shall try any cases of trespass or poaching that Mister Burns reports. He is the forester. You are a judge. And Mister Douglas' authority does not extend beyond the manor or the tenants, for now. Lilburn, as corporal of volunteers, shall continue the drills. Is that clear? Mister Burns knows how to contact me."

Gordon looked down at his plate and said nothing. Douglas smiled and said, "As it should be, Captain. All will be in good order."

In the morning, Robert, and Barkley rode south through Cawmills village towards Berwick-upon-Tweed. They stopped briefly to inform his uncle Viscount Curtis of their plans. Katie and Wilhelm were at the hospital. Karl had persuaded Katie to stay. Karl and Will would travel to Mainz to deliver Archbishop Abbot's letter. They would find Johann and send notice to Werner to come to England for the wedding.

Leaving Berwick-upon-Tweed, they joined Great North Road south. Once again, they passed the Holy Island of Lindisfarne and came midday upon Alnwick Castle. In the years the Ninth Earl of Northumberland, Lord Percy, had been banned from the north, the distinction between village and castle broke down. The walls separating the castle from the town were partially demolished, the stone being used in the growing market town. The wall supporting the main gate stood, and the towers and the fortress remained, its garrison only a memory. Alnwick Castle was centuries old with a storied history, but the neglect of many years was painfully evident.

Harold Percy, another cousin of Lord Percy, was informed Captain Curtis awaited him. As Robert strode through the door, Percy said, "Sir Geoffrey, how good..." He stopped and stared at Robert.

Robert smiled. "I am afraid you have mistaken me for my cousin Geoffrey. I am Robert Curtis of Berwick-upon-Tweed and now Sheriff of Cawmills and Warden of Cawmills Royal Forest. You have not heard the news of my cousin's misfortune. His title stripped and his land forfeit to the crown."

Robert handed the constable the letter of introduction from Lord Percy and continued. "I am here at the invitation of Lord Percy. We share common interests in science, architecture, and religion. He insisted I make use of his library here. His circumstances have kept him away for many years. He asks my opinions on the castle, perhaps some amount of restoration."

Harold Percy replied as he opened the letter, "He has said nothing of this to me,"

Robert smiled. "It was our talk that spurred his mind. Does he not say so? Fresh eyes—he asked I look at it, and my report to provide an informed opinion from fresh eyes."

Harold Percy read the letter and said, "You are welcome, Captain Curtis, please take no offense in my mistaking your identity. You mentioned your cousin's misfortune—tell me what has become of him?"

Robert struggled not to smile. "He has been found a

traitor to the King. Geoffrey was arrested and held at the English garrison of Frankenthal—he was with Colonel Vere's volunteers. I shall require a room and for my under-sheriff, Master Sergeant Barkley as well. No need for special attention, but we would ask to take our meals here—Lord Percy insisted."

"You are most welcome, Captain Curtis—Master Sergeant Barkley. A servant will show you to your rooms. You must join me for dinner—it will be my pleasure to hear the news from my cousin, the Earl, Lord Percy."

Alone in Robert's room, Barkley asked, "Science, architecture, religion? The library? What are we looking for?"

Robert replied, "We are looking for Fitzhugh's books—the box with the Bible and code. We are looking for Joseph Wright and William Winter—and any other plotters. We are looking for connections to my cousin Geoffrey and Curtis Castle and Cawmills. We are in their headquarters, Blakely. We must have our wits about us."

Barkley nodded. "One thing we know, he was expecting Sir Geoffrey."

CHAPTER 17
ANSWERS AND QUESTIONS

The view from the Tower window looked out upon rolling hills interrupted by rocky ridges. The fields were showing the first scars of the plow as men and oxen slowly made their way across, line by line, furrow by furrow unearthing gravelly soil. Below was the centuries-old long wall of Alnwick, perched precariously along a high stone ridge fencing the castle and village from Scottish invaders from the north and west. The old wall appeared ragged as it conformed to the ridge beneath it. But the irregular shape supported an excellent defense, allowing a full field of fire for its defenders. Near the tower was a large stable and kitchen. Along the wall and at the corners were roofed barracks, quarters for a large garrison, interrupted by storerooms and shops.

Robert moved his hands over the heavy stones framing the window. "Barkley, have you ever seen a tower wall as wide and strong as this?"

Barkley stood next to Robert and looked at the

narrow window and out to the horizon. "Much stronger than Berwick Castle or any we have seen in Germany. I dare say, a fair match to many a cannonball."

Glancing down at the perimeter wall, he said, "Can't be said for the castle wall—though storming it would be suicide without a large force across that field of fire. Tunneling under is not an easy option—not through the rock on which it stands."

Barkley paused. "You aren't considering an assault, Robbie, what are you thinking?"

Robert murmured, "The strongest fortress is always vulnerable from within."

Barkley replied, "Aye. That was the plan against our regiment."

"That will be their strategy again and again until they succeed. I am going to the library. You go to the stable, the smith, the working men."

"What am I looking for?"

"Why Joseph Wright, William Winter, and any who drink with them."

Robert went downstairs in search of the library. He stopped and gazed into the great hall. He marveled at the size and splendor of the room. Rows of tables tiered down from the outside walls lengthened the already immense dimensions of the room. The lower story of the chamber was richly paneled from the floor to fifteen feet. Above the paneled sides of the room towered rows of mullion windows another fifteen feet high. The vaulted ceiling rose triumphantly above in dark beams, and ceiling planks broken by immense chandeliers -great suns shining on the nobles gathered below. The eye was drawn to the end of the room with soaring floor to ceiling windows, bordered and decorated in stained glass.

Robert stood and stared. He thoughtlessly muttered, "Great—beyond great. For certain, all of Berwick's Church of the Holy Trinity could fit inside this room."

Robert was startled to hear Harold Percy reply, "Aye, Captain Curtis. Two hundred knights could dine together, all sworn in allegiance to the Earl of Northumberland. Come here at night when the moon is bright in the sky; sit beneath the great window and listen—you can hear them—knights and Lords swearing allegiance ahead of the battle. It is a sacred place to all who have Percy blood flowing through their veins."

Robert's eye caught a familiar religious pane in the stained glass. *I've seen that before.*

Harold Percy broke his concentration. "You have not come to hear Percy family legend, Captain. What is it you seek?"

"The library. Lord Percy has offered it up to me. We discovered we shared interests when we met at Petworth."

"It is this way, Captain. I will take you. The letter you bore, it is most unusual for his Lordship."

Robert followed Percy and replied, "Indeed? I did not know. I know only that his messenger had just left, and as I was to depart, Lord Percy generously wrote the note of introduction. We had only just met. Indeed, it was my great fortune to be a guest. I had never made his acquaintance. I came as a guest of a guest, and over a fine evening of cards with his close friends, we discovered many common…"

Harold Percy replied, "Interests. I know you have said so. You say Lord Percy's friends?"

Robert said, "Yes, George Calvert, Lords Henry de Vere, Thomas Howard, and George Gordon and Sir Thomas Wentworth. Great men, one and all."

"Indeed, Lord Percy is an influential man. You mentioned an interest in religion?"

Robert smiled. "That is what I seek in his library, an ancient Bible brought by the Irish Monks, works of the church fathers, Cardinal Woolsey's letters—on the right of worship."

Harold Percy stopped and turned to Robert. "And you are of the same mind as Lord Percy and his friends?"

Robert nodded. "I am of the same mind as Sir Thomas. A friend of tolerance and peace in England. I had gone to London to petition for a friend, a Jesuit who saved my life."

The constable stopped in front of a door. "The library. I shall you leave you to your pursuits."

The gilding on the many leather-bound volumes was still bright. The books were only lightly used. Robert pulled a volume on the church fathers. He blew away a thick layer of dust from the top of the book and opened it for the first time in many years. Robert smiled and thought, *the dust shall help me narrow the search.*

Robert made his way around the room, looking at the dust on the shelves in front and on top of the books. He stopped when he came to a well-worn and dustless shelf.

Barkley walked through the stable. He stopped and stroked the neck of his horse as his eyes searched. He heard footsteps and hay being pitched in the loft above. He saw the saddles neatly set on railings beside each stall. Each saddle was sitting on its blanket. *I'll have to lift each one,* he thought, and slowly walked the length of the stable silently, lifting each saddle from its blanket and returning it as he found it. Near the far end, one blanket lifted with its saddle. Looking once again, and sure he was alone, Edward loosened the leather bindings, slid his hand under the saddle, and felt a hidden pouch. *Another of Mister Cox's custom saddles.* He removed the pouch saw that it was empty and returned it to its place.

Edward stepped back and made a mental note of the horse. *Chestnut with three white stockings and a white blaze on his forehead. The right rear stocking—light brown.*

Barkley walked to the ladder up to the loft and called from below, "Hallow there! Lookin' for the stable master."

"I'm stable master, be down in a bit. Let me finish with this hay."

Barkley replied, "Aye, I can wait—well-ordered stable. I'll have me a look about while I wait."

Barkley wandered about, looked in the tack room, and noticed more saddles and blankets and polished leather saddlebags with the Percy crest. In the adjacent carriage room, he saw two carriages and half a dozen carts. Everything was clean and orderly.

The stable master joined him in front of the carriage

room. "Not much call for carriages. Lord Percy cannot visit, and his son and heir Algernon Percy is in France. Few visitors really, his friends find him at Petworth now."

"You maintain them well. The constable must be pleased."

The stable master snorted, "Harold Percy is not permitted their use. I exercise them once a month— keeps the leather soft and the grease wet. I make certain he sees—vexes him every time!"

Barkley smiled. "My Captain and I are guests of Lord Percy. Captain Curtis will need to send a letter to his Lordship. I was told you might know the whereabouts of the messenger, oh what is his name, Joseph, Joseph…"

"Joseph Wright. Useless lad. Don't know why they keep him on. Aye, he's here. You can find him at the Castle Rock Inn. Probably drunk," the stable master replied.

"If I miss him, does he drink alone? Has he any friends I might ask after?"

"If he is there, you will find him in the corner with young Will Winter and George Catesby. Ne'er do wells, all of them."

"They are all in service here?" Barkley asked.

"Aye. Winter is a gamekeeper, and young Catesby works accounts for Constable Percy."

Barkley nodded. "Well, I shall be leavin' you to your work." And he started for the door.

Barkley stopped and asked, "There is a fine horse, wonderin' if he would be for sale—the chestnut—the one with three white stockings?"

The stable master shook his head. "Not for sale. A fine animal he is—wasted on that worthless lad, Joseph Wright."

"Well, thanks. Good day to you." And Barkley was off to the Castle Rock Inn.

Robert opened the leather-bound box made to appear as a book with the title "Hay and Fodder of Northumberland." It was filled with papers—pamphlets—underground Catholic pamphlets authored by the Jesuit Superior of England. Robert scanned the documents, a call for non-violent resistance to English persecution of Catholics. Robert was surprised by the strong condemnation of violence. *I wonder how Archbishop Abbot would view this Jesuit Superior? I pray with respect and shared tolerance.*

As Robert opened other boxes on the well-worn shelf, he found similar letters and pamphlets on advice for recusant Catholics—prayer life, works of mercy, and penance. The contents confirmed the beliefs he heard from Lord Percy, a desire to worship freely and openly as a Catholic, loyal to his King and country. *This is too obvious—to easily discovered. There must be more. Where is the Ancient Irish Bible?*

Robert stepped back and scanned the room. He sat at a table in the center of the room. Next to the table was a tall candelabra. Paper and ink were set out for writing beside a small candle on the table. Robert turned from his study of the artifacts and gazed at several pedestalled busts of former Earls. He moved his chair, and the floor beneath his boot squeaked in its complaint. He looked down at the small carpet under the table and tested it with his foot once more. Again, a soft but distinct squeak. Robert stood, moved the chair, and slid the rug away. The floorboards appeared normal, but as he further moved the small rug, he noticed that three of the boards, though butts not aligned, were all short. Then Robert saw a small knot in one board just large enough for his little finger. He looked about once, got down on his knees, hooked his finger in the knothole, and lifted. The void beneath was dark. Robert lit the candle and lowered it into the darkness. He saw several boxes. Carefully, he lifted the first out, set it on the table and unwrapped the velvet cloth surrounding it. He smiled, *Identical to Fitzhugh's—it may be the same.*

Steps. Robert heard steps in the hallway. He froze for a moment before returning the box, hastily throwing the rug back over the floor compartment and sliding the chair back in place. He walked to the door and cracked it open. Someone approached. Sounds grew louder—the footsteps were careless and heavy. Clanging. What was that noise? A man turned the corner and came into view. A servant carrying a tray of dishes walked past without so much as a glance towards the library door.

Robert closed the door and returned to the desk and the hidden compartment beneath it and recovered the box. He remembered how he opened the secret compartment he found in Fitzhugh's box. He smiled as the hidden compartment opened. Inside he saw the same prayer beads and cipher. It was Fitzhugh's. He opened the

top and removed the beautifully illustrated Celtic Bible.
Inside the gilt cover, inscribed in Latin was written,
"Holy Island, Lindisfarne." Robert closed his eyes and
thought, *What a sacred text for our people! How did he come
by it? Why isn't it in Durham Cathedral with the other
Lindisfarne relics?*

Robert gently and silently went through the pages.
Magnificent bold colors—painstaking calligraphy, hand-
painted illustrations. He had only seen craftsmanship like
this in one other Bible at Cambridge. As he held the Bible
in his hand, he sighed and shook his head no, Robert was
afraid of what he was about to do. He opened the Bible
wide, the binding arched, stretching the ancient cover
away from the binding. First, he looked into the newly
formed cavity, then he carefully inserted his index finger
and pried. The smooth movement of paper inside startled
him. He pulled out a small piece of paper, unfolded it,
and read. Names—names matching Fitzhugh's cell and
others. Names that he expected and names that surprised
him. He carefully returned the Bible, wrapped it in its
velvet cover, and returned it to the void.

The second box held letters—no names, only nine
code names. Robert quickly went through the box. The
messages involved Colonel Vere's volunteers, the Spanish
campaign on the continent, and positions supported by
Spain in the English House of Parliament and privy
council. Robert nervously looked around and listened for
anyone nearby. He rose from his chair, walked over to the
shelf, and took the box of Catholic pamphlets. He spread
the documents on the desk and covered the floor

compartment with the rug. A simple matter to hide
documents under the harmless Jesuit pamphlets in case a
visitor again surprised him.

When Robert finished the letters in the second box
from beneath the floor, he returned it and opened the
third box—more notes, not coded—all calling for
action. Nine names were recorded. These letters were
different. They were filled with curses and references to
the evil tyrant, the devil ruling England, Scotland,
Ireland, and Wales. Robert read and reread them. He
could feel their hatred, but he could find no specific
plot—only a desire for the assassination of King James.

Robert copied the nine names, returned the boxes,
and the floorboard. He carefully spread the rug and made
sure the table was as he found it. He then returned the
box of pamphlets to its place on the shelf and went to his
room.

As he waited for Barkley to return, he thought about
what he had found. He looked at the long list of names
and the letters of the radicals he found in the last box.
Only Howard Fitzhugh and Father Oswald Tesimond
appeared on the long lists. The others: Joseph Wright,
William Winter, and George Catesby were new. *With
Fitzhugh dead, is this cell known only to Tesimond, or has he
passed the names along? Catesby works for Harold Percy. He
must be the one hiding these letters. He knew Fitzhugh and
Winter, Fitzhugh's guard the day we searched Fitzhugh's
Cambridge chambers. How much does Harold Percy know? Why
did he hire Catesby?*

Robert knew that Count Gondomar, Father Simon

Stock, Donald Stock, Charles Richard, Geoffrey Curtis, Howard Fitzhugh, Don Lorenzo, and Don Pedro engaged in the plot against the regiment. *Geoffrey has escaped, and one other is unknown. All the known cell members are on the long list. Likely also the missing ninth member is too. Who?*

The remaining names from the list in the Bible were the Jesuit Superior; a priest, Father Henry Clitherow; and recusant Catholics, Anne Vaux, Elizabeth Vaux, Edward Vaux, Eleanor Brooksby, and Harold Percy. Most had been accused of providing safe houses for Catholic Priests. *The missing name for the remaining plotter against the English Regiment must be one of these.*

Robert pondered the list and the boxes. *One list, three letterboxes—three cells. The first is recusant or secret Catholics. Their greatest crime, besides their faith, is providing safe houses for priests. Anyone on the list might do that—with the means. They may contribute money, a printing press, or other support. But they are opposed to violence. In their hearts, they are English. The second cell actively supports Count Gondomar and a Spanish union. Their plot was foiled. The third, the radical zealots are determined to avenge the deaths of the gunpowder plotters. Their hate overpowers their caution—reckless and careless. Yet dangerous.*

Robert paced the room before stopping by the window. There is something about viewing the horizon that brings order and clarity to one's mind—at least that is what his father said he learned as a young boy sailing cargo ships across the sea. The sun low in the sky above the western horizon captured his attention. Life went on. The sunset was as constant as the sunrise. God was in heaven—His will be done. His thoughts came together again. *Only my cousin Geoffrey from Cawmills? Does that eliminate Andrew Douglas and the others? Is Geoffrey part of all three cells? Someone is communicating with him. Gordon carries letters—where? The priests—Father Oswald Tesimond fled England when he was implicated in the Gunpowder plot. Has he returned? And Father Henry Clitherow—could he be a relation to Margaret Clitherow, a martyr to English Catholics?*

Robert's thoughts were disturbed as Edward Barkley came into the room. "Joseph Wright, Will Winter and George Catesby—you didn't know about Catesby—they are here. I have just left them…"

Robert smiled. "I know about Catesby and their fellows, Fitzhugh and the priest, Oswald Tesimond. They seek to kill the King."

Robert paused and smiled at Barkley, who was surprised and disappointed to hear his news was late in coming. "You've done well, Edward. You found them, and they do not know you. I would have given us away. My visit to the library supplied many answers but many more questions. The most urgent being, I still don't know their plan, or who to trust at Cawmills. Sit, let me tell you what I learned."

Barkley listened intently. When Robert listed those determined to kill the King, Barkley interrupted, "We have them here. We must arrest them now!"

"On what evidence? Letters of hate? We have found no plot—no conspiracy—yet."

Barkley shook his head. "There was the attempt at Bramshill. William Winter—arrest him."

Again, Robert said, "No evidence! We can prove he was there, but we cannot prove he tried to kill the King. No. We need more."

Barkley sighed. "Will you share the names with Sir John Doddridge? Allow him to take them to the King?"

Now it was Robert who sighed and slapped his hands down on the table, "I can't share the list. Not the whole list. I would not betray Lord Percy, not with Harold Percy listed. I am unable to shame a Catholic whose only crime is to practice his faith. Plotters, yes. Protectors of radical Catholic priests bent on the murder of protestants and our King—without hesitation. But the only list is long, and Wright, Winter, and Catesby are not on it. There is more to be found here. What have you learned from Wright, Winter, and Catesby?"

Barkley leaned back in his chair. His eyes closed. He took a deep breath and answered, "Nothing yet. They drank the ale I bought them and spoke only of their boredom with Alnwick."

Robert stared at the wall behind Barkley, his eyes not seeing beyond him. "Pursue their acquaintance, speak of adventure—speak of soldiering, how you spit in the eye of danger. Encourage their idealism as you fill them with ale—or good Scotch Whiskey. Let them believe you might join them."

"Aye, Robbie, try again to loosen their tongues. How would a fine Catholic kill a devil King?"

Barkley paused, looked up, and smiled. "I might mention gunpowder—that may give them ideas!"

Robert smiled. "Yes! If they are looking for revenge,

what better statement could they make? And what better opportunity to trap them! Procuring gunpowder is the job of a smuggler. And I shall send a report to Sir John, and Lord Percy, but only regarding the priest and the three lads. Perhaps they can tell us more about Father Tesimond."

Robert sat back and smiled. "Now who is the traitor to the regiment we haven't identified, and where is my cousin Geoffrey? You haven' told them your name? Tread carefully. We don't want him warned away."

CHAPTER 18
KNOWN AND UNKNOWN

Robert stood in the great hall with Harold Percy staring at the vaulted ceiling. "How many centuries have Alnwick Castle belonged to the Percy family? Consider all the lords and ladies that have supped here—the nobles and the knights that knew Alnwick as the headquarters of the English Middle March. The Percy's, trusted servants of the King—what would happen to the Percy that lost Alnwick forever?"

Harold Percy said nothing. He just stared out the great window towards the fields and the moors. Robert sighed. "Thomas Percy came close to destroying your family. After twenty years in the tower, you know Lord Henry Percy will not allow that to happen again."

Still, Harold Percy said nothing, but in his silence, Robert knew he was listening. "When I arrived, you were expecting my cousin Geoffrey. If you know where he is, you will do well for Lord Percy and every man with Percy blood in his veins, to tell me."

Robert turned in front of Harold Percy, looked into his eyes, and said, "I have no complaint against a man's religion. It is a foolish game that the King plays against his people, pitting Catholics against protestants, Church of England against the Scottish Kirk, and all against puritan non-conformists. I will not be the one to betray your faith. But treason—betraying your brothers-in-arms. Plotting with foreign powers to kidnap or kill your King—that is too far for any Englishman or Scotsman—too far for Lord Percy, Earl of Northumberland. I believe it is too far for you, Constable Percy. Do I tell Lord Percy that you helped me—or that you follow your kinsman Thomas Percy, a traitor?"

Harold Percy sat down, lowered his head, and rubbed his eyes. He sighed and said, "The message came. It said Sir Geoffrey Curtis needs a safe house until he can plead his case before the King. I do not know when he will come—or if he has been warned."

"You say a message, from whom? Who carries these messages, Joseph Wright?"

"Joseph Wright is only one messenger—others are working at safehouses."

Robert nodded. "George Gordon from Cawmills?"

Harold Percy looked up. "George Gordon, carry messages? Not here. Always Sharpe and after him, some lad would meet Joseph Wright."

"You hired Joseph Wright. You pay him and put him up."

Percy answered, "The priest. He sent him. Priests send the messengers to the safehouses. We don't question our priests. They put their lives in danger to serve us."

Robert nodded. "Yes, yes. Do you know Joseph Wright is the son of John Wright, the traitor?"

Percy nodded yes. "Aye, but the lad needs work and the priest…"

Robert interrupted, "So all who are sent by your priests are given a place, no questions asked?"

"It isn't like that. We provide refuge and work for our brothers. They are good men—hardworking. They only want to live and worship as Catholics. We must trust them, and they trust us. We are a persecuted people!"

Robert sighed. "Yes, as are the protestants in the Palatine and Puritans everywhere."

Robert took a breath and added, "Your priest, is he obedient to the Jesuit Superior of England?"

Harold Percy looked confused. Robert continued, "The Father Superior does not threaten our King. Radical zealot priests like Oswald Tesimond will bring ruin to your house."

Percy mumbled, "Father Oswald has fled to Italy."

"And where is Father Henry Clitherow?"

Percy's eyes widened. He avoided eye contact with Robert. "Father Clitherow is said to be in France."

Robert immediately asked, "One more question—and I must report to the Earl—weapons and gunpowder—what remains from the King's store and the Earl's?"

Percy looked up, his face contorted by alarm, "Weapons? Gunpowder? The King's stores from the garrison were all removed years ago, after the…"

"After Thomas Percy's treachery. That should be a

lesson in the King's trust of the House of Percy. What remains?"

"A few weapons, hunting mostly and relics from the past. Gunpowder is bought in the village as needed. His Lordship cannot visit, and his heir, Algernon, has not visited in years. What little we have is in the guardhouse."

Robert left Harold Percy seated in the great hall staring out the window.

When Barkley returned from the inn, he found Robert waiting. "I questioned Harold Percy about my cousin Geoffrey. He admitted he was expecting him. He claims Geoffrey intends to petition the King. Priests arrange the messengers and send Catholics here and other safehouses. He knows the lads' stories, but I don't believe he suspected another plot. The Percy's have too much to lose. But he knows more about Geoffrey and Father Henry Clitherow than he let on. Clitherow's name surprised him. He is scared—he will warn Geoffrey and his priest. I suspect he will send notice to the Father Superior."

Barkley replied, "The birds will all scatter."

Robert nodded. "They already know Alnwick Castle is no longer safe for priests and zealots. No, I want the Father Superior to know what the radicals are up to. Lord Percy will assure the Father Superior our real concerns. The Father Superior will help us."

Robert paused and asked himself, "I wonder if Clitherow is still in France."

Then turning to Barkley, he asked, "How did you get

on with lads?"

Barkley smiled. "Once they were well into their cups, I let slip 'the only way to get attention is with a bold plan.' I said, 'twas a pity, only bad luck, the patriots who took action against King and Parliament, did not succeed. What glory that would have been. Aye, an explosion! Gunpowder. A few barrels of gunpowder would be a proclamation to the people—a proclamation of justice being served!'"

Robert smiled. "And…"

Barkley smiled back, "They wondered where gunpowder might be had for the takin'. I mentioned, 'Well from the King, of course! The March headquarters are no longer garrisoned or provisioned, but the King has authorized a new militia in Cawmills, a militia of Cuirassiers, pistols, and arquebuses. All needin' gunpowder."

Robert asked, "Did they try to recruit you?"

Barkley shook his head. "No. I did not give them a chance. I said I would be leavin' soon with Captain Curtis, chasin' his cousin like a wild man. Always leavin' his Cawmills duties to others. The man has no cares for his duties. He collects his pay and chases about England and Scotland. No tellin' where we're off to next."

Barkley smiled. "We're known to too many others. My name slipped to Geoffrey or Stock—no, better I that I am found a drunken fool than a spy."

Robert patted Barkley's shoulder. "Good thinking."

He rubbed his chin and then continued. "Grab your riding cloak. We're spending the night in the stable. If

Geoffrey Curtis is anywhere in Alnwick, Percy will warn him and demand he leave."

A single lantern was lit, hanging in the center of the stable. It gave just enough light to safely lead, saddle, or unsaddle a horse. Robert and Barkley found comfortable positions just inside the doors at either end of the stable in sight of each other. They settled in under their heavy black riding coats, their swords beside them, ready to silently signal their intentions. The peace, quiet, and comfort made staying awake difficult. It was Barkley who quietly shook Robert's shoulder to awaken him and whispered, "No smuggler, you. Snorin' like a honkin' goose. Concentrate Robbie. What do we do tomorrow?"

Robert sighed. "Thanks, Barkley—sorry. Yes, something to consider. Go back to your station."

An hour later, Robert heard a dull thud outside the stable door. He raised his sword to alert Barkley, who at once acknowledged. Both men sat in silence and listened. Again, the dull thud. Robert stood by the edge of the door and peered out. The crescent moon gave little light, but slowly his eyes adjusted to the darkness. He could see nothing. The air was still and the yard silent. Twenty yards away was the door to the large kitchen of the old garrison. Nothing moved. Two low hollow thuds broke the silence. Robert pointed his sword at Barkley—a signal to wait. Robert slowly crept into the darkness staying in the shadow of the castle wall.

A horse stirred in its stall and began to stomp nervously. Barkley crept to the horse, went into the stall, and gently stroked its neck. Moving forward, he lightly caressed the frightened animals face. *High strung, are you? You're a handsome animal. Don't remember seein' you here before.*

Robert approached the kitchen. The large wooden door was slightly ajar. He crept to the edge and looked in. He could see nothing from the door. There was no lantern inside to aid his view. Suddenly, two low thumps exploded in his ears like canon blasts though they were softer than a visitor knocking on a door. Sword drawn, Robert entered the kitchen.

Barkley did not hear the man come up in the stall beside him. He did not see the sword being raised. His body crumbled in the stable as the gilded hilt of an officer's sword was driven down on his head.

Inside the kitchen, Robert stalked in the silence. Directly in front of him, a wooden crate—thump, thump. Robert lifted the wooden box with his left hand; his sword held high in his right hand. A young boy squealed, "Don't hurt me! Don't hurt me!"

Robert sighed, lowered his sword, and grabbed the boy, not ten years old, by the collar. "Stand up, son. Who told you to do this?"

The boy cried, "Don't hurt me. Please don't hurt me. A man gave me a penny. Said he was joking with a friend. I meant no harm. Don't hurt me." And the boy began to cry.

Just then, Robert heard a horse in the yard between the kitchen and the stable. Robert ran outside to see Geoffrey Curtis charging at him sword drawn. Robert stood firm, gripped his sword with both hands, and parried Geoffrey's blow as he rode by.

Robert stood and watched Geoffrey disappear into the darkness. He was surprised to hear his own voice cry out, "Barkley!" And he ran to the stable. Barkley was not at his station.

"Barkley!" he shouted. "Barkley, where are you?"

Robert ran up and down the stable, looking into each stall. When he found Barkley lying at the far end of the empty stall, he cried out, "Please, God!"

Robert kneeled over his friend and lifted his head, covered in blood. He felt Barkley's breath on his arm and cried, "You're alive, my friend—please God, let him live!"

Edward Barkley refused to ride in a carriage. "I am neither a maiden nor an aristocrat. If I cannot sit a horse, I will walk!"

Robert shook his head at his friend and snorted. "Then we wait another day. I won't be having you falling off in who knows where. Your hurt, Barkley! You must recover."

Barkley sat up in bed. "There is too much afoot! Geoffrey Curtis escapes—his trail grows cold. The three lads will be movin' on after our gunpowder while you, Robbie, pretend the second comin' of me mother!"

Robert shot back, "While we wait—and you grow more stubborn, there is no powder yet to steal. While you've been dreaming, I've been thinking. I have a plan. And as for my cousin Geoffrey, I know where he travels."

Robert paused. He kneeled beside his friend and hugged him. "Thank God you're alive!"

Barkley mumbled, "Don't go mushy on me, Robbie."

He paused and asked, "Why did he clobber me on the head? Why not finish me when he had the chance?"

Robert stood up and faced Edward. "It could be that he feared a scream if he stuck you, or it could be he did not want to add murder to his crimes."

"Robbie, the man is proven a traitor!"

"He seeks an audience with the King to dispute the charge. He wants his lands and title restored. We leave in the morning."

Barkley's bandaged head and tired body alarmed his friends at Berwick-upon-Tweed. His lordship, James Curtis, insisted Edward go directly to bed. The doctor was summoned, and Katie and Hulda were told to return from the hospital. Somehow, the word reached Mary Hawkins, and soon the house was filled with worried friends and determined nurses.

Katie insisted on a clean bandage and scolded Edward, "What were you thinking? A long ride after a severe head wound? Robert, you allowed this?"

Robert began to answer, "I tried..."

Barkley cut him off. "Don't badger Robbie—he would have me still abed in Alnwick Castle. There is much to do! Traitors afoot..."

Katie shamed, "You won't catch them in your condition. What good are you to anyone dead?"

"Now, Katie, don't you start on me..."

Mary Hawkins appeared and spoke softly. "Edward, listen. Would you hard ride a lame horse? No, I'm sure you wouldn't. Now I'm sure Robert values you more than any horse or anyone else. How better can you help him than regaining your strength? The race is not always to the swiftest."

Mary smiled warmly, leaned over, and kissed his cheek and said in little more than a whisper, "Get well for me— for all of us. Let Katie and Hulda care for you. No more arguing—we know you to be a man of strength and courage. Show us wisdom. Get some rest—get strong for all of us."

Barkley smiled and nodded. He closed his eyes and fell asleep.

Robert returned downstairs. Lord Curtis was waiting with a letter. "A courier from the Earl of Northumberland. There is also one from Sir John Doddridge. Before you read them—there is news-bad news from the Palatine. There has been a battle—at Wimpfen not far from Heidelberg. The Margrave of Baden has been defeated—crushed. The Catholic armies of Count Tilly and de Cordoba have combined. Duke Christian was on his way to join Georg Friedrich, the Margrave of Baden, but arrived too late. Bad luck. The battle was going well for Friedrich, but for a single canon shot—his powder magazine store was hit. The explosion panicked the cavalry and destroyed his wagenburg defense fort. Most of his men killed crossing the Bollinger Bach creek. Duke Christian retreated to Hochst and awaits the meager army of Count von Mansfeld."

Robert closed his eyes and sighed. His thoughts were with his comrades awaiting the assault to come. Robert opened the letter from Sir John first. Sir John wrote,

"Edward Vaux, Baron of Harrowden, circulated a petition on behalf of Geoffrey Curtis seeking an audience with the King. He attempted a defense of his 'misstated' actions. George Calvert has joined Sir Thomas Wentworth in condemning the petition, and no one in court is willing to carry it forward. In the face of a broader radical Catholic conspiracy, your support in court holds. There is disturbing news. Separately the King has authorized Edward Vaux to raise a regiment of volunteers to support the Spanish Army of Flanders in their fight against the United Netherlands. Admittedly, this is the work of Count Gondomar. Vaux's license denies permission for his volunteers to support any action against the Palatinate of Frederick V and the King's daughter, Elizabeth of Bohemia, or the English and Scottish volunteers on the continent."

A sigh of relief told Lord James the letter brought good news. Robert opened the letter from Lord Percy. "My dear Robert, I have shared our discussions with my friend, the Father Superior of the Jesuits in England— please understand why I do not share his name. But be heartened, his desire for a peaceful return to our religious rights remains steadfast. He agrees a Catholic murderer of King James would lead to a long and bloody civil war. That said, he offers to your service his man at Cawmills, who you will find him a great help in your current endeavors. He shall contact you. I share other news. Lord Edward Vaux busies himself, raising a regiment of volunteers for the Army of Flanders. Many sympathetic to a union with Spain and the true church join this cause. Count Gondomar's negotiations promise no engagement against the Palatine. I am assured your cousin, Geoffrey, will not be among them."

CHAPTER 19
THE INSIDER

Adam Cox saw Robert riding up the hill to Curtis Castle and waited for him at the stable. "Thought ye might have the young lad, Hawkins in tow. Finished his saddle."

Robert nodded. "Young Peter is down at Berwick-upon-Tweed fussing with the others over Barkley. Even Barkley can abide but so much caring, 'expect he'll be here in a day or two. But let me see the saddle."

Cox smiled and pointed to the saddle on a rail with the familiar red and blue Curtis blanket. Robert walked to the saddle and ran his hand over the seat. "You know where to look—where the riders know where to look. But slide your hand over here."

Robert slid his hand to the special pouch and asked, "Why, what have we here?"

Robert pulled out a letter. He recognized the hand of Lord Percy. Inside the pouch was a second sealed letter addressed to Captain Robert Curtis. Robert glanced at Adam Cox, who said simply, "I believe that is my introduction. We have much to talk about."

Robert nodded. "So you run the messenger service and?"

"Read the letter, and then I will answer your question."

Robert replied, "At least I am saved the trouble of testing who else knows the secrets of this saddle" Robert read and reread the letter and slid his hand down his chin. "Seems I was right about Douglas being the priest."

Cox sniffled. "He's not your every-day priest in hiding—he is special. Does the name Clitherow speak to your discoveries?"

Robert looked up. "Father Henry Clitherow? He is said to be in France."

"He runs things here at Curtis Castle. An occasional letter is mailed from France to some of our more talkative faithful. He stays here on your cousin Geoffrey's invitation. They share a vision. A dangerous vision. It has been my duty to watch Father Henry."

"Douglas does not surprise me. I long ago surmised he is a priest. The others, the tenants, also Catholic, I believe. Are they more than farmers, millers, and coopers?"

Cox nodded. "As you say, they are Catholics seeking protection—the ability to worship in their faith—but…

Cox paused and took a breath. "But they had to swear before Father Douglas—they did not know his true identity. To a man, they swore allegiance to Geoffrey Curtis. Before God, they swore to bear arms in his cause. How convenient for your cousin that you train, equip and pay his militia."

"I was aware of the risk. I believe in fair and just treatment—lacking by my cousin, and I thought expanding the volunteers to outside Cawmills would overcome past allegiances. Surely, not all of them are zealots?"

Cox replied, "No. Most are the honest men you thought them. But neither can you trust all of the outsiders. You can thank Justice in Eyre Gordon for that."

Robert's brow tightened. "Gordon is undoubtedly a plotter with Douglas and Geoffrey—yet you must know that his cousin, Lord Gordon, is Lord Lieutenant of Scotland and in favor with the King. Lord Gordon is one with Lord Percy in…"

Cox interrupted, "Lord Gordon has seen the damage that can be done to a loyal family by a radical member. Be assured; Colin Gordon is watched."

Robert smiled. "As the master of the messengers, an easy task for you. Tell me, young Aiden Lilburn, what do you know of him?"

"He has not sworn allegiance to Geoffrey Curtis. He was not sent here to hide among fellow Catholics. He is looking for something. I am certain of it—but what he seeks—I do not know."

Robert said, "I took a chance on him. His story—his work as a gamekeeper. It did not ring true. Though I did confirm, he comes from Lindisfarne. I wanted Lilburn where I could watch him. Though Barkley and I are both amazed at his proficiency and enthusiasm for the militia."

Robert leaned over the new saddle inhaling the fresh

leather polish. He glanced about the stable once more and said, "Here is what I learned at Alnwick Castle. My cousin was there but has fled—I believe to the estate of Edward Vaux or his relations."

Cox nodded in agreement when he heard Vaux's name.

"I identified two groups of Catholic zealots. They appear connected, but perhaps not completely. The smallest group includes the priests, Father Oswald Tesimond and Henry Clitherow. Among them was the traitor, Howard Fitzhugh, the gamekeeper Will Winter, the messenger Joseph Wright, and a clerk at Alnwick, George Catesby. I could not overlook that the three lads, I called them, were sons or relatives of the Gunpowder plotters. Indeed, we should prepare for them soon. Barkley put in their ears that gunpowder brings attention and is fitting for their purpose of regicide."

Cox was silent for a moment before he said, "The others? Others you believe radical?"

"The names were listed but kept separate. Others I deem radical are Count Gondomar, Father Simon Stock, Donald Stock, Geoffrey Curtis, Howard Fitzhugh, Don Lorenzo, Don Pedro, and Edward Vaux. There was a third list—good men whom I shall never give up—whose only desire is to practice their faith in England and Scotland with no threat to their countrymen or sovereign."

Adam Cox smiled. "The second list, they are the men who conspired against the Volunteers in the Palatine. You believe there is a connection to these other radicals?"

"Well certainly, Howard Fitzhugh is a connection. But

it was the gamekeeper, Will Winter, who brought them together in my inquiries. He has already acted once—at Bramshill, to kill King James. Someone directs him. Howard Fitzhugh is dead, yet they continue. They meet at Alnwick and plan. They have little means or knowledge of their own—someone directs them."

Cox replied, "One of the priests? Tesimond or Clitherow?"

Robert nodded. "Yes, and someone with resources."

Cox shook his head. "Not Count Gondomar—he plays the game of state—and is winning. Not Don Lorenzo or Don Pedro. The Holy Father realizes war must be short and swift—there is no bounty in a burnt land and dead peasants. There is no desire to bring new nations into the war. The strategy is to keep them out. An attempt on King James would bring civil war to England and further passion against the Pope and Emperor."

Robert asked, "Who would gain from civil war? Only madmen with a plan to steer its outcome."

Adam Cox nodded. "So we have then, Geffrey Curtis, Simon and Donald Strock and Edward Vaux. And your current plan is to draw the 'three lads' as you called them, here to Cawmills to steal gunpowder. You will need more than the theft of powder to convict them of treason—and still the others plot."

Robert and Adam stood staring silently at the straw strewn stable floor. Robert looked up. "Your messenger, Colin Gordon, where does he ride?"

Barkley was released by his captive nurses the next day on the assurance young Peter Hawkins would ride with him the one hour to Cawmills. Hawkins' continued requests to enlist in the Volunteer Company ground against Barkley's goodwill even more than the nursing. "Now, you're selfish!" Barkley barked. "You have a widowed mother. Think of her loss, not your glory."

"But Master Sergeant," Hawkins protested.

"No enlistment—Captain Curtis and I have given our word! Would you make liars of us? And of the honor of your father, who taught you to be honest? A man of integrity?"

"Then allow me to drill. Just to learn—I need no recruitment pay."

"Did you not hear the promise I made?"

"That was enlistment—not drilling on my own."

Barkley tried to change the subject. "What have you observed of the game in my absence?"

"Nothing poached—all healthy. Just allow me to be there when you drill. Mister Lilburn is not much older than me, and you have made him a corporal. We talk about training all the time. He will vouch for me."

"Corporal Lilburn will do as I say. You asked to become a gamekeeper, perhaps someday a forester. If that is no longer your desire, you can return to Berwick-upon-Tweed Grammar School and prepare for university. Tell me, son, gamekeeper, or student. That is the only choice."

Peter Hawkins sighed. "Gamekeeper."

Robert was waiting, hand on his hips, when Barkley and young Hawkins rode up the hill. "Can you dismount yourself, Barkley, or shall I call for a milkmaid to help you off your horse?"

"Not today, Robbie, not in the mood for it." Turning towards Hawkins, he continued. "This one has spent all my patience for one day. It seems Lilburn has bent his ear towards soldiering."

Robert studied the dejected young man and said, "There is no glory in soldiering, Hawkins. Pray you never are called, though the day may surely come. For now, live for those who love you."

Robert reached over and put his hand over the boy's hand. "Come with me. I have something to cheer you up."

Barkley and Hawkins dismounted and led their horses into the stable following Robert. On a rail beside the stall of the boy's horse was the new saddle. "It's yours, Hawkins. The first in the colors of the house of Curtis. It occurred to me you're going back and forth to Berwick-upon-Tweed makes you fit to be a courier as well. Letters and such. The horse is yours now as well. You need to improve your skill on horseback."

Young Peter stared at the saddle.

"Go ahead. It won't bite you. And the horse, are you happy with it? Why not take a ride about the forest this afternoon? Find Mister Burns ask him to join us for supper—sunset."

Peter ran his hand over the new polished leather. A smile broke his trance. He unsaddled his horse and carefully saddled him with his new prized possession. Not removing his eyes from his happy work, he said, "My horse? My saddle? The finest in the stable. Yes. Yes, I shall go at once—ride the forest—and, oh, yes, return with Mister Burns. Thank you, Captain Curtis!"

Once the beaming Peter Hawkins was out of the stable, Barkley asked, "That is the custom saddle, isn't it? It will bring no harm to the lad? I argued the entire ride of our promise to his mother."

Robert nodded. "He will not know. He cannot tell what he does not know. He will have his saddlebag for letters."

Robert turned towards Barkley's face and said, "The Harness maker, Adam Cox, is with us. He gave me a letter from Lord Percy. Let me tell you what I have learned."

They walked towards the tower, and Robert reached over and tenderly touched Barkley's bandaged head. "Looks like no hat for a while. Tell me, did she kiss you— whisper sweet nothings in your ear?"

Barkley spun to face Robert. "Who? What are you talking about?"

"The widow, Hawkins. The lady of your dreams—the reason you stayed in Berwick."

"Don't start with me, Robbie."

Barkley paused and smiled broadly. "A long and tender kiss."

Robert shook his head. "Well, brother, I am happy to hear it!"

As they reached the tower door, Robert said, "Oh,

someone searched the tower again while we were gone. Come inside, there is someone not of Cawmills, but here searching for something— Aidan Lilburn."

The volunteers were becoming proficient with the pistol and sword on horseback. Robert introduced cannon fire to their drills. Both the horses and riders needed to be trained to fight through volley noise, fire, and confusion. But more important to Robert was the need to reinforce the availability of gunpowder. Neither Robert nor Barkley had seen any evidence of the three gunpowder lads from Alnwick Castle. Adam Cox sent inquiries throughout his network but had received no update.

Only Barkley had the keys to the powder locker. Only he and Robert knew the small kegs of good powder were hidden in false bottoms of the water barrels. All the large, marked powder barrels held only old, dead powder, long past its useful life. Barkley prepared the training powder and issued it before each drill. With no bites on the bait, they patiently went ahead with the training. There would be no doubt to anyone near Cawmills that gunpowder was in good supply.

By mid-summer 1622, the Royal Cawmills Cuirassiers were at full strength, trained and proficient. Robert and Barkley had run horses and riders through a field of burning wagons, pounding cannon fire, gunfire, and small black powder explosions. They faced no shells or balls and only strawmen with pikes, but the men had faced everything short of battle, preparing them for combat. He taught them to build and repair baggage carts, pull and deploy the cannon, and build piked earth forts and temporary German-style 'Wagon Forts.' It was time to recognize his men.

Every new cuirassier was issued a deep blue tunic bordered in red with the letters: JR (James Regent), under a red crown, front and rear. Each horse was saddled with a similar monogrammed blanket. Robert invited all the tenants and servants of Cawmills, the people of Lamberton, Eyemouth, Cottington Abbey, and Berwick-upon-Tweed as well the Viscount of Berwick, the burghers, and friends to the Manor House of Curtis Tower for a commissioning ceremony.

Robert assembled his company and sat erect on his horse as Sergeant Major Barkley paraded the volunteers onto the field. When the volunteers came to 'company front' facing their Captain, resplendent in his gleaming half armor and horsehair crested helmet, Barkley presented, "Cawmills Cuirassiers ready for inspection," and saluted Robert. Robert smartly returned the salute and rode up and down the line. He found it hard not to smile with pride at the men before him and returned to the center of the line before his face betrayed him.

"Volunteers of the Cawmills Cuirassiers. You have proven yourself in training. And now you look like soldiers. Not just any mercenary thugs, but soldiers of the King! You are the first company called not to serve a Lord Baron or Earl but His Majesty, James, King of England, Scotland, Ireland, and Wales. Sergeant Major Barkley, a soldier, proven in battle swears by you men. Now Sergeant Major Barkley is not an easy man to impress. He is a man to whom I would entrust all that I love and my very life. You, too, have learned of his courage, strength, and skill—if you can make him proud, then I believe you can make your King proud. Today you have a choice. You can freely—for you are all volunteers—freely swear an oath to faithfully serve your King and follow the orders of your officers. You will hereafter be known as a Royal Cawmills Cuirassier, or you may surrender your tunic and weapons, leave now and never return."

Robert and Barkley rode the line together, making eye contact with each man and nodding at Corporal Lilburn at the end of the line. Robert rode back towards the center and said, "You are given a noble opportunity—to swear loyalty to the King by swearing, 'Aye,' when your name is called. Corporal Lilburn will now call the roll."

One by one, as each name was read, a loud "Aye!" responded. When Corporal Lilburn finished, Barkley called out, "Corporal Lilburn—do you so swear?"

"Aye," came the answer, and then Robert called out, "Sergeant Major Barkley, do you so swear?"

His answer, "Aye, with the help of God above," echoed across the field.

Finally, Barkley asked, "Captain Robert Curtis, do swear to lead us as a faithful a servant of the crown?"

Robert replied, "Aye, so help me, God!"

Robert returned Barkley's salute and addressed the men. "You are now the Royal Cawmills Cuirassiers. I have invited His Highness to review his company. I expect you to impress him when he comes. Sergeant

Major Parade, the Company!"

Adam Cox was busying himself in the stable when Robert was the last to lead his horse to its stall. "A fine ceremony Captain Curtis. Very fine to see. The men look proud and brave."

Robert unsaddled his horse and walked beside Cox, "They did appear truly proud and took the oath to a man."

"Aye, that they did."

Robert sighed and faced Cox. "Does the oath bind a good Catholic?"

Adam Cox smiled. "Depends."

Robert waited. "Depends?"

Cox nodded. "Depends on what his priest tells him."

CHAPTER 20
THE REUNION

Young Peter Hawkins rode up to Curtis Castle at full gallop, slipped off his horse, and rushed inside. "News for Captain Curtis!" he shouted.

Barkley was inside. "Stable your horse properly, lad, and then come with me."

Adam Cox met Hawkins in the stable. "I'll see to your horse lad, I can see you're anxious to share the news. Your smile tells me it is happy news. Go on then, tell the Captain I shall be by to see him later."

Peter ran outside, nearly knocking Barkley over as he came through the door. Barkley shook his head. "Come along. Then, I can see you won't be kept waiting."

They found Robert sitting at the table in the lower level of the tower. "Captain Curtis! His Lordship the Viscount requests your presence, and you too Master Sergeant Barkley, his Lordship says you are to come at once."

Robert looked up. "Peter, we shall certainly go. Did my uncle say why he sends for us?"

"A feast! Father Will has returned with Herr Schroeder and Pastor Johann. There is to be a feast and a wedding!"

Robert stood up. "Indeed, you bring glad tidings! Please inform Mister Burns that we will be going. He is to manage the forest in my absence with the help of Mister Lilburn. Return here once you have spoken to them."

Robert turned to Edward and said, "Barkley, go with him. Pass the word to Mister Douglas and Justice-in-Eyre Gordon. Tell Lilburn no training will be necessary during our absence."

No sooner than Barkley and Peter Hawkins had left, Adam Cox came in holding a letter. "Found this in young Peter's saddle."

Robert took the letter and said, "Sit down for a moment."

Robert read the letter and set it down on the table. "News from the court. Edward Vaux is disgraced. His volunteers return disbanded. He was compelled by the Spaniard, General Ambrosio Spinola, to send his English volunteers against the English and Scots of Sir Robert Henderson at Bergen op Zoom. This, despite his pledge and the promises of Count Gondomar, never to face English forces or forces of Frederick V or Elizabeth of Bohemia. Vaux's volunteers deserted the Spanish and even now find their way back to England. While Vaux is viewed as the scoundrel, Colonel Sir Robert Henderson is acclaimed a hero, a victor even in death. He died valiantly leading his men, his pike in hand at the front. It is reported, 'He was nothing but spirit and courage stepping into the enemy trenches—calling upon God in his injuries—he received the sacraments and very cheerfully drank five toasts. The first was to King James, the second to Prince Charles, the third to the Queen of Bohemia, the fourth to the Prince of Orange, and the last to the Earl of Marre. When he had done, he desired his brother put him into his bed, and so he took leave of this miserable life.'"

Adam Cox shook his head. "It is a good thing Englishmen, Catholic and protestant, did not raise arms against their brothers. Count Gondomar is betrayed as well."

Cox closed his eyes and took a deep breath before continuing, "If Edward Vaux shelters Geoffrey Curtis, he will be forced to flee. And still no word on the plotters, Wright, Winter and Catesby."

Cox sighed. "Go. Enjoy your friends. I know where to reach you."

Hulda Hahn sat staring at the handsome young man engaged in earnest conversation with her brother. Will smiled broadly and answered loudly as he shared with the German protestant pastor, Johann Schroeder. Will wasn't one to smile much and rarely spoke with such enthusiasm. *Who is this protestant pastor? Can anyone be so enthusiastic? So happy? How has he won over my brother? Will is usually quiet and contemplative—never sure of himself. This Johann fellow, can he always be so sure—confident? And Katie—she adores her brother. Look at how she glows!*

Hulda sighed and turned towards Karl and Lord Curtis, talking amicably. The quiet man sitting next to Karl caught her attention. His name was Werner. He sat so patiently, listening politely, and smiling at Katie. *Wilhelm knows him and greets him warmly—a friend of Karl and Katie. He looks and acts the servant, but they say he is no servant, but a friend and member of their household. There is something deep within him—I can feel it.*

Her thoughts were disturbed by Robert and Edward arriving and loudly calling out to Johann, "Welcome, brother! God has preserved you! I see Karl has found you, no doubt Werner's doing."

"Robert! Edward! You have prospered since we last journeyed together! God has been good to you both—and I am told the King has favored you! Dare I hug you, brothers, dressed in such finery?"

Robert and Edward each put arms around Johann's shoulders. Robert replied, "I see Katie and Will smiling at your return..."

Barkley interrupted, "She smiles for finally, she can marry Will. She insisted on waiting for her papa and brother."

Robert's voice turned serious. "Is it true, you bring six English soldiers with you? Catholics from Edward Vaux's volunteers?"

"It is true. The Netherlands is filled with Englishmen looking to come home. It was the Christian thing to do. Papa's network sends them to Amsterdam, and we help them."

Lord Curtis interrupted, "I will feed them, provide

them a place to bathe, new clothes, and pay their travel home. I have sent messages to other nobles. We will send a ship to Amsterdam for others. Edward Vaux abandoned them to roam the continent—he dares not return."

Robert implored, "And Heidelberg?"

Karl shook his head. "Our friend, Colonel Gerard Herbert, still holds the city and castle. The walls are now rubble from canon fire. There has been no food—provisions of any kind to enter the city in months. I fear the end is near. Relief never arrived. It is always pulled away by General von Mansfeld, more concerned with the survival of his army of the Palatinate."

Robert nodded, closed his eyes, and silently prayed. Looking up and realizing this was not the time to detract from the joy of the occasion, Robert warmly greeted Karl and Werner and asked with a new smile, "Did you believe you would see this day—Katie and Will to be married?"

Karl smiled. "Truly a blessing—and with Wilhelm's future secure, I have seen a father's prayers for his daughter answered."

Werner nodded agreement. Smiling broadly, he proclaimed, "Katie is a special woman—God's blessing on them both!"

Johann glanced at Hulda, sitting quietly across the room. "Wilhelm, you must introduce me to your sister!"

The men walked across the room, and Will took Hulda's hands and helped to her feet. "Hulda, this is Johann, Katie's brother, and my good friend. He is a fellow servant of our Lord and Savior, and I am so happy that he is to be my brother-in-law."

Hulda held out her hand and, without a smile, said, "Herr Schroeder. I am Fraulein Hahn. You seem to have a great influence on my brother."

Johann smiled. He did not bow sharply, as only the Germans can, or say politely, 'My pleasure Fraulein Hahn. Instead, he looked into her eyes with an enormous smile, took her hand and kissed it gently, "At last I meet the loving sister of my good friend. God bless you, my dear lady! I have heard such wonderful words. I pray my sister Katie has shown you great kindness."

Johann's smile disarmed Hulda. His words were warm and authentic, but she could not stop the scripted words on her tongue. "So, you, along with Captain Curtis, steal my brother from his calling."

Johann's smile only broadened. "Wilhem, do you not still serve or Lord and Savior with acts or mercy for the poor and sick? Have you forgotten your vow to serve God with your whole heart? Are you no longer a priest to God's people? I am sure that is not the Wilhelm I love."

Hulda felt the blush growing on her face. "Perhaps not his vow—but..."

Johann continued to smile. "His courage? His love of justice and mercy? His prayers for others? Where has he failed his calling?"

Hulda's eyes narrowed, and her lips tightened. "His judgment. You have taken from him his priestly discernment!"

Johann's smile could not be dislodged. He gently squeezed Hulda's hands. "Dear sister, I know no man more discerning than my brother Will. In all the days we traveled together and debated—Will, Robert and I, we have learned from each other. It was Will who saw the heart of each issue and brought us to common faith through his open heart. He expanded our faith and understanding. But as you do not value our voice on the matter, consider Will's influence. He is friend and confidant to the Archbishop Elector of Mainz, first among the electors of the Holy Roman Empire and counselor to Emperor Ferdinand II. And he is a friend too, to the Archbishop of Canterbury, primate of England. He is trusted by both and carries letters between them—letters seeking peace and reconciliation between warring members of the Church of Christ. Is this a man lacking discernment?"

Hulda was silent. The grimace on her face faded, "I love my brother. I see now that you and his friends gathered here, love him as well. Forgive me."

His smile still warm, Johann nodded. "There is nothing to forgive. I pray that you come to see our love for you as well."

Hulda managed a slight smile and said, "Truly, Katie is a godly woman. She has been most tenderhearted towards me—and she selflessly serves the sick and the poor. I see the same heart in her that I so admire in my brother."

Johann, still beaming, nodded. "They give strength to each other, together they will minister in love. We believe they are a gift from God for faithful service—matched in His will. It is a day to rejoice!"

Lord James Curtis clapped his hands but was not heard above the lively conversations. He walked to Barkley and asked, "Edward, be so kind as to command everyone's attention. It is time for the handfasting."

Barkley stomped his foot and in his perfect sergeant's voice bellowed, "Hear ye! Hear ye! The Viscount of Berwick, Baron of Tweedbridge, Lord James Curtis, demands your attention!"

Every eye turned to Barkley, and the conversations ended. A smiling Lord Curtis spoke. "Thank you, Sergeant Major Barkley. We are here today to witness, finally, for indeed, it was a long time in coming, the happy event—the handfasting of the marriage proposal of the Reverend Wilhelm Hahn and the beautiful Katharina Schroeder. But before the handfasting, I distinctly recall the fair Katie demanding her father's and brother's approval of this marriage. Karl has approved. I see our friend, Johann Schroeder, Katie's brother is here. I believe our waiting has earned our opportunity to see our friend Will ask Johann's permission. Of course, if he denies it, it will make a short night of celebration. Johann, Will, let's hear it."

Will blushed as he walked over to Johann. "Pastor Schroeder…"

Someone shouted, "Louder! We all waited to hear this!"

Still blushing, Will spoke louder. "Pastor Schroeder, I ask your permission for the hand of your sister Katharina in marriage."

Johann was smiling. "Can you care for my sister?"

"Yes, and God willing, we shall prosper."

Johann smiled. "And do you love my sister?"

"With all my heart!"

Johann turned to Katie and said, "Katie, will you have this man?"

Katie shouted, "Oh, Hans, you know I love him."

Johann nodded and said, "Then you have my blessing." And he grinned a toothy smile.

A smiling Lord James spoke up. "Katie, Will, you are new to England, and we welcome you warmly. It is our tradition that a betrothal of marriage is sealed with a handfasting until the marriage in church. It is our custom that no wedding takes place until thirty days after handfasting."

Katie interrupted, "Must we wait? We have already agreed."

Lord Curtis shook his head. "Only a maiden with child would wed sooner. Scandal!"

Katie sighed.

Lord Curtis continued, "Both of you. Please come forward. Stand in front of me. Will take Katie's right hand. Now hold it tight, Katie. Do you Will and you Katie accept each other as husband and wife?"

Two, "I do's" were spoken.

The Viscount smiled. "It is customary that gifts be exchanged now."

Will slipped a ring on Katie's finger and kissed her cheek. He then gave her white lambskin gloves wrapped in a red ribbon. When he finished, Katie slipped a ring on Will's finger and gave him a simple wooden cross with a leather neckband. After hanging the cross around his neck, she kissed his cheek.

Edward Barkley shouted, "Katie, you can do better than that. Give him a real kiss!"

The exuberant Katie hugged the red-faced Will tightly and kissed him full on the mouth to the cheers of all present. A smiling Lord Curtis said, "One month from today, Katie Schroeder and Wilhelm Hahn will be married in the Church of the Holy Trinity. All here are invited to witness this joyous event. Now, I believe there is a feast awaiting us in the great hall!"

After the ladies were seated, Lord Curtis directed Barkley to the seat beside Mary Hawkins and said, "I believe Missus Hawkins would like to hear the progress of her son at Cawmills."

Mary Hawkins looked up and smiled. "Edward, what a pleasure to see you on this happy occasion."

The next morning found Karl staring out a window in the quiet sitting room. Robert greeted him as he came in. "The house has not been this quiet in months."

Karl turned and smiled. "They are all still asleep. The celebration went on long into the night. I have seen only your uncle, Lord Curtis, going out the door. A private matter, he said."

"His habit is to slip out early in the morning—talks to himself as he walks. I would like to continue our conversation from yesterday..."

Karl sighed. "About the war. Indeed, it goes badly. The armies meet to fight—break off to regroup and return to fight again. It is the people—peasants and townspeople who suffer the most. Fields are destroyed, villages burned—the only paying work is to join one of the mercenary armies. Even then, their pay is withheld, or the money forged and worthless."

Robert shook his head. "Last year, England's crops were poor, and this year will be little better. But God has blessed Cawmills, and a fine crop ripens in the field— God willing the weather holds through harvest."

Robert walked beside Karl and stared out the window, "The ship my uncle intends to send to Amsterdam—if it carried wheat, barley, and oats—could it find its way safely to markets where the people need it? And can a fair price be returned in a true coin?"

Karl faced Robert and said, "Our captain friend still has his boat. The network still moves among the cities of the Palatine. My friend, Moses, and I can assure silver and gold in payment. What is your plan?"

"The tenants of Cawmills Forest have been treated poorly by my cousin. I am determined to be generous with them—but I must return a good profit to the King. It seems to me, the property of the King cannot be taxed or charged by customs. The market in Scotland will be strong, but the price on the continent, stronger still. I would give, but the crop is not mine to give."

Karl smiled. "There are others with the means to help the suffering. You just deliver us the crop."

Barkley made his way slowly into the room, yawning as he walked. "You two are up early. It was a most pleasant evening. I slept like a baby and awoke to the sweet calls of songbirds. All is right with the world!"

Robert laughed. "Can it be the company of Mary Hawkins has brought this joy to your soul?"

"None of your jabs can touch me this morning, Robbie. Give it your best if you must."

"No more cuts. I am glad for you, my friend. I have been asked to officiate at the wedding. I am off to the church to arrange with the vicar. Come along with me and hear our plans."

As they walked, Robert began, "With your efforts, the company of volunteers is a well-trained militia. It is only their loyalty that troubles me."

"To the man, they have sworn their loyalty to the King."

Robert nodded. "A good sign, yes. But the Cawmills men have also sworn allegiance to my cousin. We know they are Catholic. Their religion does not concern me, which oath they hold to does. My cousin provided them a Catholic refuge, but he did not treat them fairly. I intend to do better and in the same doing to help our friends in the Palatine. I intend to market the crop there. The ship's my uncle sends shall carry the grain, and Karl shall see it finds it way safely. Our trap for the radicals has not sprung. We need the loyalty of the Cawmills men."

Barkley nodded. "Aye, a good plan. But Robbie, loyalty is built on trust, and trust, like respect, must be earned."

"Spoken like a good officer! It is time to assign leadership to some of the men—a good sergeant and several corporals, while you, my friend, become my lieutenant."

"Now, Robbie, I am no officer. Master Sergeant suits me just fine!"

"You, better than any man, know the makings of a good officer. You know what the men expect—how to earn their trust. I know you admire the Colonel and trust him. I am not asking you to change only now you will lead with a stern eye and soft voice."

"Robbie, you ask a hard thing."

"Have you considered Mary Hawkins?"

"What are you saying?"

Robert stopped and faced Barkley. "What do you know about her? Do you remember the day we met her? How did she dress? How did she speak? Her speech was no different than any woman on the land. And her dress—common to the tradesman's wife."

Barkley squinted and replied, "Her house was clean and orderly, and she was teaching her children to read."

"Which won our respect. But how does she dress here? And her speech here? The woman speaks perfect French and knows her way about a Lord's table! Barkley, she is refined! She is comfortable among the wealthy and the nobility. Now, I believe she has taken to you and will have you as you are, but as an officer and a man with Royal duties, well, she and her children will find greater welcome in the great houses of England and Scotland."

Barkley trudged on a few steps in silence before asking, "It was always my mother's desire for me to act the gentleman. And I would want the best for Mary if she would have me. Being your sergeant—having responsibility for men has grown on me. I am not sure I can change."

"My friend, I am not asking you to change. I have grown to like the Edward Barkley, I know. You are more than my sergeant. I could not act without you. You have always been my lieutenant—my right hand accomplishing our work. Now we must find others to grow."

They came to the church, the highest point in the city. Robert kept walking to the ancient city wall behind it. "Here. The city wall over the beach. To the east, our comrades starve during sleepless nights, unable to stop the cannon fire raining down on them. I cannot help but believe that somehow God took us away and brought us here for a reason—for His plan. We must not be selfish; rather, we must grow determined to walk the path He lays before us with faith."

Barkley placed his hands on the wall and stared out across the German Ocean. "I never planned on being a soldier. Being a master sergeant was good; lieutenant will be better. Lilburn is the natural choice for sergeant—if we can trust him."

Robert stepped back and put an arm on Barkley's shoulder. "I must speak with the vicar. You wait here. Adam Cox tells me Lilburn is searching for something. We need to find out what that is. We must know if we can trust him. There must be a way."

Robert left Barkley to his thoughts. The sun was rising in the sky, and the heat of the late summer fought against the cool breeze off the sea. Barkley kept his eyes on the sea, took a deep breath, and thought, *What to do about*

Lilburn. I believe him a good lad and an enthusiastic soldier. How can we be sure?

Words broke Barkley's concentration, a conversation—no, only one man talking. *What's he mumbling about?*

Barkley turned and looked. No one was in sight. He heard the voice again. *It must be coming from the cemetery on the other side of the church.*

Barkley walked around the back of the church. There under the shade of a large oak, a man was sitting beside a grave. Rounding the corner, he recognized the voice. Lord James Curtis was talking to the grave. "Happy days indeed. The house is filled with joy. And Edward—oh, you would be so proud of your son! A man of accomplishment and integrity. It was your doing, of course, I tried to help him in his troubled days, but it was you who taught him right and wrong and showed him a kind and loving heart. What a help he has been to my nephew, Robert. Always thought the young Robert withdrawn—no backbone—never knew his own mind. They have grown into fine men—soldiers of the King, sheriffs, and wardens. Rejoice in this my love, Edward has drawn the affections of a fine woman. Reminds me of you—reads and writes, she knows her mind—always doing for others. Edward will not repeat my mistake. He has no title to inherit. How I regret agreeing to the marriage, my father arranged. I lost my son last year, but I feel I have gained two fine sons in Edward and Robert."

Edward tried to back away quietly, but he stepped on a branch, and the snap alerted Lord Curtis. "Who's there," he shouted. Turning, he saw Edward standing, confusion painted on his face.

James smiled. "Edward. I don't know how much you heard, but its time you knew everything. Please, come sit with me beside your mother's grave, the woman we both loved."

CHAPTER 21
TRUST BUT VERIFY

The fields of Cawmills Royal Forest were ripe for harvest. Robert called all the tenants together in the great hall of the manor house. Looking at Andrew Douglas, Robert said, "When I came to Cawmills, it was said, 'my cousin Geoffrey Curtis was a generous landlord.' I was told you had a poor harvest, and I heard some dispute on the price he paid each of you. Also, it was said he charged you for your seed grain."

Andrew Douglas glared as Robert spoke but remained silent. Low murmurs were heard among the tenant farmers. Robert smiled. "Well, my duty is to the Crown—a good profit must be returned."

Robert paused. "As the King's Warden, I have shown you generosity—pay for enlistment in the militia, pay for stabling the King's militia horses…"

Tom called out, "You charged a bailiwick for the game. You required grain to feed the deer herd and told us to fence rather than poach game in our fields!"

Robert nodded. "Aye, you saw the King's game protected. So today, you shall hear the rent."

Robert walked to a window and looked out towards the fields below. Turning around, he said to Andrew Douglas, "A good crop, would you agree, Mister Douglas?"

Douglas' brow tightened. "Fair to good, Captain Curtis—the estate has seen better."

Robert turned around and faced the farmers. "Have I not said, His Majesty is generous to those who serve him loyally? These are the terms: You shall set aside your seed for the spring planting without charge. Did not Geoffrey Curtis charge you full price for seed? Geoffrey Curtis took half your crop. The King asks, but one third. Geoffrey Curtis set the price, as Mister Douglas claimed, not the best market price in Eyemouth, only for second-grade grain. The King gives you a choice. You may market your grain in Eyemouth on your own, or you may sell it to the Crown at ten percent higher than the Eyemouth first grade price. The King will have a fair profit if you gather every kernel, and you shall prosper as his tenants."

Tom called out, "The seed you say is free—how much seed?"

Robert nodded. "Same as you purchased last year. If you wish to plant more, the added comes from your share. My men will witness your harvest for the account."

Another called out, "How can His Majesty pay more than the Eyemouth price?"

Robert replied, "His Majesty's grain will not be sold

in Eyemouth. Another buyer has come forward."

"And two-thirds of the crop after keeping seed is ours?"

Robert nodded. "Just as you say—a reward for loyalty and faithful service."

"And the sisal?"

Robert replied, "Same division but at the King's market price in Berwick-upon-Tweed."

The farmers gathered and talked among themselves. Finally, the outspoken Tom called out, "Captain Curtis, your word has been true. We agree to sell all our crops with His Majesty's. God save the King!"

Douglas spoke up. "Captain Curtis, you have told us that the King requires worship according to the Church of England at his estates. And did you not announce to the militia company an invitation to the King? When will the tenants have to take communion in the Church of England?"

Immediately the room was alive with anxious voices.

Robert raised his arms and called out, "Good men of Cawmills, please hear me!"

When the room quieted, and every eye was on Robert, he continued. "I have not hidden my identity. Many of you know that I am also vicar of the hospital, the orphanage, and the poor house in Berwick-upon-Tweed. It is common knowledge I have taken Holy Orders in the Church of England. If His Majesty, King James, honors us with a visit and desires a service of the Eucharist or Even Song, I will preside before him and all who come."

The murmuring resumed. Robert raised his voice and

continued, "But this is Scotland, not England. I do not hold anyone here to the Church of England. The King recognizes the Kirk in Scotland. Indeed, you are free to worship in any church. I do not judge you. Just as my faith is common knowledge, so it is known that there are Calvinist's—followers of John Knox outside the Scottish Kirk, and there are, about this land, non-conformists, the so-called, 'Puritans,' and there remain throughout the country Catholics. Good and loyal men all. This is my word to you: I will not impose the Church of England on any man, though I will serve His Majesty and his guests."

Andrew Douglas turned and walked out of the room.

The room quieted, and the tenants began to make their way out. Again, Robert lifted his arms and said, "Men of Cawmills see that no corn is lost—the world is hungry and prays to be fed!"

When the room was empty, Barkley whispered to Robert, "Nothing like a good profit to buy loyalty. Are you sure you were not too generous?"

Robert put his arm on Barkley's shoulder. "They are good men who have been treated unjustly by my cousin. He gave slave wages to his Catholic brethren. We will not take away their worship, but we must open their eyes."

Robert smiled. "The King's price will be fifty percent higher than the Eyemouth price. His Majesty shall see his profit, and our friends in the Palatine will have food."

Barkley nodded. "But a high price for Karl and our friends."

Robert looked into Barkley's eyes. "Have you

considered the price of grain in the Palatine after export taxes, going through four, five, or six trader's hands? If any is even available? And delivered on my uncle's ship? No, my friend, we take only from the profiteers. Karl finds this price is a gift from God."

Barkley asked, "And Douglas, the priest?"

Robert smiled. "Douglas will not know the profit. We will report only to the Royal Treasurer in Edinburgh."

Adam Cox met Andrew Douglas at the entrance to the manor house. Douglas barked, "What is it you need?"

Cox smiled and said, "Captain Curtis is setting rents and accounts. I have come to settle with him for saddles and harnesses."

Douglas mumbled, "You will find him in the hall with his Sergeant Barkley."

At the door to the great hall, Cox called out, "Captain Curtis, a word if I may."

"Come in, Mister Cox."

Cox walked towards Robert. As he came near, he slipped a letter from inside his sleeve and passed it unseen into Robert's hand. "I come to settle accounts on saddles."

Robert smiled and replied, "I was about to retire to the tower, come along, and we shall talk."

Safely in the tower, Robert asked, "Word from your Father Superior?"

Cox replied, "There is news. I leave it for you to read."

Cox paused and then said, "I passed the tenants returning from your meeting. You have proven yourself a fair man in their eyes."

Robert nodded. "But will they be dissuaded by their priest?"

Cox took a deep breath, "I think you have won them. Douglas, or shall I say Father Clitherow, is more loyal to Catholicism than he is to other Catholics. You have confirmed their suspicions about Geoffrey and Douglas and removed the threat of forced communion. You framed Geoffrey and their priest in their sight. The two have treated the men of Cawmills as mere vassals to their traitorous purpose."

"Please, sit, Mister Cox. "Tell me the news."

Adam Cox sat down and smiled. "Geoffrey Curtis was seen. He has abandoned Vaux's, Harrowden Hall. And the three gunpowder lads have returned to Alnwick Castle. They had some story of being off to a sick relative who lingered long in death. In truth, they were at Harrowden Hall as well."

"Where is Cousin Geoffrey now?"

"We don't know. But when he seeks refuge in a safe house, we will hear."

Robert sighed. "I pray it is soon. I fear the King may indeed visit his Royal Forest and review his new company of Cuirassiers once his profit is made known."

Cox appeared confused. "The Royal visit was not a ruse?"

Robert shook his head. "Our friends have put a Royal Hunt at Cawmills before His Majesty. Lord Percy and Lord Gordon make it known King James has not come north in many years."

"Well, my friend, you must have the plotters before

His Majesty comes."

Once Robert and Barkley were alone again, Robert said, "Lilburn is our immediate problem. We need to know if he can be trusted."

Barkley shook his head. "I will deal with Aidan Lilburn. He is not my greatest concern. No, my greatest concern right now is you. Yes, there you have it. It's been troubling me. You condemn your cousin for abusing the servants, tenants, and tradesmen. Are you different, Robert? You think you can buy them with money and a blind eye to their Catholic faith. Fine words about gaining trust and opening their eyes. What do you know of their needs? Do you know Tom's wife is ill? Open their eyes, indeed? How? If you are unwilling to live out our faith, what can they see?"

Robert bit his lip. "You too? You sound like Will."

"Robbie, you are a priest, though I fear a reluctant one. Do you still pray? You told me a priest's duty is to intercede for the people. Do you share the eucharist? Are you withholding communion from those who may come forth and seek it? People expect more from a priest than honesty, more than integrity—these can be found among the people. They expect a priest to seek God's blessing on them."

Both men sat silently. Confusion contorted Robert's face.

Edward continued, "Robbie, I would lay down my life for you. You have been my friend and teacher. But you, too, must learn. You told me God judges the heart. And your heart is true. Just as you found boldness soldiering, you must become bold as a priest. Do you doubt the power of God's Spirit within you? It is not enough to confess with your mouth, you must believe in your heart. And then trust God, who gives you the power to do His will."

Robert looked up at Edward and nodded. "You want me to open the church in Cawmills."

Edward smiled. "I want you to offer yourself as a priest as well as Warden."

Robert's head bobbed up and down as he gathered his thoughts. "It is a hard thing to be a warden, a captain, and a priest."

Barkley agreed. "Aye, yet here you are. They are three roles, and you must be true to each or give them up."

Robert stood up and placed his hand on Barkley's shoulder and said, "Let's take a walk to the church."

Walking down to Cawmills village, Robert asked, "I don't recall speaking of 'confessing with your mouth and believing in your heart,' though it speaks to a passage in the book of Romans."

Barkley looked up. "Perhaps it was Mary who said such."

Robert stopped. "Mary? Mary Hawkins?"

Barkley blushed. "She is a most wise and godly woman. We pray for you, Robbie. She speaks the Bible from memory, like no one else I know. More so than even my mother!"

The heavy oak door of the church was closed but not locked. The hinges creaked, annoyed at being awakened after years of sleep. Peering in, Robert turned to Barkley and said, "Unshutter the windows. Let's have some light inside."

The dust-covered floor was disturbed by footprints. "*Lilburn's been here as well.*

Robert stood and faced the altar, a simple table at the far end of the church in the middle of a raised platform surrounded by a railing and kneeling board. Alongside the altar was a modest pulpit. An open Bible was the only object on the altar. On the wall behind the altar was a wooden cross. An alcove in the wall was empty. The graying white walls were interrupted by white shadows where objects had been removed.

Robert walked to the altar and looked at the Bible. The dust had been disturbed on the left side and cover by some recent hand. He smiled at the old Geneva Bible, favored by Calvinists and Puritans, before the printing of the King James Authorized Translation of 1611.

Light entered the room as Barkley opened shutter after shutter. Robert's eyes followed the footprints in the dust to a closet beside the rear wall. Robert opened the door and saw a large crucifix leaning against the wall and several wooden boxes. It was clear that each box had been opened.

One box held a statue of the Virgin Mother resting in a bed of straw. Others held large tiles depicting the stations of the cross. Robert smiled as he considered the honest and straightforward teaching of the crucifixion of Christ in pictures the people, unable to read, could understand. They were beautiful tiles, well-executed by talented artisans. Robert peered over each one and said to no one listening, "One is missing. There should be fourteen." Going through them carefully, he spoke. "Station four is missing." Then looking at the others—"Yes, I have seen it. Why is it there, above the fireplace in the Great Hall, and not here with all the others? Station four, 'Jesus meets his mother, Mary.'" Then he smiled and whispered, "Of course!"

Barkley joined Robert in the church. "Our young friend, Lilburn, has been here as well—looking, but he has taken nothing."

"Yes, I will deal with Lilburn straight away."

Robert continued, "It will need some cleaning, and I will request some articles from Vicar Widden in Berwick-upon-Tweed, but soon we will worship here again. We must be respectful of what our Catholic brothers have left behind."

Robert, hands on his hips, looked up and all around, nodding as he scanned the sanctuary. "Ask the lads, Peter and Aidan to help us clean…"

Robert paused and turned to Edward. "To do this right, I must write to the Bishop of Durham. If this is to be a Church of England, it must be consecrated."

Barkley asked, "Does that mean a ceremony?"

"Yes, Barkley. The rite of consecration is a ceremony. I have letters to write. You can set about cleaning up."

Aidan Lilburn sat nervously across from Barkley and wondered why he was summoned. "Corporal Lilburn, have not Captain Curtis, and I treated you justly?"

"Aye, Sergeant Major, most justly."

"Have we not shown you our trust?"

"It is just as you say, Sergeant Major."

"And you have sworn allegiance to His Majesty, King James?"

"Aye, Sergeant Major… why am I here? What have I…"?

Barkley did not let him finish. "Do you know the fate of one who betrays his oath to the King? My own eyes have seen a man hanged, drawn, and quartered for betraying His Majesty."

Lilburn sat silently, visibly shaken as he listened.

Barkley leaned forward, his focused eyes burning into Lilburn's face. "You have been entering places you do not belong. You have been in the tower—though it is off-limits. You have searched the manor house, the powder room—even the church. Is this how you reward our trust? The property you violate belongs to the King! Shall I turn you over for justice?"

Lilburn cried out, "No, please. I have taken nothing!"

Barkley remained stern. "We know you have taken nothing—nothing but the right to be trusted. Now, you will tell me what it is you seek, or you shall become an example of one who betrays the trust of the officers of the King."

Lilburn began to cry. "I honor the King -it is…I seek what was stolen—we believe Geoffrey Curtis has hidden a holy relic—he stole the Lindisfarne Bible! We seek to recover what has belonged to my people for centuries."

Barkley was taken aback. "This Bible, is it an ancient Bible—from the Irish monks—gilded and painted throughout?"

Lilburn's eyes widened. "Aye, it goes back to the days of Saint Aidan and Saint Cuthbert. Many on Lindisfarne hold to the old ways."

Barkley stood up. "Come with me. You will tell Captain Curtis what you have told me."

Barkley found Robert at his writing-table in the tower. "Corporal Lilburn tells me he seeks an ancient Bible stolen from Lindisfarne by Geoffrey Curtis."

Robert looked up from his letter. "Geoffrey Curtis took a relic Bible from Lindisfarne? When? On what pretext?"

Lilburn stood at attention and replied, "The Bible has been venerated and protected. It was hidden in the abbey until the notorious King Henry VIII took the lands and abbey. The monks stayed, and some even married. We worship as we always have—in our language, not Latin. Sir Geoffrey heard of the Holy relic and took it by the edge of his sword. He said it should be studied by the scholars and promised to return it."

Robert asked, "When did this happen?"

"It would be more than two years now."

Robert nodded. "Please, continue."

Aidan was calmer now. "When the Holy Book was not returned, our elder confronted Sir Geoffrey. Geoffrey told him the Holy Book was the property of the Pope who has gifted it to one more deserving."

Robert mumbled, "I can think of no man less deserving than Howard Fitzhugh."

Barkley nodded. "If the word was that of the pope."

Robert asked Aidan softly, "You are named after Saint Aidan, your father…"

Aidan smiled. "Aye. It as you say. My grandfather was a monk when the wretched dissolution occurred."

Robert closed his eyes and thought, "You argued with your father before you ran off from Lindisfarne."

Aidan was surprised. "Aye, my temper got the better of me. I told my father I would search until the Holy Book and would not return without it. My father scolded, 'It is but a copy of God's Word—made by man. We place no faith in relics. Our trust is in the Lord of heaven and earth.'"

Robert smiled. "Your father is a wise man."

Robert stood up and walked to the front of the table. "Corporal Lilburn, will you honor your oath to the King?"

Lilburn looked into Robert's eyes and said, "Aye. You and Seargent Major Barkley have treated me fairly and trusted me. His Majesty cannot be blamed for the past. Yea, I will serve faithfully."

Robert grasped Lilburn's forearm. "I believe you. Master Sergeant Barkley and I can help you. We saw the Bible. I expect it is still in its hiding place. I will help you return it to Lindisfarne—and we shall talk more of worship. For truly, it was the longing to hear the Word of God in English and worship in our English language that brought us the Church of England—a church which honors both Cuthbert and Aidan as true saints."

Lilburn muttered, "You have seen it! You will return it to Lindisfarne? God bless you, Captain Curtis, God bless you indeed!"

Robert smiled. "That will be all Sergeant Lilburn."

Lilburn replied, "Aye, sir! Wait...sergeant?"

Barkley replied, "And I will wantin' your recommendation for two corporals."

Robert patted Lilburn on the shoulder and said, "Now be off with you sergeant, I have work to do."

Robert sat down and sealed his letter to the Bishop of Durham. He took another sheet of paper and wrote, "Dearest Lady Eleanor...."

CHAPTER 22
REBUILDING THE CHURCH

Robert knocked on the door of Tom Pritchard's cottage. The door cracked open a few inches, and a young girl peeked from behind the edge. "Papa and my brothers are in the fields."

She started to close the door, but Robert put his booted foot inside the jamb. Robert smiled. "Is your mother home? Is she well?"

The frightened girl remained hidden behind the door. "Mama is in bed, though she does not sleep."

"Has the doctor come to see her?"

"Papa says the doctor costs money we do not have. The pr... that is, Mister Douglas has come and prayed for her."

Robert nodded. "I shall pray as well. Please tell your father that I am sending for a doctor."

Robert prayed as he walked to the church. Barkley, Lilburn, and Peter Hawkins were inside sweeping. Robert called out, "Mister Hawkins, ride to Berwick-upon-Tweed and bring the doctor back with you. Tell him I sent you and he must come without delay. Take him to the Pritchard cottage where Mrs. Pritchard lies in a sickbed. Now Hawkins! No delays—ride hard!"

"Yes, Captain Curtis!" And young Hawkins ran out the door.

Barkley and Lilburn stood and stared. Robert snorted. "What are you gawking at? Back to work. I want the walls white-washed and see about new candles. Draw them from the estate manager."

Adam Cox saw Robert call on the Pritchards and watched him walk to the church. When he saw Peter Hawkins run off towards the stable, he set down the harness he was repairing and walked to the church. Robert was in the closet bent over a box when Cox stopped outside the church door. Robert did not look up from the box. "Barkley, tell Mister Douglas we are cleaning and restoring the estate church. Tell him that the tile above the fireplace in the Great Hall should be carefully removed and returned to the church where it belongs. Tell him if it is damaged a replacement—and it would be a hard thing to replace—a replacement will come from his pay."

Barkley stared. "Tile? Above the fireplace?"

Robert stood up, turned around, and stared at Barkley. "The missing station of the cross tile. Station number four, Jesus and Mary. It announces to Catholics that Cawmills is a safe house. The same station was displayed at Alnwick Castle."

Adam Cox called out, "Good day Captain Curtis! Intending on reopening the church?"

"Mister Cox, welcome! Yes, a wise man has convinced me of a sin of omission. I have been mistaken in my zeal for freedom to worship. I have not availed my call to holy orders for the good of all that call Cawmills their home."

Edward looked at Robert and silently went back to work.

Adam Cox came in and looked about the church. "You still favor conscience—freedom, as you say?"

Robert smiled. "Of course. Does freedom require everyman's religion to be a secret?—though it may be kept so. With no religious intercourse, our brothers and sisters are told vicious stories, rumors, and lies about their neighbor's faith. This is the devil's doing. But the body of Christ, the Church, will prevail—through prayer, love, mercy, goodwill, and the Spirit's leading."

Cox replied, "You seek to build trust, love for your neighbor through showing your worship?"

"And listening and loving. I long that we see each other as brothers and sisters loving God and one another. Aye, I would have us rejoice in our brother's worship, though it is different."

Cox added, "Break down fear and division between neighbors?"

Robert looked up, his thoughts elsewhere. "A school. What are your thoughts on schooling? Sunday, there is no work. Sunday afternoon, after all, worship. We teach our boys and girls to read and write. We teach them their numbers for the market—and we teach them the stories of our people."

Adam   Cox   smiled.   "You   stopped   at   the

Pritchard cottage."

Robert nodded. "I heard she was ill. I sent young Hawkins for the doctor. We must all pray for her recovery. All those young children and poor Tom."

Cox nodded. "The school would be a good thing."

"I would give them the joy of reading Scripture—prayers and…"

Cox interrupted, "Perhaps the saints and Church fathers?"

Robert was smiling. "Just as you say—even the encouragement of the Jesuit Father Superior. Mister Cox, I would show my faith, my prayers, and love for my neighbors in my Church of England. I intend to intercede on their behalf, as is my duty. I leave all else to God."

Robert paused. "Speaking of the faith we share, I have uncovered these wonderful tiles—stations of the cross. They must be returned to the walls and then—a good woodcarver, do you know one? I would place tablets, the ten commandments, and the Lord's Prayer on the wall either side of the cross. The creed, too. And I must find a place for the statue of Mary, blessed mother of God."

Adam Cox smiled. "I know of a carver, I shall send for him. I should very much like to' teach in your Sunday school. What will you name this church?"

Robert replied quickly, "Not my school, our school—it is the Cawmills school. As for the church, I think I should like it to be Saint Aidan, no, better—Saint Cuthbert."

Cox nodded. "A local man and saint to all of us."

Robert's eye caught Aidan Lilburn look up in surprise.

The sound of clomping boots running up the path broke the silence. Neil Burns appeared in the doorway, "Captain Curtis—poachers!"

The carcass of the young deer was lying beside a salt lick and grain drop. Poaching was a rare event in the open terrain of Cawmills but leaving a carcass in full view of a feeding station was unheard of. The poacher was either incredibly naïve or making a bold statement. Burns pointed to footprints, "One man, Captain. Knew how to gut and cut cleanly. Leavin' a carcass—it's not like a poacher. Nay, your poacher will be wantin' to leave no evidence—wants to return again. Trail leads to the Blackadder River. Likely had a boat waiting—the man surely did not swim off with a young stag."

Robert stared at the carcass and nodded. "Take Lilburn and see what you can find. If it was a boat, did he go upriver to Coldstream or downriver to Tweedmouth? With luck, someone saw something—some stranger. This is not the work of a Cawmills man."

Robert scanned the valleys below turned and said, "Only the lord of a manor would leave a carcass for others to deal with. This is a message from Geoffrey Curtis—'I will take what is mine.'"

Barkley looked to the southwest. "If it is Geoffrey, there is no refuge for him in Berwick or Tweedmouth. No, he is off to the south or west—Coldstream, Kells Abbey, Roxburg, or Dryburgh. Or a short boat trip to his horse. I say Mister Burns should follow the river to Coldstream. I will ride to Kells Abbey, Roxburg and Dryburgh."

Robert nodded. "Very well then—before the trail grows cold."

Robert thought aloud, "Would he return to Alnwick Castle? The reports said the three lads had returned."

Robert returned to Cawmills village. Peter Hawkins was tending to three horses outside of the Pritchard cottage. "Is the doctor with Mrs. Pritchard, then?"

Peter nodded. "Aye and Miss Hulda, who insisted she come along."

"Hulda?"

"Miss Hulda was about her nursing in the hospital with the doctor. She was most insistent."

Robert shook his head. "When the doctor comes out, send him to the church. I would have a word with him before he departs. And Peter, have one of the children fetch Mister Pritchard from the fields."

Robert walked to the church, went to the rail, kneeled, and prayed. He did not hear Adam Cox approach quietly and kneel beside him. When Robert raised his head and opened his eyes, he turned to Cox and said, "There is much to pray for."

Cox nodded. "I see the doctor has come, may God grant him wisdom."

Robert breathed deeply. "My cousin sends me a message—he seeks to take back what he claims is his. Where is he? Who is with him? I am at a loss of what to do."

Cox put a hand over Robert's still on the communion rail, "Captain, continue to do as you are. Your judgments are true. Continue your prayers. Have we not been taught, 'The prayer of a righteous man accomplishes much?' I will leave you—there are things I must do."

Cox stood up, paused a moment, and said, "After you speak to the doctor, come and see me."

Robert bowed his head and prayed. After several minutes he stood up and gazed about the church. Then he closed his eyes and made a mental list of what he needed.

The doctor found Robert in the church. "She struggles, but she is a strong woman, Her fever, her sweats—much like the sweating sickness of twenty years ago. Hulda will stay with her. Cold compresses—they must find the coolest water. And drink—she must drink often more than she asks."

"Thank you for coming doctor. I shall cover the fee. Has Tom, her husband, come?"

The doctor nodded. "He is with her now. I have spoken with him and the children. Hulda has taken charge of her care. They listen to her, despite her poor English and her heavy German accent."

Robert smiled. "They recognize the authority of a nun."

"Yes, well, do call me at once if anyone else shows signs of the same illness."

Barkley returned three days later. Like Burns, he found no one who would admit to seeing Geoffrey Curtis in many months. No one reported a man bearing a young stag for the market or otherwise. The trail of the poacher went cold at the river.

Robert kept busy with Barkley, Peter Hawkins, and Aidan Lilburn at the church. With the walls whitewashed, the fourteen stations of the cross were rehung as they had been in decades past. Reverend Witten visited, bringing Robert an altar cloth, a large King James Bible, ten copies of the Book of Common Prayer, silver candlestick holders, and a silver tray bearing a chalice, ciborium, and bowl for the Eucharist.

Robert helped Reverend Witten bring welcomed gifts into the church. Witten said, "When we heard you were reopening the church, your uncle, Viscount Curtis, determined it was time for new vessels at the Church of the Holy Trinity, and perhaps Cawmills could use these."

Robert laughed. "Did he indeed. Well, we shall endeavor to put them in God's service here."

Witten smiled and said, "It occurred to me you may need an Alb, cincture, and stole. I brought several of mine if you will accept them. You will need them for the wedding of our dear friends as well."

"Father Witten, you are most generous. Thank you. So, what do you think?"

Witten looked about and said, "It will make a fit place of worshipping of our Lord."

Witten paused. "Of course, the Church is not a building—this is but a place of worship. Building the Church, making disciples, will mean changing hearts. You must have patience and perseverance, Robert—but mostly love."

Robert nodded and replied softly, "So Wilhelm and Edward have taught me."

Witten smiled. "Have you written to the Bishop? Will there be a consecration? Will it be church or chapel?"

Robert took a deep breath, "I have invited the Bishop to come the Sunday following Will and Katie's wedding. Perhaps it is selfish of me, but I want it to be a part of the celebration. There is as yet no parish. I will obey the Bishop, of course, but I propose a chapel until the people desire a parish. A chapel will impose no church tax."

Witten nodded. "Your desire appears well thought, and the two events are both long in coming for good friends. I leave you to your work."

Adam Cox called to Robert as he walked by his shop. "A word Captain Curtis regarding reins for the baggage carts."

Robert stepped inside Cox's shop. "What word Mister Cox?"

"Your gunpowder ruse has failed. I missed the first message, but I have seen another from Mister Gordon's saddle. It reports the poaching of the stag shook you. Douglas, I am certain it is Douglas who writes, tells Geoffrey Curtis a strike against you cannot fail. He calls you toothless, with only dead powder, and reminds Geoffrey that most of the militia have given their oath to him. He tells Geoffrey a Royal visit was requested, but perhaps the consecration of the devil's church you restore would send his message to the King."

Robert took a breath and thought. "My cousin wants more than a message to the King. An attack on the King's property would not return it to him and would seal him as a traitor and an outlaw. No, if Geoffrey cannot be restored, he must face the King himself."

Robert looked up. "How did he learn of the dead powder?"

Adam Cox exhaled. "I don't know. Perhaps the merchant, your supplier?"

Robert replied, "I found it in Edinburgh. The man was happy to have it out of his storehouse. He promised to a word to no one."

"Colin Gordon has many friends and relations in Edinburgh. What will you do now?"

Robert smiled. "Grow teeth."

The following evening, Robert saw Hulda coming out of the Pritchard cottage carrying wash to hang on a line. He approached and asked, "Is Mrs. Pritchard on the mend?"

Hulda turned around and said, "Oh, it is you, Captain Curtis. Yes, but she is still weak. The fever has broken, and she no longer sweats, but she is tired and sleeps much of the day."

Robert replied, "God has heard our prayers and blessed your service."

Hulda stared at Robert a moment and said softly, "It is good that you sent for the doctor. The Pritchards are thankful. Mister Pritchard finds you an honorable warden and righteous man."

"They are good people—all of them. Any Christian would do as I did."

Hulda shook her head. "No one else did."

Hulda paused. "I prayed the rosary with them, day

and night. We prayed to Jesus and Mary and the saints."

Robert smiled. "Did she find comfort in your prayers?"

Hulda nodded. "Yes. Very much so."

Robert said, "Then I am glad. I am glad you were with the doctor when he was called. Our Sovereign God made it so. Thank you for giving her comfort. Will you stay long?"

Hulda went back to hanging the laundry. "I will stay until she is strong enough to do her chores."

Robert nodded. "I will let you return to your work."

Robert turned to leave. Hulda spoke up. "Wilhelm was right about you. He insists you have a good heart and a love for people though you fear to show it."

Tom Pritchard came to the door. "I thought I heard your voice, Captain Curtis. May I have a word, sir?"

Robert replied, "Come walk with me, Tom. I need your advice."

Tom came out and asked, "Where are we going?"

"To the fields."

Tom matched Robert's cadence as they walked down the lane. "Thank you, Captain, for the doctor and Hulda. You know she..."

Robert interrupted, "That Hulda is a novice nun, yes. I am very close to her brother, once a Jesuit priest—still a priest—he will always be a priest."

"Hulda spoke of your influence on her brother."

"Did she speak of his influence on me?"

Tom sighed. "You will reopen the church—Mister Douglas says you will take a parish tax and require we take communion."

"Mister Douglas says that. Did I not say I will not take a tax or force communion in the Church of England on any here? Have I broken my word?"

"Aye, Douglas has never been generous, but…"

Robert stopped. "Tom, you are a man who speaks his mind. You tell me what others fear to say. Of all the men in Cawmills, to you, I owe the truth. It shall be a chapel, not a church. There will be no parish church tax. Consider, we are in Scotland. The Scottish Kirk and the Church of England have yet to come to common terms. I serve as a vicar in Berwick-upon-Tweed under the Bishop of Durham. He has authority over me but not the people of Cawmills. The forest is the King's estate. It is my duty to see the King and his guests have a place of worship, and I, too, must worship and serve. My prayers are for the people of Cawmills, but I compel no one—and a school. I earnestly desire to teach the boys and girls too—men and women if they so wish—to read and write. Perhaps your son shall be a scholar or Royal clerk!"

Tom walked along, his eyes cast down on his feet. "The poacher. You never searched Cawmills for the stag."

Robert shrugged. "Why waste my time or yours. I know there are no poachers among us."

They came to a golden field of wheat. Robert put an arm on Tom's shoulder and said, "Tell me, Tom, can we not begin the harvest? My buyer is most anxious and the weather—I dare not tell a farmer about the weather. I would not risk any loss."

Tom laughed. "You fear a turn in the weather before we gather the wheat. So do I and every tenant. We will begin in the lower fields tomorrow. They are the most vulnerable. The higher fields can shed any rain and will dry faster."

Robert asked, "I can hire more carts and wagons—better to move quickly to the buyer."

Tom nodded. "Yes, if we can harvest to wagons without storing, that will save time and risk."

Robert smiled. "I would like you to go to Eyemouth, on my behalf—I will give you a letter—go to Eyemouth and establish the price. The others will trust you."

Tom sighed. "You must come with me—you are an Officer of the King. I am a tenant farmer."

Robert patted his shoulder. "We will go together. And then you shall find work in the fields for Barkley, Lilburn, Peter Hawkins and me."

Tom looked surprised. "What do any of you know about swinging a scythe?"

Robert smiled. "We can drive the wagons. Tom, I taxed your grain for the King's deer. Let me return the cost."

As they walked back to the village, Tom said, "A school for my children. Mrs. Pritchard will be pleased."

CHAPTER 23
BRINGING IN THE SHEAVES

The lower fields were harvested before the rain. Wagons filled with forty-pound sacks of first-grade grain made their way to Charles Curtis' warehouse on the wharf in Berwick-upon-Tweed. After three days of autumn rain, and another three days of sun and wind, the upper fields were ready for harvest. Robert walked alongside Tom Pritchard as they made their way to the last wheat field.

Tom's step was lively, and a wide grin shone on his face. "The price per sack half again more than last year and a good crop. Next year's seed in our barns and two-thirds coming to the tenants! There will be new shoes and clothes for everyone. Mrs. Pritchard will be buyin' fine cloth for curtains and new blankets—and I will buy another milk cow, sheep, and goats, maybe hogs as well. A fine thing you have done for us, Captain. A fine thing indeed!"

Robert added, "And a good profit for His Majesty, King James!"

Robert paused and said, "Perhaps there will be more time to school the children after the harvest."

Tom nodded. "Can a grown man be taught to read and write?"

"Tom, It's amazing what a grown man can learn."

Robert and Barkley delayed the return of the last wagons from Berwick-upon-Tweed until late at night. Peter Hawkins helped them unload barrels of good gunpowder, cases of flint, cord, wadding, pistol balls, and even cannonballs for the old cannon. The armory was filled. The Royal Cawmills Cuirassiers were provisioned for a campaign.

Robert slipped away to Edinburg to settle accounts with the Royal Treasurer.

"Your account shows deductions for enlistment pay, provisions for the company of Royal Cawmills Cuirassiers. I see you have withdrawn all of the expenses, and you bring the Crown a profit of eleven hundred thirty-nine pounds."

The treasurer looked up. "A very tidy sum, Captain Curtis! I know this year's prices are good against a below-average crop, but your results—how did you do it?"

Robert smiled. "By doing the best for tenants and King,"

Robert paused. "I have another request. Sergeant Major Barkley, I would have him commissioned Lieutenant of Cuirassiers. I would buy the commission as the King requires."

The treasurer nodded. "It is true, any commission not

granted by the King directly must be bought. One hundred pounds, Captain, and I will issue the commission. His full name?"

The chilly morning air of late September could not dampen the high spirits of Robert, Barkley, and Peter Hawkins as they rode to Berwick-upon-Tweed two days before the wedding of Will and Katie. Royal Cawmills Forest was left under the vigilant care of the Forester, Neil Burns, and the eager Sergeant Aidan Lilburn kept a wary eye on the armory. The road to Berwick followed the Whiteadder River, sheltered by a coastal ridge blunting blasts of cold, wet winds off the German Ocean.

Entering lower Berwick-Upon-Tweed, where the Whiteadder added its water to the Tweed at Tweedmouth, a ship, a large three-masted carrack, with an English pennant showing proudly in the breeze, could be seen mooring at Charles Curtis' wharf. "That would be the ship that my uncle has hired. Following the wedding, Karl and Werner will sail with our wheat to Amsterdam. Karl will return at once with the soldiers abandoned by Baron Edward Vaux. Werner will go with the grain to the Palatine."

Barkley spoke up through rising wind. "A daring and dangerous plan, Robbie. It will require all our prayers and God's mercy. If any man can move a boatload through war, blockade, and a starving country, it is Werner. The man moves like a phantom, silent, and..."

Robbie finished, "Resolved. Yes. His strength comes from his unshakable faith."

The men turned their mounts and rode through the narrow gate in the high wall up the cobblestoned street into old Berwick. The sun began to bore its way through the morning fog as they dismounted in front of Viscount Curtis' manor house. The door servant directed them to the small dining hall where the Viscount was having his breakfast.

"Ah, you're here! Did you see the ship? She will carry back every Englishman Karl finds. The grain loading will begin today. Young Mister Hawkins looks hungry. Did you feed the lad? Thomas, bring breakfast for my three guests."

The servant bowed and left. "Sit—there is much to be arranged and much to do."

Robert nodded to Barkley and Hawkins, each found a chair and sat down. "Yes, uncle, a grand ship she is. There shall be room for many."

Robert paused. "There will be no trouble with the customs inspector?"

Viscount Curtis grunted, "He works for me! I am the King's collector of customs! It is all perfectly legal. The contract for the King's grain calls for it to be delivered in Amsterdam. The grain in the warehouse, aye until it arrives, is still the King's and not subject to customs. The fact that it was paid for in advance and the buyer accepts all risks of the voyage, well, that is just good business. Now we have other issues to discuss."

Viscount Curtis paused to eat the ham piled before him. "There are more letters for you, Robert. After breakfast! They will wait. Now, before you are all off about your business, you will dine with me this evening. We shall eat early. I will not have my guests walking in the dark. There is good news to celebrate, and I would have this celebration before we become overwhelmed by the joyous wedding to come. Karl and Werner will sail the day after the wedding, so you see, it must be this evening."

The servant returned with platters of food. "Ah, your breakfast, gentlemen—go ahead, eat! Good man, Hawkins, never let your food grow cold!"

Robert read his letters, and smiling broadly, left for the church to see Vicar Witten. Barkley and Peter walked to Mary Hawkins' house. Mary hugged Peter. "Have you had your breakfast?"

Peter nodded. "Viscount Curtis insisted we eat. May I go down to the wharf and see the ship? I have never seen anything so large upon the water. I should like to ask if I may make the voyage—imagine what I could learn!"

Mary sighed. "No voyages for you, young man. But you may go down to the wharf. If Karl is there, you may ask if you can go aboard."

Peter was out the door. Barkley stood inside the door, smiling. "He's a good lad—a fine gentleman in the making."

Mary wore the sad smile of a mother as she watched Peter run off. "Soon he will be off on his own—I miss him so."

Turning to Barkley, her smiled brightened. "Edward, it is good to see you. If you are here to tell me of the Viscount's invitation, he has already made it clear that my attendance is needed. Do you have any idea what his great news is?"

Barkley shook his head. "I was going to ask you."

Barkley sighed. "Peter is doing well. Neil Burns praises his work, his diligence, and his character. I hope we have not interrupted his schooling too much—that is if he should decide to become the scholar."

Mary smiled. "Edward, you have opened so many doors for him."

Barkley looked down and nervously shuffled his feet. "I must be going. I look forward to tonight."

Barkley started for the door, then paused. "Mrs. Hawkins—Mary, may I call you Mary? I was wondering—perhaps—may I..."

Mary asked, "Yes, Edward, you may call on me."

.   Barkley looked up, blushing. "I must be going—much to do for Robbie. Tonight."

Mary called out, "Wait! Edward, before you go—if you are going to call on me—there is something I must tell you."

Robert and Barkley met as scheduled for lunch at the Hen and Chickens Inn tucked in the city wall just inside the wharf gate. Barkley was clutching a tankard of ale, smiling ear to ear. "I never knew a man could be so happy. Joy, Robbie, so much joy—Katie and Will, the good Viscount Curtis and now, well now, I feel like singing!"

"Spare me and all the good company of the inn, your voice! Tell me—no, I will tell you—you are encouraged by the lovely Mary Hawkins."

"As you say, the fair lady consents to my calling. Robbie, she agreed before I asked!"

Robert laughed. "Well, it is good she did—seemed you would never get up the courage to ask her. She knew of your desire."

Robert slapped Barkley's shoulder. "All of Berwick knows you have fallen hard."

Barkley blushed. "I am all the more fortunate, for she is indeed the lady of refinement you suspected."

"She has opened to you? You can be sure she will not deny you."

Robert lifted his tankard. "To my good friend, Edward Barkley, may your happiness carry you through a long and blessed marriage!"

Edward stared at Robert. "Marriage—it will come to that?"

Robert laughed while Edward became quiet, staring at the old panel above the fireplace. Barkley read the words aloud. "'Wysedom and science, which are pure and kynde, should not be writ in books but in mynde.'"

Barkley turned to Robert and said, "I will write to Mary: 'Wysdome and love in which so pure thou art, should not be writ in books but in my heart.'"

"Poetry, Barkley? You are smitten!"

When Robert and Barkley arrived at Lord Curtis' manor house, a carriage was being backed into the carriage house. Robert was greeted inside by Hulda dressed in an elegant new dress with white lace encircling her deep cut bodice. Her hair coiled atop her head added six inches to her petite frame. Robert could smell sweet perfume and noticed the white makeup and reddened lips on her smiling face.

Beaming brightly, she said in accented English, "Captain Curtis, Robert. I am so happy you will be with us this evening. The Viscount has told me it will be special indeed. You must be my escort this evening."

"Fraulein Hahn, you look so enchanting. Not like the drab novice I first met."

"Why sir, you never saw me in Vienna! You will see there is more to me than…"

"Than a reluctant nun. Tell me, Hulda, the carriage…"

Hulda shook her lovely head. "Just some guest of your uncle—business most likely."

Robert smiled. "Business, you say. Well, I shall see you at dinner."

Robert came down when Mary and Peter Hawkins were announced. Will, Katie, Hulda, Karl, Werner, and Barkley were gathered in the sitting room. A servant was lighting candles. Robert's father, Charles, and his uncle Viscount James Curtis came in together. Lord James said, "Are we all here then? Right. It is a special night, but you will learn nothing here. No, first dinner, and then you shall hear my news. My dear Katie, perhaps you and Will should lead us into the great hall."

Hulda made her way towards Robert and stood smiling beside him. Slowly the party made their way by twos through the sitting room door into the hall and moved towards the great hall. As Will and Katie passed by Lord James could be heard. "Ah, our missing guest—

always one to make an entrance, Lady Eleanor Montclair, please join us."

Hulda looked up the stairs and then clasped Robert's arm to her side. Eleanor came down, smiling, radiant in the emerald green dress she knew Robert adored. "Apologies, Lord Curtis."

She walked under the gaze of all present and took Robert's other arm. "I am sure Captain Curtis would not let a lady dine unescorted."

Barkley started to say, "I say, Robbie…"

Mary Hawkins discreetly kicked his shin, her smile as pleasant as ever, said, "Lady Eleanor, what a pleasant surprise."

Eleanor smiled at Mary and replied, "My dear Mary, it's been too long!"

Hulda could not hold her smile, but she clung to Robert's arm, and he escorted both of the beautiful women into the great hall. Lord Curtis chuckled. "Well, Captain, the thorny stem between two rose blooms. I am jealous!"

Robert struggled through dinner, trying his best to be warm to the tender and enthusiastic Hulda, whose bold plan seemed to be crashing before her sensitive eyes. And there was Eleanor, beautiful, beguiling but a woman he knew to be just as tender and vulnerable. Looking across, he saw Mary Hawkins sitting beside Barkley. *How does Mary know Eleanor? Barkley said she opened up to him. I should have asked.*

Viscount Curtis rose, holding his wine goblet. "Friends, this is a special evening. There is precious little time we all have together. My dear Katie, your day is but two dream-filled nights away, and then Karl, Johann, and Werner will be off to Amsterdam and beyond. So, forgive a sentimental old man. I have been given so much—we begin life receiving gifts. Gifts from God and gifts of love from others. The gift of loving mothers and proud fathers. But there comes a time we must become the giver rather than the receiver of good gifts—this is a lesson of the Lord our God. So today, we are here to give honor to a man I have watched grow to become a true gentleman. Robert, you have something to present."

Robert stood up and said, "Master Sergeant Edward Barkley, please rise."

Barkley cautiously stood up. Robert continued. "Edward Barkley, be it known that His Majesty, King James, commissions you as Lieutenant of Cuirassiers in service to the Royal Cawmills Cuirassiers. Do you, Edward Barkley, swear allegiance to His Majesty?"

Barkley replied, "I so swear."

"Please be seated, Lieutenant Barkley. I yield to the Honorable Viscount Berwick."

Robert sat down, keeping his smiling gaze upon his friend Edward. Lady Eleanor placed a hand on his thigh and whispered in his ear, "I missed you, Robert. Aren't you glad to see me?"

Robert kept smiling at Barkley. Eleanor continued, "You've been a very busy boy. Really Robbie? She is little more than a girl."

Hulda kept smiling and squeezed Robert's arm even tighter than before. She did not notice Johann's smiling face across the table. He could not take his eyes off of her.

James Curtis clapped his hands, and a servant appeared bearing in his arms the half-armor and plumed helmet of a Royal Cuirassiers Officer. "Edward, please accept this armor. Wear it honorably. As a gentleman of Berwick-upon-Tweed, you are granted a seat in the company and the position, Inspector of Customs."

The Viscount raised his goblet. "To Lieutenant Barkley, a gentleman of Berwick-upon-Tweed, and my dear friend!"

"Huzzah! Huzzah! To Lieutenant Barkley."

A smiling Mary Hawkins squeezed Edward's hand. "I'm so very proud of you, Edward. May I kiss you?"

Not waiting for his reply, she kissed his cheek.

Viscount Curtis called out, "Come, Mary, show our dear Edward your true feelings!"

Mary pulled Barkley's head close and kissed his blushing face, full on the lips.

Robert whispered to Eleanor, "You never told me you knew Mary Hawkins."

Eleanor, still smiling, watching Mary's hearty kiss on blushing Edward's lips, replied, "I leave it to her to tell her story."

Eleanor's face turned serious for a moment. "There is news. I must tell you."

Robert glanced at her face. Eleanor smiled. "If you can tear yourself away from your German schoolgirl."

Robert smiled. "Don't underestimate Hulda; she is Will's sister—a determined young woman with the heart of a lioness."

Robert turned to Hulda and smiled. "Lady Eleanor is a close friend. You have made her jealous. Your beauty is hard for any man to ignore. Look how Johann watches you! Two things about Johann, no three. He has not taken his eyes off you all night. He always smiles in your presence and…"

Robert paused and stared into Hulda's doe eyes with a warm and genuine smile.

Hulda looked back at him, her face open. "And? You said three things."

Robert placed his hand on top of hers. "And he would never leave you or forsake you. Johann is a man after your own heart. He is your match. Do not let him leave for Germany before you speak with him. You love your brother Will. You will find the same heart in Johann."

His friends surrounded Edward. Robert stood and hugged him. "My friend, no, my brother! I am so proud! Where would I be without you?"

"Ahh, Robbie, don't make me go mushy."

Will and Johann hugged Edward. Karl wrapped an arm around his shoulder and said, "Well done, Barkley, well done indeed!"

Werner stood silently, nodding nearby.

Johann came over and got in line to congratulate Edward. As he waited, his smiling eyes rested on Hulda.

Hulda's eyes met his. After a few moments, a small smile grew on her pretty young face.

CHAPTER 24
PREPARATIONS

The wedding of Katharina Schroeder and Wilhelm Hahn was a joyous event. The inexperienced Reverend Robert Curtis officiated without mistake. The beaming newlyweds and merry friends made their way back to Lord Curtis' grand stone house. Unaccustomed to clerical robes, Robert excused himself and went upstairs to change his clothes. He returned to an overflowing great hall filled with music and guests enjoying English country dancing. Scanning the room, he found Lady Eleanor seated beside Mary Hawkins and Edward Barkley.

Robert bowed and asked, "May I join you, Ladies? Lieutenant Barkley?"

Eleanor and Mary, deep in conversation, glanced at Robert and smiled. Barkley pointed to a seat and said, "Sit here, Robbie, between these two, I can't get a single word in the conversation."

Mary smiled. "Captain Curtis, please join us. Lady Eleanor and I were just catching up."

A smiling Eleanor made room for Robert between her and Mary. When Robert sat down, Eleanor took his arm. Mary continued, "Lady Eleanor and I grew up together. The Earl brought me into his house to tutor Lady Eleanor, though I am but four years her elder. I was more companion than tutor as she was ignored and alone in his castle."

Eleanor smiled. "My only friend."

Mary nodded and continued, "You wonder how I came to be a gamekeeper's wife on a country estate."

Mary closed her eyes for a moment, sighed, and explained, "My father was the vicar at the Earl of Montclair's estate church. He was a vain, self-righteous, and ambitious man. My father coveted respect—he loved expensive robes and acted the moral and religious superior. He saw placing me in the Earl's house to his benefit. But it was there. I found my friend, and I met Peter Hawkins."

Eleanor smiled as she listened to her friend's story. Mary patted Edward's hand and continued. Peter was the Earl's nephew. He came as a ward to the Earl when the pox orphaned him. Peter loved the estate—he was drawn to the wildlife, the forest, and the wonders of nature. He claimed that God's revelation came to him in creation. Well, his uncle sent him to Oxford—to be schooled for the church. It was at Oxford that Peter met non-conformists—puritans whose love of God was genuine—so quite different than what he saw in my father's church."

Edward spoke up. "He had questions, Robbie, much

like you."

Mary smiled. "When Peter returned for a visit, he challenged the Earl and my father. He claimed that the Word of God, the gospel of Jesus' love, was not preached or lived there. I loved Peter. And he loved me. Though I was but sixteen, he asked permission to marry me—of course, it was denied. My father accused Peter as a recusant. Peter would not attend the estate church and would only take communion with fellow puritans. We married without permission. Peter was forced to leave Oxford. The Earl barred Peter from the estate. But secretly, the Earl arranged for Peter to work at Bramshill. Lady Eleanor befriended Lady Mary Zouche so that she could secretly meet me in the village during her morning ride."

Robert nodded. "Young Peter is fourteen years old. For all those years, she maintained this friendship?"

"Peter taught our children and me the gospel of love and the habit of reading the Scriptures. Robert, your friends: Will, Katie, Karl, the Viscount, and sweet Edward, all of them, show the love that Peter taught. God above has taken my first love, but he has sent Edward and this happy company to comfort me and bring new life."

Robert smiled. "Edward…"

Barkley replied, "So now it's Edward and not Barkley?"

Robert laughed. "Brother, you must marry this woman!"

Barkley grinned. "And so I shall—if she will have me!"

Mary leaned over and kissed Edward. She whispered in his ear, "You know I will."

Eleanor smiled and then said, "Oh," and she pulled on Robert's arm. "Have you considered the news? I have done my best—as have your friends in London. The King makes his way north as we speak. He left York with Prince Charles and the court as I passed through on my way here. His Majesty stayed but one night at the Archbishop's palace in Durham. He travels north into Northumberland, though his itinerary is not published. The Marquess of Huntly, Lord Lieutenant of Scotland, Sir George Gordon, travels with him. They will surely visit Scotland. A hunt at Cawmills Royal Forest has been suggested and a review of the Royal Cawmills Cuirassiers. You must have everything ready. You will receive no more than a few days' notice as is His Majesty's practice."

Robert stared thoughtfully at the ceiling. "The Castle Manor is ready. The Cuirassiers are ready. The hunt shall be a success—if only..."

Eleanor looked worried. "If only what?"

Robert remained silent. Barkley spoke for both. "If only we found the traitors or knew their plot. They have seen through our trap and remain at large."

Robert and Barkley saw Karl, Werner, and Johann off at the wharf. Hulda, Katie, and Mary arrived with Lord James Curtis in his carriage. Hugs were exchanged, and tears fell from the ladies' eyes. Robert watched Hulda standing in front of Johann. The back of her head barely reached his shoulders. Her eyes were drawn up to his and his head down listening. Johann's face was bright with the same warm smile he always gave her. Somehow, Robert knew Hulda saw it afresh.

When Karl and his party scrambled aboard, the crew let loose the lines, raised the sails, and the ship slowly made for sea. Mary stood beside Edward. "You are off then to Cawmills? We shall come for the consecration of the church on Sunday."

Mary turned to Robert. "Lady Eleanor will come Sunday, as shall we all."

Robert nodded. "I am glad. It is the opening of a new chapter in my life, and I pray the lives of the good people of Cawmills."

Mary did not smile. She stared into Robert's eyes and said, "Do not hurt her."

The Bishop of Durham arrived on Saturday. He was cordially, if not warmly, received at the dinner in his honor by Mister Douglas, Mister Gordon, and Mister Burns. Douglas made sure the Bishop's wine goblet never emptied but otherwise sat quietly. Learning Robert's request to name the King's Cawmills Chapel after Saint Cuthbert, Bishop Neile engaged Robert in polite conversation about the relics of Lindisfarne held at the Durham Cathedral.

When the Bishop paused to taste his lamb, Edward asked, "Your Grace, we have heard that His Majesty travels north to Scotland. You received him in Durham. Is it true that he will visit Cawmills Royal Forest? We have invited him and would be honored if he visits, but we received no word."

Bishop Neile smiled. "You are well informed, Lieutenant Barkley. The invitation to a hunt and a review of your cuirassiers was well received by His Majesty. Of course, his travels are not made widely known, but you may expect a courier with news happy several days in advance."

When the dinner was over, and the Bishop retired for the night, Andrew Douglas approached Robert, and seeing they were out of earshot of any others, said, "A word, Captain. A friend in London—I speak of Lord Percy, sent word to me. He writes that you pursue radical Catholics zealots plotting against His Majesty, the King. I have kept my true duty here secret until now. I warn you of danger. The radical priest, Father Henry Clitherow, hides in plain sight here in Cawmills. He is a compatriot of your cousin, Geoffrey. I was sent to watch then and report their activities."

Robert held up his hand, asking Douglas to wait. "You said, friends. You mention Lord Percy; what others know of this plot?"

Douglas smiled. "The Marquess of Huntly, Lord Gordon. It was his cousin, Colin Gordon, who brought word."

Robert waited for Douglas to pause and asked, "And who is the imposter?"

Douglas whispered, "The harness maker, Adam Cox. He keeps to himself, but in truth, he conducts his business through secret couriers—letters carried in special saddles he makes."

Robert nodded. "I should arrest him at once—send him to Edinburgh Castle or the Tower in London, where surely they will loosen his tongue."

Douglas shook his head. "I would not be so hasty. Say nothing to him of the King's visit and permit me to catch him in my net. I will deliver the scoundrel to you!"

Robert smiled. "I shall say nothing."

Sunday morning dawned damp and foggy. By breakfast, the fog had lifted, and patches of blue appeared in the sky. Dignitaries and guests made their way down the heather-covered hill to the small, whitewashed stone church in Cawmills Village. The first pew on the right was reserved for Reverend Witten, the Calvinist pastor of the Kirk in Eyemouth and their wives. To the left, Lord James and his brother, Charles Curtis and Barkley, accompanied Katie Hahn, Hulda Hahn, Mary Hawkins, and Lady Eleanor. The Hawkins children chaperoned by Peter, and friends from Berwick-upon-Tweed, sat behind them. Neil Burns, Colin Gordon, and a reluctant Aidan Lilburn represented Cawmills.

The old bell in the church tower called the faithful to worship at eleven o'clock. At the first peel, Father Wilhelm Hahn led Robert followed by Bishop Neile in procession into the old church. Each clergyman bowed at the altar. Will stood to the left of the altar, Robert to the right, and the bishop went to the carved oak bishop's throne at the foot of the cross. Bishop Neile's green and gold mitre, his magnificent shimmering robe, and wooden shepherd's crook were resplendent against the newly whitewashed wall.

Robert and Will wore identical white albs, their hoods resting on their shoulders behind their necks. Both priests' robes were girdled at the waist by white braided wool ropes, knotted at the side, and hanging below their knees. Green stoles with an embroidered gold cross were draped from their necks and floated freely as the men moved. Will was in his element. He was accustomed to clerical robes and rituals. Robert was barely recognizable, his determined expression as out of the ordinary as his dress.

Robert opened the Book of Common Prayer and began the rite of consecration. Will assisted as Robert read the liturgy between prayers, Psalms, and Scripture. At the appropriate time, Bishop Neile rose, prayed, turned to Robert, and loudly asked, "By what name will this Chapel of King James be known?"

Robert replied, "This place of worship shall hereafter be known as "Saint Cuthbert's Chapel at Cawmills.""

Bishop Neile lifted his hands and prayed a prayer consecrating the chapel to the worship of Jesus Christ in the Church of England. After the amen, he took a silver aspergillum and sprinkled the altar with holy water while saying, "In the name of the Father, the Son, and the Holy Ghost I consecrate this Saint Cuthbert's Chapel at Cawmills. Amen!"

When he finished, he returned to the bishop's throne while Will sat at the priest's chair, and Robert walked in front of the altar to preach. Robert looked at Adam Cox, sitting alone inside the door. He could not see Tom Pritchard, the cooper and three other tenant farmers sitting under the windows outside, listening to their captain-priest.

Robert turned first to the bishop and thanked him for making the long journey from Durham. He acknowledged vicar Witten and the pastor of the Eyemouth Kirk. He bowed to his uncle, the viscount, and then said, "Friends and good people of Cawmills welcome to Saint Cuthbert's Chapel at Cawmills, a house of worship always open to all Christians for prayer and worship. I see among us Englishmen and Scotsmen. We are all loyal subjects of the King though our faith be the Scottish Kirk, the Church of England, puritan—any non-conformist or Roman Catholic. Our King heads the Church of England, where I am ordained, but I desire this chapel to be a safe haven for all the body of Christ."

Robert smiled and stepped down from the altar. "Before there was an England, before there was a Scotland, there was a Kingdom here in the north— Northumbria. When Christians fled Britain with the Romans, an Irish Monk came to our shores and brought the light of God to a dark land and forsaken people. A young nobleman saw a vision. He sought out that monk named Aidan, believed and was baptized a Christian. The young man's name was Cuthbert. Cuthbert was different than the other Irish monks; he went into the villages and homes of the pagan people and shared the love of Christ. Cuthbert taught them the Scriptures, the word of God in their language. He led them in worship, a simple liturgy, not in Latin, but the common tongue. Saint Cuthbert, under the leadership of Saint Aidan, brought Christianity to Northumbria, and when priests from Rome finally came north, they found a vibrant church. The Roman priests could not establish the trust of the local people, they relied on Cuthbert, a man of God who was trusted because he listened, he cared and would not recite a liturgy in a foreign language, he would not turn his back on his flock. Saint Cuthbert interceded for our ancestors because of a shared language, a shared community, a shared love, and a shared faith."

"Friends, it is my prayer that the mission of Saint Cuthbert is practiced in this chapel."

After his sermon, the first Church of England communion was served. One by one, Robert served them the bread, and Will served the cup. Aidan Lilburn knelt with his arms crossed. Robert waited and smiled when the last congregant came, kneeled at the rail, and crossed his arms. Robert placed his hand on Adam Cox's shoulder and blessed him.

Robert followed Bishop Neile in procession after the end of the service and stood outside the door, greeting congregants as they filed out. Most had encouraging words of congratulations for the priestly role of Robert rarely seen. Lady Eleanor lingered inside the door. She was the last to go through.

Lady Eleanor was smiling as she faced Robert. With a tight smile of recognition, she sighed and stood silent in front of him. Eleanor reached around Robert's neck and straightened his stole, which hung unevenly to one side. Her eyes peered into his, and she whispered, "I saw your heart today. A lovely heart and strong."

She paused and said, "You look so much the priest in your robes, oh, not so grand as the bishop, but trustworthy and good. The thing is, Robbie, and I love you so…"

She closed her eyes for a moment and exhaled a breath. "The thing is, Robbie—I cannot be a vicar's wife."

Riding south on the Great North Road, Robert, Barkley, and Lilburn discussed what lay before them. Robert spoke. "We must act quickly. We will not stop, though I told Douglas we are off to Berwick-upon-Tweed, he may yet warn of our visit."

Barkley replied, "Aye, a long ride. Do you believe his accusation against Adam Cox? How would Douglas know we are on to the plot and that Father Clitherow hides at Cawmills? Do you trust him? Can we trust Adam Cox?"

Lilburn said nothing. He hid his surprise, his eyes focused on the trail ahead. He listened carefully and wondered what it all meant, and why he was with the Captain and Lieutenant."

Robert kept scanning the road as he answered Barkley, "The constable of Alnwick Castle, Harold Percy—he knows we are on to the plotters. He knows we seek Geoffrey. Harold Percy knows I searched the castle. He may know Cox's identity and passed the word. Remember, the zealots use the Catholic couriers, Joseph Wright, and Colin Gordon. And Marquess Gordon may not know his cousin Colin is a radical."

Barkley turned to Robert and asked, "Why does Douglas come forward now?"

Robert turned to Barkley and smiled. "Exactly! Lord Percy's letter informing me his man would contact me came months ago. Douglas came forward now because the King's visit was just made known. It must not be canceled. And then there are the men. Douglas is no one's friend. He sees only his mission. Adam Cox, well, I see the heart of a brother priest. Douglas could not bring himself to attend the consecration. Attending would help his claim, but he could not violate his unbending hatred for the Church of England."

Robert turned to Lilburn. "Sergeant Lilburn, we ride to Alnwick Castle to arrest three men who plot against the King. I have brought you with us because I believe your oath is true. But there is more. I have seen the stolen Lindisfarne Bible. It is hidden in the castle. I will fulfill my promise to you. You will return the Bible to Lindisfarne."

Aidan Lilburn's confused stare only allowed a direct, "Aye, Captain, arrest scoundrels and return the Bible to Lindisfarne."

Robert smiled, and Lilburn stuttered, "You will return the Bible to Lindisfarne? Not send it to Durham Cathedral?"

Robert nodded. "You must assure me that it is secure—safe from thieves and scoundrels."

Lilburn nodded excitedly and said, "Aye. We will defend it with our lives!"

Robert smiled. "It is a strong reminder of Saint Aidan and Saint Cuthbert. But remember, Lilburn, the Bible is in Latin. Cuthbert taught in our English."

Lilburn nodded. "Aye."

"Perhaps you shall invite me to worship with those who follow Saint Cuthbert's ancient liturgy. I would think it is much like the Church of England liturgy."

Lilburn smiled. "Captain you, and Lieutenant Barkley would be welcome to join us."

When the tower of Alnwick Castle came into sight, Barkley asked, "What is your plan?"

Robert stopped. Barkley and Lilburn came close alongside. Robert said, "Barkley, you go directly to the inn where they drink. If they are there, keep them there. If not, wait. Lilburn is not known. He will wait at the stable in case they make a run when I am announced. He shall not let anyone ride off. I will go to the castle tower."

Barkley scratched his head. "Can you can arrest more than one man on your own? It seems dangerous."

"I shall require Percy to assist me. I believe the man more loyal to the Percy family than the plotters—and I believe the man a coward. I shall call for Sergeant Lilburn if I make the arrests."

Barkley and Lilburn nodded.

Robert looked at Lilburn and said, "No one leaves Alnwick Castle by order of the Sheriff of Cawmills. Charge your pistols and light the cord. Have your sword at the ready."

"Aye, Captain. At the ready."

Barkley rode alone into Alnwick village and made his way to the inn. Robert and Lilburn followed five minutes behind him. Robert dismounted at the Castle keep gate. Lilburn led Robert's horse to the stable. A stable servant met him and took Robert's horse to a stall. Lilburn called after him, "No one is to leave this stable under orders of the Sheriff of Cawmills."

The servant called back, "Ain't nobody here but me."

Lilburn nodded. "Close the stable doors and wait inside. No one is to enter."

The servant stared at Lilburn. "Sheriff of Cawmills? Not Alnwick?"

His eyes found the lit cord of his pistol. "As you say, close the doors and wait inside."

Lilburn called, "No saddle on any horse!"

"None of the horses are saddled—you can look for yourself."

The far door creaked as it slowly rolled shut. The near door sounded the same before an uneasy silence settled on the yard.

A servant led Robert to Constable Harold Percy. "Captain Curtis! Your cousin, Geoffrey, is not here. He knows he is no longer welcome."

Robert nodded. "Constable, I require your assistance. I am here to arrest George Catesby, William Winter, and Joseph Wright. You shall take me to them at once."

Percy's face drained of all color. "Catesby works. He is in the library. I shall take you to him at once. Come. You know the way."

As they made their way to the door, Robert asked, "And Winter and Wright?"

"Joseph Wright left with letters—he said to Lord Percy, but I ..."

"Yes, he is not a man to be trusted. And

William Winter?"

"I haven't seen Winter. Catesby might know."

At the door to the library, Robert drew his pistol and stepped into the room. Catesby was leaning over an estate book, pen in hand. "George Catesby, you are under arrest for treason against His Majesty the King!"

Catesby spun in his chair and began to slide away from the desk. He stopped when he saw Robert's pistol pointed at him. "There must be some mistake. I am a loyal servant to Lord Percy and His Majesty."

Robert kept his pistol pointed at Catesby. "Where is Will Winter?"

"Will Winter? I do not know a ..."

"Will Winter, a sometime gamekeeper. You drink with him at the inn. Tell me, Catesby; the Tower guards will persuade you to talk, but with far more pain."

"I haven't seen him in days. He went off lookin' to find work on a hunt."

Robert nodded. "A hunt for His Majesty, no doubt. And Joseph Wright—where is he?"

Catesby was pale white. "He doesn't tell me. He's a courier. He goes where the message takes him."

Catesby turned slowly and stood facing Robert. Robert turned to Percy. "Is there a jail or dungeon for prisoners?"

Before Harold Percy could answer, Catesby bolted for the door. Robert turned and fired. Catesby screamed and fell to the floor, his hands grasping his bleeding leg.

Robert raised his second pistol. "Do you want to die, son?"

Catesby clutched his leg and cried. "What will become of me?"

Robert walked over to Catesby, looked down, and said, "If you help me, I will petition the King for mercy. I know that after your father's rebellion failed, he took his own life. I know they dug up his body, and he was beheaded and quartered. I watched Fitzhugh be hanged, drawn, and quartered. It is not the death you want. Help me, and on my word, I shall do what I can for you."

Catesby sat on the floor, blood flowing from beneath his hands, squeezing his wounded leg, sobbing.

Robert turned to Percy and said, "Tell the servant standing outside the door to go for the surgeon."

Percy stuck his head out the door and saw a man leaning against the wall, just outside. "Do as Captain Curtis says, bring the doctor at once!"

The servant ran off without a word. Robert stared at Harold Percy. "I do not want to tarnish the reputation of Lord Percy. Now you must decide your loyalties. Lord Percy stands with the King. Do I have your word, Constable?"

Percy nodded and said, "Aye. I am a Percy first."

Robert took off the silver girdle sash from his waist and tied it tightly around Catesby's leg wound and mumbled. "Lady Eleanor would not approve—it was an expensive girdle."

Looking once again to Percy, he said, "Tell Sergeant Aidan Lilburn who waits by the stable I have urgent need of him. Tell him to bring his saddlebag. Then find Edward Barkley, you know the man, at the Castle Inn and bring him to me."

Robert, alone with Catesby, prayed, "O Lord of all Mercy, spare the life of this young man. Heal him, body and soul."

Catesby cried, "I am a dead man. Better to let me bleed out."

Robert shook his head. "Hope in the Lord, Mister Catesby. No one knows the mind of God."

The heavy thuds of Lilburn's boots echoed in the hall as he ran into the room. "Captain Curtis, Is all well?"

"Not so well for Mister Catesby. I sent for a surgeon and Lieutenant Barkley. The other birds have flown. Lilburn, you see the desk in the center of the room. Push it aside and pull away the rug. There is a small finger hole in a floorboard. Pull it up. You will find some boxes beneath. Bring them here."

Lilburn's eyes widened, and his breathing stopped as he saw the Lindisfarne Bible through the glass cover of the first box.

Robert smiled, took the box and opened it. He removed the Bible, opened it to the center, reached into the arched binding, and slid out the folded paper. Robert handed the Bible to the awestruck Lilburn, "As I promised. Put it in your saddlebag."

Robert slid the folded paper into his doublet. He then removed the rosary and code ciphers from the secret compartment and set the box down. Lilburn recovered the two remaining boxes, and Robert removed the documents. "Put these in your bag as well. Never let it out your sight!"

Lilburn nodded. "What are they, Captain."

"The evidence to convict Mister Catesby and his confederates."

Pointing to the hole in the floor, Robert asked, "Is there anything else down there?"

"Nay, Captain. Nothing."

"Then replace the board, return the rug and desk. No need troubling Constable Percy."

The doctor arrived before Barkley and examined the wound. "The pistol ball went through the leg, missing the bone. A clean wound. I can sear it if you like."

Catesby silently stared.

Robert replied, "On with it, then."

The doctor followed Percy to the kitchen, where he heated a blade in the coals. The wide-eyed Catesby screamed when the blade seared both entry and exit wounds.

"Keep it bound tight, and he likely he'll recover. If fever sets in, call for me. Good day gentlemen."

Robert replied, "Thank you, doctor. Can he travel?"

"Aye, on horseback or wagon. Keep a sharp eye on the bandage. Must be dry and tight."

Barkley arrived as Catesby screamed, "Oh, it's only the surgeon. Cheer up, lad. The sooner the wound is seared, the better chance there will be no fever. Seen it on the battlefield. Is that not right, Captain Curtis?"

"Just as you say, Lieutenant Barkley. We shall be leaving straight away. The others are not here."

Barkley nodded. "My visit was not in vain. I learned..."

Robert interrupted, "Not now, too many ears. Constable Percy, we shall require a horse for Catesby, it shall be returned."

"Tell the stable master—Catesby's usual mount."

Robert turned to Lilburn. "See to the horses and help Mister Catesby mount. Bind his hands. You hold his reins. The prisoner is in your custody, sergeant, be sure he does not escape!"

Lilburn threw his now heavy saddlebag over his shoulder and said, "Aye," as he marched through the door.

On the road north, Lilburn led the way, leading Catesby's horse. Barkley and Robert trailed behind. Robert asked, "What news from the inn?"

Barkley smiled. "Innkeeper has not seen Winter or Wright in several days. But he did say, when I asked of their friends, of a gentleman been drinkin' with them."

"Gentleman?"

"Robbie, the man had a servant! The servant sat behind, only spoke when asked. Was sent off and would return, whispering only in his master's ear. Had to be a gentleman."

Barkley added, "Was a captain. The innkeeper heard Winters call him captain and was scolded, he was. The gentleman said, 'No names, no titles.'"

"You're thinking, my cousin, Captain Curtis. Don't remember him traveling with a servant. Captain Stock had a servant. Never out of earshot."

Barkley asked, "Where are we taking him? Can't bring him to Cawmills, it would alert too many enemies."

Robert scratched his beard. "Can't take him to

Berwick-upon-Tweed either, too much coming and going. Some tongue is sure to wag before the wrong ears. Eyemouth. We take him to the Sheriff of Eyemouth. A solitary cell beyond anyone's ears."

Robert rode alongside the prisoner. "You are fortunate. It was a clean wound and treated promptly. You shall soon walk again."

Catesby glared and spat out in reply, "Oh, I feel so very fortunate. You would have me walk to my execution."

Robert sighed. "Your fate is not determined. The King may show mercy. Why, Lord Gordon took up arms against the King as Earl of Huntly. He repented and begged the King. Today he is the Marquess Huntly and Lord Lieutenant of Scotland."

Catesby shook his head. "Lord Gordon is rich and powerful. He had something to give His Majesty— influence. How many great lords followed him in swearing allegiance?"

"But you do have something to offer—information. Help me stop this attempt on the King's life—yes, I know you plan a bold attempt—tell me. You have my word the King will know of your sincere change of heart."

"Change of heart? Have I changed my heart? He hunted my father and desecrated his body."

"So, revenge is better than life? Many are the men who will swear there is no peace in revenge."

Catesby cast his stare down to the dirt road, "I will think on your words."

An hour later, Lilburn led Catesby's horse over the high, stone Berwick bridge. He did notice Catesby's horse move to the edge of the bridge. He heard only the stomping of hooves and the cries of the frightened animal and then the splash.

Robert and Barkley could only watch in shock as George Catesby flung himself from his horse over the side of Berwick bridge. Dismounting, they could see his bloodied, lifeless body floating downstream.

Barkley spoke for both. "The rocks, Robbie. I'll take Lilburn and recover the body."

CHAPTER 25
A ROYAL VISIT

The body of George Catesby was taken to the Berwick-upon-Tweed coroner. Robert, Barkley, and Lilburn made sworn statements to his arrest and circumstances of his death. Robert told the coroner he would send the death notification to Alnwick Castle, Catesby's last known address for notice to his family.

Barkley spoke up. "As a member of the council and guild, I know you will treat this death as confidential as our investigation into serious treachery continues."

The coroner bowed. "As you wish, Lieutenant Barkley. Not a word to anyone."

Outside the ornate guildhall, Robert instructed Lilburn. "Sergeant, ride south to Alnwick Castle and give notice to Constable, Harold Percy. You have two days leave. I believe you have something to deliver to safety in Lindisfarne. Two days, Lilburn. I need you at Cawmills!"

Lilburn smiled. "Aye, and thank you, Captain. The other documents?"

"Bring them to me and then be off."

With Lilburn on his way, Robert said to Barkley, "I will spend the night with my uncle. Is there anyone in Berwick you would visit?

Barkley smiled. "Ask the Viscount to save me a bed. I am off to see Mrs. Hawkins."

Charles and James Curtis were seated by the fire enjoying imported fine wine when Robert entered the sitting room. Lord James Curtis spoke first. "Robert! Back so soon? Is all well?"

Before Robert could answer, his father, Charles, said, "Lady Eleanor has left us. Said nothing—called for her carriage and rode off yesterday. She is a fine woman, son, and things were going splendidly between you. What happened? Did you say something?"

Robert looked down and shook his head. "I fear my calling puts her off. I hoped to see her again. It has been a harrowing day. My prisoner jumped to his death without giving up his knowledge. His fear of the King's judgment drove him to suicide. I could not persuade him to hope for mercy. And now, I will not face Lady Eleanor and give her the assurance she seeks."

Lord Charles asked, "So you are no closer to uncovering the plot?"

Robert shook his head. "Only that another plotter has been to Alnwick. The innkeeper heard it slip—a lad called him, 'Captain.' Barkley believes him a gentleman—seems he traveled with a servant. My only thought is Captain Stock—always with a servant, but could he have returned from the Palatine? Don't recall Cousin Geoffrey traveling with a servant."

Charles Curtis put down his wine cup and said, "Son, you don't know that the attack, if it is an attack on His Majesty, is it planned for Cawmills? It could be anywhere."

Robert shook his head. "Too many zealots at Cawmills. The renegade priest—and his watcher."

Robert paused. "Alnwick Castle and Cawmills—the two safehouses of the plotters. The King will not visit Alnwick—the plotters know the ground at Cawmills."

Lord James asked, "What will you do now?"

Robert mumbled, "Prepare for the worst."

Robert closed his eyes and thought for a moment, then said, "When do you expect the ship to return from Amsterdam? Do you think..."

Douglas stood smiling when Robert and Barkley rode up to Curtis Castle Manor, dismounted their horses, and left them with the stablemaster. "Welcome back, Captain. If you would, Captain, a short word in private?"

"Go on then, Barkley. I shall hear Mister Douglas."

"I have a plan to net the renegade priest, Father Clitherow, I can..."

Robert interrupted, "Please, Adam Cox. I do not want that name heard by anyone. Loose lips. Might be heard, and he is warned we are on to him."

"Right you are, sir. My plan..."

"I am glad you put me on to him, Douglas. In the last few days, I have considered your words. His recent actions now make sense. Do you know, he warmed to me while I was cleaning the village church? And he came to the consecration service, even coming to the rail for communion. Of course, as a priest, he would not take the elements from a protestant and merely accepted the blessing, but he is a clever man. I now see how he seeks to earn my favor. No, Douglas, we shall do nothing to warn him. But I shall know everything he does, and Lieutenant Barkley shall deal with him. You have not seen the brutality Barkley is capable of when angered or threatened. War has a way of hardening a man. Leave the renegade to us. But I shall remember your words and engage you more fully in the days to come."

As Robert and Douglas finished their conversation, both men saw a rising trail of dust from a fast-riding horseman. Both watched as he turned up the road to Curtis Castle. The rider carried a standard which they soon recognized as the Royal Standard of King James.

The Royal messenger galloped up to them, dismounted, and called out, "From His Royal Highness, King James. I carry as a dispatch for Captain Robert Curtis."

Robert stood tall and replied, "I am Captain Curtis."

The messenger reached into his bag for a sealed letter, which he handed to Robert. Robert looked at the letter, bearing the royal seal, and said, "Please, come inside. You must take refreshment from your hard ride, while I read."

The messenger nodded. "Very good, sir. I am to wait for your reply."

Douglas bowed slightly to Robert. "I shall leave you to your business."

Robert had unsealed the letter and began to read as he walked towards the manor house door. "Stay, Douglas. There is much to do. The King and Court arrive in four days. A large number—too many for Cawmills. We will bed some with my uncle the Viscount in Berwick-upon-Tweed. We will need every bed. Barkley will stay with me in the tower. Mister Gordon must return to Edinburgh. There is no room for him—just as I warned him."

Douglas nearly interrupted. "Colin, that is the Justice-in-Eyre can stay with me. It would be unfair to deny him this great opportunity."

Barkley saw the courier arrive and stood and listened silently by the door.

Robert did not take his eyes from the letter, his mind weighing its impact. "As you wish. And the house servants must be sent off, also the stable servants. So many servants to board!"

Douglas asked, "Who will cook? Who will serve? And Johnny, my head servant?"

Robert lowered the letter and looked at Douglas. "The King brings his cooks and servants. You shall carry the keys and work for the King's head man unless it is beneath you. Your quarters would be most useful, and you could spend some days away."

Douglas' face flushed. "I shall support His Majesty just as I am needed—can't have a stranger wanderin' about blind in the house."

Robert let his hand holding the letter fall to his side as he continued. "Move the horses from the stable. Only my horse and Barkley's stay. Arrange it with the tenants. And fodder—we must tend horses of those staying here and coming from Berwick. Now, the cook, he lists what he needs. You must see to the provisions."

Robert stared at Douglas. "There is much to do! Get to it, man!"

Douglas' body snapped rigidly, and he nearly shouted, "Aye! Right away—Captain, you did not say, how long will His Majesty stay? And will there be a hunt?"

Robert glared. "His Majesty will spend but one night, perhaps two. I shall arrange the hunt with Mister Burns. You will need your wits about you, Douglas. Best be about your business. I must write a reply."

Robert wrote his reply, graciously accepting the honor and gave it to the thirsty courier who finished his second mug of ale. "I have written His Majesty that many will bed in Berwick-upon-Tweed. I say it is an hour at an easy pace. You have ridden by, tell me, will his courtiers ride faster?"

The courier wiped his mouth with his braided coat sleeve, and replied, "If they leave their women in Berwick-upon-Tweed, they will make the distance faster. Most enjoy a hearty ride. Tell me, Captain, is there an inn with clean accommodation and good ale in Berwick-upon-Tweed—for friends of the courtiers?"

"Several. The Hen and Chickens Inn will suit them well. The friends you speak of will find the Inn inside the city gate near the Lord Curtis' Berwick house. I trust you to make an exact report."

Alone inside the tower, Barkley wiped his forehead

and said, "You told Douglas all."

Robert sat down. "Let him believe we trust him—keep him close under our eyes. I want no alarm sent to the plotters."

Robert smiled. "We sent off his household staff—that cuts the odds a bit."

Barkley sat down across from Robert. "He was quick to keep Colin Gordon here."

Robert nodded. "Yes, roommates—like us. Now, if his horse gets loose from a paddock, say the day before..."

Barkley looked around the tower and thought aloud, "What say? Twenty men here in the tower? Perhaps fifteen with Neil Burns and fifteen with Adam Cox. You are certain on Adam Cox?"

Robert nodded. "Fifty men come in quietly in the night. Another fifty come in the morning after the courtiers leave. One hundred infantry added to our one hundred cavalry. We shall be ready. Now, Lilburn and the best with crossbow and arquebus shall man the tower. We must plan for the others. The cannon shall be the signal. Once my cousin and his scoundrels show, we will come at them by surprise."

"It is not as we hoped, Robbie. Very risky for the King."

"We have the advantage of clear sight all around."

"Can we trust the tenants not to hide them?"

"Regular inspections of the horses in their barns and fields. You, Lilburn, and Burns must patrol. And there is Cox. The man sees everything in the village. It is up to the Royal Cawmills Cuirassiers—will they stand by their oath?"

There was a knock on the tower door. Barkley opened it and ushered Neil Burns into the tower guard room, Burns tipped his hat and said, "Word is a Royal Visit and hunt. Thought you would be sendin' for me. I came with troublin' news."

Robert's eyebrows tightened. "News?"

"While you were away, a lad came by lookin' for work. Said he heard talk of a hunt—many noblemen. Said he was an experienced gamekeeper, offered to help."

Barkley interrupted, "Sandy hair, cowlick? A northerner like us?"

Burns nodded. "Told him to wait in Eyemouth. I would find him at the inn and give an answer when the Warden returned. He insisted I better not bother the Warden, too much on his mind. Just keep it between the men that work. I agreed, said he should wait for my word in Eyemouth."

Robert smiled broadly. "Well done, Burns. Well done indeed!"

Barkley rubbed his forehead and sighed. "Just Will Winters? A one-man attack? 'Doesn't make sense. He tried once at Bramshill and failed. The land is open, hard to find cover for an assassin."

Robbie replied, "We know where he is. We know his fellows know. Perhaps he is a diversion, or perhaps they see two opportunities. No, Barkley, it is good news. The question is, when do we arrest him?"

Robert turned to Burns. "Mister Burns, His Majesty indeed arrives in four days. He will spend but one night.

Let's plan for the hunt in the early morning before his courtiers arrive. We shall lunch afterward and review the Cuirassiers in the afternoon. We shall need you to bed fifteen English volunteers, returning from the Palatine the night the King arrives. They shall come in secret and must remain hidden until the cannon signals my cousin, Geoffrey's attack. Barkley shall give you the details."

Neil Burns nodded. "Aye, Captain. A good hunt and a good show for His Majesty!"

The waning half-moon lazily slid in and out through the black clouds of night, as it fell behind the western horizon. Three horses carried weary riders in the damp night air, silent and still before the coming dawn.

Barkley raised his head and wondered aloud, "If we take him, they'll know. They may scatter, and all connections to them lost."

Robert's reply was whispered through the dark. "The risk to His Majesty is too great. Our first duty is to protect the King. Gunpowder as bait is one thing, but the King? If the plotters are put off, we shall follow them, find them, and bring them to justice. No, we know the intent of Will Winters, we must arrest him while we can."

Entering Eyemouth, they made their way to the stable behind the Abs Head Inn. Slowly opening the door, as quietly as possible, they lit a lantern hanging inside. Barkley was the first to spot Joseph Wright's saddle and blanket on the stall rail beside the beautiful chestnut horse with three white stocking legs. The saddle blanket for the horse beside it also bore the Percy family crest.

"Two birds, Robbie! Both lads, Winters, and Wright," Edward whispered.

"Check the pouch,"

"Seems there is something," Barkley replied as he slid a note into his doublet.

"Lilburn, help Barkley. Take the saddles and blankets and lead the horses.

"Where we goin'?" Barkley asked.

"To the sheriff. Quiet but quick as you can. It's almost dawn."

Three men led five horses behind the inn and down the street to the house and office of the sheriff of Eyemouth. They took the horses and saddles behind the two-story stone house as the sun broke in the eastern sky. Robert saw a candle in a rear window extinguish, and curtains pulled opened. He lightly rapped on the back door.

The door opened a crack, and a voice asked, "Who's there?"

"I'm Captain Robert Curtis, Sheriff of Cawmills and my men. Forgive the early visit. We are here on urgent business and seek your help."

"Come in, Captain Curtis." Looking at Barkley, Lilburn, and the horses, he added, "Your horses are safe in my paddock."

Inside the kitchen, Robert said, "We have come from Cawmills to arrest a man we believe has made one attempt on the life of His Majesty, and we are convinced intends so again when the King visits Cawmills in two days."

"How can I help?"

"We learned our man and a fellow conspirator lodge at the Abs Head Inn. They are to meet with the Royal Cawmills Forester this morning. We have taken their horses and saddles as a precaution. We need to hold them here in Eyemouth, secretly until the King and his court move on from Curtis Castle and Cawmills."

"Secretly?"

"Aye, there may be other traitors afoot, and we would not raise their alarm."

"I am your servant, Captain Curtis. I know such a place. I ask only to assist you in the arrest. The Abs Head is full and has many doors and windows, an easy place to escape."

The sun was halfway to zenith when Neil Burns entered the inn. He spotted Will Winters, eating a late breakfast alone in the empty room.

"Late night, my friend? A workin' man, aye, a good gamekeeper is about his business with the sun."

Will Winter smiled. "So you see the benefit of an experienced gamekeeper on a Royal hunt. Sit, tell me when to come I would hear all you know."

"Let me get an ale to wet my throat after my morning ride, and I shall tell ye all."

Burns moved to the bar as Robert appeared in the door. "Will Winter, you are under arrest! Put your hands on the table where I can see them and stand up."

Winter slowly pushed his chair away from the table and leaned over. Jumping to his feet, he threw the table forward, pulled his pistol from beneath it, and fired at

Robert. His wild shot tore through the mutton sleeve of Robert's doublet. Robert fired back, hitting the running Winter in the shoulder. Winter dropped his pistol and stopped when he came face to face with Barkley coming in through the back door.

The room became silent. The acrid smell of powder smoke blanketing the air. Heavy footsteps of someone running upstairs broke the silence. Robert ran forward and grabbed Winter, throwing him to the floor. "Barkley, after him!"

Barkley was out the back door in time to see the back of a man running to the stable.

Robert shouted, "Burns, hold the prisoner!"

Neil Burns unsheathed his hunting knife, ran across the room, kneeled on Winter's back, and put the blade to Winter's throat. "Aye, captain. Mister Winter will be stayin' where he is if he values his life."

Robert followed Barkley into the stable. Joseph Wright stood in the center next to the empty stall where his horse had been. Barkley was walking, with pistol drawn in front of Robert. The sheriff of Eyemouth, with Lilburn behind him, was walking, his pistol drawn, from the opposite side.

Robert called out, "Joseph Wright, you are under arrest. Kneel and put your hands behind your back."

Lilburn ran back into the inn and tied Winter's hands behind his back. Even with his prisoner's hands tied, Burns sat on Winter's back, holding the blade against the sobbing man's throat.

The prisoners were marched to the sheriff's jail. Burns

went for the surgeon. While Lilburn watched the wounded Winters, Robert and Barkley followed the sheriff of Eyemouth lead Joseph Wright to the end of the hall, past the jail cell. He moved aside the guard's chair, kicked away a rug, reached down, and pulled up a trap door. The sheriff took the lamp from the guard station, lit it, and told Wright to go down the stairs. One by one, the men clambered down to a silent passage below. Ten feet back, the passageway opened into a small room with three doors. Barkley laughed. "Smuggler storerooms under the sheriff's office! Brilliant!"

The sheriff unlocked and opened the door to the left. "Inside."

"You can't leave me here in the dark!"

The sheriff slammed the door behind him and locked it. "There will be a lantern outside the door. The window in the door may seem small, but your eyes will adjust. You have light. Expect no visitors."

The sheriff lit a lamp in the anteroom, turned and smiled at Robert. "The rooms came with my office. I won't speak to how they were used in the past."

When the doctor had finished with Winters, the still sobbing prisoner was led to the hidden storeroom to the right. Once locked inside, the sheriff said, "No use yellin' boys. No one will hear you."

Robert left Barkley, Burns, and Lilburn to plan the security of the Royal party during the visit, believing the risk to the King during the hunt and review of his militia was now low but recognizing that Geoffrey and other traitors were still at large. Robert was confident that no one knew the ground, trails, and potential hiding places of Cawmills, better than Burns and Lilburn. Barkley understood soldiers, their minds, and their methods. He understood the danger of crossfire and keeping defensive perimeters. But Robert was tired. His exhaustion and repeated questions seemed only to interfere with his lieutenants' planning. After another sleepless night, he decided to review their plans when he returned from Berwick-upon-Tweed.

As Robert rode into the lower city of Berwick-upon-Tweed, his eyes scanned the waterfront for the masts of the carrack that sailed five days earlier. Seeing no sign of the large ship, he turned his horse through the city gate and rode up the hill to his uncle's Stone Manse.

Finding his father and uncle in their usual high back chairs facing the fireplace, he asked, "What news of the ship? Is there any word from Karl?"

Lord Curtis replied without turning his head. "Patience, Robert. It is two days sail there, a day to unload the grain and board the men, and then two days sail back—with fair winds and a mild sea."

"It's been five days," Robert replied.

"Yes. The ship could arrive at any time."

"Well, I have some good news. We have captured the two other lads—friends to Catesby from Alnwick. But still nothing substantial on Geoffrey. Their courier, a lad called Joseph Wright, insists Cousin Geoffrey went to Ireland in search of recruits—mercenaries more than willing to kill our King."

Charles Curtis replied, "Well, there you have it. All will be well."

"Father, he left a month ago—more than enough time to have returned. Wright was carrying a letter that read, 'Proceed with plan.'"

Lord Curtis asked, "Who wrote the letter."

"The lad would not say. He denied any knowledge of the letter."

Robert walked over and leaned with arms outright, both hands against the stone fireplace. Gazing into the embers, he said, "I'm here to discuss the returning soldiers. We must convince fifty to join us before they return home. They have shown their loyalty to their countrymen—we must seek their allegiance to their King. I propose we march in fifty during the darkness the night the King arrives. If you can muster more, march them to the church in Cawmills village the next morning as soon as the courtiers leave for Cawmills."

"We shall do our best. I will offer a bonus and payment home for each who agrees to serve."

"Thank you, uncle. You have seen the number of courtiers; can you bed them all? And I must warn you, their wenches follow after them—I have recommended The Hen and Chickens Inn, it is close and well perhaps..."

Lord Curtis laughed. "Nephew, you do not alarm me. I know the ways of courtiers."

"Yes. Please do your best to encourage your guests to get an early start for Cawmills. The King shall hunt early morning before most of his guests arrive. Lunch after the hunt and then the Royal Cawmills Cuirassiers pass in review. With the gamekeeper and would-be assassin, Winters, in prison, I most fear the parade with the King in full view reviewing his cuirassiers as opportune for an attack against his person."

Lord Curtis stood up, walked to Robert, and put his arm on Robert's shoulder. "We have every confidence in you."

Charles Curtis echoed, "You make us proud, son."

Robert feigned a smile and said, "I shall wait here today for the ship. I bid your leave. I would make a call on Will and Katie."

Robert's mind wandered as he walked down the cobblestone street through the arched gate and into the lower city. He turned left on the wharf street and came to the handsome stone house where he grew up. Katie answered his knock on the door.

"Robert. Come in. Will is at the table eating lunch."

Robert kissed Katie on the cheek and said, "I come by to congratulate you once again, and…you look lovely, Katie, I see your happiness in your radiant face."

"Robert, you always flatter me. Will, Robert has come to visit!"

Robert heard Will's chair sliding from the table, and he called out, "Don't get up, friend, I know my way."

Katie smiled and said, "It must feel strange to visit us in this, which was your house. A gracious gift from your father—I feel like we have taken your inheritance."

Robert smiled. "Do not feel that way. I am welcome at my uncle's house and have been assured that one day it will be mine. No, it is a proper gift to two dear friends who have given up home, friends, everything to serve here. And Will, here, eating lunch is proof! It is but a few steps to the hospital and orphanage, and also to the workhouse."

Will stood up and said, "Robert, sit with me. Katie, a plate for our dearest friend."

Katie was at the cook fire, her back to Robert. She replied, "Yes, yes, I am already about it. Robert, you must have fond memories of this house."

Robert sighed. "A few. I remember my mother standing before the cook fire. I remember her smile and how she smelled, like sweet flowers and ocean air. But it was her hug and smile for me, different than her smile for anyone else. Once she died, the house was never again happy. My father wanted only one thing—to become as wealthy as my uncle, to show him he was the better man."

Will replied, "They are so close today. There is genuine affection between them."

"Yes, God be praised. And God be praised that you and Katie find joy here."

Robert sat down, and Katie placed a steaming bowl in front of him. "It is only porridge, but it is warm and filling."

Will looked across at Robert and remarked, "Something troubles you, brother."

Robert laughed lightly, but his smile drained away. "I come to you for counsel. I need your wisdom."

Robert paused, his eyes staring down at the bowl in

front of him. "So many doubts. I feel I have strayed from our calling. I lay in my bed at night, kept awake by guilt. I come to my priest seeking help and intercession."

Katie said softly, "I shall leave you two…"

Robert shook his head. "Please stay, Katie, have we three not journeyed through tumult and trial together?"

Will looked at his friend and said, "Only a fool, never doubts himself or his motives. Three things: God's Word, the witness of His Spirit in our hearts, and the counsel of trustworthy brothers. But too often, the handmaiden of doubt—guilt, becomes the devil's weapon against us. Forgive me, Robert, I do ramble on—first listen, then speak. Please, tell me what worries you."

Robert looked up. "The vision we share has been unity in the holy catholic church with love and tolerance for its different expressions. The business of the church is to make disciples of Jesus, spreading his gospel of love, mercy, grace, and forgiveness. I cannot forget our days in Eberbach."

Robert sighed and cast his eyes on unseen sights. "I fear I have gone down another path. My days are spent in intrigue, serving a King who stands against the very vision I pursue. And it is worse, I fear even in my service to the King, I put him at risk in my zeal to capture his enemies. I pray to our Lord but hear no answer."

Will looked into Robert's eyes. "For certain, the threat to His Highness, which you uncovered is a true cause of worry, but you should find no guilt in your service. Do you think that your one prayer or one brave and righteous deed would move our Heavenly Father to remove all trials, tribulations, and injustice? Don't you see that your vision, our vision, is but a dream that will never come wholly true in this world? All the powers that be see our vision as a threat. They fear freedom—they will always fear it and try to take it away. What is it that every King, prince, governor, and nobleman seeks? Stability. They try to preserve and pass on to their heir what they have gained by inheritance, power, and wealth. It is the same for every Bishop, Archbishop, the Pope, Abbott, and priest. They do not see unity as something to be gained. No, they see their interests attacked."

Will paused, Robert sat across from him with his eyes closed. Will began again, "When we met, Robert, you had nothing to lose. You had no inheritance, no office, and no prospects. Now you are an officer of the King and a friend to the Prelate of all England. You have opened correspondence between the Archbishop of Canterbury and the Elector Archbishop of Mainz! Do not abandon your calling. Do not assume what your detractors will not surrender. Find in yourself what you showed me."

Robert smiled. "Yes, I should not be discouraged or expect too much, too soon. I so admire your patience, Will. But the guilt—my head tells me I have been covered in God's mercy and immersed in His Grace, but still, I judge myself and carry a burden of guilt."

Will laughed. "Now you sound like a good Catholic! I can tell you all about guilt! It has forever been a cudgel of the church to maintain its power and stability and stifle the freedom and unity we so earnestly seek."

Katie reached over and took Robert's hands in hers

and said softly, "The hospital has taught me the cure for guilt."

Robert looked at Katie, concentrating on her words. "What is it every person on their death bed seeks? Assurance. Robert, we all seek assurance. We know we are sinners, and the promise of God's grace is too good to believe. We feel we must become better—pray more—love more and serve more. We look to ourselves to become more worthy, but we never do because we can never be worthy of our God. But on the sickbed, we know there is nothing more we can do. On the deathbed, we find the assurance so clearly told to us in Scripture. Robert, look for the assurance of God's love as if you were on your deathbed. In this assurance, there is grace. In His Grace, there is no place for guilt."

Robert smiled. "What a special gift God has given you in this woman!"

Will nodded. "Amen. And may God send such a gift to you as well, my friend."

Robert got up to leave. "There, my friend, I have nothing on you. It seems Lady Eleanor has left with no word—no goodbye, and I have sent your sister Hulda—a woman who will never be a nun—to chase Johann."

Katie shook her head. "Robert, ever the matchmaker!"

Katie cocked her head and said, "I see Lady Eleanor a good match for you, Robert. The way she looks at you—it is more than friendship."

His spirit lifted. Robert smiled. "Thank you, my friends. Thank you for restoring my soul."

CHAPTER 26
TOWER OF REFUGE

Robert was through the gate of Berwick-upon-Tweed on the Great North Road, riding to Cawmills when the masts of the carrack appeared on the horizon. The advance party of the King's servants, cook, and the housekeeper would arrive this day. The preparations for the Royal visit would demand most of his time. He would need Barkley, Burns, and Lilburn to oversee the hunt and military review while he kept a close eye on Douglas and the manor house preparations. Stopping first at the harness shop, Adam Cox told him he had not intercepted any new messages from Colin Gordon's saddle.

As Robert went to leave, Cox said, "The tenants, the good people of Cawmills are with you, Captain, we pray for you."

Robert nodded. "I am grateful. My prayers are for Cawmills. I have grown quite fond of the place and its people. It feels like home."

Barkley and Burns greeted Robert at the tower.

Barkley asked, "' News of the ship?"

"Not yet, should return any day now."

Barkley sighed. "We don't have many days."

Burns tipped his hat, and spoke up. "I have sent all of the tenants into the forest. Told them to look for any livestock that may have wandered off—can't have them mistaken for game. Of course, they know to report any strangers to me. I'll have them patrol each day before the hunt."

"Very good, Mister Burns. Now, on the hunt, I will not have Peter Hawkins driving game. His life is more valuable to me than the King."

Robert saw the surprise in Burns' eye, and sighed. "We will protect His Majesty with our lives. The King is old and has a healthy, robust heir. Young Peter would be first to do as his father and sacrifice himself for the King. I will not have it. Barkley, are you with me on this?"

Barkley replied, "Aye. We shall not put the lad to risk. Lilburn will drive game with Mister Burns."

Burns smiled. "I planned to have Peter lead the hunting party. The lad will be safe from an errant bolt."

Robert's voice softened. "You are ahead of me, Burns, well done. Now, Barkley, the review…"

The morning of October first was chilly under gray skies. A stiff sea breeze climbed to the roof of the Cawmills hills, stretching straight the King's standard flying proudly from the tower. Robert faced the wind and stared out at the German Ocean. *Not a day for a sea voyage.* His thoughts were interrupted by the sight of a rider at full gallop coming from Berwick-upon-Tweed. *Young Peter Hawkins, you are in a hurry. You bring news.*

Barkley joined Robert as he waited for Hawkins between the manor house and stable. Barkley said nervously, "Well, Robbie, it begins."

Peter galloped to the front door and pulled hard on his reins. His horse locked its legs and skidded to a stop. Young Hawkins flew from his saddle, and in three steps faced Robert. "His Majesty, King James is in Berwick-upon-Tweed. His baggage cart and bed make their way behind me. He shall sleep here tonight."

Robert turned to Andrew Douglas, who appeared behind him and said, "Have the house servants standby to receive the King's baggage. Have a meal prepared for them. Have everything ready for His Majesty. He will dine in the great hall this evening."

"Aye, Captain, all will be ready," he answered, and Douglas disappeared into the house.

"Has Lord Curtis given you word?"

"Aye, Captain, he tells you he tours the old castle garrison with His Majesty. They reminisced the King's last visit when he came south to be crowned. The King remembered when he lay across the border, saying it shall be a border no longer."

Robert nodded. "Yes, and the garrison was removed from Berwick forever."

Robert paused. "And my father? Any word from him?"

Peter shook his head. "Charles Curtis is with the King's party and Lord Curtis."

Robert nodded. "Well done, Hawkins. Take

refreshment and return to Berwick. Beg his Lordship's pardon. I would know when the King can be expected."

Robert turned to Barkley and said, "With this weather, there will be no ship today. I fear we must make the best of it."

Hawkins turned around. "But Captain, the ship has arrived. It came the day you were last in Berwick. Soldiers, many soldiers, they are fed and clothed. We thought you knew."

Robert smiled. "Thank you, Hawkins, no word of it to anyone in Cawmills, understand?"

"Aye, Captain. I shall be on my way now. No need for refreshment."

Gray dusk quickly followed the dreary day. The King's bed and baggage were barely in place when the Royal Party made its way to Curtis Castle Manor. All the chimneys of the great house sent dirty gray smoke into the autumn sky. The smell of roasting meats tempted the nose of the hungry King upon his arrival.

King James dismounted, gazed around the horizon, and said, "An excellent strategic location. The tower, does it go back to the Normans?"

"Aye, Your Majesty," Robert found himself replying. "The first Barron Curtis arrived with King William the Conqueror."

King James smiled. "Yes, I remember your face. You are Captain Curtis." King James stretched his muscles, took a deep breath and said, "A pleasant aroma tells me supper awaits. Very well then, I shall dine within an hour."

The King's houseman stepped forward. "This way, Your

Majesty. I shall show you to your bed chamber."

One by one, the Royal party followed the servants into the house. First the of Marquess of Buckingham, George Villiers, followed by the Marquess of Huntly, George Gordon, then the Earl of Suffolk, Thomas Howard, the Earl of Northumberland, Henry Percy. The King's secretary, George Calvert, followed.

Robert was surprised to see Sir John Doddridge, who waited to speak with him privately. "Sir John, it is good to see you. I need your wisdom and influence."

Pausing, he said, "The Crown Prince, is he not coming?"

Sir John replied, "Returned to London—bored with the travel."

Sir John came close and whispered, "Is it true you have the mystery gamekeeper of Bramshill, Will Hugh, and another plotter in custody?"

Robert replied, "His true name is Will Winters. The other is Joseph Wright. They, along with a third, dead by suicide, sadly, one George Catesby were sons of the Gunpowder conspirators. They sought to finish their fathers' work. All three were in league with Fitzhugh, my cousin Geoffrey Curtis and the radical priest, Clitherow. He is here, in Cawmills, not in France. I have their correspondence. Names—proof."

Sir John looked up, nodded his head, and smiled.

"We thwarted their plan to kill His Majesty during the hunt. The lads confessed that Geoffrey went to Ireland seeking men, but that was a month ago. He is still afoot. I have taken precautions, of course, but the threat remains."

Sir John stared in thought at the western horizon, before saying, "The proof, the correspondence, it shall put to rest the petitions of your cousin Geoffrey along with Edward Vaux. Buckingham has been listening to Captain Stock. He has not taken Stock's petition to the King—he can't, not while Sir Henry Vere's regiment remains under siege in the Palatine—abandoned by Stock."

Sir John clasped Robert's shoulder. "I will put a few words to Buckingham. Now, let's join the feast."

Robert's mind was not on the rich food set before him. He did not join the King and the lords of his court in the card game. He spent the night with Barkley and Burns rehearsing the day to come.

King James was both learned and athletic. He believed physical activity stimulated the body, mind, and soul. Of all his athletic pursuits, hunting was his favorite. Burn's plan for the hunt would have the King and Royal hunting party ride through the woods on the western side of the Royal Forest. The gamekeepers would drive the deer towards a feeding area on an open hillside below the woods. The King would have both clear sight and open fields for the kill.

Robert was mounted, riding between Burns and the hunting party when a panting Aidan Lilburn ran up beside him and struggled to say. "In the hollow, beside the Blackadder, a stranger. He ran off as we approached, Burns stayed behind to watch, I have come..."

Robert dragged Lilburn up behind him on his horse

and rode off to find Burns. Lilburn continued, "We were tracking the big stag. He often spends the night there. The man was afoot. Alone—but would not answer our hail."

Robert found Burns in the hollow. "Which direction?"

Neil Burns pointed. "Lost him in the rock scramble. Can't be far off."

Lilburn slid off Robert's horse and started towards the rocks. Robert called out, "No! Burns, take Lilburn, and continue the hunt. I will go after our visitor."

Robert dismounted and led his horse through loose stone and around a towering rock. Remounted, he followed a trail along the Blackadder Flow one hundred yards to a small clearing where he saw a man encamped, sitting beside a small fire. Robert could see neither crossbow nor any weapon. He rode into the camp and said, "You are in the Royal Cawmills Forest—do you know the penalty for poaching the King's game?"

The man looked up. "Not poachin' my Lord, just followin' the flow from Coldstream."

Robert dismounted and walked about the camp looking for weapons. "You were seen downriver. You disobeyed the orders of the forester. Tell me the truth. Who are you? Why are you here?"

Robert pointed his pistol at the stranger and waited. "I hoped to see His Majesty, King James. I heard of his visit and came to petition His Highness."

Robert kept the pistol pointed and said, "Tell me more."

The stranger looked up. "Lordship, the victuallers took

my hog. He promised a good price but never paid. My last hog and me havin' no money for grain with winter close at hand. Should my child starve while the King sups on my pig?"

"Who was this victualler?"

"Came from Curtis Castle, one on foot and one on horseback—name was Douglas."

Robert lowered his pistol and took two silver coins from his pouch. Handing them to the man, he said, "One for the hog and one for your trouble. Go home and if you lack grain this winter, come to Curtis Castle and ask for Captain Curtis."

Robert returned to the hunt in time to see King James measuring the antlers on a large stag. "Ah. Captain Curtis. Most satisfactory hunt. A fine animal. Good Sport! Have it dressed out. I shall enjoy venison in Edinburgh."

When the hunting party returned to Curtis Castle Manor, horses filled the paddock behind the stable, and elegantly decorated carriages lined the courtyard. Cawmills had never seen such an event. The mayhem in the house silenced when the King was announced. James strode through the door, ignoring the bowing courtiers and went upstairs to his bedchamber to change his clothes.

The luncheon would begin when the King reappeared and made his way to the table. Robert hurried to the tower and the waiting Lieutenant Barkley. It had been many years since Curtis Tower was filled with soldiers, a citadel awaiting attack. Thirty volunteers recently arrived from the continent were peering through arrow slits watching the manor and the approaches to the hilltop estate. Sergeant Lilburn was standing on the parapet, a crossbow at the ready. Barkley led Robert to a wounded soldier, a bandage around his forehead. "Lad, please tell the Captain what you told me."

The soldier stood at attention and tipped an imaginary hat, before casting his eyes down to the floor. "Captain, I have news from Heidelberg. The city and the castle have fallen. Colonel Sir Herbert is dead."

The blow struck Robert hard. "Sit down soldier. Tell me how many..."

"Not sixty of us walked away, paroled we were—told to leave. A German—looked more a smuggler than a merchant—called Werner—came with a boat and ferried us to Amsterdam. Left the severely wounded in hospital. Put us on a ship for Berwick."

"Captain Richard?"

"Dead, sir. Died fighting at the breach in the wall."

The soldier looked up. "When we heard of the threat against the King, well, we want to do our part."

"Thank you. Have you eaten?"

"Aye, Viscount Berwick, and Lieutenant Barkley have seen to all."

Robert grasped the soldier's shoulder and nodded. Turning to Barkley, he said, "Send Lilburn down to hear his orders."

Aidan Lilburn scrambled down the tower stairs and stood at attention before Robert. "Sergeant Lilburn, you command the tower. It is the strongest position and the only safe refuge for the King. You will not abandon this position. If there is any sign of trouble, the King will be brought here. Do not be drawn away except by my order. Is that understood sergeant?"

"Aye, Captain. Hold the tower as a fortress and safe refuge for His Majesty."

Robert nodded. "Remember, any sign of trouble coming up the hill—one cannon shot to alert the company."

Turning to Barkley, he said, "Time to muster the company."

Soon after Robert and Barkley had left, servants began moving chairs outside the manor house to the garden between the house and tower. More servants, men, came out, many walking towards the stable. Lilburn did not remember so many servants, but then the Royal party was large. The servants continued to exit the house, some he recognized as Curtis Tower Manor household servants walking to the stable in small groups. Lilburn continued to watch as first two, then five, ten men, saddled horses in the paddock.

The King and came out into the garden and walked to the high backed festival chair brought for such occasions. Once he was seated, and his guests found their chairs, the doors of the stable opened to reveal twenty or more mounted men. Lilburn fired the cannon. King James nodded and settled back in his seat, pleased that the review would start promptly.

At the sound of the cannon, veteran soldiers, their long pikes in hand, poured onto the street of Cawmills village. Down the road to Berwick-upon-Tweed, another column of soldiers heard the cannon blast and double timed their pace. Robert ordered Barkley, "Lieutenant—lead the infantry. Establish a corridor to the tower."

Then turning to his mounted cuirassiers, he shouted, "Royal Cuirassiers, your King is threatened! For King James!"

At the top of the hill, Robert was shocked to see a band of forty or fifty mounted men and one saddled horse facing the seated King. As he came closer, he saw another ten men on foot standing behind the seated King and couriers with pistols drawn. Robert signaled for his men to slow. One hundred mounted Royal Cawmills Cuirassiers, each with two pistols and a sheathed saber halted, surrounding the attackers ten yards behind. A mounted man in front of the rebel band turned and called to Robert.

"I'm afraid you're late for our review, Captain Curtis. Never to quick, not the brightest man, eh, Robbie, old chum? His Majesty was about to hear my terms."

Robert shouted, "Captain Donald Stock—a coward who deserted his Colonel and comrades in Mannheim, you cannot expect to succeed. Have your men put down their weapons."

Donald Stock rode his nervous horse in lazy circles in front of King James, "Your Majesty, pay no mind to Robbie; he will not risk your person. As a loyal subject, I will direct my men to escort you safely to Holyrood once you have signed a simple contract. One that I know you will find most agreeable."

King James replied, "If I will find it agreeable, why are weapons drawn against me?"

Donald Stock nodded. "Sadly, your Majesty, your court would not permit my petition or those of like mind. You shall have your treaty with Spain. You shall agree to the Spanish conditions for the marriage of Charles, the Prince of Wales, to the Infanta Maria Anna. The Prince shall return to the Roman Catholic Faith and his heir raised Catholic. All property stolen from the church, whether chapel, church, cathedral, or abbey shall be restored, and the true faith once again will be practiced in England, Scotland, Ireland, and Wales. And one small favor, Sir Geoffrey Curtis will be restored as Baron of Cawmills, and I shall accept a due title, my reward in your service."

King James stared at Donald Stock and replied, "He is no King who would bow to threats by little men of no honor. I am well in my years. Charles, Prince of Wales, my heir, is hale and hearty. I see no opportunity for your escape. I do not fear death, Mister Stock, I would not honor you as captain. I should simply order Captain Curtis to show no mercy. I suggest to you that you lay down your arms. Your cause is lost."

Barkley's infantry marched onto the hilltop, moving between the tower and the Royal Party.

From the parapet atop the tower, Lilburn looked down in worry and frustration. Many English pikemen and courtiers were in the tower's line of fire. He ordered his men, armed with long arquebus muskets to hold fire until his order. As Lilburn watched, he instinctively reached for his crossbow.

Stock continued to circle about nervously. "Your Majesty may find Captain Robert Curtis an unreliable ally. His company is with us!"

Two of Stock's mounted riders moved forward and threw off hooded riding cloaks. Geoffrey Curtis and Andrew Douglas raised arms as Geoffrey called out, "Good men of Cawmills you have sworn allegiance to me, protector of your true priest, Father Clitherow, and your Roman Catholic faith! Ride forward and join your fellow soldiers of God!"

Silence fell upon the manor.

Geoffrey called out, "A reward for the man who kills Robert Curtis!"

Robert called to his men, "Weapons at the ready!"

Pistols were aimed at each of Stock's men. Barkley had moved the infantry close to the Royal party and now formed an unbroken line of veteran pikemen to the tower. Lilburn's line of fire began to open up. Robert felt his stomach rise into his chest. He had no plan. His mind failed him. Was it instinct or fear? Perhaps it was hid training, or pure determination to see justice done. Robert rode alongside his cousin Geoffrey, who drew his sword. Robert fired one shot, and Geoffrey Curtis fell to the ground.

Immediately the King was encircled by infantry, their long pikes extended like thorns on a giant thistle, as they marched him to the safety of the tower. The shocked Donald Stock spurred his horse towards the seated guests, his horse jumped the frightened nobles, and he galloped off to the west.

As Robert reined in his rearing horse to give chase, the now exposed Henry Clitherow drew a small double barrel pistol and fired one shot. The ball drove Robert forward on his horse. He wrapped his arms around his steed's neck and spurred him on in chase of Donald Stock. Clitherow took aim for a second shot when he fell to the ground, a crossbow bolt in his back. Lilburn quickly readied his crossbow for another shot.

One by one, Stock's men dropped their weapons and lifted their arms, their hands behind their heads. Viscount Curtis walked over to his nephew Geoffrey. He knelt beside him, seeing him breathing, he helped him to his knees. Lord James Curtis stood, drew his sword, and with all his strength, swung it towards his nephew. Geoffrey's headless body fell to the ground. His lifeless eyes staring up beside it.

"Better it be by the hand of a Curtis."

Robert gave chase down the western slope towards the Blackadder. He saw Stock disappear behind the large crag at the rock scramble. Robert rode to the scramble, dismounted, and continued on foot. He had not walked ten yards when he fell to the ground in a pool of his blood.

Tom Pritchard was the first Cuirassier to follow. He found Robert unconscious but breathing. "Don't die on me, Captain. You have won a great victory! You must live!" Pritchard tightly bandaged the wound to Robert's left shoulder, slung him gently across his horse, and led him back to Cawmills.

Robert lay in a gray world of hazy faces and distant voices. His muddled mind somehow found a vision of Lady Eleanor, instructing him as she so often had on what he must do and who he must be. Slowly the voices grew distinct, prayers. His father and uncle were praying. Tom Pritchard was demanding someone send for a doctor. He recognized faces. He smiled as he saw Eleanor's face leaning close to his, whispering, "You must not leave me alone, Robbie. You know I am no good alone. I cannot go on without you. I will not be satisfied with a dead hero."

Robert could feel her breath on his face. He could smell her sweet perfume and see the tears in her eyes. He smiled. "An angel has come to carry me away."

Lady Eleanor hugged him, her face against his, her tears falling on his cheeks.

CHAPTER 27
POMP AND CIRCUMSTANCE

As Robert recovered, Barkley recounted what happened. The Royal Cawmills Cuirassiers escorted the King to Holyrood Palace in Edinburgh. The renegade priest, Henry Clitherow, known in Cawmills as Andrew Douglas, and Robert's cousin Geoffrey were dead. All of Donald Stock's men were taken prisoner to Edinburgh Castle, as were the two lads, Will Winter and Joseph Wright. When Robert heard this, he interrupted, "His Majesty must know that I plead mercy for them."

Barkley nodded. "Yes, the word was passed. There is time for that after their trials."

Robert nodded and settled back in his bed. Barkley continued, "Sir John Doddridge has the lists, messages, names, and codes recovered from Alnwick Castle. Colin Gordon is under arrest in Huntly Castle. Lord Gordon has given his word that Colin will die if he ever ventures out."

"What of Donald Stock?"

"Escaped. Though he is a hunted man."

"I shall find the cowardly traitor if..."

Barkley interrupted, "There will be time for that. First, you must heal. His Majesty commands our presence at Holyrood Palace as soon as you are fit to travel."

Barkley glanced up as he heard the door open. "Ah, your angel has returned with hot soup and wine. I shall leave you in her tender care."

Robert smiled at Eleanor. "There are servants to bring my food. Why must you..."

Eleanor shook her head. "Shush. You rest. I find joy in serving you."

Robert smiled and sat up in bed. "I thought I was dreaming—that you were an angel. You left without any word. I feared you would never return. When? How?"

Lady Eleanor put the tray on the table, sat on the bed beside Robert, and said, "I went to the King. I told Sir John all that you learned. I begged His Majesty to remember all that you do. I urged him not to return to London, as Prince Charles was asking, but continue to Cawmills and honor you with the Royal visit."

Robert smiled. "I did not know you returned."

"I came from Berwick-upon-Tweed with the Ladies of the Court while you were with the hunting party."

Eleanor paused. "A letter came for me from Montclair. My father is dead. I am alone in the world."

Robert took her hand. "Eleanor, I am sorry, I..."

Eleanor laughed in pain. "His Majesty, King James, told me he would be my guardian and second father."

Robert replied, "Truly, he favors you."

Eleanor smiled. "Now sit up and open your mouth. I want to feed you. You need your strength—your sovereign awaits you."

Three days later, Robert and Edward, dressed in new finery, were led into the throne room of Holyrood Palace. Lords and Ladies stood on each side of the room. King James I of England but James IV here in Scotland, sat upon his throne, his right hand holding a sword, its point on the floor. Two guards swung open the doors, a third inside slammed the staff of his halberd on the floor and announced, Captain Robert Curtis and Lieutenant Edward Barkley, Royal Cawmills Cuirassiers!"

Robert and Barkley both kneeled and bowed.

King James called, "Arise Captain Curtis and come forward."

Robert walked forward to the foot of the King's throne, kneeled, and bowed his head. King James stood up, lifted his sword, and holding it out over Robert, touched his shoulder with the blade. His voice echoed through the quiet chamber. "I dub you, Sir Robert."

The King moved the sword blade to Robert's other shoulder and rested it there. He looked out at his court and said, "It is with sadness I note the recent death of the Earl of Montclair with no male heir, and I must disestablish his family title. As guardian of Montclair's daughter Lady Eleanor and concerned for her well-being, I dub you, Earl of Montclair, if you will have Lady Eleanor as I know she would have you. Arise, Sir Robert Curtis, Earl of Montclair!"

Robert stood up, bowed, and backed away to the door to cheers. "Huzzah, Huzzah to Sir Robert, Earl of Montclair!"

When the room silenced again, the King called out, "Lieutenant Edward Barkley, come forward."

Barkley walked forward to the throne, kneeled, and bowed before the King. King James lifted his sword and tapped Barkley's shoulder. "I dub you, Sir Edward Barkley." The King placed the blade on Barkley's left shoulder. He said, "Lord Curtis, Viscount Berwick, Baron of Tweedbridge, has generously redeemed Cawmills Royal Forest from forfeiture against his kinsman, the traitor Geoffrey Curtis. Therefore, with his blessings, I dub you, Baron of Cawmills. Arise, Sir Edward Barkley, Baron of Cawmills,"

A wobbly kneed Barkley stood up, backed to the door next to Robert while the room erupted in, "Huzzah! Huzzah! Sir Edward, Baron of Cawmills!"

King James sat down on his throne and said, "Lord Lieutenant of Scotland, Marquess Huntly, I now command you to employ my Royal Cawmills Cuirassiers as my Royal Guard in Scotland. I commend their fidelity, courage, and bearing in my service. If Parliament funded a standing army, I would take them and all the returning volunteers to London."

Sir George Gordon, Marquess of Huntly, stood and bowed to the King. "It shall be as you say, Your Majesty. They are a credit to all of Scotland."

The King sat back on his throne, stared out at Lady Eleanor, smiled, bid her forward curling his finger. He said warmly, "Lady Eleanor and Sir Robert come forward."

Robert and Eleanor, came forward, then kneeled and bowed. King James smiled and said, "Arise."

As they stood smiling before him, the happy King James said, "Lady Eleanor, I find Sir Robert an acceptable match. As your protector, I give my permission to wed!"

Robert and Eleanor stood smiling at each other.

The King paused a moment and said, "Sir Robert, you shall not withhold me the joy of Lady Eleanor's presence in court."

Robert smiled. "As you wish, your Majesty."

King James' smile widened. "On with it, man! Kiss her!"

As Robert and Eleanor kissed, Mary Hawkins found her way beside Edward. Sir Edward smiled and asked, "Would you be my Lady Mary, Baroness of Cawmills?"

A speechless Mary, with happy tears, nodded yes. He took her in his arms and kissed her passionately.

EPILOGUE

Sir Edward swore to the tenants and tradesmen of Cawmills the same generous terms that Robert had given them. He opened more land for tenants who wanted additional fields. Neil Burns became the estate manager. Lilburn continued as head gamekeeper with Peter's continued service. Barkley told his assembled tenants that the Chapel of Saint Cuthbert was theirs alone on Sunday after 11:00 AM. The manner of their worship was between them and God. He invited Adam Cox to stay and teach reading, writing, and good Christian behavior to all in Cawmills. He asked only for their goodwill and earnest prayers for his stewardship. He appointed Neil Burns, Tom Pritchard, and Adam Cox to decide the fitness of anyone seeking employment or tenancy at Cawmills.

Lord Edward gifted the tower back to Lord Curtis as a permanent house of the Curtis family. He kept the name Curtis Castle in honor of his friends and benefactor. And he accepted Robert's award of his commission as Captain of the Royal Cawmills Cuirassiers.

The Marquess of Buckingham arranged Sir Robert's appointment as Inquisitor General of the Royal Bench, working with his friend, Sir John Doddridge. Sir John welcomed Sir Robert, reminding him, "This for the only man to question what happened at Bramshill. The only one to ask: 'Why would a cautious and experienced gamekeeper put himself between hunter and quarry? It makes no sense!'"

The Reverend Father Wilhelm Hahn conducted a double wedding ceremony at The Church of the Holy Trinity in Berwick-upon-Tweed. Pronouncing in his heavy German accent, he said, "What God has joined together, let not man put asunder."

APPENDIX

ARCHAIC TERMS

Arquebus, a long smooth-bored, matchlock gun fired from the shoulder, supported on a pole.

Carrack, a three or four-masted ocean-going sailing ship, typically recognized by its large aft castle at the stern, a high forecastle, and bowsprit.

Cuirassier, Mounted cavalry wearing cuirass armor (torso plate half armor), armed with pistols and sword.

HISTORIC PEOPLE

Count Gondomar, Diego Sarmiento de Acuna. Spanish Ambassador to England 1613—1622

Sir John Doddridge, Justice of the Kings Bench. Led the inquiry of the Bramshill Homicide

George Villiers, Marquess of Buckingham. King James favorite, later 1st Duke of Buckingham

Prince Charles, Prince of Wales heir to James I

Infanta Maria Anna. Daughter of King Phillip of Spain, possible wife for Prince Charles.

George Calvert, Secretary of State under James I. Converted to Catholicism at retirement.

Baron Cranfield, Earl of Middlesex, Lord High Treasurer under James I

Edward la Zouche, 11th Baron Zouche, diplomat. Hosted hunt at Bramshill

John Thorpe, Architect of Bramshill House

Peter Hawkins, Gamekeeper at Bramshill accidentally killed by Archbishop George Abbot

George Abbot, Archbishop of Canterbury, member of the privy council—sidelined by inquiry

William Laud, Bishop of St. David's, confidante of Buckingham, foe of George Abbot

Lancelot Andrewes, Bishop of Winchester, Led KJV Bible translation, friend of George Abbot

Frederick V Elector Palatine. Assumed the of the crown of Bohemia starting the 30-year war

Countess Elizabeth, Elizabeth of Bohemia, daughter of James I wife of Frederick V

Anne of Denmark, Queen consort, Wife of James, rumored deathbed conversion to Catholicism

Tobias Matthew, Archbishop of York

Lady Catherine Howard, Countess of Suffolk, noted beauty, took bribes at court, Catholic

Admiral Thomas Howard, Earl of Suffolk, Lord Treasurer jailed and fined for bribery Catholic

Count of Tilly, Johann Tserclaes, field marshal of Catholic League forces, 30 Years War

General Ernst von Mansfeld, A Catholic, he led the protestant army of Frederick V

Duke Christian of Brunswick, Raised an army to for the protestant cause in 30 years war

Emperor Ferdinand II, Austrian Hapsburg. Holy Roman Emperor 1620-1637

Colonel Sir Horace Vere, Commander English Regiment Palatine, headquartered Mannheim

Colonel Sir Gerard Herbert, Commander English Volunteers at fall of Heidelberg Sept. 1622

Johann Schweikhard von Kronberg, Archbishop-Elector of Mainz, 1604-1626.

Richard Neile, Bishop of Durham 1617-1628

Saint Aidan of Lindisfarne, Irish monk, and missionary about 590 to 651

Saint Cuthbert, Northumbrian Angle convert of Aidan, later Bishop of Lindisfarne

John Knox, Scottish reformer, 1514—1572

Henry Percy, Earl of Northumberland, Catholic uncle of gunpowder plotter Thomas Percy

Henry de Vere, Earl of Oxford, member of James I council of war. Later served in the Palatine

Sir Thomas Wentworth, Earl of Stratford, member of Parliament of 1621

George Gordon, Marquess Huntly, Lord Lieutenant of Scotland, Chief Gordon Clan, Catholic

Thomas Wintour, John Wright, Robert Catesby, members of the gunpowder plot

Thomas Percy, Constable of Alnwick Castle, member of the gunpowder plot

Oswald Tesimond, Jesuit priest, linked to gunpowder plot. Famed for escape from the Tower

Anne and Elizabeth Vaux, Eleanor Brooksby, Catholic recusants, Safe housed Catholic priests

Edward Vaux, Baron Vaux of Harrowden, sent a regiment to support Spanish Army of Flanders

Margaret Clitherow, Catholic Saint. Pressed to death for refusing to plea for harboring priests

Algernon Percy, Heir to Henry Percy, Earl of Northumberland

Georg Friedrich, Margrave of Baden, raised a protestant army of 12,000 30-Years War

Gonzolo Fernandez de Cordoba, Spanish Commander 30-Years War

Ambrosio Spinola, Marquess of Los Balbases. Italian. Captain General of the Army of Flanders

Sir Robert Henderson, Colonel, English volunteers, hero siege of Bergen-Op-Zoom

Maurice of Orange, **Prince of Orange**, Dutch Republic 1585-1625

HISTORIC PLACES NAMES

Westminster Palace, Ceased use as a Royal residence after a fire in 1512. First Lords and later House of commons met there. Destroyed by fire in 1834, rebuilt as House of Parliament in 1868.

Berwick-upon-Tweed, found on the Scottish border at the mouth of the River Tweed. Site of a castle fortress and garrison. Many buildings of the 17th century remain.

River Tweed, Flows across the border region of Scotland and England, flows to the North Sea.

German Ocean, North Sea

Tweedbridge, Village at Stone bridge over the River Tweed southwest of Berwick-upon-Tweed

Berwick bridge, Stone bridge over River Tweed at Berwick-upon-Tweed

Lambeth Palace, London residence of the Archbishop of Canterbury sections date back to 1435.

Bramshill House, Opened in 1612, Hampshire home of Baron Zouche. Site of a hunting accident where Archbishop Abbot killed gamekeeper Peter Hawkins, July 1621.

Cawmills, Hilly area in southeast coastal Scotland, just north of Berwick-upon-Tweed.

The Great North Road, The main highway between London and Scotland. It ran through York then along the Coast, over the Tweedbridge through coastal Scotland. Route close to modern A1.

Petworth House, West Sussex home of the Percy family, Earls of Northumberland

Alnwick Castle, Northumberland Castle, garrison, and residence of the Earls of Northumberland

Church of the Holy Trinity, Berwick-upon-Tweed built 1652, consecrated 1660.

Hen and Chickens Inn, Berwick-upon-Tweed. Long history in Berwick-upon-Tweed.

EVENTS

Fall of Heidelberg, September 19, 1622, the English garrisoned city and castle fell the combined Spanish forces of Tilly and Cordoba. Garrison commander, Sir Gerard Herbert was killed.

Battle of Wimpfen, May 6, 1622, forces of Spain and the Catholic League under Tilly and Cordoba, defeated the protestant forces of Georg Friedrich, the Margrave of Baden

Siege of Bergen-op-Zoom, July 18, to October 2, 1622. The Dutch under Maurice of Orange with support of Ernst von Mansfeld and Sir Robert Henderson broke the Spanish Siege.

ABOUT THE AUTHOR

David Martyn retired from a career in the Maritime industry and lives in Gig Harbor, Washington (nicknamed *The Maritime City*) with his wife Karen. David writes Christian fiction.

David's historical fiction series, *The Robert Curtis Mysteries*, take place during the 17th Century Thirty Years War (when the Church was at war with itself) and the lead up to English Civil War. These mysteries include: *Called Into Service, Soldiers of the King: the Bramshill Affair,* and *Lords and Ladies: the Banqueting House Plot.*

His Biblical series of novels, the 'Hall of Faith' series, include*: The Praise Singer: a Disciple of Melchizedek, The Oak of Weeping: the Story of Isaac, Deborah, and Rebekah, and The Epistle: a Story of the Early Church..* David also wrote a pocket novel, *Huldah and the Last Righteous King,* and a collection of short stories, *A Light in the Darkest Night.*

David's short stories can be found in Blue Forge Press anthologies: *Unconditional: Ten Stories of Enduring Love, Unnerving: Volume 2,* and *Unnerving: Volume 3.* A complete listing of David's works can be found on the website: blueforgepress.com